Praise for Rosie's previous books

'Goodwin is a master of her craft: she excels in writing about the complexity of relationships, the hardships of life, the ties of family and the joys of love and friendship.'
Lancashire Evening Post

'Rosie is a talented storyteller.'
Dee Williams

Other titles by Rosie Goodwin

The Bad Apple
No One's Girl
Dancing Till Midnight
Moonlight and Ashes
Forsaken
Our Little Secret
Crying Shame
Yesterday's Shadows
The Boy from Nowhere
A Rose Among Thorns
The Lost Soul
The Ribbon Weaver
A Band of Steel
Whispers
The Misfit
The Empty Cradle

Catherine Cookson titles

Tilly Trotter's Legacy
The Mallen Secret
The Sand Dancer

Rosie GOODWIN

Home Front Girls

Canvas

Constable & Robinson Ltd
55–56 Russell Square
London WC1B 4HP
www.constablerobinson.com

First published in the UK by Canvas,
an imprint of Constable & Robinson Ltd, 2013

This paperback edition published in the UK by Canvas, 2013

A copy of the British Library Cataloguing in Publication data is available from the British Library

ISBN: 978-1-47210-101-3 (paperback)
ISBN: 978-1-47210-102-0 (ebook)

Printed and bound by CPI Group (UK) Ltd, Croydon, CR0 4YY

1 3 5 7 9 10 8 6 4 2

For Yasmin, my faithful, loving little companion for sixteen years. I hope you are happy and playing with your mum in doggy heaven.
I miss you. xxxxx

Acknowledgements

A huge thank-you to Victoria, Martin and everyone at Constable & Robinson for making me feel so very welcome. Also my lovely editor Sheila Crowley and the brilliant Joan Deitch, my copy-editor, who is so wonderful at picking up on any mistakes I may have made!

Not forgetting my dear friend Jane and everyone at 'The Thursday Club' at the Mary Anne Evans hospice who tried to come up with a title for this book.

And, last but never least, to my family for their ongoing patience each time I disappear into my study.

Chapter One

Coventry, November 1939

'I'm sorry, darling, but the long and the short of it is, you will have to find yourself a job immediately.'

'*What!*' Annabelle Smythe's beautiful blue eyes stretched wide with horror as she stared back at her mother, who was nervously wringing her hands. They were in Annabelle's bedroom and the young woman leaped up and began to pace up and down the length of the soft flowered carpet as her pure silk dressing-gown swirled about her slim legs. Annabelle was twenty years old and had never done a day's work in her entire life. Nor did she intend to. The only child of wealthy parents, she had been indulged in everything she had ever wanted from the moment her mother had held her in her arms, and she was not going to let that change now.

'But why, Mummy?' she whined as she raised a perfectly plucked, pencilled eyebrow. 'Is it the latest clothing bill I ran up in town yesterday? I know I was a little extravagant, but I won't do it again, I promise. It's just that after I'd bought the new dress I had to have shoes and a handbag to go with it – and a coat, of course, didn't I? And if what people are saying is true, then it's going to be very hard to get hold of any decent clothes soon and you wouldn't want me to walk about like a tramp, would you?' She gazed at her mother imploringly.

'Oh, Annabelle!' Miranda Smythe sank down onto the bedroom chair, which was upholstered in a soft pink colour to match the bedding and the curtains. 'You must realise, surely, that the war has affected Daddy's business badly. People aren't buying luxury cars any more and the thing is . . . Well, the truth of the matter is – we're struggling a little bit.'

'Hmph!' Annabelle snatched a silver-backed hairbrush from the dressing-table and began to yank it through her shoulder-length blonde hair, which only that afternoon had been primped and teased into marcel waves at a hairdresser's in the city centre. 'Is that why you've sacked Mrs Fitton? It's going to be horrible now, having no one to do our washing and ironing.'

'I'm afraid it is,' her mother replied as patiently as she could. She adored her daughter and would have walked over hot coals for her if need be, but sometimes, just sometimes, she wondered if she hadn't spoiled her just a little too much. However, now she had started she ploughed on, 'And you may as well know, Mrs Brookes will be finishing at the end of the week too.'

'*What!* But who will do the cleaning and cooking then?'

'We shall have to learn to do it ourselves,' her mother replied steadily.

'You must be joking, Mother!' Annabelle spluttered,

utterly horrified. She was not capable even of boiling an egg, and the thought of having to do menial things like cleaning and cooking was more than she could comprehend.

'You have to accept that the war is affecting everyone, darling. We have been very lucky up to now, but we must all make sacrifices. I'm sure we shall manage admirably once we get into some sort of a routine. After all – how hard can it be?'

Annabelle glared at her mother as she slammed the hairbrush back down, barely able to take in this unwelcome news. Her mother had always been so easy to get round. Usually the girl had only to drop her bottom lip and pout, and Miranda would give in to her every demand. But here she was now, telling her that she must learn to do her own cleaning and cooking *as well* as getting a job! It was preposterous! They had never taught her how to do domestic tasks at the expensive schools Daddy had sent her to. Needlework and piano lessons were the most gruelling things she had ever had to tackle up to now.

'And just what sort of a job do you expect me to do?' she snapped as she threw herself onto the bed.

'Well, as it happens I heard that they are looking for staff in Owen Owen. You might enjoy shop work,' her mother added hopefully.

Annabelle couldn't imagine anything worse than having to bow and scrape to awkward customers. She herself had often given shop staff a hard time; making them run here and there for things she wanted to look at, and now here was her mother daring to suggest that the roles should be reversed.

'I don't think Daddy would be too happy with your suggestions,' she spat peevishly.

'Actually . . . it was Daddy's idea.'

Annabelle felt the bottom drop out of her world. She had been praying that at any second her mother would chuckle and tell her it had all been a silly joke, but one glance at Miranda's pale face told her that she was dreadfully serious.

'And what if I refuse?'

Her mother shrugged. 'Then there would be little we could do to force you to go out to work. But I'm not at all sure how you would manage. You see, Daddy can't afford to give you your allowance any more.'

This was the final straw and Annabelle scowled as her mother looked about the room and sighed. Yesterday's lingerie littered the floor, and clothes that Annabelle had tried on earlier in the day then discarded were lying crumpled in the bottom of the wardrobe.

'You perhaps ought to hang those back up,' her mother suggested tentatively. 'Now that Mrs Fitton has gone you will have to be responsible for your own washing and ironing too, and there's no point in making unnecessary work for yourself.'

And with that the woman turned and walked from the room, closing the door quietly behind her as Annabelle stared after her. Throwing herself off the bed, she stormed to the window and flicked the snow-white net curtains aside to stare down gloomily into the tree-lined avenue where they lived in Cheylesmore in Coventry. It was one of the very best areas in the city, and the home she had grown up in was magnificent – a rambling Victorian four-bedroom detached house set in half an acre that had been tastefully furnished from top to bottom by her mother. A sweeping drive led up to the heavy oak door, and on it was parked her father's gleaming Triumph. Annabelle smirked. That would give people something to talk about, if her father were to drop her off at some shabby workplace in *that*. But now as she calmed down a little she was sure that it wouldn't come to that. She would give it half an hour and then go downstairs and turn the tears on, and all this silly nonsense would be forgotten. She had always been able to wrap her father around her little finger before, so why should now be any different?

Humming to herself, she began to rummage through her wardrobe again to find the new dress. She must wear something decent at tonight's party at her friend's house. It was Jessica's eighteenth and if her dishy brother, James, was going to be there, Annabelle was determined she would look her best. Sadly, since the war had started there had been a shortage of young men, since a lot of them had already been called up. James had only missed it because of a minor heart defect, but Annabelle could live with that. He was one of the most eligible chaps she knew and his family were positively rich, occupying an even larger house than the Smythes. In a much happier frame of mind, she continued to rummage, taking no notice of her mother's suggestion of hanging up her other clothes.

Downstairs, Miranda entered the drawing room to find her husband staring into the fire with a glass of brandy in his hand and a dejected expression on his face. He was worried for the future, for his family; the comfort they had always known was under threat. He glanced up as his wife entered the room and his face instantly softened as it always did when he caught sight of her. Even after twenty-four years of marriage he was as besotted with her as he had been on the first day he had set eyes on her.

'How did she take it, darling?' he asked as his wife crossed to the decanter standing on the highly polished mahogany sideboard to help herself to a small sherry.

Miranda sighed as she joined him. 'Not well, I'm afraid – but then I think we expected that, didn't we?'

At forty-three years old, Miranda was a striking-looking woman. Her hair was still a lovely shade of pale blonde with barely a grey hair in sight, her face was unlined and she had retained her slim figure. Annabelle's hair was a darker shade of blonde and her eyes a deeper blue, but she was also a very beautiful young woman. Richard loved them both to distraction, although he was aware that the gossips said he had married above himself – which he knew to be the truth.

Richard Smythe was proud of the fact that he was a self-made man. He had started life on a slum terrace on the other side of the city, and after leaving school at the earliest opportunity he had got taken on in the stables of a big house near Shilton, eventually graduating to the garage when his employer acquired a Hispana-Suiza. Years passed, and he left to work for an old gentleman who owned an automobile business. Sales boomed in the 1920s and by scrimping and saving, Richard eventually managed to buy the garage from the old gentleman who had trained him.

The start of this war, a mere twenty-one years after the 'War to end all Wars', was causing sales to drop off alarmingly due to petrol rationing and, as far as he was concerned, it was time for them all to pull their belts in – especially Annabelle. Money dripped through that one's fingers like water, which was why he had ordered his wife to have words with her.

Miranda had been very good about it and was happy to let the charlady and daily help go and to tackle the chores herself, even though she had never had to do so before. But then she had a totally different nature from Annabelle – kind and thoughtful despite having enjoyed a very privileged upbringing. Richard could still remember the look of horror on Mrs Hamilton Gower's face when Miranda had first introduced him to her. At that time, he had just bought the business and was painfully aware that he, with his oil-stained hands, was not at all the sort of chap Miranda's parents had planned for her. Even so, because he was their daughter's choice they had grudgingly accepted him, and that had spurred him on to work even harder to prove to them that he could give her the sort of lifestyle she was accustomed to. He had even changed his name from Smith to Smythe as Miranda's mother felt it had a better ring to it. He had known that what she *really* meant was that Smith was too 'common' for her daughter, but eager to be accepted, he had gone along with it.

They had married eventually and the wedding had been a lavish affair paid for by the bride's father. The newly-weds had been ecstatically happy and planned to have a large family straight away, but then years of heartache had followed as Miranda sobbed each month when she found that she was not pregnant. At last, after five long years, Annabelle had come along – and finally Richard could do no wrong; his in-laws had even come to admire him, especially as his business grew and they saw that he genuinely loved their daughter. Sadly, Annabelle was destined to be their only child, so she had been shamelessly spoiled by both her parents and grandparents. But now all that was going to have to stop. Things were, in fact, even worse than Miranda knew. Richard had tried to keep the bad news from his wife for as long as possible, but now it was time to make some serious economies or he could see them losing not only his business but the house as well – and then where would they be?

'Try not to worry too much, darling,' his wife said softly. 'This war cannot last forever and Annabelle will survive. She might even enjoy working, once she gets used to it. She is often very bored stuck at home when she has nothing to entertain her, and at least she can look around for a job that she wants to do. Most girls her age are working in munitions factories now.'

'Hm, well, I'd like to think you're right – but I can't see it myself,' he replied glumly as she took his glass and went to refill it.

Miranda handed him the glass back and then they both sat down on the velvet upholstered settee as they waited for Annabelle to put in an appearance, which they were confident she would, given time.

Half an hour later, Annabelle breezed into the room in a waft of expensive French perfume, looking as if she had just stepped out of the pages of a fashion magazine. She was wearing the outfit that she had bought the day before – a very pretty red pleated cocktail dress that was cinched in at the waist by a broad belt, which showed off her slim figure. On her feet were her new high-heeled court shoes, and her face was made up to perfection.

'How do I look then? Do I pass muster, Daddy?' She twirled in front of him before bending to plant a kiss on his cheek. A little display of affection never usually failed to melt him; he was like putty in her hands. But she was quick to note this wasn't the case tonight.

Frowning slightly, he eyed her up and down before asking, 'And how did you manage to buy all this, miss?'

'With my allowance, of course. At the moment there are still some nice outfits in the shops, but once these stupid clothes coupons come into force there will be nothing decent left to buy,' she answered, trying not to sound resentful. 'How are we expected to look smart if we can't just go out and buy what we need? Half of the shops don't have anything worth buying in them any more!'

'It's a case of make do and mend at the moment,' her father answered, uncharacteristically sharply. 'In case you hadn't noticed, there is a war on. Even as we speak, young men are being killed. And here you are, Annabelle, worrying about the lack of choice of clothes in the shops. Why, if you didn't buy another single thing, you would have enough to last most people for the next ten years. I happen to know that your wardrobe is bulging at the seams.'

'But I just had to have a new outfit for tonight,' Annabelle said resentfully. 'It's Jessica's birthday party and you wouldn't want me to go looking a mess, would you?'

When her father didn't respond as he usually did, Annabelle looked towards her mother for support, but for the first time in her life she didn't find it. Deciding to try a different tack she lowered her head and said quietly, 'I'm sorry. I didn't think. But don't worry – I'll be really careful from now on, honestly I will. You're quite right – I don't need any more new clothes and I won't buy anything else for ages.'

'I'm pleased to hear it, because as your mother has informed you, things are going to have to change around here for the foreseeable future.'

'I know, but you didn't really mean what Mummy said, did you? About me getting a job?'

'I'm afraid I did,' Richard said firmly. 'And I suggest you go about it as soon as possible, because as from now, I am stopping your allowance. I have no choice, I'm sorry.'

Annabelle's mouth gaped open. Things were not going at all as she had planned, but she guessed that she would only annoy her father more if she pursued it now, so she swallowed her temper and asked instead, 'Could you give me a lift to the party, please, Daddy?'

'No, I can't, dear. Petrol is getting very hard to obtain and Jessica only lives ten minutes' walk away.'

'But I can't be expected to walk there in *these* shoes,' Annabelle gasped. 'And it's so dark outside.'

'Then stay in. It's not wise to go out after dark at the moment anyway. And if you must go, don't forget to take your gas mask.'

Her new resolution forgotten, Annabelle stamped her daintily shod foot. 'Now you're just being mean!'

'No, I am not. It's called being sensible. And if the air-raid sirens go off before you get to Jessica's, make sure that you head for the nearest shelter.'

Annabelle had never seen her father in this mood before, and realising that for now at least he was not going to be swayed, she turned on her heel and marched off to fetch her new coat and the hated gas mask. She detested having to carry it everywhere with her and saw little point in it anyway. Word had it that the Germans would be targeting the factories on the other side of the city, so she didn't see why she should have to lug the damn thing everywhere. For a moment, a sense of the enormity of what was happening to them all overwhelmed her in a wave of fear about the future. Then she pulled herself together and brushed her feelings to one side.

Blasted war – I'll be glad when it's over and things can get back to normal, she thought, and in no time at all she had slammed the door and was making her way through the icy, darkened streets.

Chapter Two

'Come along, Miss Kent. Get this lot tidied away now. An untidy counter will not do, now will it?'

'No, Mrs Broadstairs,' the mousy-haired girl muttered as she hastily shuffled the gloves the customer had tried on into pairs. The woman had been difficult to say the very least, trying on nearly every pair of gloves available and then leaving without even buying any – a fact of which Mrs Broadstairs was acutely aware. Not that she was surprised. Dorothy Kent was a timid little thing, hardly suited to serving the public in her opinion, with barely any social graces at all, but then if Mr Bradley felt that Miss Kent was up to serving, who was she to argue?

Percival Bradley, the manager, ruled his shop like a sergeant-major – not that he could do any wrong in Mrs Broadstairs's eyes. She had been in awe of the man, and more than a little enamoured of him, ever since the day she had started at Owen Owen as his assistant. Unfortunately, he never seemed to notice her – which was a shame as she'd been widowed for the last four years and now felt ready to look for a suitable replacement – and Mr Bradley more than fitted the bill. As far as she was aware, he had never been married, although she couldn't understand how he'd managed to escape the net. Nearing sixty, he was still a fine figure of a man, and seeing as she wasn't far behind him in age, her chances of finding a new husband were narrowing significantly, although she prided herself on being as smart as a new pin. Unfortunately, up to now, all her best attempts at flirtation had come to nothing, and each time this happened she tended to take her frustrations out on the shop girls – as she was doing now with young Dorothy.

As well as being Mr Bradley's assistant, Mrs Broadstairs was also responsible for deciding which girls would work in which departments, especially the new employees. It was a task at which she excelled. Usually she could tell within minutes which department a particular girl would be best suited to. Not that it always worked out as she would have liked any more. Now that they were so short-staffed, the girls had to go where they were most needed for much of the time.

The girl was fumbling in her haste to tidy the counter and after tutting, Mrs Broadstairs swept away.

Dotty, as she was known, sighed with relief. This was only her second month at Owen Owen and she was still doing her best to fit in. It was her first job and although there was an element of excitement in working for a living, it was still all rather strange too. Dotty had had a lot of adjusting to do over the last few months. She had been dumped in an orphanage on the other side of the city by her mother when she was a very new baby, and had stayed there until just before her eighteenth birthday. Her welfare worker had then found her lodgings in King Edward Road in Hillfields, and had also helped her to get this job so that she could become independent and pay her own way.

Dotty could clearly remember how excited she had been when her welfare worker had told her about the room, but when she took her along to see it, Dotty's first glimpse had been somewhat of a disappointment, to say the very least. It was an attic room situated in a large Victorian terraced house that had been divided into three floors, and it was barely big enough to swing a cat around in, consisting of a small bedsitting room and a kitchenette that housed a sink and two grimy gas-rings. A grubby settee pulled out to make into a bed at night with the addition of pillows and an eider-down, but then she had consoled herself; at least the place would be all hers and she wouldn't have to share it with anyone, which was a first for Dotty. To get to the attic meant a long climb up a number of steep stairs. The bathroom, which was shared by all the residents, was on the second floor, but after one glance inside, Dotty knew that she would rather die than ever use it. She would make do with a good strip wash each night and then visit the public baths once a week.

Dotty had always shared a dormitory with other girls and she had become used to keeping herself to herself, so she'd decided that she would look at 'going it alone' as an adventure. The only person she had ever been remotely close to was Miss Timms, a gentle woman who had worked at the orphanage for as long as Dotty could remember. Miss Timms had been a great favourite there, especially with the younger children, for she would read to them at bedtime and sit them on her lap and rock them when they were feeling unwell. In actual fact, Dotty realised that Miss Timms was the only person she would really miss, although the woman had promised to visit her often, which had made the parting bearable. And the fact that the room was so run-down would give her something to do each night after work, Dotty told herself. She would buy some paint and brighten it up no end, and it was quite exciting to think that she could choose any colour she wanted – *if* she could get hold of the paint, that was. Everything was suddenly in short supply since the war had broken out.

The next big step had been when Miss Wood, the welfare worker, had taken her along for an interview at Owen Owen. Dotty had been quaking in her shoes and sure that she would never get the job in such a posh department store. All the other shop girls they passed on the way to the office looked so pretty and so smart that she didn't think she stood a chance. But much to her amazement she had got the job, although she did wonder if it was because many of the shop girls had now gone into munitions factories, where they were paid better money.

Miss Timms had taken her shopping to purchase two black skirts and two white blouses as well as a pair of sensible black shoes that would be suitable for work, and in no time at all she had been deposited in the flat. For the first time in her life she was truly alone and it was more than a little daunting. Dotty had become institutionalised over the years and was used to following a strict routine. Admittedly, the staff at the orphanage had never been cruel to her, but apart from Miss Timms the rest of them had been too busy to give any one particular child any special attention, and so she had become used to doing as she was told and obeying orders. And now suddenly here she was, free as a bird to do whatever she chose and it was taking some getting used to.

Up until now, the other girls she worked with had more or less ignored her, although Dotty would find them huddled in small groups, smoking and chatting about what film they had been to see or what music they liked, in the staff dining room at break. She herself had never been to the cinema and longed to go but was too afraid to venture into a picture-house on her own. The other girls would glance at her and smile but rarely tried to include her in their conversations, for on the few occasions that they had, Dotty had blushed furiously and become tongue-tied. And so she would sit and watch enviously, wondering how they managed to get their hair looking so nice and their make-up so perfect, painfully aware that she was a real plain Jane. Her hair was as straight as a poker, as Miss Timms had used to tease her, and she was so slim that she was almost boyish.

Coming back to the present, she renewed her efforts when she saw Mr Bradley glance her way, and in no time at all the gloves were replaced neatly beneath the glass counter. Through the window she could see that it was growing dark and she knew that it must be getting on for home time. Other girls were bustling about tidying the hats that were strategically placed for best effect about the shop, and others were dusting their counters whilst keeping an eye on Mr Bradley's movements. They all knew that he would not allow any of them to go home until the whole place was spotless, and so they scurried about like ants, putting the shop to rights.

At last Mr Bradley was satisfied with their efforts and he waved his hand dismissively as Mrs Broadstairs followed him about like a lovesick puppy. The girls trooped away to the staff room where they chatted animatedly about what they were going to do that night as they wrapped up warmly. Dotty listened wistfully as she shrugged her arms into her drab brown coat. It was the one that the orphanage had supplied; plain but serviceable, as were all the clothes that the children there were given. I'll perhaps save up and get myself a new one, Dotty thought as they all began the long trek through the department store. They passed the lingerie department and the bridal department where the shop assistants were still throwing snow-white sheets across the gowns on mannequins that were dotted about, and Dotty sighed dreamily as she tried to imagine how it would feel to wear such a dress – not that she was ever likely to find out. She needed no one to tell her that she was as plain as a pikestaff. The mirror told her that every time she glimpsed herself in it.

A doorman stood at either side of the exit when the girls finally reached the ground floor. The doors had been closed to the public for the day now, but they unlocked them for the staff to leave, flirting outrageously with the prettier ones. But no one bothered Dotty or even seemed to notice her for that matter; it didn't trouble her, she was used to it by now.

The cold outside took her breath away and after pulling her collar higher she set out for the Pool Meadow bus station. Frost was already forming on the pavements and the thought of going back to a cold empty room and making herself a meal was not appealing. At least at the orphanage she had had her meals prepared for her, and had been surrounded by people. Still, there was no going back; so she knew she would just have to make the best of it.

The smell of boiled cabbage and the sounds of babies crying met her when she entered the house. She was cold and tired by then and she trudged wearily up the steep staircase. Once inside the tiny room she hastily lit the gas-fire, then went to rummage in the only cupboard the room possessed. Her search came up with a tin of soup, so after taking the lid off with a tin opener, she put it in a saucepan on the gas-ring to heat up, then peeled off her layers of outer clothing before turning the wireless on. The sound of Bing Crosby floated around the room as another lonely night loomed ahead of her. The only visitors she had had since moving in were her welfare worker and Miss Timms.

Placing the kettle on the other gas-ring, she then turned to the bucket of cold water that she stood her milk in, only to find that it had curdled. She wrinkled her nose as she sniffed it before tipping it down the sink, then turned the soup off. There was nothing else for it; if she wanted a cup of tea that evening she would have to go to the corner shop, although she didn't fancy venturing outside into the cold again. She pulled her boots and her coat back on then hurried out onto the landing, locking her door behind her. It should only take her ten minutes, if she hurried.

She had reached the landing below when a door opened and a harassed-looking woman appeared clutching a wailing baby in her arms.

'Ah, I thought I heard yer comin' down the stairs, luvvie,' she said. 'You ain't off to the shop by any chance, are yer?'

'I am actually,' Dotty answered.

'Ooh, then yer couldn't do me a big favour an' fetch me a loaf back, could yer? This 'un's been yarkin' her head off fer the last 'alf an 'our. I reckon she's hungry an' I ain't been able to get out 'cos the other two are down wi' the measles. Poor little mites. Still, I suppose I shouldn't grumble. At least it's stopped 'em from bein' evacuated, fer now at least.'

'Of course I will, Mrs Cousins,' Dotty responded kindly. She felt so sorry for the poor woman. Her husband had been one of the first victims of the war, being killed in an accident just four weeks after joining up. Mrs Cousins had been forced to leave their home then and had ended up here with three small children to care for and barely tuppence to rub together, from what Dotty could make of it. It seemed such a shame, but then she was only one of many who were suffering because of the war, and Dotty supposed she should think her own self lucky. There was some compensation to being alone: at least she had no one else but herself to worry about.

Taking the money that the older woman held out, she smiled and hurried on her way, grimacing as she passed the bathroom. The smell that issued from it was appalling and she wasn't surprised that no one ever used it. All the residents preferred to go to the outside privy, which at least had the benefit of a strong flush and fresh air coming through a broken window. Dotty thought it was probably her turn to cut up squares of newspaper to hang on the string there.

The frost on the pavements had thickened now and her breath floated in front of her like lace, but soon the corner shop came into sight and she hurried inside to get the bread and milk.

Once back at the house she toiled up the first two flights of stairs and tapped on Mrs Cousins's door. The baby was still crying as Dotty thrust the loaf towards the woman, along with the half-a-crown she had given her.

'But you've not taken anythin' for it,' the woman protested. She was dressed in an old pair of men's trousers and a baggy Fair Isle jumper that Dotty supposed might be her late husband's, the only thing she had ever seen her in, and a scarf was tied turban-like around her hair.

'Oh, the shopkeeper let me have it for nothing because it's yesterday's and a little stale, but I'm sure it will still be all right if you eat it tonight. Oh, and there's a bottle of milk here too that he was going to throw away. He was just about to shut.'

Mrs Cousins looked puzzled as she squeezed the bread. 'Well, it feels fresh enough to me. Are yer quite sure it didn't cost yer nowt?'

'Absolutely.' Dotty began to move away, clutching her own pint of milk. Her feet felt as if they were going to drop off after being on them all day, and all she wanted was to settle down by the fire for the night with the wireless for company. She didn't want to give Mrs Cousins an opportunity to question her too closely either. She had treated the poor woman to the milk and bread, but what was the harm in a little white lie if it was doing someone a kindness? As she hurried on, she realised with a little start that Mrs Cousins was the only person who had spoken to her all day, apart from Mrs Broadstairs when she was issuing her orders, of course, and the customers she had served.

The flat was warm when she got back up to the top floor, which was something at least, so she turned the heat back on under the soup and sighed with pleasure as she kicked her boots off, sat down and stretched her feet out by the fire.

'Now then, Miss Kent, there's been a slight change of plan for today,' Mrs Broadstairs informed her when she got into work the next morning. 'One of the girls in the lingerie department is off sick, so I've told the floor manager that you may help out down there today. Do you think you can manage that?' Personally, she had grave reservations about sending Dotty to that particular department. All the girls who worked there were so much more glamorous than her, and seemed to have so much more about them. But then desperate times called for desperate measures. The whole store had been operating on a skeleton staff since the outbreak of war, and Dotty was the best she could manage. She certainly wasn't going to send one of her more experienced girls. It wouldn't do at all if sales were to be down on her own floor.

'Yes, Mrs Broadstairs, I'll be fine,' Dotty assured her meekly.

'Then run along, dear. We don't want to upset the floor manager now, do we? Her name is Miss Norton. Just tell her I sent you.'

Mrs Broadstairs then scurried away, leaving Dotty to turn and head for the stairs. The lingerie department was down on the next floor and she had often wondered what it would be like to work there. Admittedly, there was not the same wide selection of underwear and nightwear displayed as there had been before the war, but there were still the odd few extravagant items in pure silk. Dotty couldn't even begin to imagine how it would feel to wear anything so expensive. The orphanage had always made sure that the children were adequately turned out, but their budget had not run to anything other than hardwearing materials, and the habits of a lifetime were hard to break. Dotty still tended to go for sensible shoes and clothes, partly because she had no fashion sense whatsoever. She hadn't needed to be fashionable in the orphanage. She had just been one of many. Now as she entered the lingerie department she felt slightly out of her depth as she gazed about at the mannequins strategically placed to catch the customers' eyes; a blush rose into her cheeks. It seemed strange to see such personal items displayed so blatantly, but then men rarely ventured into this particular department, which Dotty felt was just as well.

Glass-topped counters were placed all along one wall. In one was a selection of cotton knickers – very serviceable and very much in demand since the outbreak of the war. Another counter contained brassières of various sizes and colours. There were nightdresses in flannelette and cotton, and pyjamas, dressing-gowns, and stockings, which were getting much harder to come by and ridiculously expensive.

Along the opposite wall were the counters containing the more exclusive items in silks and satins, some trimmed with guipure lace. There was even an exquisite negligée set on display that got Dotty's pulse racing, and she flushed at the thought of anyone daring to wear it. She was also terrified at the prospect of having to show it to anyone. It was so delicate that she was sure it would tear if she so much as blew on it. But thankfully, Miss Norton took one look at her and guided her to the other side of the room. Dotty seemed a nice, helpful enough sort of girl but she was hardly the sort to show off Miss Norton's treasured exclusive lines.

The day passed slowly and Dotty was glad when it was time to go home. No one in the lingerie department had bothered to talk to her even at break-time, and it was a relief to escape into the chilly early evening air. The streets felt eerie now that everyone had blackout curtains up at their windows. Even the display windows on the shopfronts no longer turned on their lights and Dotty imagined she could have been walking through a ghost town. She quickly found herself making up stories in her head as she moved along. It was something she had done for as far back as she could remember, and she was never happier than when she was writing her stories down. Writing went a long way towards easing her loneliness. The imaginary characters she created were all beautiful, exciting people, nothing at all like herself, and sometimes she got so involved with them that they actually became real people to her, like the family that she had never known. Her English teacher and Miss Timms had always encouraged her and had urged her to carry on with it when she left school, but of course she didn't have so much time now, although she still tried to write a few pages each night before she went to sleep.

Dotty had become so engrossed in the latest plot growing in her mind that it was almost a shock when she found herself at the bus station. She paid her fare and climbed aboard, then sighed sadly. This being independent wasn't turning out to be quite as satisfying as she had thought it would be. In fact, if she were to be honest with herself, she was lonelier than ever.

Chapter Three

Lucy Ford sat with her handbag balanced primly on her lap as she discreetly glanced at the other girl in the waiting area. The girl was positively beautiful and so well dressed that she might have been a model. Surely she couldn't be here for a job interview too? She certainly didn't look as if she needed a job, but then who was she to judge? The world seemed to have turned upside down since Hitler came to power.

She gulped as she thought of her older brother, Joel, who had joined up only the month before. He had been sent to a training camp on the shores of Lake Windermere, but other than a brief letter from him that had arrived the previous week, that was all she knew. The letter had been heavily censored and she had a terrible feeling that once he had completed his training, Joel would join the other forces that had entered France. In September the British Expeditionary Forces had been taken by troop trains and lorries to ports in the south of England where ferries and transports escorted by destroyers had taken them across the Channel to take up position alongside the French army. Poor Joel, she thought, he must be finding it so difficult. He had always been such a shy, reserved sort of chap, although he had been her rock since they had lost their mother and father almost five years ago following the birth of Mary, the youngest family member. They had moved almost immediately to a smaller house on the other side of Coventry and Joel had worked hard to support them all, until his call-up papers dropped on the doormat; after which Lucy knew that, from then on, it would be down to her to earn a living to keep herself and Mary until, God willing, Joel returned.

Now, as she peeped at the other girl again, her heart dropped. If it were a choice between her and this girl, she would never stand a chance. At that moment the girl glanced up, and seeing Lucy looking at her, she asked, 'Here for a job interview, are you?'

She was very well spoken, which made Lucy feel even worse. 'Y-yes,' she stammered, suddenly feeling very dull and dowdy.

'Hm, so am I,' the girl said, sounding none too pleased about it. 'I must have been here for *hours* already. I wonder how much longer they'll keep us waiting? I'm Annabelle Smythe, by the way. How do you do?'

Lucy managed to flash a weak smile. 'I'm very well, thank you, and I'm Lucy – Lucy Ford.'

The conversation was stopped from going any further when the office door suddenly opened and a middle-aged woman with a tight bun on the back of her head and a sour expression called out, 'Miss Smythe.'

As Annabelle rose, Lucy noted that she didn't look the least bit nervous, whereas her own heart was thumping so loudly that she was certain everyone within a mile radius would surely hear it.

Annabelle straightened her skirt and followed the woman without a qualm as Lucy swiped her sweaty palms down the side of her dingy navy-blue coat. I may as well go home now, she thought despondently. I stand no chance against that one if there's only the one job going, but she forced herself to carry on sitting there. The savings that Joel had left behind to tide her and Mary over were dwindling fast now, and Lucy knew that she would *have* to find a job – any job, even cleaning public lavatories if that was all she could get – or how were they to live? Her thoughts moved on to Mary – poor little scrap. Already it was apparent that there was something not quite normal about her. The health visitor at the clinic had told Lucy quite callously that Mary was 'backward'. Lucy hated that term. Mary was very slow in her development, admittedly, but Lucy still had high hopes that the little girl would catch up with other children her age, given time. Still, at least she had found someone who was prepared to care for her sister, if and when she found a job. Their kindly neighbour, Mrs Price, affectionately known as Mrs P, was an amazon of a woman with a heart to match, and since the Ford family had moved in next door to the Prices, the woman had been a godsend. The two younger Price children, Barry and Beryl, had been evacuated to the country a couple of months earlier, and now the big woman was happy to pour all the love she usually reserved for them onto Mary.

Momentarily forgetting her nervousness, Lucy grinned as she thought back to the day she had been told that Mary was 'backward' and Mrs P's indignation.

'Silly buggers,' she'd declared angrily. 'What do they know? Happen the poor little mite is just a bit slower at graspin' things than other kids her age, but she'll catch up – you'll see.'

Lucy's thoughts were dragged back to the present and the nervousness returned with a vengeance as the door opened and the striking blonde reappeared. She whispered to Lucy as she sailed past in a gust of Chanel No. 5, 'Looks like I just got myself a job,' but Lucy had no time to do anything other than nod before the stern-faced woman appeared again.

'Miss Ford,' she barked.

Lucy shot to her feet and almost stumbled in her haste to follow the woman into a room where a gentleman with the most enormous bulbous nose she had ever seen was sitting at a desk waiting to interview her.

Ten minutes later, she left the place in a daze. She was to start as a shop assistant at eight o'clock sharp the following Monday morning.

'So 'ow did it go, sweet'eart?' Mrs P asked when Lucy went to pick Mary up half an hour later.

'I got the job,' Lucy informed her.

'Well, what yer lookin' so glum for then?' Mrs P raised an eyebrow as she jiggled Mary up and down on her plump knee. 'That's good, ain't it?'

'Oh yes,' Lucy assured her hastily. 'I suppose I'm just feeling a little . . . Oh, I don't know – nervous, I suppose. Most of the girls who work there seem very glamorous and pretty. I just wonder how I'll fit in. And are you *quite* sure that you won't mind caring for Mary whilst I'm at work?'

'Huh, I've hardly got a lot else to do to pass the time, have I? An' this little soul is as good as the day is long. It'll be a pleasure, so don't you go frettin' about that. As fer you fittin' in . . . . Well, yer as good as any o' them an' better than most,

I don't mind bettin',' Mrs P replied as she eyed the girl up and down.

Lucy really was an extremely attractive girl, although she appeared to be completely unaware of the fact. She was tall and slim with lovely shoulder-length auburn hair that turned to fiery red in the sunshine, and big green eyes that looked almost too big for her heart-shaped face. Given smarter clothes and with a little bit of make-up on, Mrs P was certain she could have been quite striking. But then she supposed the poor kid didn't get an awful lot of time for titivating as most girls her age did. She was too busy caring for Mary and keeping her home running, which was a crying shame as far as Mrs P was concerned.

In actual fact, the Ford family were a little bit of a mystery and very tight-lipped about their past. All Mrs P knew about them was that they had lost both their parents five years ago, although she had no idea how they had died, and whenever she asked any questions about them, Lucy closed up like a clam. Mrs P supposed it was too painful for the girl to talk about. But there was no doubt she was as good as gold to her little sister, like a little mother, and she kept their tiny terraced house as neat as a new pin. Mrs P still felt that it was an awful responsibility for such a young woman, even more so since her brother had been called up. Now Joel was a nice lad an' all. Good husband material for some lucky girl, although he'd not have much chance for romance now till this damn war was over.

The big woman sighed as she thought of her own son, who had also gone to fight for his country. With her two youngest sent off to the country too, she and her husband Fred were rattling around like peas in a pod and sometimes she felt that her life had no purpose any more. Were it not for little Mary, she was sure she would have gone stark staring mad. She had been used to the small house teeming with kids and noise, and laughter bouncing off the walls, but now the quietness often threatened to choke her. And she was painfully aware that things could get much worse. All the young men, including her oldest son, Freddy, had already been called up, but if the war didn't end soon then there was a faint chance that her husband might be called too, even if he was working in a munitions factory and was a bit long in the tooth. It just didn't bear thinking about.

She put Mary down and struggled out of the easy chair at the side of the fireplace. A fire was licking up the chimney and despite the fact that the furniture had seen better days, the room was cosy and welcoming.

'I'll make us a nice cuppa,' she declared as she headed for the kettle, then on a more serious note she confided, 'I've half a mind to get the kids back from the country. I mean, there ain't nothin' happened here as yet, is there? An' so they might as well be at home, the way I see it.'

'That doesn't mean that nothing *will* happen though, Mrs P,' Lucy pointed out. 'And at least you know they're safer there.'

'Yes – but what if they ain't bein' properly looked after?' the woman fretted as she rinsed the heavy brown teapot and carefully spooned tea leaves into it.

'I'm sure they are.' Lucy's heart went out to her. Mrs P adored her family and she could well imagine how hard being separated from them all must be for her.

In no time at all, she and Mrs P were sitting at the kitchen table enjoying a cup of Typhoo as Mary played with a pile of brightly painted wooden bricks on the hearthrug. She'd had a beaker of milk and a Royal Scot biscuit from Mrs P's polka-dot biscuit barrel.

'Now then,' Mrs P took a noisy slurp of her tea before

asking, 'What are you to wear for work then? Do you have to wear a uniform?'

'Not a uniform exactly but a white blouse, a black skirt and sensible black shoes.' Lucy hadn't given it much thought up until now, but she suddenly realised that she didn't possess such a thing as a white blouse, and with funds being as tight as they were, how was she going to afford one?

'I've got the shoes and a suitable skirt, but I don't know what I'm going to do about a blouse,' she said worriedly.

Mrs P chuckled. 'Well, you've no need to worry on that score. I just happen to have two good white linen pillowcases that would make a lovely blouse, and thank Gawd I'm a dab hand wi' a needle an' thread. I've had to be, wi' my tribe over the years. I'll get me old Singer sewin' machine out from under the stairs an' I'll run you one up in no time.'

'But I couldn't let you do that,' Lucy objected. 'You do more than enough for me already.'

'Rubbish!' Mrs P topped their cups up and stirred in another spoon of sugar each, saying sagely, 'I dare say this is somethin' else we'll have to get used to doin' wi'out soon. My Fred loves his sweet cuppa, but the ration we'll be allowed won't last a day, let alone a week. Still, on a more cheerful note I heard from our Freddy today. Now that he's done his trainin' he's been sent to Preston an' he thinks they'll be shippin' 'em over to France any day.'

Seeing the deep concern on the older woman's face, Lucy's heart went out to her. She knew how much she worried about Freddy, but then most women with sons the same age were in the same position. Each of them dreaded seeing the telegraph boy cycling towards their house and prayed that he would pass them by. Freddy was actually a very nice young man and had made it more than clear that he liked

Lucy, but the girl wasn't interested in having a boyfriend, much to Mrs P's disappointment. Her boy could have done a lot worse than take up with young Lucy as far as she was concerned, but then who knew what might happen when the war was over? She could live in hope.

'I'm sure he'll be fine,' Lucy said as she patted Mrs P's hand. The words sounded so inadequate even to her own ears, but what else could she say? Rising from her seat, she began to gather Mary's things together now, and once they were ready to leave, she gave Mrs P an affectionate hug.

'Thanks so much for having Mary and I'll see you tomorrow, shall I?'

'You will that, luvvie.' The woman forced a smile as she saw Lucy out, then moving back to the table she took up Freddy's letter again and reread every word, wondering if the whole damn world had gone mad. The war won't last for long – it can't do, not after the last lot, she told herself, and helped herself to a Garibaldi biscuit to dunk in what remained of her tea.

Chapter Four

'Right then, young ladies,' Mrs Broadstairs said the following Monday morning as she eyed the new recruits critically. 'A few rules before I show you to the departments where you will be working. First of all, you must remember that the customer is *always* right! You must never, and I repeat *never*, argue with a customer even if you feel their choice is unwise. Customers are hard to come by in these difficult times. And Miss Smythe, I have to say those shoes are *most* unsuitable. You were told to wear flats, not high heels. I have no doubt you will wish you had by the end of the day when your feet are aching.'

Annabelle stared back at her haughtily. 'I don't own any flat shoes, nor do I wish to.'

Mrs Broadstairs positively bristled. She could see that she might have problems with this one. Miss Smythe was a right little madam if she wasn't very much mistaken, but then no doubt she wouldn't be quite so cocky after a long day on her feet. The other girl, Miss Ford, looked all right though. Her clothes were plain but smart and her auburn hair was tied neatly back into a ribbon at the nape of her neck. She didn't appear to have a cocky attitude like the other girl either, which was something to be thankful for.

'You two will have your morning break at eleven a.m. The staff dining room is located on the top floor but you will be back in your departments at eleven fifteen promptly. Your lunch break is from one to one thirty, and afternoon break three thirty until three forty-five. Is that quite clear?'

When both girls nodded, Annabelle somewhat resentfully, Mrs Broadstairs went on, 'Neither of you will have access to the tills until you have more experience – you are junior sales personnel. And you will both do exactly as the shop-floor manager tells you, be it dusting or stock-taking.' She got a little thrill of satisfaction when she saw the look of horror that flitted across the blonde's face. She obviously wasn't used to such lowly tasks if her clothes were anything to go by, especially the white ruffled blouse she was wearing, which looked suspiciously like pure silk; Mrs Broadstairs wouldn't have minded betting that they'd probably cost more than the girl would earn in a whole month here. Still, there was a war on and everyone was having to make sacrifices, so why should this young woman be exempted?

'For now you will both work on whichever floor you are needed on, on any particular day,' the woman continued. 'It could be that one day you may find yourselves in the shoe department and the next on lingerie or wherever. Sadly, many of our gentlemen employees have gone to join the war, so we have to do our best to keep the shop running efficiently whichever way we can. Working in different departments will also give you a wider knowledge of the way the store is run. As I have explained, for the first few weeks you will probably do the more menial jobs, but when the floor managers feel that your skills are sufficiently developed, you will be allowed to start to serve the customers.'

Mrs Broadstairs was quick to note that Annabelle was looking gloomier by the minute, although Lucy appeared quite happy with the arrangement. 'Come along then, girls,' she told them. 'Before you begin work I will give you a brief tour of the store and introduce you to the various floor managers. Follow me.'

Patting her hair, which was so thick with setting lotion that it looked as if it wouldn't budge even in a gale-force wind, the woman turned about, heading for the lift that ran from the ground floor to the very top of the store. The lift stopped at each floor and in no time at all both girls were wondering how they were ever going to find their way about. The shop was enormous and there was so much to remember. But eventually, Mrs Broadstairs stopped in the men's department and told Lucy, 'This is where you will be working for today. Mr O'Dell is the floor manager and I've no doubt he will find you plenty to do.'

Lucy looked over to see an elderly man coming towards them with a broad smile on his face and she thought perhaps things wouldn't be so bad, after all. He looked nice enough.

'Hello, my dear,' he greeted her. 'Mrs Broadstairs informed me that I would be having a temporary new assistant today, and I must say I was glad of the fact. We are seriously short-staffed at present with all our young men disappearing. But there we are, we shall just have to make the best of things, won't we, and pray that the war will soon be over.'

Lucy warmed to him immediately. He looked like everyone's favourite grandad although he was very smartly turned out in a dark grey suit, a crisp white shirt and a pale blue tie. He was slightly shorter than her and plump, with wispy grey hair and startlingly blue eyes.

'So come along then,' he said pleasantly.' I'll show you where everything is so that you can get your bearings. Over on this side are the suits, and over there are the shirts and ties . . .'

Seeing that Lucy was now safely in her colleague's capable hands, Mrs Broadstairs turned back towards the lift, abruptly telling Annabelle, 'Right, we'll go and get you settled now. You will be working in the lingerie department for the rest of this week.'

Mrs Broadstairs was experienced enough to know that Annabelle would be perfectly suited to this department. Women who shopped there were usually looking to be a little extravagant and they liked to be surrounded by young attractive women, so Annabelle would certainly fit the bill.

Once in the lingerie department they were met by Miss Williams who, along with Miss Norton, had that particular department running like clockwork. Tall and slim, she looked to be in her late thirties and was known for being fairly strict with her staff. As she was keen on telling them, 'There is a place for everything and everything has its place.'

She was exactly as Annabelle had imagined a spinster to be – tall and thin with a nose so sharp it could have cut butter, and she was impeccably dressed in a smart two-piece costume that was, however, quite old-fashioned. Her hair, which was fair, was pulled back into a tight bun on the back of her head and large rimless spectacles were perched on the end of that knife of a nose.

Despite the daunting floor manager, Annabelle was actually secretly pleased to be in this particular department.

At least she had nice things to look at here. It would have been awful to have been stuck in household wares or somewhere boring like that.

Her eyes flicked appreciatively over the display stands and came to rest on a young mousy-haired girl who was busily dusting the tops of the glass counters as if her very life depended on it. The girl offered her a nervous smile but Annabelle stuck her nose in the air and turned her attention back to what Miss Williams was saying, wondering how such a dowdy-looking girl had ever got to work in such a glamorous department. They really must be short of staff!

And then a customer emerged from the lift, and forgetting all about Annabelle, Miss Williams almost pounced on the woman with a smile so wide that her plain face was quite transformed, trilling, 'Hello, madam, how may we help you?'

Crikey, she could be quite attractive if she'd take a bit of trouble with herself, Annabelle thought as she crossed to examine a pretty lace bra that had caught her eye. It was on a stand quite close to the counter that the mousy-haired girl was dusting and now she looked at Annabelle and said shyly, 'Hello, I'm Dotty.'

'Annabelle Smythe,' Annabelle introduced herself imperiously and Dotty was completely bowled over by her. The girl was so beautiful that she might have been a model out of one of the magazines she was so fond of. In fact, Dotty wondered if perhaps she *was* a model come to model some of the lingerie.

'Worked here for long, have you?' Annabelle asked now. She was bored already.

'Not very long,' Dotty admitted. 'But it's quite nice here.'

'Hmm, well I could certainly think of better ways of spending my time,' Annabelle said petulantly. By now,

Miss Williams had passed the customer over to a senior member of the sales staff and was bearing down on Annabelle again.

'Right then, Miss Smythe. Let me show you around so that you are properly acquainted with where everything is when the time comes for you to serve the customers. Over here we keep the knickers, ranging from cotton to pure silk, and over there are the brassières. Later on I shall show you the correct way to measure a customer for those. You would be shocked at how many women don't wear the correct size. And over here . . .' Her voice droned on as Annabelle reluctantly followed her about. It looked set to be a very long day.

At last it was time for the morning break. To Annabelle, who was usually still in bed at this time, the morning had passed interminably slowly. As she entered the lift, Dotty followed her in, but Annabelle didn't bother to speak. She just wanted to go home. And when she did she would tell her father how unreasonable he was being. She was even prepared for him to cut her allowance if it meant not having to come back to this place again. There had only been four customers who had actually bought anything all morning, although the foot traffic through the lingerie department had been quite heavy. But that didn't mean that Miss Williams had allowed her to stand idly about. The blasted woman had had her in the stock room for the last hour unpacking the underwear that had been delivered to the store the day before, and after the break she had informed Annabelle that she must transfer it all to the correct places on the shop floor.

'Do you think you will like working here?' Dotty plucked up the courage to ask when the lift started to rise.

Annabelle glared at her as if she had taken leave of her senses. 'How could anyone *like* working?'

Dotty gulped and wished that she had kept her mouth shut, and the rest of the ride to the top floor was made in silence.

When the lift stopped, Annabelle found herself in a large staff dining room. It was nowhere near as nice as the restaurant that the customers used, but she made her way to the counter all the same and ordered a cup of tea. Then she stood indecisively looking around. Tables covered in plain oilskin cloths were dotted all about the room, but she saw that the place was saved from looking drab by the panoramic views of the city from the windows. The rest of the staff were sitting in little groups chatting and laughing, and she suddenly felt like a fish out of water; all her confidence fled.

Seeing that Annabelle was looking uncomfortable, Dotty decided to forget her haughty attitude in the lift and suggested, 'Why don't you come and sit with me? We could go over there – look. There's a table by the window.'

Annabelle followed her gaze and shrugged; she didn't have any better option and there was only one other girl sitting there. As they walked towards her, wending their way through the tables, Annabelle saw that the girl was actually quite pretty, or at least she could have been if she'd known how to look after herself. She had quite striking green eyes and her hair was a lovely auburn colour, but she had pulled it back into a ponytail; she seemed to be the only person sitting alone in the whole room.

'Would you mind very much if we joined you?' Dotty asked politely as they neared the table and the girl smiled.

'Actually, I'd be really grateful if you would,' she admitted. 'I'm feeling a bit strange sitting here all on my own but I only started today and I don't know anyone.' She beamed at Annabelle.

'So how are you finding your first day?' Annabelle asked eventually, although she wasn't really that interested.

'I'm quite enjoying it actually, but I'm not so sure my floor manager is that pleased with me,' Lucy confided. 'There's so much to remember and I keep putting things in the wrong places. He sent me downstairs for something earlier on and I actually got lost trying to find my way back. The store is huge! Still, it's early days, isn't it? I dare say I'll get the hang of it, although I never realised there was so much to shop work. I thought the assistants just stood about all day until there was a customer to serve.'

'Oh, there's much more to it than that,' Dotty piped up. 'We aren't allowed to be idle for a second, especially since they are so short-staffed. I've been here for two months already, but I'm still only allowed to serve a customer if the rest of the senior staff are busy.'

'Well, I think it's disgusting!' Annabelle rubbed her sore feet under the table. She had to grudgingly admit that Mrs Broadstairs was right when she said that high heels weren't a good idea for work. Her feet were throbbing already and she still had the biggest part of the day to get through. '*I* certainly don't intend to spend my days dusting and stocking shelves,' she huffed.

Lucy and Dotty exchanged an amused smile. Both of them were just grateful to have jobs, but it certainly didn't appear to be the same for Annabelle. They watched as she took a cigarette from her bag and lit it, then she stared at them through a haze of blue smoke as she asked, 'Do you both live locally?' She felt she ought to at least make an effort to be friendly.

The girls nodded in unison but before they could answer, Annabelle went on, 'I live in Cheylesmore with my parents and I don't mind telling you, this job wasn't *my* idea!' She sniffed indignantly. 'Daddy has cut my allowance so I had to get a job. And all because of this bloody stupid war! It's all a waste of time, if you ask me. After all, nothing's even happened yet, has it? No bombs – nothing! And half of the kids who were evacuated are coming back already. I mean, what's the point of them staying away anyway? I reckon it will all be over in no time and then we can get back to normal – and the sooner the better, I say!'

'I'd like to think you were right but I'm not so sure,' Lucy replied pensively. 'I was reading in the newspapers that some of our ships are already being sunk by magnetic mines out at sea. I'm afraid this is only the beginning and I think things will get far worse before they get better.'

'Hm, and in the meantime *we* have to suffer.' Annabelle took another long drag of her cigarette. 'They're ruining the city in the meantime, digging up shelters for everyone. Have you seen the trench one they're working on in Cox Street on the corner of Grove Road? It will shelter two hundred people when it's finished apparently, but it's a right old eyesore! Then there's another being dug in Bird Street on the old bowling green that will accommodate six hundred and forty-five people when it's finished. That's to name but a couple, not to mention the ugly Anderson shelters that are appearing in people's gardens everywhere.'

'I suppose it's just a precaution in case they're needed,' Lucy said sensibly, but Annabelle just shook her head.

'I disagree. Why would the Germans want to bomb the city centre? If they do drop any bombs, they're going to aim for the factories on the outskirts of the city, surely?'

The conversation was stopped from going any further when Dotty nervously pointed to the large clock on the wall above the counter. The catering staff, who were robed in long white coats and hairnets, were now collecting the dirty pots and the majority of the staff had already disappeared off back to their departments. 'I think it's time we were going, otherwise we'll be late.'

'Oh for goodness sake,' Annabelle groaned. 'I haven't even had time to go to the ladies yet!' Even so she ground her cigarette out and followed the other two back to the lift with a martyred expression on her face.

It was almost lunchtime when Annabelle was approached by a customer as she was arranging a nightdress on a mannequin.

'Is that pure silk, my dear?' the middle-aged woman asked her imperiously. The fur coat she was wearing looked like mink and Annabelle saw that her handbag and shoes were of the finest leather. Annabelle glanced about. She had been told that the senior staff would serve the customers, but as none of them appeared to be about she couldn't see the harm in helping the woman.

'Yes, it is,' she answered, flashing a bright smile. 'Would Madam like me to take it down so that you can see it?'

'*I'll* take over from here, Miss Smythe.' One of the senior assistants had appeared at her elbow from nowhere and Annabelle glared at her resentfully as she ushered the customer away. From the look on the assistant's face, anyone might have thought that Annabelle had committed a cardinal sin, but what was she supposed to have done? Just left a customer standing there unattended? She frowned as she glanced at the clock. Roll on lunchtime!

She was secretly pleased when she found Lucy and Dotty already sitting at the same table they had shared during the morning break when she entered the staff dining room some time later, and after buying some sandwiches and a cup of tea she joined them.

'How did your first morning go?' Dotty asked pleasantly as Annabelle sat down.

'Huh! Apart from almost getting my head bitten off when I started to serve a customer, all right I suppose,' Annabelle grumbled, then pointedly ignoring Dotty, she looked at Lucy and asked, 'How about you?'

Lucy smiled. 'Really well, considering I was dreading it. I think I might like working here. One of the girls on my floor told me they do staff outings from time to time. They all went to Southend for the day in the summer apparently, and the store laid on the bus and everything.'

Annabelle shrugged. It would take more than a promise of a day at the seaside to raise her enthusiasm. She had always been privileged to spend her holidays abroad with her parents, and after that a day out to Southend sounded positively dull, although Dotty, she noted, looked quite excited at the prospect.

'I was actually allowed to serve my first customer today,' Dotty told them now with a wide smile.

Lucy grinned. 'That's nice,' she said. 'And the other girls on my floor have been really helpful. I'm sure we'll get the hang of it eventually.'

Annabelle wished she could be so optimistic but held her tongue while Lucy and Dotty rattled on. They seemed to be getting on like a house on fire but then she had to grudgingly admit that they were nice, even if they weren't the types she usually mixed with.

She noticed in the lift after lunch that some of the other girls spoke to both Lucy and Dotty, and wondered if perhaps she shouldn't make more of an effort – but then why bother? she asked herself. She didn't intend to come back here again.

*

'I have *never* been so bored in my whole life!' Annabelle complained as she took a seat at the table in the canteen during the afternoon break and lit another cigarette. 'I don't think a day has ever passed so slowly.'

'Actually, I'm still quite enjoying it,' Lucy responded. Up until now she had spent her days cleaning the house and caring for Mary, so it was a pleasant change to have something different to focus on. She just hoped that caring for Mary would not be too much for Mrs P.

'I like working here too,' Dotty admitted shyly.

'Then you must both be crackers!'

Lucy and Dotty giggled. They had felt at ease with each other from the first moment, and seeing as both of them had led rather sheltered lives, they hoped that a friendship might develop between them.

Observing that Annabelle had now lapsed into a fully-fledged sulk, Lucy asked Dotty, 'Do you live with your parents?'

'Oh no. I was brought up in an orphanage and I've just got my own little place in Hillfields. It isn't much at the moment,' she added hastily, 'but I'm trying to do it up in my spare time. How about you?'

'Well, my parents are gone too and until he was called up I lived with my older brother and my little sister in Tile Hill.' Lucy sighed as she thought of her brother so far away. They had been very close and she missed him dreadfully. 'A neighbour is looking after my little sister now so that I can come to work.'

Even though Annabelle had appeared to be disinterested she had obviously been listening to the conversation because she now asked, 'But why hasn't your little sister been evacuated?'

'Because she isn't quite old enough, and anyway even if

she was, Mary is . . . well, she is sort of special. You know, not quite as bright as other children her age.'

'What – you mean she's backward?'

Lucy bristled. 'No, she isn't!'

'Ah, poor little thing,' Dotty said quickly, seeing that Lucy was offended. 'It must be very hard on you having to care for her and keep a home going all on your own.'

'Not really.' Lucy glared at Annabelle as she answered Dotty politely. 'Mary is a beautiful child and both Joel, that's my brother, and I think the world of her.'

This time it was Annabelle who rose from the table first, telling them, 'Right, I'm off to the ladies before we have to go back to the treadmill. Bye for now.' In fact, she doubted she would ever see either of them again because when she got home that evening and told her father how boring the work was, he would surely relent and not make her come here again.

'I don't think Annabelle is too happy to be here,' Lucy remarked as they watched her totter away on her high heels.

'Mm, I know what you mean, but needs must when there's a war on. Personally I'd rather be here than stuck in my flat on my own. I've been a bit lonely since I left the orphanage, to be honest.'

'Then you must come round to meet Mary one evening,' Lucy said kindly.

'I'd like that, thank you.' Dotty blushed and Lucy thought how different she looked when she smiled. Dotty wasn't pretty in a conventional sense but her skin was flawless, like peaches and cream, and when she smiled her eyes twinkled.

Glancing at the clock, they both rose and hurried towards the lift feeling that a new friendship had just been born.

Chapter Five

Annabelle arrived home to find her mother tackling a large pile of ironing. She looked as if she had been crying, which didn't help Annabelle's bad mood one little bit.

'I've had the most *awful* day you could ever imagine,' the girl complained bitterly as she kicked her shoes off and slouched into a chair. 'Is there a cup of tea going, and what's for dinner? The sandwiches they sold in the works canteen tasted like bloody sawdust.'

'In answer to your questions, no, there isn't any tea in the pot and I haven't even thought of what we're going to have for dinner yet,' her mother replied. 'And please don't swear, Annabelle. It really doesn't become you. Why don't *you* put the kettle on? I could do with a hot drink too. I've been washing and ironing all day.'

'Then you shouldn't have let Daddy sack Mrs Fitton,' Annabelle said nastily as she dragged herself out of the chair and headed for the sink.

'Daddy didn't have any choice. In fact, you may as well know, your father is joining up. It's barely worth keeping the garage open the way things are at present, and he wants to feel he's doing his bit towards the war.'

Annabelle spun round on her heel and stared at her mother incredulously. 'Daddy's *what?* Joining up, did you say? But he can't! Who will look after us?'

'As most other women are having to do, we shall have to look after ourselves,' her mother replied. She was obviously upset about the development but trying to put a brave face on. Deep inside, Miranda was terrified at the thought of her husband going to war. What if he was injured, or worse still – what if he never came back? But she didn't say this to Annabelle, of course, and she admired him for his decision. And so if he was prepared to be brave she had decided that she would be too, and for the first time in her entire life Annabelle would have to accept that things were going to be different from now on. She was a little shocked that Annabelle's first concern had been for herself when told of her father's decision, rather than concern for his safety, but then Miranda knew she had only herself to blame for that. Annabelle had been allowed to become utterly selfish, and having to work for a living was not going to be easy for her.

As she lifted the shirt she had been ironing to place it on a hanger, Miranda stifled the sob that rose in her throat. Soon there would be only her own and Annabelle's ironing to do and it was hard to contemplate.

Now Annabelle looked in danger of throwing one of her famous fully-fledged tantrums as she filled the kettle and slammed it on the gas-ring to boil.

'I can't believe that Daddy is just going to go away and abandon us,' she wailed as if her father was going on holiday. 'Isn't he too old to join the war?'

Miranda shook her head wearily. 'Not at all. Admittedly they called up all the younger men first, but as long as he passes his medical there is no reason why your father shouldn't join.'

'And when he is going to have that?' Annabelle snapped.

'Next Monday, after he's had time to put all his affairs at the garage in order. It will remain shut then until after the war. As your father rightly pointed out, there isn't much call for prestigious cars when petrol will soon be rationed.'

'So that means I shall have to carry on working then?'

'I'm rather afraid it does. And furthermore, I intend to do something to make myself feel useful as well.'

'Such as *what?*' Annabelle was getting crosser by the minute. She couldn't take much more of this.

'Well, I haven't really had much time to think about it, but drivers are in very short supply at the moment what with all the men being away. I could perhaps drive an ambulance or something.'

'I can't see Grandma and Grandpa being very pleased with that idea,' Annabelle said churlishly.

'Actually I've already told them what I intend to do and they think it's a wonderful idea – and they're also very proud of your father,' Miranda answered as she swiped the iron over one of Annabelle's silk petticoats. 'And don't start getting the notion that you can go running to them for hand-outs either, because even they are going to have to tighten their belts for the foreseeable future.'

Annabelle put the sugar bowl on the table so angrily that some fell on the lino and she had to bend down and sweep it up, which did not improve her temper.

Lucy hurried towards Mrs P's house, eager to see how the first day of her caring for Mary had gone. A lot rested on it because she had no intention of farming Mary off on just anybody. Joel and Mary were all she had left in the world now – well, almost – and there was nothing she wouldn't have done for them. She tapped at the door tentatively and when it was opened by Mrs P herself seconds later with a broad smile on her face, she sighed with relief.

The woman placed a finger on her lips, 'Shush, pet, the little 'un is fast asleep, bless her heart. She went out like a light not ten minutes since, so you've got time fer a nice hot cuppa while yer tell me all about how your first day's gone.'

Lucy gratefully flopped into a chair while Mrs P hurried away to return seconds later with two mugs.

'I guessed you'd be back about now so I just made a brew,' she said cheerfully as she tugged down the brightly coloured knitted tea cosy on the heavy brown teapot. She then lifted the strainer and carefully poured out the tea before pushing the pressed glass milk jug and sugar bowl across the table to Lucy.

'Help yourself,' she told her, and as Lucy spooned sugar into her tea she thumbed towards Mary and went on, 'That one has been as good as gold. Hardly known I've had her, I ain't.'

Lucy glanced towards the child who was curled up fast asleep on the sofa with her finger jammed in her mouth. When she was asleep she looked no different to any other child her age, and Lucy's heart ached afresh for her. She had already been told that Mary would never be able to lead a normal life and would always need someone to care for her, which placed a huge burden on her own young shoulders. Not that she minded. She would have walked through fire for the little girl if need be, but it seemed unfair that Mary would have to miss out on so much.

'Take that tea an' go an' sit over by the fire, yer look frozen through,' Mrs P told her now. 'You've no need to rush away. Mary's had her meal an' I've got you a plate o' stew an' dumplin's ready. I didn't think you'd be in the mood to stand cookin' when you've been on yer feet all day.'

'Oh, Mrs P, whatever would I do without you?' Lucy said almost tearfully. She was pleased not to have to rush off. The house felt so empty now with Joel gone.

It was some time later when she was finishing her meal at the table that the door opened, letting in a blast of icy air, and Mr Price walked in. Like his wife, the man had a heart of pure gold and he beamed at Lucy.

'Hello, luv, come an' have a brew,' his wife welcomed him as she helped him off with his coat. Fred was the love of her life and she had insisted on naming their oldest son after him, so now the two men were referred to as Big Fred and Little Freddy.

Mr Price worked at the Dunlop, a large factory in Holbrook Lane, and he sighed with pleasure as he kicked his heavy boots off and massaged his aching feet.

'Had a good day, have yer?' Mrs P asked as she scuttled over to the oven to fetch his dinner, which she had kept warm.

'Same as always. We've been workin' on parts fer tanks today.'

Mrs P shook her head sadly. Almost all of the large factories were making either aeroplane or tank parts now, which only made them all think of how things had changed since the outbreak of war. It seemed that there was no getting away from it.

Lucy rose and carried her plate to the sink, but when she started to wash it Mrs P shooed her away. 'Leave it in soak,' she told her. 'You've done enough fer one day.'

'Well, if you're sure.' Lucy began to put her coat back on.

'I'll get madam there round home now then and get her ready for bed.'

Mrs P chuckled. 'That's if you can wake her up. Here, let me help yer get her coat on. Better still, rather than disturb her we'll just wrap it around her, eh? You've only got to go a few steps an' she looks so peaceful it's a shame to disturb her.'

With Mary clutched to her chest, Lucy stood aside while Mrs P opened the back door for her, then after planting a quick kiss on the woman's cheek she stepped out into the cold yard they both shared and rushed across to her own back door.

As she entered the tiny scullery she shuddered, but after quickly going into the back room which served as a kitchen-cum-living room, she smiled when she saw that Mrs P had been round and lit the fire for her. The woman was a real angel.

After laying Mary, who didn't stir, onto the small settee, she then hurried across to make sure that the curtains were firmly drawn before dashing upstairs to fetch Mary's pyjamas and warm them on the fireguard. Eventually the little girl was tucked up nice and cosy in Lucy's bed, a habit she had adopted since her big brother had been gone. Lucy didn't mind in the least, in fact she liked having Mary's little body to cuddle up to on a cold night. Now she looked around her modest living room and felt contented. It was only an ordinary terraced house, but she and Joel had worked tirelessly on it to turn it into a home since they had moved in. Joel had scoured the second-hand shops to find the three-piece suite, which had come up a treat with a good scrub, and Lucy had then brightened it up with cushions. She had bought the curtains for a snip from a rummage sale along with the hearthrug, and all in all the room was now very comfortable. But it just didn't feel the same without her brother.

The nights were the worst, when Mary was in bed. That was when the loneliness would close in on her and why she had not been averse to getting a job. She and Joel had always kept themselves very much to themselves, but at least now she would have someone to chat to apart from Mary and Mrs P. She wondered what Joel would be doing now and hoped that he was all right, then she set to tidying the room and getting Mary's clothes ready for the morning.

Dotty was hurrying through the deserted streets with her coat collar turned up against the cold. She hated going out after dark, particularly since the blackout had been in force. Even the streetlamps were turned off and the odd people that were out and about loomed up out of the darkness like spectres.

I wouldn't be surprised if it didn't snow soon, she thought to herself. It certainly felt cold enough. The pavements were white over with frost and they glistened eerily in the gloom. At last the house came into view and she fumbled in her bag for her key. Once inside, as always the smell of stale cabbage met her. She was sure that cabbage was the staple diet of Mrs Cousins and her children, but at least they would have something different this evening. She had called in to the corner shop on the way home and picked up some milk, bread and a tin of corned beef along with a few apples for the woman.

'Why, hello, luvvie,' Mrs Cousins greeted her when Dotty tapped on her door. 'What can I be doing for yer?'

'Nothing,' Dotty responded with a shy smile. 'But I just realised if I don't get rid of these few bits they'll go off before I can eat them. I thought you might be able to make use of them. You'd be doing me a favour and if you can't I shall have to throw them away.'

'Then in that case I'd be glad to take 'em off yer hands.' The woman flushed. She guessed that Dotty had bought them especially for her and thought what a lovely young lass she was. It was a shame that she didn't seem to have any friends though. She had never once seen anyone visit her since the day she had moved in, apart from a woman who Dotty had told her used to look after her in the orphanage, and she tended to keep herself very much to herself. But then she was a quiet sort of girl and happen she wasn't one for gallivanting about like most girls her age did.

'Thank you very much,' she said as she took the brown paper bag from Dotty's gloved hand. 'Would yer like to come in fer a warm an' a cuppa?'

'I won't, if you don't mind. I'm just longing to put my feet up, but thanks for asking,' Dotty replied as she headed for the last set of stairs.

Once in the privacy of her own little flat she hurried to light the gas-fire and put the kettle on to boil. She had quite enjoyed the day and having someone to talk to for a change during the breaks and the lunch-hour. She grinned as she thought of Annabelle and Lucy. They were as different as chalk from cheese but she liked them both, especially Lucy, with whom she somehow felt an affinity. Admittedly, Lucy had a family, or at least a brother and sister, but there was something sad about her eyes that made Dotty feel that Lucy was no stranger to heartache. She could remember as a child how she would try to imagine what her own family was like, and her young imagination had run riot. Perhaps she was the daughter of a princess who had been stolen away by a jealous godmother? And maybe one day, her mother and the prince, her father, would come and find her. Soon after that she had started to write, and invariably her stories were of abandoned children who eventually made good. Sometimes the stories had been so touching and heartfelt that they had moved Miss Timms to tears when Dotty showed them to her, and from then on the kindly woman had encouraged her to write at every opportunity.

Dotty had never given up hope that one day her natural mother would come back to claim her and she would be whisked away to a life of happiness, but as the years had passed and Dotty saw other children at the orphanage being chosen for adoption by loving families, her dreams had dimmed to a dull flicker of hope. She could well understand why the other children had been chosen over her. Most of them were pretty and cute, something that Dotty could never claim to have been. Once Miss Timms had found her crying about it and she had wrapped her in her arms and assured her that it was always the ugly ducklings that turned into swans and that Dotty was beautiful inside. But that had been a poor consolation. One day in her early teens, Dotty had spent her meagre savings on face cream, powder and rouge and plastered it on in front of the little mirror in her dormitory, but all it had done was make her resemble a clown, so after that she gave up and accepted herself for what she was. Her thoughts moved on to Annabelle, who was everything that Dotty longed to be – pretty and confident. A little full of herself admittedly, and undeniably spoiled – but then who could blame anyone for spoiling Annabelle?

Sighing, she lifted her writing pad and soon all the sad thoughts disappeared as she became lost in the story she was writing.

Chapter Six

'Good morning,' Dotty said the next morning as she made a beeline for Lucy who was hanging her coat up in the staff cloakroom. 'Is Annabelle not here yet?'

'Well, if she is I haven't seen her.' Lucy glanced around before grinning. 'And between you and me I wouldn't be surprised if she didn't come back. I don't think she much enjoyed her first day.'

But the words had barely left her mouth when the door opened and Annabelle strolled in, looking none too pleased with herself or the world. Her hair didn't look quite so immaculate today and both girls noticed that she was wearing only the minimum amount of make-up, unlike the day before. She made her way over to them and started to take her coat off.

'I can't *believe* that we have to be here a whole hour before the shop opens,' she said, grumbling as usual. 'I had a job to get up this morning at such an ungodly time.'

'You'll soon get used to it,' Dotty told her encouragingly. 'I wonder what departments we'll be working in today?'

'I don't know and I don't much care,' Annabelle replied. 'Just so long as they don't stick me in the hardware department.' She couldn't think of anything worse than having to spend her day amongst buckets and bowls.

The room was buzzing with laughter and noise as the staff chatted to each other about what they had done the night before and tidied themselves in readiness to go to their departments. Before the doors were opened, the head of each floor would inspect them all to make sure that they were respectable and then that the department was neat as a new pin before the customers were let in.

Annabelle thought it was a ridiculous waste of time. After all, it was hardly as if the customers were going to appear in droves at that time of the morning, especially when it was so bitterly cold outside.

'Did you notice what they're doing outside now?' she asked in disgust as she took a lipstick from her bag and expertly applied it. 'Stacking sandbags against all the shop-fronts! They look appalling and I really don't know why they're bothering. What with them and all the shelters, the whole place is beginning to look a total mess – and what about those awful barrage balloons they've got floating above the city! Why, they remind me of great grey elephants flying. And all for what, I ask you? We haven't had a sign of a single bomb yet.'

'And let's hope we don't,' Lucy said quietly. Without another word she turned and left to go to her department, thinking what a self-centred young woman Annabelle was.

At morning break-time they all sat together again in the canteen and Dotty treated herself to a slice of toast with a thin layer of margarine spread on it to go with her cup of tea. She was actually finding the canteen quite handy. At lunchtime you could get a warming bowl of soup for a penny and it certainly beat trying to cook herself anything when she got home, dead on her feet. They had all been surprisingly busy as people were trying to get their Christmas shopping done early before the rationing came strictly into force.

'Where are you today?' Annabelle asked Lucy as she joined her and Dotty at the table. Thankfully, she herself had been in the lingerie department again.

'I've been in childrenswear,' Lucy beamed. She had loved working in there and only wished that she could afford to buy some of the lovely garments they stocked for Mary. Most of their clothes came from jumble sales, not that Lucy was complaining. There were some rare bargains to be had if you were prepared to look carefully enough, and she was proud of the fact that she had always managed to keep her little sister well turned out.

'Oh you poor thing, how *ghastly*.' Annabelle looked horrified but Lucy shook her head.

'Actually I love working in there. I've asked Mrs Broadstairs if I could stay there permanently if it's possible.'

Annabelle stared at her as if she had lost her marbles. She had never had a lot to do with children, having no brothers or sisters, and nor did she wish to.

'But how could you possibly enjoy serving brats?' She shuddered dramatically. 'All those runny noses and tantrums.'

Lucy chuckled. 'There is a little more to children than that,' she assured her. 'My Mary is a little sweetheart and as good as gold.'

Annabelle frowned as she took a packet of Players and a box of Swan Vesta matches from her bag. 'Don't you feel resentful of the fact that you have to care for her? After all, at your age you should be out dancing, going to the cinema and enjoying yourself.'

'Not at all,' Lucy said evenly. 'Family is family at the end of the day and you do what you have to do.'

'Well, rather you than me,' Annabelle retorted, lighting her cigarette. 'I don't think I shall ever want children.'

'Really?' Dotty gazed at her in amazement. Surely every girl dreamed of getting married and starting a family? Not that she thought there was much chance of that happening to *her*. She had never even had a boyfriend and doubted that she ever would. But now, sensing the tense atmosphere, she hastily changed the subject, telling them: '*I've* been in the fabric department.' Her eyes were shining and she looked really pleased. 'Ooh, you should just see some of the material they have in there,' she went on. 'It's really beautiful. They've got such a selection too. There's raw silk in all the colours of the rainbow and satin as well as lace and the more everyday materials. It almost makes me wish I could sew, but I've never been very good with a needle. I prefer to write myself.'

'What sort of things do you write?' Lucy asked with kindly interest.

Dotty flushed. 'Oh, just stories and poems really,' she said self-consciously. 'And I'm not that good at it . . . I just enjoy it.'

Again, Annabelle raised her eyebrows. It seemed that anything that didn't involve going out and having a good time was of no interest to her.

'I shall have to get you to show me some of your stories sometime,' Lucy said. 'I love to read when I get a spare minute. I often go to the library.'

'Oh? What sort of books do you like?'

Lucy shrugged. 'Anything I can get my hands on really, although I do love a good soppy love story and of course the classics – Jane Austen, Mrs Gaskell, Dickens – any of those. In fact, I've read *The Olde Curiosity Shop* three times. That's one of my very favourites.'

'Mine too,' Dotty admitted, but their conversation was stopped from going any further when Annabelle butted in with, 'Well, give me a trip to the cinema any time. I'm going to the Gaumont tonight as it so happens to see that new Clark Gable film with my friend Jessica. Don't you think Clark Gable is just the *handsomest* man you've ever seen? Now find me a fellow with his looks and a fat wallet and I shall be happy.'

Both Lucy and Dotty giggled.

'So will the man you marry have to be rich then?' Dotty asked innocently.

'Oh absolutely.' Annabelle tossed her head. 'You'll never find *me* in some grotty back street surrounded by a herd of kids. I want to enjoy myself and see the world.'

'In that case I wish you luck, but this perfect man might prove difficult to find with most of our chaps away fighting the war,' Lucy said as she took a sip of her tea.

'But the war can't last forever, can it?' Annabelle stubbed out her cigarette and rose from the table. 'Right – I'll see you both at lunchtime,' she said. 'Bye for now.' And with that she stalked off to the ladies, her smartly clad rear wiggling provocatively.

Lucy chuckled. 'She's a bit of a one, isn't she? But you know, I like her for all that and I hope she manages to meet her ideal man. I can't see Annabelle settling for anything less. But come on, we'd better get a shufty on otherwise we'll be late. See you later, Dotty.' And with that she hurried off to the lift with Dotty close at her heels.

*

It was as they were all leaving the store that night that Lucy turned to Dotty and offered, 'Would you like to come home with me for a bit of tea and to meet Mary?' She sensed a deep loneliness in the girl and had taken to her, which was unusual, as Lucy had always kept herself very much to herself, especially over the last few years. Since moving to Tile Hill, Joel and Mary had been her whole world, but now that Joel was gone there were times in the long evenings when she longed for another grown-up to talk to. Of course, there was Mrs P, but when she had put Mary to bed, that was the worst time. 'It will only be sandwiches,' she rushed on quickly. 'Mrs P, that's my neighbour who looks after Mary whilst I'm at work, will have given Mary a hot meal and I don't usually bother cooking just for myself weekdays.'

Dotty's cheeks glowed with delight at the unexpected invitation. 'I . . . I'd love to,' she stammered. After all, there was no one to rush home to and they didn't live that far apart – so why not?

Soon they were sitting side by side on the bus as it crawled through the darkened streets with its headlights shielded, giving off the merest hint of light. Once again it was bitterly cold and both girls shivered as they gazed through the windows, not that there was much to see. All the houses had blackout curtains tightly drawn across the windows now and it brought home to both of them just how much the declaration of war had changed so many lives. Lucy was suddenly worried about what Joel would say if he were to find out that she'd invited someone into their home. He'd always been fiercely private before he went away and guarded Mary and Lucy possessively. Of course, she knew that he had good cause to be as he was, but what harm could it do, making a friend in Dotty? Anyway, it was too late to do anything about it now so she decided she might as well make the most of it. It would certainly be nice to have someone to talk to.

'You'll like Mrs P,' she said conversationally. 'She's got a heart of pure gold, and between you and me I think she's quite enjoying caring for Mary. Her oldest son has been called up and her two younger ones have both been evacuated to the country. I know she misses them terribly. In fact, she keeps saying that she's going to fetch them home because nothing's happened as yet, but I don't think that would be such a good idea.'

'How sad.' Dotty thought how difficult it must be for a mother to be parted from her children, although her own mother had obviously found it easy to abandon her. Lately, the fantasies she had woven about her true parentage had faded somewhat and she had started to feel some bitterness towards the woman who had left her at such a tender age at the orphanage. Not that the people there hadn't been kind to her, but it wasn't the same as having your very own family.

The bus had arrived at their stop, and soon they were hurrying along the row of terraced houses on the street where Lucy lived. Dotty wondered how she could know which house was hers, since they all looked the same. They stood in two straight regimental lines like soldiers standing to attention, and as all the doors opened directly onto the pavement and all the windows were covered in blackout curtains, it was hard to distinguish one from another. However, Lucy obviously knew exactly where she was going, and soon she turned into an entry that was so dark they had to feel their way along the whitewashed walls to the gate. The entry was acting like a wind tunnel, and by the time Lucy tapped on Mrs P's back door, the girls' teeth were chattering with cold.

'Come on in, luvvie,' Mrs P invited, then her smile widened as she saw that Lucy had someone with her.

'This is Dotty, my friend from work, Mrs P,' Lucy introduced her. 'She's come to meet Mary – and you, of course,' she added hastily.

'Well, 'ow nice is that?' Mrs P beamed at Dotty, putting the girl at ease. She'd never heard Lucy mention a friend before and was delighted that the girl had someone her own age to talk to. She'd often worried about her being all on her own with a little girl to care for and thought it was healthy that she was now mixing with other young women. This Dotty might even persuade her to have a night out and a bit of fun if she played her cards right – not that Dotty looked the fun type, if she were honest. She was a mousy little thing, but then anyone was better than no one at the end of the day.

'Come on, sit yourselves down and have a warm while I get you both a cuppa,' she urged them.

Dotty quickly did as she was told while Lucy unwrapped the scarf from about her neck and bent to tickle Mary's chin. The child stared up at her, her mouth hanging slackly open as she continued to pile the colourful wooden bricks one on top of the other until they toppled over. Then the whole process began again and Dotty's heart twisted in her chest for the poor little mite. Lucy had warned her that Mary was 'special' and now she could see exactly what she meant. It was a shame because the child was quite beautiful, with soft curly auburn hair, much the same colour as Lucy's, and strikingly green eyes. But those eyes, when she looked up at Lucy, were vacant. It almost broke Dotty's tender heart just to see her. There had been a little boy in the orphanage who had been much the same, and she wondered what would have happened to him now. He had been a great favourite amongst the staff, and the other children were always very protective towards him, but now Dotty was forced to ask herself what would become of him when he was too old to stay in the safe confines of the orphanage? It didn't bear thinking about because, just like Mary, he would never be able to look after himself. Perhaps he would end up in a mental institution somewhere?

These gloomy thoughts were interrupted when Mrs P pushed a mug across the table to her and pointed to the milk and sugar. 'Help yourself, luvvie,' she said pleasantly.

During the next ten minutes, as the girls drank their tea, Mrs P kept up a running commentary about Mary. 'Little angel this one is, just like her big sister,' she told Dotty, making Lucy blush. 'She's so good you don't know you've got 'er. But now tell me what you two 'ave been up to today.'

The girls willingly told her about the departments they'd both been working in and Mrs P listened attentively until the front door opened and Fred walked in.

'Got company then, 'ave we?' he asked good-naturedly as he threw his snap tin onto the table and shrugged his long arms out of his coat.

'This 'ere is Dotty, young Lucy's friend.'

'Pleased to meet yer, Dotty.' The huge man shook Dotty's hand until she was sure it would fall off as Lucy began to collect Mary's things together.

'Yer could always leave her here fer the night if you two fancied goin' out,' Mrs P offered hopefully. She had never known Lucy go out without Mary before, apart from a couple of hours each Sunday afternoon, that was, when she willingly looked after Mary for her. She still didn't know where the girl disappeared off to, but felt that it would do her the power of good to have a proper night out.

However Lucy shook her head. 'Thanks for the offer, but we're just goin' to have a cosy night in,' she told the kindly woman.

Minutes later, after Mrs P had closed the door behind them, she dished up Fred's dinner while he hastily washed at the deep stone sink.

'It would have been nice fer young Lucy to have a night out,' she remarked. ''T'ain't natural fer a young 'un like her to have so much responsibility on her shoulders.'

'Well, it don't seem to bother her none, Glad,' Fred pointed out as he took a seat at the table and lifted his knife and fork.

The woman sniffed. She knew how much Lucy was worrying about Mary, and she was dreading her going away herself; the little scrap had kept her sane since her own children had been evacuated. But the child would be five years old in the New Year and then Lucy would have no choice but to have her evacuated too – if the war wasn't over, that was, but there didn't seem much chance of that any day soon. But then, at least Lucy would have more time to herself afterwards and perhaps she would start to have some sort of a social life?

''Ow do yer think young Lucy will cope when little Mary gets sent away?' she asked her husband now and he swallowed a mouthful of boiled spud before answering. His Gladys had a heart as big as a bucket, and if she wasn't fretting over their own children she always seemed to be fretting about someone else's.

'Thing is, she ain't like other kids her age, is she?' she went on.

'Kids are a lot more adaptable than folks give 'em credit

for,' Fred replied, pushing a piece of bread around his plate to mop up the gravy. 'Mary won't really understand what's goin' on an' that won't be a bad thing.'

'I suppose yer right,' Mrs P conceded, knowing he wanted to put her mind at ease, then she bustled away to get him his pudding. She'd done him his favourite tonight – jam roly-poly steamed in a basin – and custard so thick it clung to the spoon. If that didn't put a smile on her Fred's face, nothin' would!

Next door, Dotty was looking around admiringly at Lucy's little home. The back door opened directly into a small scullery, and they passed through that into another room that served as a kitchen-cum-sitting room. Lucy was relieved when she saw that Mrs P had popped round to light the fire for her again and had drawn the blackout curtains across the window. She motioned for Dotty to take her coat off while she settled Mary in a chair by the fire. Mrs P had already got her into her pyjamas and the little girl was yawning now.

'Make yourself comfortable while I get Mary some warm milk, then when I've tucked her into bed I'll make us both something to eat.'

'Oh, don't get worrying about me,' Dotty said hastily. 'I don't want to put you out of your routine.'

Ten minutes later, Lucy set off upstairs with Mary in her arms and while she was gone, Dotty took the story she was currently writing out of her bag and began to work on it. She was so engrossed that she didn't see Lucy appear from the stairs door that led up from the room and she started when the other girl asked, 'So what are you doing then? Writing a letter to someone?'

'Oh no.' Dotty squirmed uncomfortably. 'It's just another

story I'm writing. It helps to pass the time when you live alone.'

Lucy went to fill the kettle at the sink and set it on the stove to boil. 'I'm absolutely useless at that sort of thing,' she admitted. 'Although I think I told you, I do love to read when I can find the time. To be honest, since my older brother Joel went away, the most I've managed are bedtime stories to Mary, and I don't even know if she understands them really. I think it just soothes her to hear my voice. May I have a look at it?'

'Oh no!' Dotty rammed the sheets of paper haphazardly back into her bag. 'They're really not that good.'

'How do you know, if you've never let anyone see them?'

Dotty shook her head adamantly, then hoping to change the subject, she asked, 'So how long have you lived here?'

Now it was Lucy's turn to become flustered. 'Oh, since shortly after Mary was born.'

'Is that when you lost your parents?'

Lucy gulped deep in her throat. This was exactly the reason why Joel had always insisted that they keep themselves to themselves. Thankfully the kettle began to boil just then and she was saved from having to answer, although Dotty was eyeing her curiously. The girl was wondering how Lucy's parents had died. Lucy obviously didn't want to talk about it, but then it was probably too painful. She promised herself that she would never ask again. Hopefully, if they did become good friends, Lucy would tell her in her own time one day – and if she didn't? Well, at the end of the day it was really none of her business.

Chapter Seven

On a cold blustery morning before she left for work one day, Annabelle said her goodbyes to her father. Richard Smythe had packed a small case, telling his wife that this was all he would need to take as he would be supplied with a uniform as soon as he arrived at his destination. He had passed his medical with no problem, as Miranda had anticipated, and during the days leading up to his departure she had maintained a cheery attitude. However, this morning, she could not stop the tears from falling as Annabelle looked on, at a loss as to what to say. Personally she couldn't understand why her mother was so worried. The British Isles remained untouched and as yet there had been no sign of an air invasion, although Australian and Canadian troops had been arriving in droves to help the mother country. It was rumoured that Adolf Hitler was waiting for the better weather before he began his attacks, but Annabelle was certain that the war would be over by then and her father would be home safe and sound. Was it really necessary for her mother to get herself into such a state? The girl was also acutely aware that if she didn't get her skates on, she would be late for work so now she pecked her father on the cheek, telling him, 'Good luck, Daddy. Write to us, won't you? And take good care of yourself.'

He nodded as he hugged her and then she was swinging off down the drive leaving her parents to say their goodbyes in private. She supposed that she should be feeling more upset than she was, but then she was going to the cinema that evening with Jessica to watch Joan Crawford in *The Ice Follies*, and she was already wondering what she should wear.

Before the girls knew it, Christmas was racing towards them and Owen Owen was packed with shoppers each day from early morning when the doors opened to when they closed each evening. The store took on a festive atmosphere and small Christmas trees popped up in each department as if by magic. The staff were allowed to bring in colourful paper chains, which they festooned around the fronts of the counters, and with which they decorated the staff dining room.

Annabelle was now actually enjoying her job, as Mrs Broadstairs had placed her permanently in the perfume and cosmetics department. She seemed to have a flair for knowing which perfume would suit a particular customer, and as she was allowed to sample the goods she sold, she was in her element. She never tired of gazing into the glass display cabinets at the lipsticks and the arrays of cosmetics, and she kept her own counter as neat as a new pin.

Dotty was now permanently placed in the fabric department, a job that she too thoroughly enjoyed. So much so that she had actually treated herself to a second-hand Singer sewing machine from a stall in Coventry market, and was teaching herself to sew. She was working on a nice tweed skirt that she hoped would be ready in time to give to Miss Timms for Christmas, and Mrs P had been marvellous, showing her all the basics of how to work the machine and cut out a pattern. She would have liked to buy some pretty cotton and attempt to make Miss Timms a blouse too, to go with it, but felt that this was a little adventurous yet. Even so, she loved handling the bolts of material. A long brass tape measure was fixed to the edge of her counter and after helping a customer to choose what they wanted, she would then carefully measure the material from the roll, cut it neatly and parcel it up for them.

Lucy still tended to be sent to whichever department she was needed in, although whenever possible Mrs Broadstairs would place her in the children's department, which was the girl's favourite. From her wages she had bought Mary a smart red wool coat with a matching bonnet for Christmas as well as a dear little blue velvet dress and a pair of white tights to go under it. She knew that she had been rather extravagant – but then, who could tell what the following year might hold for them? And so she spent her money and smiled, as many other people were doing, intent on enjoying themselves whilst they still could.

A strong friendship had formed among the three girls now, and without even thinking about it they would head for what had become known as their table each break and lunchtime.

It was during a morning break two weeks before Christmas that Annabelle joined Lucy and Dotty with a face as long as a fiddle.

'You'll never believe what happened to me last night,' she

grumped as she took a seat and lit up her first cigarette of the day. 'I was going to see my friend, Jessica, when this ARP warden appeared out of nowhere and asked me where I was going after dark! I mean, what business was it of his? Why shouldn't we go out after dark if we wish to?'

'I suppose he was only doing his job,' Dotty said cautiously. She was actually longing to move the conversation on because only the night before she had finally allowed Lucy to take one of her short stories home to read, and she was waiting to hear what she thought of it.

'Did you get time to look at my story?' she questioned her when Annabelle eventually stopped complaining long enough to draw breath and take a puff of her cigarette.

Lucy beamed from ear to ear. 'I most certainly did – and I don't mind telling you, Dotty, I thought it was *brilliant*. So good, in fact, that I think you should send it away to a magazine. I'm sure they'd want to publish it.'

Dotty looked delighted and embarrassed all at the same time. Up until now, the only person she had ever allowed to look at her work was Miss Timms, who had always said much what Lucy was saying now.

Her brush with the ARP warden forgotten, Annabelle leaned forward, her curiosity aroused. 'I wouldn't mind reading it too,' she said. 'I hardly ever go out any more and I get *so* bored in the evenings. Half of the dance halls have shut down and even when they're open it's mainly girls there, which isn't much fun. All the decent chaps are away fighting this bloody war. Do you think you might let me see it too?'

Lucy looked at Dotty questioningly and when she nodded she took the story out of her bag and handed it to Annabelle. 'You're in for a treat,' she told her, and Annabelle quickly tucked it safely away.

'So why don't you both come round to my house after work this evening for supper?' Lucy suggested now. Annabelle had visited Dotty's flat, but up to now she had never been to Lucy's house. 'I got four lovely pork chops from the butcher's on my way home last night and I need you girls to come and help me eat them.'

Annabelle considered the invitation for a moment. Her mother was going out that evening to some voluntary thing she had got herself involved in, so she would be in on her own again with only the wireless for company. Miranda had kept herself busy since her husband had gone off for training some weeks previously, and even when she was in, she wasn't much company, Annabelle thought. She was too busy worrying about Richard.

'I suppose I could if you're sure you don't mind,' she said. 'But what about your little sister?'

Dotty and Lucy chuckled. Annabelle had made no secret of the fact that she wasn't that keen on children, and Lucy had a sneaky suspicion that was why she had turned down her invitations before.

'Believe it or not, she doesn't bite,' she told Annabelle and the girl had the good grace to flush.

Lucy had explained that Mary was 'special' as she termed it, and Annabelle was envisaging some little monster with two heads or something equally as horrible.

'Actually, Mary is a little sweetheart,' Dotty chipped in. She had become very fond of the little girl during the time she had known Lucy, and was now a regular visitor to the house, as much to see Mary as Lucy, if truth be known. She had bought her a lovely rag doll, with yellow woollen plaits, for Christmas from the toy department, and could hardly wait to give it to her.

And so it was decided, and after their break the girls

went back to their departments with smiles on their faces.

By the time the shop was due to close, all three of them were exhausted. Dotty had been measuring and cutting material all day for people who hoped to make themselves or a family member a new outfit in time for Christmas. She had also spent ages helping customers to choose patterns that would be compatible with the fabric they had bought, and her feet felt as if they were about ready to drop off. Her arms ached too from lugging the heavy bolts of material to the counter.

Lucy had been equally busy as people rushed in to get their children new outfits to wear on Christmas Day and the sound of the big brass till opening and closing became like background noise by mid-afternoon. But it was Annabelle who made them giggle when she met them outside on the chilly pavement.

'Good grief, I could smell you the minute you stepped out of the door,' Lucy said, wrinkling her nose.

'I suppose I do smell a bit strong,' Annabelle admitted, sniffing each wrist in turn. 'But the men are the worst customers to serve. They come in wanting to buy their wives some perfume for Christmas but can't choose which one, so I have to spray some on myself for them to choose.'

'Then all I can say is you must have been busy too,' Lucy joked. 'You must have a whole bottle-full sprayed up and down your arms.'

They set off through the chilly streets for the bus station, which as usual was in darkness. They were getting used to it now though.

'So what are you two planning on doing over Christmas then?' Dotty asked once they were on the bus.

'Well, I wanted to go to London and see a show in the West End,' Annabelle sighed, 'but Mummy isn't keen on me going. She's such a worrier, especially since Daddy went away. I would have liked to see Ivor Novello's *The Dancing Years* but I doubt it will happen. I was hoping my friend, Jessica, would come with me and we could have a couple of nights in a hotel, but she informed me last night that her mother is sending her to stay in Devon with her grand-parents next week until this damn war is over. All I can hope for now is that the man of my dreams – tall, dark, handsome and *extremely* rich – will appear from nowhere and take me away from all this. And of course, I'll settle for nothing less!'

She looked so glum that Lucy squeezed her arm and grinned. 'Well, if it's any consolation, I shan't be doing anything special either,' she remarked. 'With Joel being away it will be just me and Mary this year.' In actual fact, she was dreading the holiday and beginning to really worry about her brother now. It was weeks since she had heard from him and she didn't even know if he had been shipped out to the front yet. But then she tried to console herself that no news was good news. The best Christmas present in the world at that moment in time would have been to arrive home to find a letter on the doormat from him.

Soon they were tripping towards Mrs P's house, but when they entered, Lucy's face fell as she saw that there was no sign of Mary.

Mrs P herself seemed to be in a high state of excitement.

'Where's Mary?' Lucy's voice was edged with fear but Mrs P only giggled like a schoolgirl. 'Never you mind about Mary fer now. Get yerself round home an' happen you'll find a nice surprise waitin' for you there.'

'But Mary is all right, isn't she?'

'Right as ninepence, but now be off wi' yer. Go on . . . shoo!'

With her heart pounding, Lucy turned and hurried

through Mrs P's back door as Dotty and Annabelle exchanged a concerned glance and hurried after her.

Seconds later, Lucy was fiddling with the back-door key, but her hands were shaking so badly that she struggled to get it in the lock. Whatever could Mrs P have meant by 'a nice surprise'? And where was Mary?

After flashing an apologetic smile at Dotty and Annabelle, she stepped into the scullery then hurried towards the kitchen and flung the door open. The light was on, and as her eyes settled on a large kitbag to the side of the door her heart began to pound even harder and she dashed into the room, praying that what she was hoping for was right.

Joel was sitting in the fireside chair with Mary snuggling contentedly on his lap and Lucy suddenly felt as if her Christmas had come early as her heart threatened to explode with joy.

'Joel!' She was across the room in a second and her arms went tightly around his neck, threatening to choke him as he chuckled.

'Calm down, sis, I can't breathe.' But then the laughter died away as he caught sight of Dotty and Annabelle.

Following his eyes, Lucy hastily told him, 'Oh sorry, Joel. These are my friends from work, Dotty and Annabelle. They've come for tea. I didn't know you'd be here, you see. But how long are you home for? Why didn't you let me know you were coming? And are you all right?'

'Whoa with the questions, eh?' he said, very conscious of the two strangers. 'I got two days' leave but I didn't know about it until this morning.'

'Only *two* days? But that means you won't be here for Christmas. Why couldn't they have given you longer?' Lucy could not keep the disappointment from her voice.

'Because we're being shipped out the same day I go back

to camp,' he told her calmly. 'And before you ask, I have no idea where we're going.'

His eyes moved back to the two girls standing uncomfortably in the doorway then, and without even realising he was doing it, he sniffed at the air.

'Oh, that's Annabelle you can smell.' Lucy giggled now. 'She works in the cosmetic department and she has to spray herself so that the customers can decide which perfume they want to buy.'

But Annabelle didn't hear a word she said because her eyes were glued to the flame-haired young man sitting by the fire; the weirdest sensations were coursing through her. He looked at her and suddenly he too felt colour flood into his cheeks. She was undoubtedly the most beautiful girl he had ever set eyes on, and for no reason that he could explain, his stomach flipped. They both seemed to realise that they were staring at each other at the same time, and both hastily averted their eyes, wondering what the hell was going on. It was as if an unspoken message had passed between them and they were both confused and bewildered – a rare experience for Annabelle at least, who had had more boyfriends than she cared to remember. Yet none of them had ever made her heart dance as this Joel did. It was all very strange. He certainly wasn't the best-looking young man she had ever seen, but there was something about his shorn red hair and the intense green eyes that she found mesmerising.

'Look, you two have an awful lot of catching up to do. Annabelle can come to my flat for tea,' Dotty said tactfully.

'Oh no, there's no need for you to go, is there, Joel?' Lucy asked as she stared up at her brother. He had placed Mary in the chair and was standing now, and Annabelle saw that he was tall; so tall that he towered over her.

'No, of course there isn't. You're very welcome to stay,'

Joel said immediately, but Dotty would not be swayed. She could see how thrilled Lucy was to see her brother and thought they deserved some time alone. She and Annabelle could always come for tea another day and it wouldn't take very long to get back to her flat, although she couldn't offer pork chops. In fact, they might have to stop at the local chippie on the way and take their meal home with them. Taking Annabelle's elbow in a firm grip, she was surprised to find that the girl was shaking. Annabelle was staring at Mary now and was relieved to see that she was actually a very pretty little girl. Nothing at all like the freakish monster she had imagined her to be.

'No, really. We'll do this another time,' Dotty said decisively, turning Annabelle about and giving her a little nudge in the back. 'Goodbye, Joel. It was nice to meet you.' And then without another word she steered Annabelle out through the front door. It was not until they were out on the pavement that Annabelle began to breathe again.

Dotty stared at her curiously. 'What's wrong?' she asked with concern. Even in the dim light she could see that Annabelle was as white as a bleached sheet.

'I er . . . nothing,' Annabelle stammered as she struggled to regain her composure. 'I just felt a bit faint, that's all. I didn't have any lunch, that's probably what did it. Come on, let's go and find something to eat. I'm sure I'll be all right then.'

Dotty peered at her from the corner of her eye. She had seen the look that had passed between Joel and Annabelle, and had the strangest feeling that she might just have witnessed the start of something beautiful.

Back inside, Lucy was clinging to Joel with tears streaming down her cheeks as he absently stroked her hair, his thoughts fixed on the gorgeous blonde-haired girl who had just left. Joel had never had the time or inclination for girlfriends – he had been far too busy for the last few years caring for Mary and Lucy and keeping them safe. But if he *were* to look for a girlfriend . . . he stopped his thoughts from going any further. As if a girl like her would ever look at the likes of him! Joel was under no illusions. He knew he wasn't ugly, admittedly, but he was also aware that he wasn't the most handsome chap in the world. He was tall and muscular, but he considered his nose to be a little too long and his eyes a little too far apart for him to be classed as handsome in the conventional sense. His hair didn't help either. Red curly hair might be considered attractive on a female – Mary and Lucy were proof of that – but he had always hated it on himself, although it did look slightly better now that it had been chopped off for the Army. Then he gave himself a mental shake, thinking what a soppy devil he was, and asked Lucy, 'Who were they then? I thought we agreed to keep ourselves to ourselves. You haven't told them anything, have you?'

Lucy pulled away from him, her expression hurt. 'Look, as I said, they're friends from work. And of course I haven't told them anything! I'm not an idiot, you know. But you can't expect me not to speak to anyone now that I'm working.'

Joel was instantly contrite. 'Sorry, love,' he mumbled. 'Of course you have to have a life, especially now that I'm gone. It's just that I worry, that's all. We've worked so hard to put the past behind us.'

She reached up to stroke his cheek, promising, 'It's all right, I understand, and never fear – I'm not about to blab to anyone.'

They stared at each other for an instant and then she asked, 'Are you quite sure you don't know where they will be sending you when you get back to camp?' It was hard to keep the edge of fear from her voice.

'I honestly don't know.' He spread his hands in a helpless gesture. 'It seems to be a closely guarded secret at present, but I'd put my money on France.'

She nodded. She now read the newspapers avidly, something she had never done before, and was aware of how bad things were out there, although up until now the war did not seem to have touched the people of Coventry. She could only pray that it would end before it did, or better still before Mary reached the age where she would have no choice but to let her be evacuated.

Joel seemed to pick up on her gloomy thoughts. Glancing at the child, he said, 'She looks well, Lucy. You're doing a fine job with her and I do realise how hard it must be for you, what with having to work now too.'

She shrugged. 'It's not so bad now that I'm getting into a routine, although I'd never manage without Mrs P. She's been absolutely marvellous.'

His head dipped in agreement as he took a Park Drive out of a packet and lit it. 'She is a real pal,' he readily agreed. 'And when this is all over, we'll try and make it up to her. But now, how about a bit of home cooking, eh? The Army food is diabolical, I don't mind telling you, and I could eat a scabby horse.'

'In that case it's a good job I just happen to have four nice juicy pork chops going begging,' she grinned, her eyes twinkling, and leaving him to watch over Mary she sped away to start the evening meal, thinking how wonderful it was to have her brother back, if only for a short time.

It was quite late when Annabelle eventually got home after spending time with Dotty at her flat, but the house was still in darkness. It felt as if she scarcely ever saw her mother any more. She was always off somewhere or other doing voluntary work.

After letting herself in, the girl made for the kitchen, and once she had ensured that the curtains were firmly drawn, she put the kettle on. She had just spent a pleasant couple of hours with Dotty and had only left because a visitor had arrived. The woman was called Miss Timms; she was a quiet, unassuming sort, but it was clear she thought a great deal of Dotty. Dotty had been delighted to see her, but then she had admitted to Annabelle a while back that Miss Timms was the nearest thing to a mother she had ever known. Annabelle actually felt quite sorry for Dotty. She couldn't begin to imagine what it must have been like, being brought up in an orphanage. There were times when her own mother and father had driven her to distraction, but she loved them both dearly all the same, although she wasn't always good at showing it.

Kicking off her shoes, she bent to massage her aching ankles. She had actually treated herself to a new pair of shoes with slightly lower heels, but her feet still throbbed at the end of each day and the icy pavements didn't help. Her mother had tried to persuade her to get a pair of the fur-lined flat boots that were so popular at the moment, but Annabelle had drawn the line there. The shoes she had purchased were as low as she was prepared to go.

Now as she watched the kettle gently steaming, her thoughts returned to Lucy's brother and once again her heart did a funny little flip. Joel was certainly not the best-looking bloke she had ever seen, and nothing like the sort she was normally attracted to, but all the same there was something about him . . . The kettle began to whistle and she jumped up to make herself a pot of tea. She was just getting a cup from the smart oak dresser that took up almost the whole of one wall when she heard the front door open and seconds later her mother appeared huddled up in a thick coat, a warm scarf and a pair of woolly gloves.

'Hello, darling. Brrr, it's cold out there, isn't it? Have you been back long?'

Annabelle took another cup from the dresser. 'No, only a few minutes. Dotty and I went to Lucy's for tea, but when we got there she found her brother home on two days' leave, so we went round to Dotty's then – and would you believe it – she had a visitor too, some woman who used to look after her in the orphanage where she was brought up.'

'That was nice for them then, wasn't it?' Her mother took her coat off and placed it neatly over the back of a chair before saying tentatively, 'Actually, I joined the WVS this evening. I'm going to collect my uniform in a couple of days.'

Annabelle stared at her in amazement. 'But I thought you'd put your name down for ambulance driving!'

'I have,' her mother said calmly. 'But thankfully up until now there hasn't been much need for me to do it. And even if or when there is, I'm sure I can fit the two in perfectly well.'

Annabelle was taken aback and it struck her then just how much their lives had changed in such a short time. Just a few months ago, the most she had had to worry about was where she was going that week and what she would be wearing. Now her father was away God knew where, preparing to fight for his country, she was a shop girl, and her mother was about to become an ambulance driver and a member of the WVS!

Seeing her daughter's stunned expression, Miranda reached out to pat her hand. 'Don't look like that,' she urged.

'I did tell you I wanted to do my bit. But now, about these two friends you've made at work – I've heard you mention them so many times I thought it might be nice if you invited them over for tea at the weekend. Do you think they'd come?'

Annabelle pictured Dotty's tiny flat and Lucy's little terraced house in her mind. They would probably both fit into half of the downstairs here, but seeing as she had nothing better planned for the forthcoming weekend, she decided it wouldn't hurt to ask them to Primrose Lodge, though she seriously doubted that Lucy would come.

'I think Dotty might come,' she answered. 'But I doubt Lucy will be able to.'

'Oh, why is that then?'

'Well, she has to look after her little sister, doesn't she? As far as I can gather, she never goes anywhere without her, apart from to work.'

'I can't see that need be a problem; she could bring her with her too. The more the merrier, I say.'

'In that case I'll ask them both tomorrow,' Annabelle replied, and then with a heavy sigh she got out the ironing board and plugged the iron in to start the job she detested the most. She still missed having her ironing done for her, but she had soon found out the hard way that if she didn't do it, no one else would.

Chapter Eight

The girls met up outside the store the next morning and went in together.

'I didn't expect to see you today,' Annabelle commented as she glanced at Lucy. 'I thought you might decide to have a day at home with your brother, seeing as he hasn't got a very long leave.'

'I must admit the thought did cross my mind,' Lucy admitted with a guilty grin. 'But then it will be nice for him to spend some time with Mary, and I shall see him tonight, shan't I? This place is short-staffed enough as it is, and I wouldn't have felt right making things worse.'

'Then you're a better person than I am,' Annabelle growled. 'Just give *me* a good enough excuse and I wouldn't set foot in this place again, apart from to shop here. I tell you, this job has been a real eye-opener for me. I never realised how much work went into keeping a store running smoothly.'

'Things will calm down again after Christmas,' Dotty said hopefully. 'People are spending money at the moment like it's going out of fashion. I'm sorry about last night, Annabelle. I wasn't expecting a visit from Miss Timms, but you would have been quite welcome to stay.'

'Yes, and I'm sorry too,' Lucy piped up. 'You could have knocked me down with a feather when I found Joel at home, and after I'd promised you both dinner as well.'

'It doesn't matter.' Annabelle led the way into the cloakroom. 'In actual fact, my mother has sent you both an invitation. She thought you might like to pop over and have tea with us on Saturday. That's if you haven't got anything better planned, of course?'

Just as she had expected, Lucy frowned. 'That would have been lovely. But the thing is, after Mrs P has looked after Mary all week, I don't like to impose on her more than I have to at the weekends as well.'

'That won't be a problem. Mummy said you're quite welcome to bring Mary too,' Annabelle assured her.

'In that case I'd love to,' Lucy responded.

'And so would I.' Dotty was grinning from ear-to-ear. She usually spent her weekends tidying the flat and writing, and so the thought of going somewhere other than to work was appealing.

Mrs Broadstairs entered the cloakroom then and suddenly there was a flurry as all the girls scattered like flies to their different departments.

By home-time all three girls were exhausted after being run off their feet all day.

'I never thought I'd say it, but I shall actually be pleased to get home and put my feet up tonight,' Annabelle told them as she pulled her coat on. She was missing her friend Jessica badly, but tonight she wouldn't have wanted to go out even if she'd had the chance to. 'I shall be glad when the Christmas rush is over now,' she said, never missing the chance to have a grumble.

'Hmm, the problem then is we have the January sales and after that, we have to stock-take. Mrs Broadstairs told me so today,' Dotty confided. 'And apparently that's no easy task. Still, I dare say we'll survive it.'

'It's going to be a strange Christmas anyway with Joel away,' Lucy said gloomily, and then she instantly felt guilty. Here she was feeling sorry for herself, but she still had Mary, whilst Dotty had no one. Perhaps she should invite her over for Christmas dinner? She decided she'd give the idea some thought.

'At least we've only got five more days to go until we break up,' Dotty said, ever the optimist. 'And then we can enjoy a few days off work.'

'Oh whoopee doo! We finish late on Christmas Eve and then we're back in again the day after Boxing Day to start getting ready for the January sales. I cannot wait!' Annabelle sighed as if the weight of the world was on her shoulders, making the other two burst out laughing. Annabelle could always make them smile without even trying.

It was as they stepped outside the store onto the icy pavement that someone suddenly stepped forward and Lucy gasped with pleasure to see Joel standing there clutching Mary's hand.

'We thought we'd come and meet you out of work,' he explained, keeping his eyes fixed on Lucy, but he was painfully aware of Annabelle standing directly behind her. 'I thought Mary would like to see the displays in the shop windows. Not that there's much to be seen now that it's dark,' he added.

'Oh, that's lovely, but I hope you've got her warmly wrapped up,' Lucy fussed as she bent to tighten the ribbons of Mary's bonnet beneath her chin.

'She could go to the Antarctic and not feel cold with the layers of clothes she's got on,' her brother assured her wryly. 'But now why don't I treat you all to a nice cup of tea before you go home? I noticed there's a café open just a bit further along in Trinity Street.'

Annabelle's tiredness was suddenly forgotten and she was glad of the darkness that would hide the colour that had risen in her cheeks. Her heart was thumping painfully again. I'm acting like a love-struck kid, she scolded herself, but she followed the others along the pavement all the same.

When she entered the steamy café, she blinked as her eyes adjusted to the light inside. Apart from the *Open* sign outside she might have passed it without even knowing that it was there, for the place had blackout blinds that effectively blocked all the light from leaking outside and sandbags propped all across the front of it.

Joel scurried to the counter to get them all a drink as they found an empty table, and Annabelle quickly got out her compact and powdered her nose while he was gone, much to the amusement of Lucy. Dotty, meanwhile, was fussing over Mary, who had totally captured her heart.

Soon Joel was back with a tray loaded with mugs of tea, a glass of milk for Mary and five scones.

'There wasn't much choice in the cake department,' he apologised. 'But these should keep us all going until dinnertime.'

He found himself with no choice but to sit next to Annabelle and now it was his turn to feel self-conscious, but soon they were all chatting as if they had known each other for years. As Dotty and Lucy looked after Mary, Annabelle told Joel about her father joining up and her mother's voluntary work.

'I think she's doing it to keep her mind off what might be happening to Daddy,' she confided and he nodded.

'I can understand that. It must be really hard after being married all those years to be suddenly apart. Are you er . . . married?'

Annabelle threw back her head and laughed. 'Oh goodness me, no. I don't even have a boyfriend.' She instantly wished that she hadn't told him that in case he thought she was setting her cap at him, but he seemed to take it in his stride. He began to tell her all about what his training had involved and some of the chaps he was stationed with, and she listened raptly until Lucy coughed gently to get their attention.

'I think the lady is waiting to close up,' she told them, pointing towards the counter where they saw the owner standing with her arms crossed, tapping her foot. Glancing around, they were shocked to see that they were the last customers in there. They had been so engrossed in conversation that they hadn't even noticed that everyone else had gone. They all hastily rose and bundled little Mary ahead of them until they were once more outside on the cold pavement.

'Look, I have to go back to camp the day after tomorrow,' Joel said. 'So why don't you two both come round for dinner after work tomorrow? After all, I made you miss your meal what with turning up out of the blue like that yesterday, so I'll do the cooking to make it up to you.'

Lucy's mouth gaped. She had never known Joel to volunteer for cooking before, but then she wasn't going to argue.

Annabelle and Dotty glanced at each other before nodding

in unison. 'That would be lovely, if you're quite sure.' And so it was decided and as Annabelle headed for the bus stop she found that she had a spring in her step.

The next day she took especial pains over her make-up and set off for work feeling like a schoolgirl going on her first date. This is ridiculous, she berated herself as she stared out of the window of the bus. Joel isn't even my type. He looks nothing like Clark Gable and he's certainly not rich! But she still couldn't stop herself from feeling excited at the thought of seeing him again.

The day seemed to pass interminably slowly and she found herself glancing at the large clock above the lift doors in her department every ten minutes. If Lucy and Dotty noticed how quiet she was during the day they tactfully didn't comment on it.

'I have to say, Joel seems quite smitten with Annabelle,' Lucy confided to Dotty as they travelled down in the lift together following the lunch break. 'I've never even known him to look at a girl before but he must have mentioned Annabelle at least a dozen times over breakfast before I left for work.'

'Well, judging by the way she was looking at him in the café last night, I'd say his feelings were reciprocated,' Dotty chuckled, her romantic mind working overtime. 'Although I have to say your brother doesn't seem anything at all like the sort of man Annabelle is always telling us she wants to snare. No offence meant, of course. It's just that she always says she wants a rich, handsome older man who will spoil her shamelessly and keep her in the lap of luxury.'

'I know exactly what you mean,' Lucy responded. 'And a young private in the Army hardly fits the bill. Still, they do say love is blind. We'll just have to see what happens, although it won't be easy for them, what with Joel going off to God knows where the day after tomorrow.'

Her face became solemn then and Dotty squeezed her hand. 'Miss Timms always told me that everything happens for a reason, so let's just sit back and see what happens, eh? If they're meant for each other, love will find a way.'

'Speaking of love, I'd love to get my mitts on another of your stories. It would give me something to look forward to, for when Joel is gone.'

'That can be easily arranged,' Dotty promised her as the lift creaked to a halt and then they parted and headed for their different departments.

Dotty had a particularly difficult afternoon. One customer made her lift down almost every bolt of material in the shop before finally deciding on a length of pale blue satin. She then spent the next hour poring over the patterns, dismissing every one that Dotty suggested would suit the fabric before finally deciding on one that Dotty was sure would be totally unsuitable. By then Dotty had gone past caring and was just glad to see the back of her. It took her almost half an hour to replace all the different materials, and by then she was thoroughly cheesed off and longing for her afternoon break, although she was still looking forward to going around to Lucy's that evening. Anything beat sitting in an empty flat.

When they finally met up in the canteen it appeared that the other two hadn't had a very good day either.

'I had this one woman who had me spray at *least* eight different perfumes,' Annabelle complained. 'And then at the end of all that, she *still* couldn't make her mind up and left without buying a thing! Between you and me, I just wonder if she ever intended to in the first place. And they were all expensive ones too.'

'Well, you can't win 'em all,' Lucy said matter-of-factly, grinning as she spotted the tiny bit of mistletoe that had dropped into Annabelle's hair, behind her ear. 'It's been manic in the children's department too and I heard one girl say that they've been run off their feet in the food hall. I reckon people are beginning to hoard stuff before the food rationing comes properly into force. They're stocking up on packets, tins and bottles and jars of things like there's no tomorrow.'

'That's all down to this bloody war again,' Annabelle said crossly. 'They're calling it "the phoney war" now so why is everyone panicking? It's not as if it's affected us yet, is it? And now we're all going to be issued with identity cards. I mean, for God's sake! It's bad enough having to cart those damn gas masks about everywhere.'

'Better to be safe than sorry,' Lucy said sensibly. 'I still have an awful feeling that things are going to get a whole lot worse before they get better.'

Annabelle lit a cigarette and stared morosely down into her tea as the other two chatted about this and that.

The rest of the afternoon proved to be as busy as before, and by the time the end of their shift came around, the girls were all worn out. Then, to crown it all, they ended up having to stay behind for fifteen minutes extra to do the tidying up that they had been unable to do whilst the customers were milling about. Admittedly the cleaners came in once the shop was shut, but the staff were still expected to put everything neatly away before they left.

'We'll have missed the six-fifteen bus now,' Lucy wailed as they put their outdoor clothes on in the staff cloakroom. 'And I only have tonight with Joel too. He'll be gone again in the morning.'

Dotty nodded sympathetically. Joel and Lucy seemed to

be very close and she must be so worried about him being shipped off somewhere.

'I'm sure he'll write to you regularly to let you know how he's getting on,' she said comfortingly.

Lucy nodded although her face was grim.

They got outside to find it had started to snow, and right on cue, Annabelle groaned, 'That's all we need!'

'It might not settle,' Dotty said hopefully, although the flakes seemed to be as big as dinner plates. She glanced down at Annabelle's shoes. The heels were not as high as she had used to wear admittedly, but they were still totally unsuitable for walking on slippery pavements. But she didn't dare say anything. The mood Annabelle was in, she was afraid of getting her head bitten off.

Just as they had feared, they had missed their bus and the bad weather conditions made the next one late, which meant they didn't get to Lucy's until gone seven o'clock.

Joel sighed with relief when they all trooped into the cosy back room.

'Where have you been? I've been worried sick,' he said as he helped Lucy off with her coat.

She quickly explained as she crossed to warm her hands at the fire and kiss Mary. She then sniffed at the air appreciatively. Something smelled good and it made her stomach rumble with anticipation.

'So, what culinary delight have we got for tea then?' she asked with a twinkle in her eye. Her mother had used to tease Joel that he could burn water, before— She stopped her thoughts from going any further. This was his last night at home and she didn't want anything to spoil it.

'I've made us a cottage pie.'

He flushed when Lucy raised her eyebrows then admitted sheepishly, 'Well, Mrs P did help a bit.'

'Whoever cooked it, it smells delicious.' Lucy ushered Annabelle and Dotty to the table. Joel had laid the cutlery on the oilskin cloth and had even managed to find a few pink chrysanthemums at the local florist. He had placed them in a vase which now took pride of place in the middle of the table.

'If I'd known you were this domesticated I'd have given you a few more chores to do before you went away,' Lucy teased her brother as he hurried to fetch the pie and the vegetables.

The meal was a light-hearted affair with a lot of giggling and chattering. Once it was over, and Lucy had gone off to put Mary to bed, Dotty insisted on doing the washing up on her own, which left Joel and Annabelle to entertain each other for a while.

'The papers are full of doom and gloom today,' he told her. 'Have you read them?'

Annabelle had never been one for reading newspapers, she much preferred a fashion magazine, but not wishing to appear ignorant, she shook her head and said simply, 'No, I don't get time now I have to be out for work so early.'

'It seems the Russians have bombed Helsinki,' he told her quietly. 'And the German battleship, the *Graf Spee*, has been sunk in the South Pacific. I can't see Hitler being any too pleased about that. I've no doubt there will be serious repercussions.'

Annabelle tried to look interested, although she really couldn't see why this should affect them. Finland was miles away. But of course she nodded gravely before asking, 'What exactly have you been doing during your training? Is it really awful?'

'It's not exactly a picnic.' He shook his head. 'The worst thing for me has been having to learn how to handle a gun.

I mean, it's one thing to do target practice when you're aiming at a board, but quite another to know that soon you may be aiming at another human being, be he German or otherwise. We'll be using rifles too – Lee Enfields. Powerful beasts, I don't mind telling you! The physical training is all right, although by the end of the day all you're fit for is to collapse on your bunk. The assault courses are quite tough.'

Annabelle looked horrified and he said immediately, 'Sorry, I didn't mean to scare you.'

Speaking to Joel had suddenly brought it home to her just how dangerous the war could prove to be. Up to now it had scarcely affected her part of the world, but what if that changed? And would her father stay safe? Joel's words had brought the reality of the war much closer.

When the other two eventually rejoined them, Joel and Annabelle were still deep in conversation. Lucy made them all a cup of tea and they sat around the fire together to drink it.

'I think I ought to get off now,' Dotty said some time later, glancing at the clock on the mantelshelf. 'The buses are going to be all over the place with the weather as it is, and I don't want to end up walking home.'

'Hm, you could be right. I suppose I should be making a move too,' Annabelle agreed.

Lucy went off to fetch their coats as Annabelle self-consciously held her hand out to Joel, saying, 'It's been really nice to meet you. We'll perhaps meet again on your next leave.'

'I hope so.' He held her hand for a fraction longer than was necessary and Annabelle felt as if it was on fire. Then quite unexpectedly, he leaned forward and brushed her cheek with his lips, making Annabelle blush furiously.

'The mistletoe,' he explained, pointing to her ear, and she

laughed, pulling it out of her hair. She had had no idea that it was there, and the two others had naughtily not mentioned it.

Joel then said his goodbyes to Dotty too and settled back into his chair as Lucy saw the girls to the front door. He was determined to make the most of his home comforts while he had the chance. God knew how long it might be before he was home again – *if ever*, a little voice in his head whispered, but he thrust it away. It wouldn't do to get all maudlin on Lucy and upset her any more than she already was.

'They're nice, aren't they?' Lucy said when she came back to join him. 'I thought Annabelle was a bit stuck-up when I first met her, but she's all right when you get to know her.' She helped herself to a digestive biscuit from the plate between them.

'They are nice,' Joel agreed. 'And I have the feeling you're quite enjoying your job. But . . . well, it wouldn't do to get too close to them. You know what I mean, don't you?'

Lucy bit her lip. 'I'm very careful what I tell them,' she assured him.

He nodded with satisfaction. 'Good. I don't mean to be a spoilsport, but if they ever found out . . .'

'They won't! At least not from me. But let's not discuss it on our last night together. All that is in the past now, and I try not to think too much about it.'

Joel pursed his lips now and told her, 'I went to see Mum today. I told Mrs P that I was going to do a bit of shopping and she looked after Mary for me. She doesn't seem any better, does she? Do you still go every Sunday?'

'As much as I can,' Lucy told him in a small voice. 'But I can only go if Mrs P is able to look after Mary. It upsets her too much if I take Mary along.'

Her brother reached out to squeeze her hand, sensing that

she was getting emotional. 'And is my money coming through all right?' he asked.

'Oh yes,' she assured him in a slightly wobbly voice. 'Your wages arrive every other week but you really shouldn't send so much. You must hardly keep anything for yourself, and now that I have a job I'm managing fine.'

'It's not as if I have anything to spend it on, is it?' he said ruefully. 'And I need to know that you and Mary have enough to get by on. But what's going to happen after her birthday? She'll be five soon.'

'I know.' Lucy's eyes brimmed with tears. 'I try not to think of it too much because I'll have no choice but to let her be evacuated, and I don't know how she'll cope with it. She's never been away from us before.'

Joel too was worried sick at the thought of it. 'I'm sure they'll be kind to her, whoever takes her in,' he said gently, and hoped with all his heart that that was true.

And then they went on to talk about other things as the short time they had left together ticked away.

Chapter Nine

Dotty met Lucy and Mary in the bus station on Saturday afternoon and they caught the bus together to Cheylesmore. Mary was looking very pretty in her Sunday best outfit, and anyone seeing her would have thought that she was just a normal little girl, until they looked into her eyes and saw the vacant expression there.

'Oh Lucy, she looks just *lovely,*' Dotty cooed as she bent to plant a kiss on Mary's cheek. Then: 'I wonder what Annabelle's home will be like?'

'Really posh, I should think,' Lucy replied as she paid the conductor. 'Which is why she's probably invited us,' she went on with a grin. 'I think Annabelle likes to think of us as the paupers.'

'I reckon you could be right,' Dotty agreed, then giggled. 'But she's nice when you get to know her, isn't she? Though I have to admit I wasn't all that keen on her at first. She really hated her job to begin with, she said that it was beneath her, but between you and me I reckon she quite enjoys it now. At least she doesn't grumble so much, and when I went through the perfume department the other day I saw her arranging her counter without being told. When I teased her about it, she said that she was only doing it so that she knew where everything was, but I didn't believe her for a minute. I think she takes a pride in her own counter now.'

Lucy nodded in agreement as she pointed out St Michael's Cathedral to Mary from the window, not that the child took much notice of it, but Lucy never gave up trying to reach her – although deep down she knew that she never would.

Eventually they arrived at their stop and the bus trundled to a halt. Lucy and Dotty ushered Mary off between them then Dotty took a scrap of paper from her pocket and peered at it. It was only three thirty in the afternoon but already the light was fading and it was bitterly cold, although thankfully they hadn't had any more snow as yet.

'Ah, that's Leaf Lane over there – look,' Dotty pointed. 'And the house is called Primrose Lodge.'

'Doesn't it have a number?' Lucy asked as they set off with Mary between them.

Dotty scoffed. 'No, none of them along here do, by the look of it. Numbers are common, didn't you know? Crikey, they're really posh, aren't they?'

They moved on, looking at the names on the gates of the houses, which all seemed to be hiding at the end of long, winding driveways.

'Ah, here we are,' Dotty said a good ten minutes later. 'This is it.'

They set off up the drive in silence, each of them nervous as they glimpsed the size of the house they were approaching.

'It's more like a mansion than a house,' Lucy whispered in awe.

Lucy rang the doorbell and almost instantly Annabelle opened the door with a wide smile on her face.

'Ah, so you found us then. Come on in out of the cold. Mummy is so looking forward to meeting you.'

Lucy couldn't help but glance enviously at their friend. It was the first time she had ever seen her out of her white blouse and black skirt, and the other girl looked lovely in a calf-length skirt in a shade of deep blue, with a very pretty lace-trimmed blouse. Her hair had been brushed till it shone like spun gold and Dotty was sure that she could have been a fashion model. She certainly had the looks and the figure.

Annabelle helped them off with their coats as the two other girls stared shyly about.

'Blimey, I reckon this entrance hallway is as big as my whole flat put together,' Dotty quipped.

There was a wall-to-wall patterned carpet on the floor and a huge gilt-framed mirror stood above an ornate hall table. Lovely smells of baking were issuing from a doorway further along the hall and Annabelle shooed them towards it, telling them, 'Mummy is in the kitchen making cakes. She thought Mary might like one for after her tea. We used to have a cook but since she left we've discovered that Mummy is actually a very good cook.'

When she threw open a door the two girls found themselves in the most enormous kitchen they had ever seen. Cupboards were ranged around the walls and a huge scrubbed oak table with six chairs placed about it stood in the centre of the room. On the far wall was a large oven and as the girls entered, a woman who was in the process of taking some small sponge cakes from the oven smiled at them in welcome. Once she had placed the baking tray on a rack, she ushered the visitors towards a fireplace where a blazing fire was licking up the chimney.

'Now which of you is Dotty and which of you is Lucy?' she asked pleasantly. 'I've heard so much about you from Annabelle. I've been really looking forward to meeting you.'

The girls introduced themselves and then the woman bent to Mary's height and said kindly, 'And you must be Mary?' Her eyes were gentle as she looked at the child, who stared blankly back at her. Poor little mite, Miranda thought. Annabelle had told her that Mary was 'not quite right' as she had put it.

'Well, I'm Miranda,' she told them now as she bustled about getting cups and saucers laid out. 'And I insist that is what you call me. Mrs Smythe is so formal, isn't it?'

The girls felt themselves begin to relax despite their luxurious surroundings. Miranda was so easy to talk to that she put them at their ease as she began to carry the food to the table. It turned out to be quite a feast. There were sandwiches with cucumber or meat-paste fillings and sausage rolls fresh from the oven followed by home-made fairy cakes and scones.

'Now do please help yourselves,' she urged them. 'Otherwise Annabelle and I shall be eating this lot for the next week.'

They were only too happy to oblige, and as the meal progressed the girls found themselves relaxing even more and talking to Miranda as if they had known her for years. Annabelle's mother was nothing at all like they had imagined she would be. She had no airs and graces whatsoever, unlike her daughter. It was soon very obvious that Miranda had completely fallen in love with Mary and she kept encouraging the little girl with tasty titbits. In fact, Lucy became concerned that Mary was overeating and worried about her being sick, but she didn't like to say anything. Miranda was clearly enjoying having a little one to fuss over.

'Our neighbour, Mrs P, is having an Anderson shelter built in her back yard next week,' Lucy told them when the conversation turned to the war.

Miranda clucked and shook her head. 'It's perhaps for the best,' she said. 'You know – just in case. We're lucky that we have a large cellar. I've already taken down there everything I thought we might need if there's an air raid. Candles, blankets, pillows and that sort of thing. I've put some containers of water and tins of food and a tin opener down there as well, but I pray we'll never have to use them – although it's looking all the more likely that we shall. It might be quite scary for Mary though – if we have an air raid, I mean,' she said worriedly. 'All those loud explosions and everything. Bless her, she won't understand what's happening. How old is she, Lucy?'

'She'll be five in a few weeks' time,' Lucy responded and Miranda saw the fear in her eyes.

'Ah, so she'll be evacuated then?'

As Lucy nodded her head, she swallowed tears. Just the thought of it struck terror into her heart.

'I'm sure she'll cope admirably,' Miranda said reassuringly as she patted the girl's shoulder. 'After all, even Princess Elizabeth and Princess Margaret Rose have been evacuated.'

'Yes, but they're at Balmoral with servants to wait on them who they probably already know,' Lucy said hotly. 'Once Mary goes I shan't even know where she's been sent till the person who is taking care of her sends me her address on a postcard. She could end up anywhere – and with total strangers too!'

Seeing that Lucy was becoming distressed, Miranda said calmly, 'Well now, let's not talk of sad things any more. Why don't you two girls tell me all about the departments that you work in at Owen Owen?'

So for the next half an hour that's exactly what Dotty and Lucy did as Miranda listened with interest.

'And what hobbies do you both like?' she asked.

Lucy fell silent and lowered her eyes. There was little time for hobbies in her life with looking after Mary, holding down a full-time job and running a home.

'Well, I know that you like writing, dear,' Miranda said, turning her attention to Dotty. 'In fact, I hope you don't mind but Annabelle gave me the short story you lent her and I read it straight through. I couldn't put it down! I think you have a rare gift for storytelling and I'd really love to read some of your other work – if you wouldn't object, that is . . .' Her voice trailed away uncertainly as Dotty blushed a dull pillar-box red.

'I er . . . I've never shown anyone my work before until Annabelle and Lucy,' she stammered self-consciously, 'apart, that is, from Miss Timms at the orphanage where I was brought up. It was she who encouraged me to write in the first place. I always found it hard to mix and show my feelings, but she told me that I could put all my dreams and feelings down on paper and it does really work. I find that when I'm writing I can go anywhere and be anyone I want . . .' She lowered her eyes and started fidgeting, but not before Miranda had seen how animated she had become when she spoke of her writing.

'I read it too, last night,' Annabelle chipped in. 'And I have to say I agree. It really was first-rate.'

'Then in that case I suppose I could let you both read some more.' Dotty was almost cringing with embarrassment and pleasure, and not used to being the focus of attention, wasn't at all sure how to act.

'I shall look forward to that then. But now Annabelle, why don't you show your friends up to your room and listen to some music or something. I'll keep little Mary here with me.'

Lucy opened her mouth to object but Miranda held her hand up. 'She will be perfectly all right down here,' she promised her with an indulgent smile in the child's direction. 'Go on, off with you and enjoy a little free time while you can. I shall tell Mary the story of Goldilocks and the Three Bears while we have a cuddle in front of the fire. It used to be one of Annabelle's favourites when she was a little girl, and if I had a pound note for every time I'd told it to her, I would be a very rich woman by now.'

The girls obediently followed Annabelle from the room, their eyes on stalks as they moved through the beautiful house. It was like entering another world, especially for Dotty, brought up in the austere confines of an orphanage.

Lucy whistled quietly in awe when Annabelle showed them into her bedroom. The main colour scheme varied from the lightest pink to a deep rose, and it looked warm and inviting.

'I have to admit it's not usually as neat as this,' Annabelle said truthfully. 'At least, not since Mummy had to let our cleaner go, but I had a tidy-up because I knew you were coming.'

'It's really beautiful!' Lucy gasped. 'You're so lucky, Annabelle.'

'I know I am,' Annabelle said, and her chest swelled. She loved to be the centre of attention.

Dotty was standing at her dressing-table admiring the

array of cosmetics there whilst Lucy had wandered over to stroke the velvet floor-length curtains.

Meanwhile, Annabelle had crossed to a small record player and in no time at all the soft strains of a Vera Lynn song were floating around the room. 'They're calling her "the Forces sweetheart" now, you know,' she commented and the girls nodded in agreement.

Annabelle then opened the doors of the enormous rosewood wardrobe and the girls' eyes goggled as they saw the selection of clothes hanging there. There was everything from ballgowns to riding breeches.

'I used to have my own pony,' Annabelle told them airily. 'His name was Copper and when he died Daddy offered to buy me another one, but I'd tired of riding by then and I was more interested in dancing so I didn't bother. I really must get you two to a dance,' she went on. 'You don't know what you're missing. There's nothing like having a queue of handsome young men waiting to dance with you.' But even as she said it, a picture of Joel's face floated in front of her eyes and she immediately blinked to clear it.

Both he and Lucy were obviously as poor as church mice, and Joel was nothing at all like the sort of husband she had decided she would eventually have, so she really must try to stop thinking about him. But even so she suddenly blurted out, 'I don't suppose you've heard from Joel, have you?'

Lucy shook her head, her lips set in a prim line, and Annabelle got the impression that she didn't like her to mention him, which was strange. After all, he was only her brother, not her husband. But then Lucy answered shortly, 'No, I haven't, but he only left a few days ago. Even if he had written, I doubt the letter would have had time to reach me yet.'

'Oh no, no, of course not.' Annabelle was flustered and

now pointed to a tiny ornate desk in the corner, hoping to change the subject. 'Daddy bought me that for my fourteenth birthday. It's an antique and worth a fortune apparently.'

'It's lovely.' Lucy looked at it appreciatively. 'Is it a Chippendale piece?'

'I believe it is.' Annabelle was astonished that Lucy would know about things like that.

'I thought it was, by the shape of the legs. My mother loved—' Lucy stopped abruptly and a shadow flitted across her face, then forcing a smile again she said, 'Let's have a look through your record collection then. Do you have any by the Ink Spots? I love their music.'

They spent the next hour pleasantly but then when Lucy saw the clock on Annabelle's bedside table, she said regretfully, 'I'm afraid I shall have to be making tracks now. By the time we get home it will be Mary's bedtime. I don't want her to fall asleep on me on the bus. I might end up having to carry her and she's a right little heavyweight now.'

'I'll come too,' Dotty told her. 'And then we can get the same bus into the city centre. I hate walking about the streets on my own now at night. It's so dark.'

Downstairs they found Miranda with Mary tucked on her lap and it was hard to tell who was enjoying the cuddle the most.

'She's such a sweetheart,' Miranda said with a trace of sadness in her voice. 'I always hoped for a large family but unfortunately it wasn't to be. Not that I'm not grateful for Annabelle, of course,' she added hastily when she saw her daughter frown. 'But I suppose you'll want to be off now, will you? I think Mary is getting tired if her yawns are anything to go by.'

She bundled the child up in her outdoor clothes whilst Lucy and Dotty put their own coats on, then saw them to the door with Annabelle, where she kissed them all soundly. 'It's been an absolute pleasure to meet you,' she told them sincerely. 'I do hope you'll come and visit us again. In fact, why don't you all come and spend Christmas with us? Have a think about it and let Annabelle know what you want to do.'

The girls thanked her as they headed off down the drive, and Miranda and Annabelle waved them off.

Once they were back on the pavement, Dotty remarked, 'Annabelle is such a show-off, isn't she? I think she liked taking us around her house.' She tittered. 'Primrose Lodge, eh?'

'Well, you can hardly blame her, can you?' Lucy answered. 'I think I might be a show-off in her position and it's clear she's been doted on by her parents. It must be nice to be born with a silver spoon in your mouth.'

They then bent their heads and with Mary marching between them they set off for the bus stop through the darkened streets.

Back at the house, Annabelle was pensive as she helped her mother to tidy up. She wondered why Lucy had seemed so put out when she had mentioned Joel, but then she shrugged. Perhaps all sisters were possessive of their brothers? Never having had one she could have no way of knowing so she put it from her mind.

'Annabelle's mother was lovely, wasn't she?' Dotty said as they stood waiting for the bus some time later. 'And it was so kind of her to invite us to spend Christmas with them.'

'It was, but I doubt we'd be able to get there with no buses running,' Lucy reminded her.

'Ah, you have a point there,' Dotty answered, looking crestfallen.

'It isn't so far to my house though,' Lucy went on. 'So why don't you come and spend the day with me and Mary? Perhaps you could borrow a bicycle from someone? It would be much better than spending the day on our own.'

Dotty nodded enthusiastically. In truth she had been dreading spending her first Christmas all alone. 'Thanks – I'll see what I can do,' she promised, and then they ushered Mary forward as the bus drew up.

Chapter Ten

On Christmas Eve it was mayhem in Owen Owen from the second the doors were opened. Shoppers who had left it until the last minute to buy their presents poured inside in a frenzied wave.

'Crikey – I didn't think we were even going to get a morning break,' Annabelle puffed as they finally managed to catch a few minutes in the staff dining room late in the morning. 'The way things are going, we won't have any stock left for the January sales. I sold out of Evening in Paris within the first half an hour.'

'It's been the same in the children's department,' Lucy agreed. 'I'm sure I've sold more pairs of pyjamas and nightdresses today than I've sold in the last month. And the children's dressing-gowns are going like hot cakes too. In fact, I've already sold out of some ages.'

'It's not so busy in the fabric department,' Dotty told them, 'but that didn't get me off the hook. Because it was quiet,

Mrs Broadstairs has had me helping out down in the food hall. Lordy, you should just *see* what people are buying! Everything and anything they can get their hands on. I'm sure I've sold enough food in the last few hours to feed the entire British Army! If it goes on like this, I doubt I'll be able to make the staff party this evening. My feet are killing me already.'

'Oh yes, you *will* make the party,' Annabelle told her bossily. 'Even if I have to drag you there kicking and screaming. I'm certainly not going to let you miss out on a free drink; we'll have earned it by the time we close.'

All around them the staff were in fine spirits, partly at the thought of the promised party and partly because they were in a festive mood. Some of them were wearing silly party hats. Others were already dressed in their finery, with tinsel necklaces strung about their necks, but just for today Mrs Broadstairs had chosen to turn a blind eye.

'She couldn't really do any other, could she?' Annabelle said dryly when Lucy commented on it. 'Seeing as she's done up like a dog's dinner herself. Poor Mr Bradley won't stand a snowball's chance in hell of escaping her when she's had a few drinks.'

They chuckled as they glimpsed Mrs Broadstairs sashaying across the dining room close on the heels of her unsuspecting prey as he headed for the counter. Her skirt was so tight that she looked in danger of bursting out of it at any minute, but she still managed to beat him to it and they heard her trill, 'What would you like Mr Bradley? Tea? Coffee? My treat. It is Christmas Eve, after all.'

The girls suppressed their laughter as the woman batted her eyelashes at him, and suddenly Dotty began to look forward to the party, after all.

At last the doors to the store were closed and there was a

mad rush for the ladies cloakroom so that the girls could touch up their make-up; some of them even got changed and the staid black skirts and white blouses were hastily discarded. Half an hour later they began to emerge and head for the staff dining room where the party would be held, looking like multi-coloured butterflies. Annabelle had changed into a very becoming pale blue dress that showed off her slim figure to perfection. She had also changed her lower heels for much higher ones, but both Dotty and Lucy settled for tidying their hair and adding a touch of lipstick.

As soon as they got out of the lift they saw that the dining room had been transformed. Balloons dangled from the ceiling and the tables had been laid with a miniature banquet all along the length of one wall. Someone had brought a record player in and in no time at all people were dancing to the music, and the free wine that the store had supplied for the staff was flowing like water.

'This is more like it,' Annabelle said happily as she helped herself to another glass of wine, but then a hush fell on the room as Mr Bradley stopped the music to give them their customary Christmas speech.

'I would like to thank all of you,' he boomed, 'for working so very hard in the build-up to Christmas. We have been extraordinarily busy in Owen Owen and I am happy to be able to tell you that despite the present grave circumstances, the takings are up. It seems that the public are intent on making this Christmas a time to remember. Who knows what the coming year holds for us all? On that sombre note I would like you all to raise your glasses in a toast to loved ones who are absent at this special time, fighting for us, our king and country.'

Lucy's eyes filled with tears as she thought of Joel, and everyone solemnly made the toast, then Mr Bradley concluded, 'It only remains for me now to wish you all a very Merry Christmas. Please enjoy the food and drink we have laid on, and have a very happy holiday.'

A cheer went up as the music resumed and then Dotty dug Lucy in the ribs and hissed. 'Look over there – quickly!'

Lucy followed her eyes and laughed out loud as she saw that Mrs Broadstairs had penned Mr Bradley against the wall whilst she dangled a piece of mistletoe above her head. Seeing no alternative, the poor man leaned forward and pecked her hastily on the cheek and instantly another cheer went up as Mrs Broadstairs simpered with delight.

'Let's hope she gets her man,' Dotty whispered. 'She's not such a bad old stick really, is she?'

In that moment, it hit the girls how settled they now were at Owen Owen. They might have the occasional grumble admittedly, but it had become a sanctuary to them and through their jobs they had found each other.

'I'd like to make a toast to us,' Annabelle shouted above the loud music as she raised her glass. 'Friends forever, eh? No matter what the future has in store!'

'Hear hear!' Dotty and Lucy chorused and then they all joined in with the party spirit.

When the girls finally left the store well after nine o'clock that evening they all kissed each other on the pavement and exchanged gifts to be opened on Christmas Day, then went their separate ways, all exhausted, yet in a happy frame of mind.

Once Dotty arrived home she turned the small gas-fire on and was in the process of removing her coat when there was a tap on the door. It was rare for her to have visitors, especially this late at night, and as she hurried to answer it she wondered who it might be. She opened the door to find Miss Timms standing there.

'Hello, what a lovely surprise!' she said as she ushered the woman into the room. 'I wasn't expecting to see you until after Christmas, but I'm so glad you've come. I have a little gift for you.'

'Oh, you shouldn't have gone spending your hard-earned money on me,' Miss Timms scolded her, but she was beaming with pleasure as Dotty closed the door firmly behind her.

'I've only just got in,' Dotty told her now as she went to put the kettle on. 'It's been absolute bedlam at the store today. I think every single person in Coventry must have remembered someone they hadn't got a present for. That's what it felt like anyway, and the tills haven't stopped ringing all day. Then when the store finally closed, we had a staff party.'

'It's always the same on Christmas Eve, and probably even more so this year. Everyone seems intent on having a good time and be damned to what happens tomorrow,' Miss Timms replied as she took her coat off and folded it over the back of a chair. She then patted her hair to make sure that it was still neatly in place before sitting down and folding her hands primly in her lap.

'So how are you, dear?' she asked now as her eyes followed Dotty about the room. 'And have you eaten? I don't want you neglecting yourself.'

'I tend to have my main meal at work at lunchtime in the works dining room,' Dotty explained. She grinned then. 'Actually it's more of a canteen but it's much easier than trying to cook anything here. I just tend to make a sandwich when I get in from work, or sometimes I warm a tin of soup up. But how are things at the orphanage? Is everyone well?'

'In actual fact, one of the reasons I came to see you was to er . . . well, it was to tell you that I've left the orphanage now.'

'You've *what?*' Dotty was amazed. As far as she was concerned, Miss Timms *was* the orphanage and she couldn't begin to imagine how it would run without her. She had been the only stable person she had ever had in her life, and she was suddenly fearful that if Miss Timms was now no longer a part of that establishment, this might be the last time she would ever see her. The thought was unbelievably frightening: what if she had come to say a last goodbye?

'Have you come to say I won't be seeing you again then?' she forced herself to ask, but it came out as a squeak.

'Oh goodness me, no!' Miss Timms suddenly looked tearful too. 'Why, I could *never* abandon you, my dear. I have helped to care for you since you were a very young baby and I . . . Let's just say I will never leave you.'

'That's all right then.' Dotty heaved a sigh of relief as she looked across at the woman's face. Funnily enough, she had never given it much thought before, but now as she looked she saw that she wasn't as old as she had always assumed she was. Miss Timms tended to dress very conservatively and that, teamed with her rather out-of-date hairstyle, made her appear older than her years. But now on closer inspection, Dotty thought that she was probably only in her late thirties at most. Definitely too young to have spent all that time locked away with orphans. But then the girl supposed that she must have had her reasons. Perhaps she had been thwarted in love when she was younger? Here I go again, Dotty scolded herself, letting my imagination run away with me!

'In regard to your question as to why I left . . .' Miss Timms shrugged, which made her appear younger and more vulnerable. 'I suppose I just decided that I wanted a career change. I missed you a lot when you left, Dotty, so I've made a fresh start. I've started work in a bank and I'm actually quite enjoying it. It's certainly different to being at the beck and call of infants and young people.'

Dotty was deeply touched. No one had ever told her they really cared about her before, which she supposed was what Miss Timms had just done in a roundabout way.

'And so what are you doing tomorrow?' the woman asked now, clearly embarrassed. 'I do hope that you won't be spending Christmas Day alone?'

'Actually, I'm going to spend it with Lucy, my friend from work,' Dotty said as she poured boiling water into the tea-pot. 'What will you be doing?'

'I shall spend the day quietly at home with my mother,' Miss Timms responded as she fumbled in her handbag. 'She's getting quite old now and she's very set in her ways.' She handed Dotty a small package, saying, 'I wasn't sure what to get you but I hope you like it.'

'Th-thank you.' Dotty took the present and stared at it before asking, 'Shall I open it tomorrow?'

'No, you don't have to wait. You can open it now if you wish,' Miss Timms told her and so Dotty carefully began to undo the string from the gaily wrapped parcel. The paper was so pretty it seemed a shame to rip it.

Inside she found an oblong box, and when she opened it she gasped with delight. It contained a beautiful fountain pen that looked very expensive.

'It's solid silver,' Miss Timms explained. 'But if you don't like it we can always change it. I just thought it might come in handy, knowing how you love to write. I do hope you are still writing?'

'Yes, I am – and yes, it will come in very handy,' Dotty assured her. 'And thank you so much. It's really lovely. In fact, I don't think I've ever owned anything so precious and you can be sure I'll treasure it.' Finally dragging her eyes away from it, she went on, 'Oh dear, I'm afraid the gifts I have for you aren't anywhere near as valuable as this.'

'That doesn't matter. It's the thought that counts.'

So Dotty hurried away and then handed a small parcel to the woman, who opened it with a look of pure delight on her face. I bet she doesn't get many people buying her presents, Dotty thought, and it saddened her.

Miss Timms showed much the same reaction as Dotty had when the gift was finally opened. Dotty had bought her a pure silk headscarf in lovely autumn colours. It looked very bright and colourful against the drab clothes that the woman was wearing, but she seemed to be over the moon with it.

'Why, it's *gorgeous.*' She ran her hand across the smooth silk with a look of pure pleasure on her face. 'I must admit I would never have chosen it for myself, since Mother doesn't like me wearing flamboyant colours, but I really love it. Thank you *so* much!'

Dotty then handed over her last gift, saying, 'I er . . . made this skirt for you myself. I had to guess the size, so I hope it fits. I'm not the best seamstress in the world, I'm afraid, so I won't be offended if you don't want to wear it.'

Intrigued, Miss Timms opened the parcel and then her face lit up again. '*You* made this?' she said incredulously. 'Why, Dotty, is there no end to your talents? I really love it and I shall wear it for church tomorrow with my very best blouse.'

Suddenly Dotty leaned over and pecked her on the cheek and the woman flushed to the very roots of her hair and became all flustered. And then they both laughed and the awkward moment was gone. Miss Timms stayed for another hour, periodically reaching out to stroke the scarf and the skirt, and when she left, Dotty had a warm glow in the pit of her stomach. Bless her, she thought happily. My childhood would have been a lot sadder, had it not been for Miss Timms. She then settled down in front of the little fire and after carefully filling her lovely new pen from a bottle of Quink, she soon became lost in the latest story she was writing. She was attempting her first novel now and loving every minute of it.

Chapter Eleven

On Christmas Day bright and early Dotty wrapped up warmly and cycled to Lucy's house on the bike she had borrowed from one of the neighbours. It was no mean feat on the icy roads. Every time she came to a hill she had to get off and push the bike up it, and by the time she reached Lucy's home her cheeks were bright red and her fingers were so cold they had turned blue even though she was wearing mittens. She wheeled her bike up the entry and into the little yard at the back as Lucy opened the back door with a smile on her face.

'I was hoping you'd come early,' she greeted her. 'You must have heard the kettle boil – I've just made a brew. Come on in out of the cold!'

Dotty gratefully did as she was told to find Mary playing on the rug in front of the fire with a new teddy that Lucy had bought her. Even though she had already bought the child her new clothes, she had purchased the teddy bear from the toy department at the last minute and Mary had barely put it down. She was muttering away to it but none of the sounds made sense, and once again Dotty thought what a shame it was that such a beautiful child should be so afflicted. There was a delicious smell issuing from the oven and she sniffed appreciatively.

'Hm, something smells good. Is that a turkey in there?'

'It is indeed,' Lucy chuckled as Dotty took her coat off. '*And* we've got Brussels sprouts, stuffing, roast potatoes and all the trimmings to go with it. I decided to push the boat out. After all, once the rationing comes in, we might be on bread and water.'

They exchanged gifts. Lucy had bought Dotty a pair of woollen gloves and a matching scarf in a deep amber colour. It was very bright compared to the drab colours that Dotty usually favoured, but she blushed with pleasure all the same when she opened the parcel. She had bought Lucy a cardigan in a wonderful emerald green that matched her eyes to perfection, and a beautifully illustrated book of fairy stories for Mary – two perfect presents. The friends hugged each other.

Christmas dinner was great fun. The girls giggled and gossiped, and made sure that Mary had plenty to eat. But Dotty sensed that behind Lucy's smile, she was missing her brother very much. Brother and sister had apparently never spent a Christmas apart before, and it must be hard for her, Dotty thought.

Once the meal was over and the table cleared, Lucy made the fire up and they turned the wireless on to listen to the king's Christmas speech. It was a very old radio that Joel had picked up second-hand from the Coventry indoor market, and it made crackling noises before gurgling into life.

Dotty loved the royal family, and while they waited for the announcer to introduce the king, she told Lucy, 'The king is supposed to be very shy, you know. He has a terrible stammer, poor thing.'

'I daresay he never expected to be king,' Lucy replied. 'Poor Prince Albert had no choice but to take the throne when Edward abdicated to marry Wallis Simpson, and it must have been a huge leap from being the Duke of York to king. When he was simply a duke he could stay in the background up to a point, but after Edward met Wallis . . .' She remembered how the newspapers had been full of it. 'That certainly caused an outcry, didn't it? I mean, who would think that a king would do something like that? Just goes to show, they're only flesh and blood at the end of the day, the same as us.'

'Yes, you can't help who you fall in love with,' Dotty remarked dreamily as her romantic mind took flight. 'Just imagine caring enough for someone to give up the throne for them. And she's an American divorcée too!' Then she asked, 'What sort of man would you like to marry, Lucy?'

Lucy's face instantly hardened. 'I shall *never* get married,' she said shortly. 'Not to *anyone*!' She looked slightly embarrassed then as she noted Dotty's shocked expression. 'Well, what I mean is, I don't get much chance to meet anyone, do I? What with looking after Mary and everything.'

'But if someone loved you enough, they would take to Mary too,' Dotty pointed out. She just couldn't imagine Lucy never marrying; she was far too pretty to be a spinster, whereas she herself was so plain that she doubted anyone would ever want to marry her.

Much to Lucy's relief the announcer's voice brought the

conversation to an end, and both girls listened to the king stammer his way through the speech.

When it was over, Dotty sighed and they sat and watched Mary playing contentedly with her new teddy. She had refused to put it down all day, even throughout dinner, but then Lucy suggested, 'How about we wrap up and go to the phone box at the end of the road to give Annabelle a ring?'

'Good idea,' Dotty agreed as she hurried away to fetch her coat, and soon after they were in the phone box and the operator was connecting them to Annabelle's number.

'Hello.' It was Annabelle who answered the phone and when Lucy spoke she sounded pleased to hear from her. 'I'm having a dreadful day,' she complained. 'Mummy has hardly stopped crying because she's never been parted from Daddy on Christmas Day before and I'm so *bored*! I shall almost be glad to get back to work – and we still have Boxing Day to get through yet.'

Both girls chuckled as they fed their pennies into the slot and took it in turns to speak to her.

'I never thought I'd hear you say *that*,' Dotty teased, and was met with a groan from Annabelle's end.

'Well, there's nothing to do, is there, but eat. I shall be the size of a house at this rate.'

'I don't think there's much danger of that happening any time soon,' Lucy responded. 'You're so skinny you'd slip down a crack in the pavement if you turned sideways.'

Five minutes later the girls came out of the phone box.

'Poor Annabelle,' Dotty said. 'I'm afraid this war is affecting her far more than you or me. We're used to staying in, but I think she is missing a more exciting way of life now that most of her male friends have joined up. She's asked me to go to the cinema with her in the New Year to see *Goodbye Mr Chips* and I'm quite looking forward to it. Why don't you ask Mrs P if she would mind Mary and then you could come with us too?'

'It would be fun,' Lucy admitted. 'And I do love Robert Donat. He's just so handsome, isn't he? Leave it with me and I'll see what I can do.'

They then hastened back to the warmth of Lucy's little terraced house, swinging Mary between them. There were constant reminders of the war all about them, like the grey barrage balloons that floated in the sky above them. It was daunting to know that now only a strip of water divided them from the wrath of Hitler's army. Rumour still had it that he was only waiting for the better weather next spring before he instructed his army to attack, and the girls could only pray that the rumour was wrong. The alternative was just too frightening to contemplate.

'Blimey, I thought we'd have an easy day today, now that the Christmas rush is over.' Lucy eased her feet carefully out of her shoes beneath the table and wriggled her toes.

It was the day after Boxing Day and ever since arriving at work all three girls had been rushing around like headless chickens. There were nowhere near as many customers in the store admittedly, but even so each head of department had had them all marking down goods ready for the January sales.

'I know what you mean,' Annabelle answered as she took out her compact and powdered her nose. 'I was busily working away behind my counter and didn't notice a customer waiting to be served when Miss Goode swept over to me like a battleship in full sail. She gave me a real roasting, I don't mind telling you, but how are we supposed to do two things at once?'

'Perhaps we should all sprout another pair of hands?'

Dotty suggested with a wry grin. 'It's no better in my department. There are so many different rolls of material and if I get the price wrong on one of them I reckon I'll be for the high jump.'

'I doubt that would happen,' Annabelle said stoically. 'We're understaffed as it is, and they can't afford to lose any more – though if what Mummy heard was true, then things are going to get a whole lot worse soon. They're saying that in January all men between the ages of nineteen and twenty-seven will be liable for service. It won't be a matter any more of them signing up if they have a mind to, they won't have a say in the matter unless they're flat-footed or suffer from some other ailment.'

They each lifted their cup as the hum of the store canteen went on around them.

A royal proclamation made on New Year's Day declared that two million young men were about to be called up, thus proving Miranda Smythe to be right. People's spirits dropped still further as young men went in hordes to the recruiting offices.

'There soon won't be a bloke worth looking at left in Coventry,' Annabelle moaned. She and Dotty were at Lucy's house and they were all feeling a bit sorry for themselves, especially Annabelle. 'Fancy,' she said, 'I actually stayed in on New Year's Eve. No party, no dance, *nothing!*'

'I don't think anyone was really in the mood for celebrating this year,' Lucy said.

Dotty nodded in agreement. 'You're right, and the weather isn't helping either. I'm sure it's trying to snow and it's absolutely bitter out.'

'Oh super, that's all we need.' Annabelle rolled her eyes skywards. 'Everything seems to be doom and gloom at the moment.' Her eyes then rested on an envelope on the mantelshelf and suddenly forgetting all her gripes, she asked, 'Is that a letter from Joel?' Just thinking about him made her heart beat faster.

'Yes, it is.' Lucy had read it so many times in the two days since it had arrived that she almost knew it word for word. 'He's going to be shipped out within the next two weeks, but the good news is he's hoping to get another two days' leave before they go.'

'Oh, and when will that be? And I thought he was being shipped out straight after his last leave.' Annabelle was doing her best not to sound too interested and failing dismally.

'So did we,' Lucy agreed. 'And I have no idea why the plans were changed. But he could be coming home on leave any day now.' Her face lit up at the thought of seeing her brother again, although she was worried sick about him being posted abroad. But then he was only one of thousands and she knew that all across the country, wives, mothers, sisters and lovers must be feeling exactly the same.

Annabelle felt a little bubble of excitement form in her stomach. 'You shall have to ask us round to say goodbye to him and wish him well,' she remarked casually, but she didn't fool Lucy for a second.

'Of course you're always welcome,' the girl answered winking at Dotty. 'And I'm sure Joel would like to see you too.'

The January sales started the next day and when the girls arrived at Owen Owen they were shocked to see people queuing along the street.

'Looks like we're going to be busy again if the crowd outside is anything to go by,' Annabelle declared as they trudged towards the staff cloakroom. 'I've never seen such a queue! Do they think we're going to be giving the stuff away or something?'

'Well, you know what they say – the early bird catches the worm, and according to the Home Service, some people have been queuing all night in London to get the best bargains,' Lucy said. 'Think of it this way – if we're busy, the time will go quicker.'

'Trust you to look on the bright side,' Annabelle bridled as she hung her coat up and checked her hair in the mirror above the sink. They then all darted off on their separate ways, wondering if they would even have time for their breaks or their lunch-hours.

'Miss Smythe, there is another customer waiting to be served,' the head of the perfume department barked at Annabelle an hour later.

'I am well aware of that fact,' Annabelle snapped back. 'But unfortunately I haven't yet mastered the art of serving more than one customer at a time!'

'Why, *really*!' The woman was enraged. 'I shall be reporting you to Mrs Broadstairs,' she sputtered.

'Well, before you do that, why don't you get behind the counter and help me to serve?' Annabelle suggested tartly, enraging the irate woman even more. Even so, she joined Annabelle and between them the queue of people waiting to be served did start to go down a little more quickly.

There was no chance of a morning break but at last the girls were given permission to go for a shortened lunch break and they all met up in the staff dining room.

'My God, I've never seen anything like it,' Dotty said as they stood at the counter waiting to be served with beans on toast. 'I've actually had two ladies almost come to blows over a length of reduced material that they both made a beeline for this morning. I had to use all my wits to calm them down.'

'It hasn't been much better in the children's department,' Lucy said.

'Nor in perfumes and cosmetics,' Annabelle chipped in. 'I ran out of Elizabeth Arden's Blue Grass within an hour and the customers have really been having a go at me, as if it was *my* fault! I'll tell you, at one point I was ready to walk out – and blow the job!'

They all saw the funny side of it then and carried their trays to the table with grins on their faces. After all, the worst of the sales rush should be over now, shouldn't it?

It was on the third day back at work that Lucy informed them that Joel was home.

'He's meeting me from work this evening so we could all go for a cup of tea again, if you like,' she suggested.

'Unfortunately I can't,' Dotty apologised. 'I have Miss Timms coming to see me at the flat tonight and I don't want her to arrive and for me not to be there.'

'But I could come – I don't have anything planned,' Annabelle told Lucy hastily.

'Right, we'll do that then,' Lucy agreed, and for the rest of the day Annabelle found that she could think of nothing else.

When they left the store they found Joel waiting for them with a worried frown on his face. 'I've had to leave Mary with Mrs P,' he informed Lucy. 'She's got a terrible cough on her so I think we should head straight home.'

'But I invited Annabelle to come to the café with us.' Lucy said, then a thought occurred to her and she turned to her friend. 'Why don't you come home with us and have dinner? That would be all right, wouldn't it, Joel?'

'Of course it would.' He was painfully aware of Annabelle standing next to him and was secretly thrilled at Lucy's suggestion. 'I'm sure we can rustle up enough for another mouth.'

And so they set off side by side for the bus station and when their bus came in Lucy watched Joel slip into the seat next to Annabelle.

'So, Lucy tells me that you'll be off soon then?' Annabelle couldn't keep the concern from her voice and Joel stared at her in the dim light. Could it be that Annabelle was as attracted to him as he was to her? But then he dismissed that idea. What would a girl like her want to waste time on the likes of him for? She was from a different class. The way she spoke, the way she dressed, the way she held herself, and everything else about her told him so – and yet . . .

He nodded and cleared his throat. 'Yes, I will. We haven't been told officially, but it looks like we're going to be shipped out to either Norway or France – and then God knows when I'll get home again.' He refrained from saying *if ever* – but it was a fear he had. What would happen to Lucy and Mary if he was killed? He and Annabelle both fell silent then as the bus trundled on through the darkened streets.

Once back at home, Joel headed for the kitchen where he had a rabbit stew simmering in the oven. Mrs P was sitting at the side of the fire with Mary on her lap.

'Poor little lamb,' she said. 'Proper under the weather so she is, but then it's hardly suprisin', is it, wi' the weather as it is? That's why I told Joel I'd come round here to watch 'er till yer got back. Saves takin' her out in the cold, don't it? But now as you are back I'll be off. My Fred'll be shoutin' fer his dinner soon.' She stood up and handed Mary to Lucy, then with a friendly nod in Annabelle's direction, she headed for the door.

Whilst Lucy got Mary undressed in front of the fire, Annabelle asked, 'Is there anything I can do to help?'

'No, thanks, but you could stay and keep me company while I dish this up,' he responded as he lifted some plates down from the dresser.

'It must be a comfort to you to know that Lucy has Mrs P next door,' Annabelle said. 'She's lovely, isn't she?'

'She is that,' he agreed. 'Salt of the earth, is our Mrs P. But I do worry about how Lucy will cope when Mary is evacuated. You've probably noticed that she adores her, and there are only a few weeks to go now.'

'Don't worry, I'll keep my eye on her for you,' Annabelle promised and was shocked to hear herself say it. Since when had she worried about anyone but herself? She was even more shocked to realise that she meant it. 'You just worry about keeping yourself safe,' she went on, and again she could hardly believe that she had said it. She might just as well have come right out and said that she cared about him.

Joel paused to stare at her and their eyes locked, but then Lucy broke the spell when she asked, 'So how is this dinner coming along? I'm starving and I'm sure you must be hungry too, Annabelle. We didn't get to have much of a break at lunch-time, did we?'

They all carried their plates to the table, and once they had eaten Annabelle helped Joel with the pots while Lucy put Mary to bed.

Crikey, I really am getting domesticated, Annabelle thought as she dried the dishes, yet strangely she didn't mind so long as it meant being with Joel.

'Will you be able to write to Lucy from wherever you're posted to?' she asked.

He nodded. 'I dare say so, though the letters will be

heavily censored, and of course there's no saying how long they'll take to get through.' Then shyly, 'If you were to give me your address I could write to you too, if you like.'

'I would like that.' Annabelle smiled at him and they finished the rest of the washing and drying up in a harmonious silence, content just to be in each other's company.

Later that evening, Joel walked her to the bus stop and they stood facing each other awkwardly as they waited for the bus to come.

'Take care of yourself then,' Annabelle said in a voice that was barely more than a whisper.

They heard the bus coming along the road, and leaning forward, he suddenly self-consciously pecked her on the cheek. 'You too,' he muttered, and then he was striding away with his hands tucked deep in his pockets.

On 8 January 1940, for the first time since 1918, ration books were introduced. Butter, sugar, tea, bacon and all the food that had previously been taken for granted were suddenly very precious. Then to make things even worse, as the month progressed the weather conditions worsened, and on 17 January the River Thames froze over – something that had last happened in 1888.

'Brrr, it's enough to make yer want to stay in bed,' Mrs P shivered one evening when Lucy arrived after work to collect Mary. Thankfully, the child's cough had improved but she still wasn't completely better and Lucy hated leaving her, especially as the time for her to be evacuated drew closer. Mrs P's Anderson shelter was now completed and she had spent a lot of time making it as comfortable as she could – just in case it was needed, as she pointed out. Fred had built bunk-beds along one wall from pallets that he had collected from the market, and Mrs P had dragged two thin mattresses in there along with a selection of old bedding that she had stored over the years. There was also an old easy chair and candles so that they would not have to sit in the dark.

'If the sirens should ever go off, don't you hesitate to get yourself an' little Mary round here,' she drummed into Lucy. 'There ain't much protection to be had from fallin' bombs beneath a kitchen table.'

Yet more shelters had now been finished all over the city, and every time Lucy passed them she shuddered and prayed that they would never be needed. But word of what was happening in the war was not promising. The papers were full of the 152 lives that had been lost when the *Dunbar Castle* had been sunk by a German mine off the Goodwin Sands, and a further thirty-two lives were lost when German planes attacked another twelve ships, sinking three of them.

'Things ain't lookin' good,' Mrs P remarked worriedly. 'I just pray that our Freddy an' your Joel are all right, that's all.'

There had been no word from either of them, although both women waited hopefully each morning for the postman to arrive.

'It said on the wireless earlier on that the government is bein' urged to give women the same wages an' conditions as men now,' Mrs P informed Lucy as she helped Mary into her coat. 'They reckon they're goin' to be given trainin' an' that there'll be an influx of women into the war industries. Stands to reason there'll have to be, don't it? I mean, who else can do it if the men are all away at war?'

Lucy took Mary by the hand, ready to leave. 'Try not to worry too much,' the girl said gently, but she knew that it would be easier said than done. Mrs P was a 'born worrier' as her Fred was always telling her.

'Fred was sayin' that they're movin' the bomber parts they're makin' from some of the factories like the Daimler, the Dunlop, the Humber an' so on to shadow factories on the outskirts of the city to reduce the threat of aerial attacks an' bombin' away from the residential areas.'

'Well, that's good then, isn't it?' Lucy questioned.

'Aye, I dare say it is, but it makes yer realise things are gettin' worse though, don't it?'

'I suppose it does,' Lucy admitted sadly. 'But now I'd best be getting home. To tell you the truth I'm dead on my feet and looking forward to spending a night in front of the fire with another of Dotty's stories.'

Mrs P instantly perked up. Dotty was now allowing all of them to read her efforts and they were thoroughly enjoying them.

'Eeh, that girl can spin a good yarn, can't she?' she breathed. 'I don't mind admittin' that one yer lent me the other day moved me to tears.'

'Her books should be in the Central Library – she's brilliant,' Lucy agreed as she moved towards the door. 'Night, Mrs P, and thank you.'

Chapter Twelve

At that moment, Dotty was entering her flat. Once inside, she snapped the light on and hurried over to light the gas-fire. She had collected her mail from the table in the hall as she usually did, not that there was ever a lot for her. Now, after placing the kettle on to boil, she glanced curiously at the envelope she had collected. It had a London postmark, but she couldn't for the life of her think who it might be from. Her name and address were typed and it looked quite official, which puzzled her even more. She slit it open. Inside was a single sheet of paper, again typed, and she quickly began to scan the page.

Dear Miss Kent,

Having read your delightful submission, The Soldier's Girl, *it gives me great pleasure to inform you that both myself and a senior editor at* Woman's Heart *magazine consider it to be worthy of publication. We would like to include the story in our March edition and in the meantime would be pleased to look at some more of your other stories as we feel your writing has great potential and we may well be interested in giving your stories a regular slot.*

If you would kindly ring us on the number below we will be happy to discuss your fee and arrange a meeting.

Yours sincerely,

Mr R. Brabinger

Dotty blinked, then read the letter through again just to make sure that she hadn't imagined it. She had lent *The Soldier's Girl* to Annabelle's mother to read just a couple of weeks ago but had no idea how it could have landed up on the desk of a magazine editor . . . unless Miranda had sent it to them, of course. Yes! That must be it, she thought, as different emotions raced through her. She felt elated yet terrified at the thought of so many people reading her stories all at the same time.

There was a tap at the door then and when Dotty answered it to find Miss Timms on the doorstep she almost yanked her into the room and pressed the letter into the startled woman's hand.

'Read this,' she said bluntly, then remembering her manners she flapped, 'Oh, I'm so sorry. Hello, Miss Timms. I didn't mean to be rude but I just got home and opened this and don't quite know what to make of it. I'm afraid I'm all flustered.'

Miss Timms took off her new silk scarf, then removed her gloves and read the letter. Her face broke into a wide smile. 'Why, Dotty, this is absolutely marvellous!' she exclaimed delightedly. 'Well done. I'm so pleased you finally plucked up the courage to show your work to someone. Didn't I always tell you it was good enough for publication?'

'But I didn't show it to anyone,' Dotty said. 'At least, not to this magazine. I let Annabelle's mother read it and she must have sent it to them.'

'Then in that case well done to her for recognising talent,' Miss Timms responded. 'You really *must* telephone them, Dotty. They obviously love your work – and who knows where this might lead? I have a friend who has been trying to get some of her work published for years, so I know how hard it is. I'm so proud of you.'

Dotty shook her head, trying to take it all in. Then she paled. 'It says they want to arrange a meeting with me and they're in London,' she gulped. London sounded like the other side of the world to her. 'And what would they think of me if I was to go? I mean, I'm hardly a raving beauty, am I? I bet they'd be expecting someone really glamorous and fashionable.'

'Nonsense,' Miss Timms snapped. 'The trouble is, Dotty, you don't realise how attractive you are. Why, your skin is flawless and I'm sure if you had your hair styled and we got you a new outfit, you'd be stunning.'

'*Me* stunning?' Dotty scoffed with a nervous giggle. 'I doubt that very much.'

'Even so, I refuse to let you throw this chance away.' Miss Timms was adamant. 'We'll get that friend of yours – you know, the blonde one, Annabelle isn't it? – to take you shopping and in the meantime I insist that you telephone these people first thing tomorrow. Do you promise me you'll do that?'

'I suppose so,' Dotty said hesitantly. 'But what shall I say to them? I'm not very good with strangers.'

'Rubbish! You will just be yourself and tell them that you

would be delighted to meet them to discuss your work, and I'm convinced they will love you just as much as I . . .' The woman's voice tailed away and Dotty had to stop herself from reaching out and hugging her. She was about to tell me that she loved me, she thought wonderingly, and the knowledge gave her joy. No one had ever told her that they loved her before in the whole of her life, and the thought that Miss Timms might love her boosted her confidence.

'All right then, I'll do it,' she promised as the kettle began to sing on the gas-ring. 'And then we'll just play it by ear.' She hurried away then to spoon some tea leaves into the teapot but her hand was shaking so much with excitement that she spilled half of it all over the table. And tea is on ration too, she thought as she giggled nervously. This was turning out to be quite an evening.

Much later, when Miss Timms had left, Dotty wrapped up warmly and walked to the nearest phone box to ring Miranda.

'Oh hello, dear – was it Annabelle you were after?' Miranda asked pleasantly.

'No, it was you I wanted to talk to, as it happens.' Dotty said, then quickly went on to tell the woman what had happened.

When she'd finished there was silence for a moment before Miranda asked tentatively, 'Are you *very* annoyed with me, Dotty? I know I shouldn't have sent the story away without your permission, but you have such a talent for writing and I thought you should be recognised. I'm not at all surprised that the magazine wants to publish you.'

'No, I'm not annoyed. More shocked, I think,' Dotty admitted. 'I'm not too sure about the trip to London though. I've never ventured that far away on my own before.'

'Oh, you'll be absolutely fine,' Miranda said confidently.

'But I could always come with you if you liked? I'm certainly not going to let you miss this opportunity. Look, why don't you come here for tea after work tomorrow with Annabelle and we'll talk about it then. But meantime make sure you ring them first thing in the morning.'

Dotty assured her that she would and floated back to the flat in a bubble of pure delight.

Both Annabelle and Lucy were nearly as excited as Dotty was the next morning when they met up during their morning break at work.

'Just think, I could be sitting next to a budding bestselling author,' Lucy twinkled. 'Have you rung them yet?'

'I have, as a matter of fact,' Dotty said. 'And I've made an appointment to go and see them next week. On Wednesday.' Her face fell as she looked down at her plain black skirt and her flat black shoes. 'Miss Timms thinks I ought to treat myself to a new outfit, and get a new hairdo,' she went on doubtfully. 'But to tell the truth I haven't got a clue about what's fashionable and what's not. I've always tended to go for comfortable, practical clothes and I can't ever remember having my hair cut by a hairdresser.'

'Hmm.' Annabelle eyed Dotty's long hair, which was tied into a ponytail at the nape of her neck with a slim black ribbon. 'You know, I think a bob and a side parting would suit you,' she said thoughtfully. 'And as for a new outfit – well, we won't have to go far to get you one, will we? We can have a look around the clothes department in our lunch-hour. There's bound to be something to suit you.'

'I don't want anything too fancy,' Dotty gushed nervously. She had never been one for making a statement or wanting to stand out from the crowd.

'Just leave it to us,' the girls told her. 'We won't put you far wrong, trust us.'

And so during their lunch break the three girls headed for the ladies' fashion department and began to rummage through the clothes rails as Dotty tagged along behind them.

'What about this?' she asked, holding up a calf-length grey skirt.

'Oh *please*!' Annabelle snorted in disgust. 'You may as well go in one of your work skirts as that. It's dull as ditchwater.'

'I'm afraid I have to agree with her,' Lucy said. 'We want something sort of . . . classy! Yes, that's it – classy and sophisticated to give you confidence.' And so the search continued until Annabelle gave a sudden exclamation of delight and pounced on a suit.

'Now this would be perfect,' she declared. A lovely shade of blue, it had a fitted jacket with a peplum waist and the skirt was calf-length and flared.

Dotty eyed it doubtfully. It looked very expensive and it was nothing at all like the clothes she normally favoured.

'Just try it on,' the two girls urged as they saw her uncertainty and so Dotty reluctantly took it off them and headed for the fitting rooms.

When she reappeared minutes later wearing the suit, both girls gasped. The assistant who had been helping during the search nodded approvingly. The jacket made Dotty's waist look tiny and the skirt was very flattering.

'How does it feel on?' Annabelle asked. The suit was made of a very soft woollen material, and Dotty told her that it felt like silk against her skin.

'It makes your eyes look really blue,' Lucy commented.

'And it shows off your figure. I never even realised you had one under all those baggy clothes you wear,' Annabelle teased.

'How much is it?' Dotty asked, ever practical.

'It isn't cheap,' the assistant said, glancing at the ticket, 'but it is beautiful quality and seeing as you work here I'm sure I could get you a staff discount. Let me go and have a word with the head of department.'

She hurried back seconds later to tell her, 'Miss Marsh says you can have it for one pound seven and sixpence.'

Dotty gasped. It seemed like a fortune but as the assistant quickly pointed out, 'Once the clothes rationing really comes into force you won't be able to buy anything nearly as nice as that.'

'And it will never go out of fashion,' Lucy added. 'It's a timeless style and just perfect for what you want it for. You could wear the skirt with a blouse and make more than one outfit out of it.'

'You're having it,' Annabelle told her firmly when she saw Dotty dithering. 'And now we need to get you a new coat to go over it. There's no way I'm letting you go to London in that drab old thing you wear to work. And then of course we'll need some new shoes and a new handbag and—'

'Stop right there,' Dotty said, holding up her hand to halt Annabelle in mid-flow. 'I might afford a new pair of shoes to go with it, but I certainly can't afford a coat and a handbag too.'

'All right then.' Knowing when she was beaten, Annabelle shrugged. 'I dare say I have a coat and a bag you could borrow,' she said generously. 'You're a bit thinner than me but with the suit underneath I'm sure I'll have a coat that will fit you. We are going to get your hair styled though. I'll make an appointment at my hairdresser's for Thursday afternoon when we're off work. And I'll come with you to make sure you have something fashionable,' she added with a twinkle in her eye. 'It's high time you got rid of that ponytail, it makes you look about fourteen. But come on now, if we don't get a move on we'll be late back to work and there'll be blood on the moon. Go and pay for that suit and then we might just have time to get you some shoes on the way back upstairs.'

Twenty minutes later, Dotty hurriedly shoved the suit along with a very smart pair of black wedge shoes into her locker before rushing off to her department. She could never remember spending a quarter as much on one single outfit as she had today, but as she thought of how she had looked and felt in the suit she was very glad that she had.

That weekend, Lucy and Dotty went to Annabelle's for tea and Miranda gasped when she caught sight of Dotty. Annabelle had indeed accompanied her to the hairdresser's and now she sported a very becoming shoulder-length bob that was parted at the side, with a fringe that made her look very grown up.

'Why, you look completely different with your hair like that,' Miranda said approvingly, then, 'Did you bring your suit with you? Annabelle told me how nice it was.'

Dotty waved a bag at her. 'Yes, I did. Annabelle is going to let me borrow one of her coats. She says I'm not allowed to go in this one.'

'Well, I certainly agree with her on that point but I don't think you'll need to borrow one. She told me what colour your suit was and I think I may have the very one. I never wear it any more so if you like it you're more than welcome to keep it.' Miranda disappeared to return minutes later with a very smart swing coat in navy blue folded across her arm. 'Here, try this on,' she encouraged and Dotty slipped it on.

'It's just perfect,' Miranda told her. 'And I have to say it looks so much better on you than it ever did on me. Take it and wear it in good health.'

'But I *couldn't,*' Dotty spluttered. 'It must have cost a fortune and I really can't take it.'

'Of course you can,' Miranda said. 'What good is it to me, hanging in the wardrobe and never seeing the light of day? You'll be doing me a favour taking it out of the way and I thought you might like this handbag too.'

She then produced a lovely black leather handbag that matched the shoes Dotty had bought perfectly. 'I've got far too many,' she assured the girl with a guilty grin. 'I'm afraid handbags have always been my weakness. Richard was always scolding me about it. Take it – I promise you I won't even miss it. And now Annabelle tells me she's going to show you how to apply a little make-up. You don't need much with that lovely complexion, but you'll be surprised to see what a difference a little mascara and lipstick can make. We'll have a full dress rehearsal then before we have tea, shall we?'

Half an hour later they all stared at Dotty admiringly as she emerged in her new outfit. She was beaming like a Cheshire cat and hardly recognised herself in the mirror.

'I don't know how to thank you all,' she said, but they brushed her thanks aside.

'You don't need to,' Miranda told her kindly. 'Just go to London and do us proud. One day when you're a bestselling author, I want to be able to say, "I knew her when . . ."'

'Hmm, I doubt there's much chance of that ever happening,' Dotty answered. 'And now I have to try and persuade the head of my department to let me have the day off on Wednesday, and that will be no easy task with us being short-staffed. I don't think she's going to be too impressed at all.'

Annabelle tossed her head. 'Well, you just stand your ground and tell her you're going whether she likes it or not,' she advised. 'You might never be offered a chance like this again. Who knows what will come of it for the future?' And then they all went off to the kitchen to enjoy the cauliflower cheese and fish cakes that Miranda had cooked for them.

By Tuesday evening Dotty was a bag of nerves and not at all sure that she could go through with the trip, although she dreaded to think what her friends would say if she backed out now. She had gone to the station and bought a day-return ticket to London, Euston. It was now safely tucked away in the lovely bag that Miranda had given to her, and her outfit was hanging on the wardrobe door.

Please, please don't let it snow now, she prayed as she lay in bed, far too nervous to sleep. The weather had worsened over the last couple of days and snow had been forecast. Now she could only hope that it would hold off until she got to London.

Miss Timms had been to see her earlier in the evening to wish her luck and Dotty was concerned about her. The woman had looked tired and pale, and when Dotty had enquired if she was all right she had told her, 'Oh, I'm quite all right, my dear. Just a little tired, that's all. Mother is very unwell so I've had to give up my job at the bank to care for her as she's bed-bound now.' She had sighed regretfully then and confided, 'I'm afraid Mother isn't an easy woman to live with, especially now that she can't get about. She raps on the ceiling for me every ten seconds with her walking stick and I seem to be constantly running up and down the stairs. At least, that's how it feels. But that's enough about me. I shan't be able to stay long but I couldn't let you go off without wishing you luck. Do be careful, my dear. You hear such terrible tales about things that happen to young women travelling alone. I wish I was coming with you.'

'Annabelle's mother offered to come with me, but I feel that this is something I should do on my own and I shall be fine,' Dotty assured her with a confidence she was far from feeling. She had planned everything down to the smallest detail. The only thing she couldn't control was the weather and that was in God's hands now.

Chapter Thirteen

'I wonder if Dotty got off all right?' Lucy said as she and Annabelle hung their coats up in the staff cloakroom the next morning.

Annabelle shrugged. She wasn't in the best of moods today and had found it hard to get out of bed. Most times now she accepted that she needed to work, but at other times, like today, she still felt that the job was far beneath her and resented the fact that she had to turn in.

'I have no doubt she'll get there, but I'm not so sure she'll get back if the snow doesn't hold off,' she commented as she straightened the seam in her stockings. They were getting harder and harder to acquire now, which was worrying for Annabelle; there was no way she would ever wear the thick lisle ones that most of the other shop girls favoured. Things were very fraught at home too. She and her mother had received a letter from her father the day before telling them that he was in

Dunkirk, and Miranda had hardly stopped crying since.

'What shall we do if anything happens to him?' her mother had sobbed and Annabelle had felt useless, with no idea how to comfort her. It seemed a million years ago now since she had lived a life of leisure, but if what the newspapers were reporting was true, there was worse to come – much worse. Hitler's army was creeping closer and there was nothing that anyone could do about it.

'Come along, girls, to your departments now. It wouldn't do to keep the customers waiting, now would it?' Mrs Broadstairs had appeared in the doorway and when she clapped her hands the girls scattered like flies.

Annabelle followed at a more leisurely pace, grinning at Mrs Broadstairs cheekily as she passed her. The woman tutted. She was too full of herself by half, that one, but then she was forced to admit that she was a good worker – when she was in the mood, that was!

Meanwhile Dotty was staring from the window of the train as the fields zipped by. Her stomach was in knots and she was terrified at the thought of the meeting ahead. She had spent a whole hour getting ready that morning and done her make-up just as Annabelle had shown her, so at least she knew she looked her best, which was something. But she was under no illusions. Even now she was painfully aware that she wasn't a pretty girl, not like Annabelle, who could turn heads wherever she went.

She had remarked on this to Miss Timms and the woman had patted her hand gently. 'Beauty is in the eye of the beholder, my dear,' she had told her. 'And I for one think you *are* pretty. You really shouldn't put yourself down so much.'

Dotty smiled as she thought of the kind, comforting words

and an elderly lady sitting opposite her smiled back. 'Off to London for a sight-seeing trip, are you, dearie?'

Dotty started. Her thoughts had been miles away.

'No – actually I'm going to meet the editor of a magazine,' she said self-consciously. 'They're thinking of publishing some of my short stories.'

'Well I'll be!' The woman looked impressed. 'I've never sat next to anyone famous before. Which magazine is it?'

'It's *Woman's Heart*, but I haven't had anything published yet,' Dotty told her hastily. 'And I'm certainly not famous. I work in Owen Owen in Coventry.'

'Even so, it sounds like you might be,' the woman responded. 'I hope everything goes well for you. What's your name? I often buy that magazine and I'll look out for you.'

'It's Dorothy Kent but everyone calls me Dotty.' Unused to being the centre of attention, Dotty was squirming with embarrassment.

'I'm off to see me daughter. She lives in London,' the woman told her now. 'It's a right worry, I don't mind tellin' you. Word has it that the Jerries will bomb London first when they start the raids, but she won't move back to the Midlands. Her bloke is away in the RAF and the kids have all been evacuated, but the stubborn little bugger still won't budge.'

Dotty felt sorry for her. 'I'm sure that she'll be fine,' she said sympathetically, and they then chatted about the rations and other everyday things as the train steamed towards its destination.

At least having someone to talk to made the time go quicker. But when they drew into Euston, the nerves came back as the two women stepped down from the train onto the platform.

'Goodbye, dearie, and good luck,' the elderly lady trilled as she righted her old-fashioned hat and turned in the opposite direction. 'And don't go talkin' to no strangers, mind. London can be a dangerous place fer a young 'un on her own.' And then she was swallowed up by the passengers surging from the train and Dotty had never felt so alone or vulnerable in her whole life.

The station was enormous and she was sure she had never seen so many people all in the same place at the same time before. There were lots of entrances and exits too. Which one should she take? Eventually she stopped a porter who was trundling a huge trolley loaded with luggage towards the nearest exit.

'Excuse me, could you direct me to Russell Square, please?' she asked shakily and he instantly slowed down.

'Yes, love, it ain't but a stone's throw from 'ere,' he told her cheerily. 'Just go through that exit there then turn left an' then turn . . .'

Dotty listened carefully, trying hard to remember all he had said, then she headed for the exit and quickly began to follow his directions. The streets were teeming with people and her heart began to race again. She felt very small and insignificant, and after all the tales she had heard of pickpockets and thieves she clutched her bag tightly to her as if it contained the crown jewels.

Soon she rounded a corner and found herself in Russell Square. She breathed a sigh of relief; now all she had to do was find the right number.

Eventually, she stopped at the bottom of some steps leading up to double doors with the words *Woman's Heart* emblazoned across them. Through the windows on either side of the doors she could see a number of women busily typing.

Taking a deep breath, she straightened her shoulders and still clutching the bag containing the stories she had brought for Mr Brabinger to consider, she climbed the steps and rang the bell.

The door was opened by a woman who looked enquiringly at her but when Dotty told her that she had an appointment to see Mr Brabinger, the woman smiled and held the door wide.

'You must be Miss Kent,' she said. 'I'm Laura Parsons, the senior editor who looked at your story with Mr Brabinger. I'm so pleased to meet you, do come in.'

The woman was tall, very attractive and very sophisticated and once again, Lucy felt very small. She followed her along a corridor where pictures from the magazine were displayed on the walls until she stopped at a door and tapped on it before opening it.

'Robert, Miss Kent is here,' she told the man sitting behind the desk, then turning to Dotty again she said, 'I'll just go and organise a cup of tea for us all. I'm sure you'll be ready for one after your journey.'

Dotty stepped into the room feeling like a lamb going to slaughter as the man rose and held his hand out. She noticed instantly that one of his arms was much shorter than the other and the hand on the end of it was shrivelled. But then her eyes travelled to his and she saw that they were blue and kindly.

'Hello, Miss Kent, or may I call you Dorothy?' he asked as they shook hands. 'Laura and I have so been looking forward to meeting you. We were both very impressed with your story. Do sit down. I'm Robert, by the way.'

He motioned towards a chair in front of his desk and Dotty perched uncomfortably on the edge of it, balancing her bag on her lap.

'You can call me Dotty, if you like,' she said in a voice that came out as no more than a squeak.

'Dotty it is then.' He shuffled some papers into a pile before asking, 'Did you bring us any more of your stories to look at?'

Dotty nodded as she fumbled in her bag, suddenly all fingers and thumbs. 'Y-yes, I did.' She placed them on the edge of the desk and he took one up and began to skim through it, giving her time to study him. He was quite a nice-looking man – not too tall, she had noticed when he had stood up to meet her, in fact only a few inches taller than herself. He had a thatch of thick dark brown hair that had a tendency to curl, and a small moustache.

'This is very good too,' he said presently as he laid the pages back on the desk. 'But if we are to make your stories a regular item in our magazine, I'm afraid there are a few things I will have to ask you to do. Can you type?'

'Yes, I had lessons at school,' Dotty answered.

'Then it might pay you to invest in a typewriter,' he advised. 'It's so much easier to read typed manuscripts rather than handwritten ones. Not that there is anything wrong with your handwriting, of course,' he rushed on with a twinkle in his eye. 'Do you think you could do that?'

'Oh yes,' Dotty said eagerly. She had really enjoyed her typing lessons but up until now hadn't felt the need to buy a typewriter of her own. And it needn't be too expensive if she bought a good quality second-hand one. There were any number of them appearing in the second-hand shops and pawnshops back home as the rationing made everyone tighten their belts.

'Good.'

Laura Parsons appeared at that moment, balancing a tray containing cups of tea, and Robert told her, 'I've just said to

Dotty here – that's what we are to call her – that a typewriter might be a good investment. Luckily she can already type.'

'Excellent – and you must call me Laura,' she told Dotty as she carefully slid the tray onto the desk. 'I don't mind telling you that we're quite excited about your stories. Have you always enjoyed writing? And have you had any of your work published before?'

'No, I haven't,' Dotty answered truthfully. 'And yes, I've always loved writing. I was brought up in an orphanage, so writing gave me something to do.' She saw a flicker of sadness flash in Robert's eyes but assured him, 'We were very well treated.'

'That's good then.' He studied her more closely, making her blush and lower her eyes. She was an attractive little thing in a funny sort of way, he thought. Not pretty in the conventional sense, but there was an air of vulnerability about her that he found appealing.

She, meanwhile, was trying to judge his age and put him at somewhere around thirty.

'Do you have no family at all?' Laura asked as she handed Dotty a cup of tea.

Dotty shook her head. 'Not that I know of, but I was very close to one of the workers at the orphanage. Still am, as it happens. She was like a substitute mother to me.'

Laura felt sad. She couldn't begin to imagine how lonely life must have been for this poor girl, having come from a large family herself. But then she pulled her thoughts back to business and began to explain to Dotty how they would want their stories set out in future and what length, what sort of stories they should be, et cetera.

Soon Dotty's head was spinning. There was so much to remember. She had always assumed you just wrote a story and that was it, but it was now apparent that there was a right way to do it.

Eventually Robert said to her, 'And now I suppose you'd like to know how much we shall be paying for these stories?' His eyes were twinkling with amusement while Dotty squirmed with embarrassment. 'We thought that four pounds per story would be a fair price. Does that sound all right to you, Dotty?'

She blinked in amazement. That was almost as much as she earned at Owen Owen for a whole *month*. She was going to be rich!

'For that we would want a short story delivered to us by a certain date each month so that we could edit it and get it ready for publication: do you think you could manage that?' he went on, giving her a moment to compose herself.

She nodded, hardly able to take it all in and feeling totally out of her depth.

'Of course, I'm sure there will be some here that we can use,' Laura added, patting the small pile on the desk. 'If you don't mind leaving them with us to look through, that is. Then you won't be under pressure to deliver any more for a few months at least, and it will give you time to obtain a typewriter.'

'Right. Well, now we have all that sorted out I suggest I take you out to lunch to celebrate, young lady,' Robert told her. 'Laura has a contract all ready for you to sign. We'll get you to do that on the way out, shall we? It will be a twelve-month contract to begin with, if that's all right with you?'

Dotty merely nodded again, too dumbstruck to answer. This sort of thing didn't happen to girls like her . . . did it? Perhaps it was all a dream and she would wake up in a minute?

But then she knew that it wasn't a dream when Robert

came around the desk and, taking her elbow, steered her towards the door as he asked, 'Have you ever been to London before?'

She could feel the warmth of his one good hand right the way through her coat and her suit. 'N-no, I haven't,' she stuttered.

'Then I think a little sightseeing tour might be in order before we go for lunch. Unless you have to catch the train home, that is?'

'Not until five o'clock.'

'Good.'

They followed Laura to a desk where she had a document all ready for Dotty to sign. 'Do read through it,' she urged in a very professional manner. 'Basically it just says that you will deliver twelve short stories to us for the next twelve months.'

Dotty did as she was told before signing her name with a wobbly hand. Then Laura said goodbye and before she knew it, Robert was leading her outside. Dotty was secretly relieved. Laura had been very nice to her, but she was so attractive and efficient that Dotty had found her slightly intimidating. Once on the pavement, Robert raised his good hand and a shiny black cab almost instantly pulled into the kerb.

'Won't they mind you being away from the office for so long?' Dotty asked as she scrambled into the cab in a most unladylike manner.

Robert leaned forward and told the driver where to go before sitting back in his seat and chuckling. 'I doubt it, seeing as I'm the boss. What I should say is – I own the magazine.'

'Really?' Dotty was shocked. He must be a very rich man indeed yet he had no airs and graces whatsoever.

Soon Robert was pointing out places of interest as they cruised by them. St Paul's Cathedral, the Bank of England, then back down to Trafalgar Square and on through Whitehall past Number 10, Downing Street to see Big Ben and the Houses of Parliament, followed by Buckingham Palace and many other places that Dotty had only ever seen in pictures. And then eventually the cab drew up outside an expensive-looking restaurant and after paying the driver Robert helped Dotty out onto the pavement.

Dotty's cheeks were glowing by then and she couldn't remember ever enjoying herself so much. Robert took her into the restaurant where a smart waiter in a black suit and a bow-tie took their coats and escorted them to a table by the window.

'Please order whatever takes your fancy,' Robert told her as the waiter handed her a menu, and once again Dotty felt lost. She had been brought up on very plain food and everything on the menu looked so fancy and expensive. She couldn't even understand what half of it was.

'Would you like me to order for you?' Robert asked after a time as he saw her discomfort.

'Yes, please,' she whispered, feeling like a country yokel.

'Is there anything that you particularly don't like?'

She shook her head and seconds later, he summoned the waiter and gave him their order then told him, 'Oh, and we'll have a bottle of your finest champagne too, if you please.'

'Certainly, sir.'

Dotty's eyes stretched even wider. Champagne? She had only ever tried a glass of wine at the staff party and she had suffered for it the next day.

The meal was like nothing she had ever eaten before, and

as one delicious course followed another she began to relax a little as she found that Robert was remarkably good company and very easy to talk to.

'Do you live in London?' she dared to ask over their hors d'oeuvre, which were mushrooms cooked in garlic sauce. Dotty was certain she had never tasted anything so delicious before in her whole life.

'Yes, I have a flat in Knightsbridge,' he told her. 'It was my mother's but I inherited both the flat and the magazine when she passed away last year. It's a bit big for me really, but I suppose I'm too idle to look around for something a little smaller.'

'Do you live alone then?' Dotty asked in surprise before she could stop herself. She had imagined he would be married. He was far too nice not to be, and he had seemed so relaxed in Laura's company that perhaps there was something between them?

'Yes, I do,' and then he grinned as if he could read her thoughts. 'There aren't many women who would want to take me on full-time with this.' He jiggled his withered arm. 'And besides, to be honest I've always been too busy to think of getting married.' He peered at her. 'But what about you? Do you have a boyfriend?'

'Oh no,' Dotty told him quickly and when she fell silent and lowered her eyes, he looked at her curiously. She was very timid and obviously lacking in confidence, which was a shame as he found her quite charming. Sort of unspoiled, which he considered was a rare thing these days.

The main course came then and once again Dotty loved it. Beef cooked in red wine sauce with a variety of vegetables and crispy roast potatoes. The waiter popped the cork on the champagne and Dotty giggled as she sipped at it and the bubbles went up her nose.

Dessert was a pear flan with whipped cream and then they ended the meal with coffee. By then Dotty had drunk two glasses of champagne and her eyes were sparkling.

'Thank you so much for a lovely day and a lovely meal,' she sighed. She was so full that she was sure she wouldn't be able to eat another thing for at least a month. The meal she had just had was certainly a far cry from the penny bowls of soup she usually had in the works canteen.

'It was my pleasure,' he assured her as he beckoned to the waiter for the bill. 'And the next time you come to see us, we shall do it again.'

'Next time?' Dotty raised her eyebrows questioningly.

'Oh yes, Laura and I will want to see you every three or four months at least, so that we can discuss what sort of stories we'd like you to write.'

Dotty felt a tingle of excitement, although she noticed that he had mentioned Laura again. They left the restaurant and once outside he glanced at his watch before saying, 'You have forty minutes before your train leaves. We're only about ten minutes away from Euston: would you like to walk there or would you rather take a taxi?'

'I think I'd rather walk,' she answered. The champagne had made her feel quite tiddly and she thought the fresh air might do her good. 'But if you point me in the right direction I'm sure I shall find the station by myself,' she added. 'I wouldn't want to put you out.'

'It won't be putting me out. In fact, I'd rather like a bit of a stroll myself to walk some of that lunch off. Come on – put your arm through mine. I don't want you falling on these slippery pavements.'

She shyly slipped her arm through his, and as they were walking towards the station it started to snow.

'I've been expecting this for days,' he remarked. 'I'm just

glad it didn't come in time to stop you getting here. I've really enjoyed today.'

'So have I,' she said, and she meant it.

Once inside the station he guided her to the right platform. 'The train should be in any time now,' he told her. 'Would you like me to wait with you?'

'Not at all, I shall be fine. You've wasted quite enough of your time on me today as it is.'

'I don't consider I've wasted a single second,' he told her sincerely. 'And I hope this will be the start of a long working relationship. Goodbye, Dotty, I'll be in touch soon.'

He turned and walked away then and she stood there and watched until he was swallowed up by the crowd.

It had been a truly unforgettable day.

Chapter Fourteen

As February 1940 drew to a close the worst storms of the century swept across the country and many areas ground to a halt as people found themselves snowed in and cut off from the world. The buses and trams in Coventry were having difficulty getting about, which gave Annabelle an excuse not to turn in to work, much to her mother's annoyance.

'Come on, Annabelle,' Miranda urged one morning after entering her daughter's bedroom and shaking her shoulder. 'You still have time to get to work if you get a move on.'

'I'm not going,' Annabelle ground out, snuggling further down under the blankets.

'But you'll get the sack at this rate. You've missed two days already this week.'

'So what? I hate the damn job,' Annabelle snapped. 'There are loads of staff can't get in. They'll understand. Hardly anyone is venturing out to shop anyway,' she finished lamely.

Miranda sighed as she straightened up. She knew better

than to argue with Annabelle when she had made her mind up about something. The girl had seemed depressed and distracted for a couple of weeks, now that she came to think about it – ever since the day the letter from Lucy's brother had arrived, as a matter of fact. Annabelle had told her nothing of what the letter had contained, apart from that Joel had been shipped out, and now she wondered if Annabelle had feelings for him? He certainly didn't sound like the sort of young man her daughter usually favoured, though. She had never made a secret of the fact that she wanted a rich husband who could keep her in the manner she had become accustomed to, and Miranda really couldn't see Joel being rich.

Sighing, she went downstairs to the kitchen where she filled the kettle and put it on to boil as she stared through the window at a mountain of snow.

Upstairs, Annabelle took Joel's letter from beneath her pillow and read it through again even though she now knew it off by heart.

Dear Belle, he had written, and the abbreviation of her name made her smile. Hardly anyone had ever shortened her name before and she quite liked it when he did it. *I thought I would just drop you a line as promised. I hope you are keeping well and not suffering too much with the bad weather. I am now in . . .* The word had been censored and was unreadable but Annabelle had a funny feeling that he might be in France. The letter continued:

I hope you had a good Christmas. Mine was pretty grotty as you can imagine, being stuck here away from the family, but then I shouldn't grumble as the rest of the chaps are all in the same boat. I'd like to think that we might get leave again soon but it doesn't look likely for the foreseeable future.

Anyway, I've never been much of a one for letter-writing,

and there's not much more to tell, but I just didn't want you to think I had forgotten you. I hope you are keeping your eye on Lucy and Mary for me.

Kind regards,

Joel

Annabelle folded the letter and slid it back beneath her pillow. It was quite a formal letter really; he had even signed it *kind regards,* but she was still pleased to think he had remembered her. Sighing, she burrowed back beneath the blankets.

As Miranda read the newspaper in the kitchen she shivered, and not only from the chill air. It was bad news, and now with the bad weather to contend with as well, her spirits were at an all-time low. Annabelle's tantrums didn't help, not that she wasn't well used to them. She had been forced to admit that she and Richard had spoiled Annabelle shamelessly, and now that he was away at war it was she who was paying the price. She rose and spooned some tea leaves sparingly into the teapot, aware that the meagre ration she had left was supposed to last them for the rest of the week. Perhaps if she took a cup up to Annabelle it might coax her daughter out of bed and put her in a better mood? She could but try.

Lucy and Dotty meantime had just met up outside Owen Owen and were heading for the staff cloakroom.

'No sign of Annabelle again then?' Lucy commented as she glanced around. The place was nowhere near as busy as it usually was in the morning. Almost half of the staff hadn't managed to make it in.

'Doesn't look like it,' Dotty replied. 'I bet there were no buses running again.'

'Hmm, though I don't think Annabelle needs much of an excuse to miss work,' Lucy joked. 'We're lucky compared to most, according to the paper. Some villages are completely cut off and they're having to drop food for the villagers and the livestock by plane.'

'It must be awful for them,' Dotty said sympathetically. 'But anyway, are you still prepared to come and have a look for a typewriter with me during our lunch break? They should have cleared the main roads by then and I've seen a nice one in the window of a pawnshop a couple of streets away. It's an Olivetti.'

'Of course I'll come with you,' Lucy told her. 'I've got to pick up a few more things for Mary as well to take with her next week.' Her face fell. It was only a matter of days now before Mary was evacuated, and she could think of nothing else. It was like a great black cloud hanging over her as she fretted about how the child would cope. 'I need to pick her up one of those little cardboard suitcases from Woolworths,' she went on glumly. 'The ones I have would be far too big and heavy for her.'

Dotty patted her hand. She knew that there was nothing she could say that would make Lucy feel any better, and she felt sorry for her.

'We'll do that then. But now we'd better get to work. With so many staff off they'll probably have us running from one department to another today.'

By morning break-time both the girls were fed up.

'Talk about going from one extreme to another,' Dotty said as she paid for a cup of tea and headed towards their table. 'There we were at Christmas and New Year run off our feet, and now the store is almost empty. It's like a ghost town.'

'That's hardly surprising, is it?' Lucy answered. 'I mean, who is going to venture out in this weather unless they absolutely have to?'

'I know what you mean, but I haven't been idle although there aren't many customers,' Dotty said. 'Mrs Broadstairs has had me tidying all morning. I think I'd sooner be serving.'

'Me too,' Lucy said despondently. 'But at least we can get out for a while at lunchtime.'

Once in the pawnbrokers, Dotty stroked the keys of the Olivetti typewriter with a wide smile on her face.

'It's almost brand new,' the shopkeeper said persuasively. 'And an absolute bargain at the price I'm asking for it.'

'I'll take it,' she told him, and she and Lucy left the shop with the typewriter packed into a sturdy cardboard box.

'We've still got time to get to Woolworth's,' Dotty said. 'But we'll have to take it in turns to carry this, if you don't mind. It's heavier than it looks.'

Once Lucy had purchased the little cardboard suitcase from Woolworths they hurried back to Owen Owen. It had started to snow heavily again and Dotty cursed breathlessly, 'Damn weather. When is it going to stop?'

Once back in the staff cloakroom they put their purchases away in their lockers then hurried up to the staff dining room with just enough time left to snatch a cup of tea before they were due back at work.

'Why don't you come round tonight after work?' Lucy suggested during their afternoon break. She was feeling very down in the dumps.

Dotty shook her head. 'I won't tonight, if you don't mind. I've got my typewriter to get home and if this snow keeps coming I might not be able to get back from your house later on.'

'You could always stay the night and we could travel to work together in the morning then,' Lucy suggested, but still Dotty refused. She wanted to get home and practise on her typewriter.

That evening the buses were running very late, so it was gone seven o'clock by the time Lucy arrived to pick Mary up from Mrs P. It felt strange to think that this would be the last week she would need to do it.

'Ah, yer look all in,' Mrs P said as she stepped through the door. 'Come an' have a warm by the fire an' a nice hot cuppa, eh?'

Mary gratefully did as she was told, and noticing the package she was carrying Mrs P remarked, 'You got her suitcase then?'

'Mm, I did, but there were only two left.' Lucy glanced towards Mary who was sitting staring into the flames in the fire and her heart ached as she wondered where she might be this time next week. They were going to make her a special tea on Saturday for her birthday and she had invited Dotty and Annabelle, but she doubted Mary would understand that it was her birthday.

'I made her cake today,' Mrs P told Lucy as she passed her a mug of tea. 'An' though I shouldn't say it I'm quite pleased wi' it, though I'd have liked to have had a few more currants to go in it an' I had to use that horrible dried-egg stuff.' She grimaced. The rationing was hitting hard now and everyone was having to do without certain foods, eggs being one of them.

'Still, I've no doubt it will do once I've put a bit o' me special pink icin' on it,' she went on more cheerfully with an indulgent glance at Mary. The woman was going to miss the child almost as much as Lucy would, but she was trying not to think about it at present.

'I'm going to pack her case tonight,' Lucy said. 'Just to make sure that I've got everything.' Every spare penny had been spent on the things that Mary would need to take with her, because Lucy wanted her to go with everything brand new. Mrs P secretly thought it was a complete waste of money. The way she saw it, the clothes that Mary already had were perfectly respectable, but then, knowing how upset Lucy was about her little sister going away, she had refrained from voicing her opinion. Best let the poor lass deal with it in her own way.

'That might be a good idea,' she said tactfully. 'Then if you've forgotten anything you'll have time enough to get it.'

Later that night, when Mary was tucked up in bed, Lucy began the heartbreaking job of packing her small case, ticking off each thing as she carefully folded it.

2 vests
Spare pair of knickers
Nightdress
Petticoat
2 pairs stockings
6 handkerchiefs
Blouse
Cardigan
Skirt
Boots
Shoes
Wellington boots

And finally a wash-bag containing a brush, comb, toothbrush, soap, flannel, ribbons, and anything else that Lucy felt the little girl might need, including her teddy bear.

By the time she was done, tears were rolling down her cheeks unchecked. All that was left to do now was count down the days until it was time for Mary to leave.

Thankfully, for now at least she had a reprieve, as she got home from work the next evening to find Mrs P grinning like a cat that had got the cream.

'You've had a visit from a woman from the Red Cross today,' she told Lucy with glee. 'I went to the door an' explained you were at work an' I had young Mary, so she asked me to pass on a message. Seems half the trains ain't runnin' what wi' the weather bein' so bad, so the long an' the short of it is, Mary won't be goin' next week. The lady told me she'd let us know when the next lot of evacuees are goin'.'

'Really?' Lucy's face lit up and suddenly she felt as if a great weight had been lifted from her shoulders – for now, at least.

Everyone said that Mrs P had done Mary proud on Saturday when they came to celebrate the child's fifth birthday. The cake was delicious and Mrs P had even found some candles to put on it although Lucy had to blow them out as they all sang 'Happy Birthday' to Mary. She was off with the fairies in a world of her own as usual, and Annabelle wondered why they had bothered. The poor little mite clearly didn't even know where she was, let alone what day it was.

Once the party was over, Mrs P insisted on keeping Mary so that the three girls could go to the pictures together. They set off for the Gaumont to see *Gulliver's Travels*.

On the way back to the bus station, Annabelle almost

spoiled the night when she asked, 'Any news about when Mary might be evacuated yet?'

Dotty scowled a warning at her. Annabelle could be very thoughtless. But Lucy answered civilly enough. 'No, not yet.'

By now, the snow had finally stopped; the big thaw had set in and everywhere was slushy and dirty. It was still bitterly cold too, but gradually the country was churning back into life as roads reopened and people could get back into work again.

After the film, which they'd all enjoyed, the three girls went their separate ways, feeling all the better after the break from routine.

Two weeks later, Lucy returned home from work one evening to find Mrs P close to tears. She guessed instantly what was wrong. 'You've had a visit from the Red Cross, haven't you?' she asked.

'Yes, luvvie – or should I say *you* did. It was the same woman that came to say Mary's going was delayed, an' guessin' that you'd be at work she came to leave the message with me. They want you to have her up at the school playground for ten o'clock next Monday mornin'. They'll take the little 'uns by coach to the station, and they'll journey on by train from there.'

Lucy had known it was coming, but the news still knocked her for six. She wondered again how the child would cope with being sent away, but of course she had no answer to that question and even if she had, there was nothing she could do about it.

'Did they say where she might be going?' she asked tearfully.

Mrs P shook her head. 'I don't think they know till they

get 'em to the station. Someone from the WVS travels with 'em from there an' then you'll get a postcard givin' you the address. I'm so sorry, love.'

Lucy shrugged. 'It's not your fault. We knew it was bound to happen, and if we do get raided, I dare say she'll be safer out of the city.'

Mrs P nodded sadly, too full of emotion to speak.

The following Sunday evening, Lucy kept Mary up until the child's eyelids were drooping with fatigue, aware that this would be the very last evening they would share together for possibly a very long time. She made the child her favourite jam sandwiches for supper and rocked her on her lap in front of the fire, then when they finally went to bed she wrapped the child in her arms and held her close as her heart ached. It was so hard to try and imagine the house without Mary in it, but she rightly guessed that many more women across the city would be suffering the exact same heartache. She had tried to be strong, but once Mary was asleep Lucy lay in bed savouring the feel of the warm little body in her arms and allowed the tears she had held back to slide down her cheeks as the hours ticked away.

On Monday morning, Lucy dressed the little girl cosily in the smart red coat and tied her woollen bonnet beneath her chin, then with a heavy heart she placed the brown label with Mary's name and address on it around her neck and lifted the child's suitcase. It was almost time to go, but first she had promised Mrs P that she would call round so that she could say her goodbyes.

The poor woman tried unsuccessfully not to cry as she kissed the child but it was useless, and soon both she and Lucy were sobbing, although Mary stood quite still showing no emotion whatsoever.

'I've made her a couple o' cakes to eat on the way,' Mrs P said, thrusting them at Lucy in a brown paper bag. 'Yer did remember to do her some sandwiches fer the journey, didn't yer?'

Lucy nodded as she turned for the door. There was no sense in prolonging the agony and Mrs P followed her out onto the pavement, her head covered in a headsquare, wrapped turban-like around her metal curlers.

'Goodbye, luvvie, an' may God go with yer,' she called as the sisters set off along the cold street.

Lucy clutched Mary with one hand and the case with the other; her feet felt as if they were made of lead and she wondered if she would be able to part with the little lass when the time came. She had both of their gas masks slung across her shoulder too, so it was hard going, but soon the school came into sight and Lucy saw a bus and a number of mothers with children already there. Lucy slowed her steps, hoping to delay the terrible moment when she would have to hand Mary into someone else's care.

A woman from the Red Cross was ticking names off a list on a clipboard and then ushering the children onto the bus, and everywhere seemed to be organised chaos. Older children were screaming as they clung to their mother's skirts whilst the younger ones appeared to view it all as a big adventure and clambered aboard quite happily to wave from the windows. A man was loading the children's cases into the hold in the side of the bus and all the mothers were clearly trying to control their tears in case they upset the children even more.

There was only about half a bus full, the majority of the children having been evacuated the previous September, and in no time at all the woman with the clipboard approached Lucy and asked, 'Child's name?'

Lucy had to lick her dry lips before a sound would come through them.

'Mary Ford,' she squeaked and the woman nodded as she crossed the name off.

'Give her case to the gentleman over there and then get her onto the bus, please?'

Lucy passed her case to the man then walked towards the steps of the bus where she stooped to wrap her arms tightly around Mary. There was a huge lump in her throat and she had to blink very fast to hold back her tears.

'Now, now,' the woman scolded. 'We don't want to set the children off, do we?' She took Mary's gas mask from Lucy and hung it about the child's neck, then before Lucy could say another word she helped Mary up the steps, where another Red Cross worker settled her into a seat. All the other children were waving and shouting but Mary sat down and stared straight ahead with no sign of emotion whatsoever.

Lucy stood as if she had been rooted to the spot, feeling so bereft that she was incapable of speech. Then the final two children were put aboard and the Red Cross woman clambered up behind them and closed the door firmly.

'Do you have any idea at all where the children might be going?' Lucy managed to ask the man who had loaded the luggage, and hearing the note of desperation in her voice he smiled at her kindly.

'Well, I can't be sure but I reckon I heard them mention Folkestone.'

'But that's only across the Channel from where all the fighting's going on,' she said faintly.

He patted her hand. 'So it is, but it isn't a target like the industrial cities, is it? Your little 'un will be just fine, I'm sure. And now if you'll excuse me I'd best get them off to the station. I'm the driver, see.'

She watched him climb into the driver's seat and seconds later the bus rumbled into life and began to pull away. Lucy ran alongside it waving frantically, but Mary didn't even glance in her direction and within minutes she was gone. Lucy stood there feeling utterly devastated. She had meant to tell Mary how very much she loved her and how much she would miss her, before she boarded the bus, even though she had told her the same thing at least a dozen times that morning, but everything had happened so fast that she hadn't had time to say anything. And now she could only pray that Mary knew.

The mothers began to trickle away then, most of them openly crying now, and Lucy trailed behind them. She had to get to work, which she supposed was no bad thing. There seemed little to go home for now that Joel and Mary were gone.

Chapter Fifteen

'Look, here it is!' Dotty excitedly held up a copy of *Woman's Heart* magazine. '*A Wartime Romance* by Dorothy Kent. It feels really strange to think that this is *my* story. And Robert has already chosen the one they want to publish next month.'

'You must feel very proud,' Annabelle said with a trace of envy in her voice. After all, it was quite an achievement to see your name in print and to know that your work was going to be read by hundreds if not thousands of people. 'And I'm sure the next one will wonderful too, if *Robert* has chosen it.'

Dotty blushed furiously. 'How many times do I have to tell you? He asked me to call him Robert because it's friendlier than a surname, that's all.'

'And of course you don't fancy him a bit, do you? And you're not looking forward to going to London again at all,' Annabelle teased.

Lucy just smiled but she didn't comment. Since Mary had gone she had been very withdrawn and quiet, and the other two girls were making allowances for her. She had practically brought Mary up so they supposed she was bound to be missing her badly.

'Of course I'm looking forward to going to London again,' Dotty said. 'But it's only business. I've told you, I think Robert already has a ladyfriend – Laura, who he works with.'

Annabelle rolled her eyes but wisely held her tongue. She was sure that Dotty must have mentioned Robert Brabinger at least a dozen times a day since their meeting, and she had a sneaking suspicion that Dotty was more than a little smitten with him, even if she hadn't admitted it yet. But time would tell. Meantime, she and Dotty were doing all they could to cheer Lucy up, sadly without much success up to now. But they had persuaded her to go to a dance with them at the Locarno in the city centre that night, and Annabelle was looking forward to it. She was fed up of being stuck at home in Leaf Lane all the time.

They were now into May and the war bulletins were not good. On the first of the month the papers had reported that a German mine-carrying bomber plane had crashed in Clacton injuring 156 people and killing four Germans and two civilians. But then the following week even worse news had reached them. The Allies who had landed in Norway only two weeks before, had departed; the German army had been too powerful for them. The Allied Forces were now in France and Belgium, but what if they were unable to hold the Germans off again? It made everyone realise that there was only the Channel between Great Britain and the enemy, and the threat of an invasion became a very real possibility.

'The Jerries have invaded the Low Countries,' Mrs P told

Lucy one evening after work. She was all in a tizzy as she waved the newspaper under the startled girl's nose. Lucy still tended to go round to Mrs P's for a cup of tea each evening. It delayed going home to an empty house for a time at least. 'They're bombing Holland and Belgium and all the harbours. It says here that almost all our ships have been sunk and now they're sending in tanks and parachutists. Where in God's name is it going to end, eh?'

Lucy felt physically sick at the news, and she knew that both she and Mrs P were thinking the same thing. Mrs P's Freddy and her own Joel could be out there somewhere.

Only the week before, a young man's mother in the next street had received a telegram saying that he was missing, and now the sight of the telegram boy cycling down the road was one to be feared. Who knew whose door he might stop at with a telegram for some poor woman telling her that her beloved husband, son or brother was missing or worse still, dead?

'Churchill reckons they'll target France next,' Mrs P went on as she mopped at her streaming eyes with a snow-white handkerchief, and now Lucy's blood really did turn to ice. Joel had told her in a roundabout way that he was in France in the last letter she had received from him. She glanced towards the darkened window, her mind full of terrible images as the barrage balloons floated like pale silver ghosts in the sky above the city.

Then only yesterday they had listened to yet another radio announcement informing them that sixty Luftwaffe He-111 bombers had besieged Rotterdam, devastating the city centre. None of them could help but wonder what would have happened if they had bombed Coventry. No one was using the phrase 'Phoney War' any more. Suddenly it was all too real.

Yet for the three friends, life went on much as it had before. They went to work at Owen Owen each day and every night they returned home, hoping to hear word from their loved ones. Lucy had not heard from Joel for weeks and nor had Annabelle or her mother heard from Richard, and sometimes they feared the worst, even though they all knew that the post was taking much longer to get through now.

'You'll probably get a whole heap of letters turn up all at once,' Dotty would tell them when she saw how worried her friends were, and they could only hope that she was right. It didn't stop them fretting, however.

After work today, they all headed for Annabelle's house where they had arranged to get ready for the dance. Dotty had taken her best outfit to work and put it away in her locker, but Annabelle had promised to find something of hers that Lucy could borrow. Much like Dotty, Lucy had never had the inclination or the funds to follow fashion so she had agreed to Annabelle's offer, although her heart wasn't really in it. She would much rather have gone home and read a book or listened to Joel's crackly old wireless, but not wanting to be seen as a spoilsport, she had agreed to go along.

Miranda was waiting for them when they arrived at the charming old house in Cheylesmore. The kettle was whistling and a meal of corned beef hash was ready.

'Sorry it's corned beef again,' she apologised to Annabelle as she loaded a pile of mashed potatoes onto their plates, 'but the butcher had run out of meat when I got there and I went quite early this morning too.'

Annabelle wrinkled her nose but Lucy piped up, 'It looks delicious. Thank you.' She scowled at Annabelle, who clearly didn't realise how lucky she was to have a mother to come home to and a hot meal on the table.

Once they had all eaten, Miranda shooed them away upstairs although Lucy and Dotty had volunteered to wash up.

'No, you get away and doll yourselves up,' she told them with a smile. 'You're only young once. Oh, but before you do, I wondered if any of you would fancy doing a first aid course? The Red Cross are running it one night a week from next Thursday along in the church hall, and who knows when first aid may come in handy, the way things are?'

Dotty and Lucy both said they were interested, but Annabelle didn't seem at all taken with the idea.

'First aid!' she exclaimed. 'But won't that be rather boring?'

'It isn't meant to be exciting,' her mother pointed out. 'And what would you rather do? Stay in and sulk?'

'Well, I shall definitely go,' Lucy said and Dotty nodded in agreement.

'And so shall I. It will be nice to feel we're learning something worthwhile.'

'In that case I suppose I ought to come along too,' Annabelle said with bad grace and she then ushered her friends up the stairs ahead of her. She still had an outfit to sort out for Lucy but she wouldn't be letting her wear any of her nylon stockings. They were getting like gold dust now.

An hour later, Lucy regarded herself uncertainly in the mirror on Annabelle's dressing-table. She was wearing a cream cotton summer skirt and a lacy figure-hugging jumper in a lovely shade of cornflower blue. She had managed to squeeze her feet into a pair of Annabelle's high-heeled shoes too, although she had no idea how she was going to walk in them. To complete the picture, Annabelle had loosened her lovely auburn hair from the band she usually tied it back with and teased it into thick shimmering waves that fell about Lucy's slim shoulders. Annabelle had even persuaded her to wear a little make-up and now as Lucy stared at her cherry-red lips and her new look she scarcely recognised herself.

'I er . . . I'm not too sure I feel comfortable like this,' she mumbled, but Annabelle waved her concerns aside.

'Oh, don't be so silly. You're too used to walking about dressed like an old schoolmarm,' she chided. 'Wait until we get to the dance. The boys will be queuing up to dance with you.'

'I hope not,' Lucy retorted, horrified at the very idea. She had never had a boyfriend and had no wish to have one now.

'You *do* look lovely, Lucy,' Dotty said, quietly envious. Lucy's eyes and hair were stunning, and Dotty had never realised just how very attractive she was up until now. She made Dotty feel like a little grey fieldmouse.

'Yes, you do,' Annabelle retorted, slightly concerned that Lucy might steal the limelight. 'And now we'd better get going otherwise it will be over before we even get there.'

Dance halls tended to close a lot earlier than they had used to; when they opened at all, that was. This was to allow people to get home whilst public transport was still running. It seemed like ages since Annabelle had had a really good night out, and she was champing at the bit. She herself was wearing a silk dress in green and gold, one of her particular favourites that she knew she looked good in, and Dotty was wearing the outfit they had all now christened 'her London suit'.

'Wow!' Miranda exclaimed when they all went back downstairs to collect their coats. 'You all look absolutely beautiful. Have a lovely time, won't you? But don't forget to leave early enough to get the last buses home.'

Dotty giggled, thinking that Miranda had made them all sound like Cinderella.

Annabelle gave a martyred sigh as she yanked her coat on and added another layer of Romance, her latest bright red lipstick, in the hall mirror. 'Yes, Mother! I dare say it will be a lot more fun than this first aid class you've nagged us all into going to.'

Miranda bit back the hasty retort that sprang to her lips. She had no wish to spoil the girl's night out but at that moment she was heartily ashamed of her daughter. Admittedly, Annabelle had mellowed slightly over the last few months since being forced to take a job, but deep down the girl was still very self-centred and selfish.

Dotty and Lucy thanked Miranda again for their meal and for allowing them to get ready at her home, and after Miranda had kissed them all they set off.

Once they reached the city centre they queued to get in then made a beeline for the ladies cloakroom where they hung up their coats and touched up their make-up.

Annabelle patted her hair into place again before telling them, 'Come on, girls, I'm ready if you are. Let's go and get ourselves a drink.'

Out in the dance hall, they saw that the majority of those present were girls and Annabelle sighed. 'I thought it would be like this,' she said despondently. 'Nearly all the half-decent-looking fellows have gone to war. Still, we may as well have a drink and make the best of it.'

She crossed to the bar and ordered three drinks which Lucy and Dotty stared at uncertainly when she passed them over. It looked like water with a slice of lemon floating in it.

'What is it?' Dotty asked, mortally aware that she was showing her ignorance.

Annabelle sank down onto a chair at the nearest empty table and after lighting a cigarette she told her, 'It's a gin and tonic. Try it. After a couple of those, you might even start to enjoy yourself.'

Ignoring the sarcasm, Dotty dutifully did as she was told before wrinkling her nose.

'Ugh, I'm not sure that I like it,' she said. It certainly wasn't as pleasant as the champagne that Robert had bought her in London.

'It's an acquired taste,' Annabelle told her as her eyes scanned the dimly lit room for likely prey.

There were a lot of people already on the dance floor and Lucy asked innocently, 'What dance is that they're doing?'

Annabelle sighed inwardly. These two were going to take some educating, that was a fact. 'It's the jitterbug.'

Lucy giggled and winked at Dotty. 'Well, they all look like they've got a touch of St Vitus' Dance to me.'

Annabelle shook her head in exasperation. Some people were very hard to please.

They had been sitting there for a few moments when Annabelle suddenly dug Dotty urgently in the ribs.

'Don't look now,' she hissed, 'but there's a chap heading this way and he isn't half-bad. I think he's coming to ask me to dance. Watch and learn.' She straightened her skirt and gave him a simpering smile as he stopped at their table.

'Good evening, ladies,' he said politely, and then leaning towards Lucy he asked, 'May I have this dance, please?'

Annabelle's face fell a foot as Lucy gaped up at him, but then Dotty nudged her and she self-consciously got to her feet and followed him onto the dance floor, glancing over her shoulder as if imploring her friends to rescue her.

'Actually he wasn't that nice-looking when he got up

close, was he?' Annabelle said peevishly as she lit another cigarette.

All three of them were asked to dance on numerous occasions as the night progressed, but the first chap who had asked Lucy to dance commandeered her whenever he could.

Lucy began to look more and more flustered, particularly after he had taken her onto the dance floor for a slow waltz.

'That chap has got more hands than an octopus,' she complained towards the end of the night. 'I'm going to say no if he asks me to dance again.'

Annabelle grinned. 'Well, at least he's keen,' she commented.

Lucy crossed her arms and scowled, and sure enough, minutes later her admirer turned up yet again.

'Sorry, I was just about to go to the ladies powder room,' Lucy told him, snatching her bag and standing up.

'Then perhaps I could wait for you to come back,' he responded cheekily.

Ignoring his comment, Lucy put her nose in the air and began to sail past him, but he made the mistake of trying to take her elbow and she rounded on him furiously.

'Why don't you just leave me alone!' she said as he backed away. 'Go and find some other poor girl to maul. She might enjoy it, but I certainly don't!'

'All right, keep your hair on,' he said, looking acutely embarrassed, and turning on his heel he slammed away through the tables.

'Crikey, that was a bit of an overreaction, wasn't it?' Annabelle said in amazement, aware that people were staring at them. 'The poor chap was only trying to be friendly.'

'Perhaps I don't *want* to be friendly,' Lucy retaliated. 'What gives him the right to maul me about? All blokes are the same, that's the problem, and I don't want any of it. And now if you don't mind, I've had quite enough of this shop window. I'm off.' And with that she marched towards the ladies cloakroom leaving Annabelle and Dotty no choice but to pick up their bags and follow her. Lucy had always seemed such a placid girl that they could hardly believe the outburst they had just witnessed.

Lucy didn't even look at them as she handed in her ticket and collected her coat. The girls hastily got their coats too and ran after her, but by the time they reached the outer door, Lucy was already striding furiously away.

'Here – hold up there! Where's the fire?' Annabelle struggled into her coat and set off at a trot with Dotty hot on her heels. Lucy had nearly reached the end of the road by the time they caught up with her, and grabbing the sleeve of her coat Annabelle panted, 'Whatever's the matter with you? That poor chap looked like he wished the ground would open up and swallow him.'

'Serves him right,' Lucy spat bitterly, but she did slow down a little and the other two girls fell into step beside her. They glanced at each other and frowned, but wisely held their tongues. Lucy was so angry she was like a powder keg waiting to explode and they didn't want to start her off again.

Eventually it was Lucy who broke the silence when she said meekly, 'I'm sorry about that. I just lost my temper, but I didn't mean to show you up.'

'It's all right,' said Dotty, ever the peacemaker. 'Didn't you like him?'

'I don't like *any* men . . . except Joel,' Lucy answered. 'They're all only after one thing and they're not going to get it from me! I shan't have a boyfriend or get married – *ever*!'

'Blimey, that's a bit strong, isn't it?' Dotty was shocked.

'You're bound to meet someone you like and fall in love with eventually. You're far too attractive to stay single.'

'I won't!' Lucy was adamant. 'If you only knew . . .' Her voice trailed away then and she clammed up. They were approaching the bus station by now and all Lucy wanted to do was get back to the safety of her little rented house. The whole evening had been a mistake. Going to the pictures with the girls was one thing, but going to a dance was a different thing entirely and she was determined she would not do so again.

'Look, I'll see you both at work on Monday,' she said lamely. 'And I'll bring all your clothes with me too,' she assured Annabelle.

Annabelle shrugged. She wasn't overly worried about the clothes that Lucy had borrowed. She had plenty more. 'Whenever, there's no rush.'

She and Dotty watched Lucy head for her bus-stand then, and once she was out of earshot Dotty asked, 'What do you think brought that on? And what do you think she meant when she said, "If you only knew . . .?" Do you think she's had a bad experience with a boy or something?'

'I've no idea,' Annabelle said truthfully. 'But that's my bus just pulled in over there so I may as well get home. The night is ruined now anyway. Goodnight, Dotty.'

''Night,' Dotty responded as she stood there thoughtfully chewing on her lip.

Chapter Sixteen

On 13 May 1940, Mr and Mrs P and Lucy huddled around the wireless to listen to the Home Service news as Winston Churchill addressed Parliament. He could offer little hope to the nation as Hitler's devastation continued, and he spoke of *'blood, toil, tears and sweat'*. Yet still his determination that they would not be defeated shone through. He admitted that there would be no easy solution and did not deny that the country faced *'an ordeal of the most grievous kind'*, but he maintained that whilst every man and woman worked together and stayed firmly behind him they would achieve victory and survive. He somehow managed to make the people feel that they were all in it together and told them, *'I take up my task with buoyancy and hope . . . I feel entitled . . . to claim the aid of all and to say, "come then, let us go forward together with our united strength".'*

Once the broadcast was over Mr P switched the wireless off and began to stuff tobacco into his pipe.

'He's a good man,' he said quietly. 'We'll not go far wrong wi' him to lead us.'

Lucy and Mrs P were thinking of all the ships that were being sunk in the Channel and of Joel and Freddy, and could only pray that Mr P was right.

On the following Sunday Winston Churchill again addressed the nation, and once more Mr and Mrs P and Lucy huddled around the wireless. He called the Nazis '*the foulest and most soul-destroying tyranny which has ever darkened and stained the pages of history*'. But he ended his speech by saying, '*Together we shall win!*'

Only days later, the papers reported that France and Belgium had begun to fall as the Germans swept through to the Channel coast. Boulogne had been evacuated, Arras had fallen and Amiens had been taken. As Lucy read it, a cold finger raced down her spine. The British Army had been forced to retreat to the beaches.

'What will happen to them?' Lucy sobbed. 'There's nowhere else for them to go now. They'll all be slaughtered like lambs.'

'I dare say they'll send ships to try and bring back those that are still alive,' Mrs P answered, her thoughts full of her son. Was he even now at the mercy of the Nazis, or taken prisoner, or worse still, lying injured or even dead somewhere?

'Do you think this might be the start of the invasion?' Lucy asked tremulously and Mrs P hugged her wordlessly. Could they have known it, even as they spoke ships and boats of all shapes and sizes were setting off across the Channel to bring back the living and the wounded. There were tugs and ferries, small private yachts, larger ships, fishing boats – almost anything that could float, in fact.

*

Over in Cheylesmore, Annabelle's mother was reading the same newspaper report and she too was distraught.

'The last time I heard from your father, he was in Belgium,' she said in a wobbly voice.

Annabelle was sitting on the rug in front of the fire painting her toenails and she glanced up to say, 'Well, I'm sure he'll be all right.'

Something in Miranda snapped then. 'Don't you *ever* worry about anyone other than yourself?' she barked.

Annabelle was shocked. Her mother had never raised her voice to her before and she didn't like it at all.

'I was only passing a comment.' She sniffed indignantly. 'Isn't anyone allowed to have an opinion around here? Perhaps you'd rather hear me say I'm sure he won't be!'

'Sometimes you're just *impossible,*' Miranda retorted with tears trickling down her cheeks, and she left the room with the newspaper firmly grasped in her hand.

Annabelle shrugged before returning her attention to her toenails. She was sick and tired of the whole blasted war, and when she thought back to the carefree life she had led before it was declared, she felt like crying too.

Meantime Dotty was in a public phone box at the end of her road talking to Robert in London, who was telling her that her stories were proving to be a great success with his readers.

'I'd like you to come to see me again – and this time I want to look at the novel you're writing,' he told her.

Dotty shivered with excitement. 'If we could make it on a Thursday, I wouldn't have to ask for time off work,' she suggested and he was only too happy to agree.

'What about next week then? I could meet you off the train

at Euston if you let me know what time you'll be arriving.'

'That would be lovely,' she said shyly, and they then went on to speak of some of the ideas she'd had for some more stories.

When she finally set off for home, she was tingling with happiness. Robert was such a genuinely nice man and he was taking a real interest in her. It was a lovely feeling.

When the girls all met up again at work the next morning the atmosphere was gloomy throughout the whole store. Everyone was worried about the latest war reports and one poor woman from Dotty's department was absent following a telegram saying that her husband was missing.

'Poor Elsie,' Dotty said during their morning break. 'She's such a nice woman and she and her husband had only been married for three years. They have a baby girl, I believe, whom her mother looks after while she comes to work.'

Lucy's thoughts instantly turned to Mary, whom she was missing more than she could say. Thankfully it appeared that she had been placed with a lovely couple in Folkestone, who had written to Lucy shortly after they had taken Mary in. Lucy carried the letter around with her in her handbag and she had read it so many times that the paper was almost falling apart.

Dear Miss Ford,

I am writing to you at the first opportunity to tell you that your sister is well. My husband is the vicar of this parish and Mary is now staying with us at the vicarage until such a time as it is deemed safe for her to return home to you. We also have another little girl staying with us from the East End who has very much taken Mary under her wing. Mary is healthy and eating and sleeping well, and I am putting my address at the top of the page so that you may write to her or visit her whenever you wish. Mary is a delightful child and as good as gold, a real credit to you. I understand how hard the separation must be for you, my dear, but rest assured that Mary is being very well cared for.

Yours sincerely,

Susan Manners

Whenever Lucy thought of Mary now, which was often, she would touch the letter, which somehow brought Mary a little closer and gave her comfort – not that there was much to be felt today. Everyone was thinking of poor Elsie and the handsome young husband she had lost. War truly was a terrible thing.

The girls decided to get some fresh air during their lunch break that day and wandered around the city centre, enjoying the feel of the warm May sunshine on their faces after the harsh winter they had just endured. They were now all allowed to serve the customers in their various departments and felt as if they had been working at Owen Owen forever.

'I'm going to London again on Thursday,' Dotty told them casually after a time and Annabelle winked at Lucy mischievously.

'Oh, are you now?' she teased. 'And are you still writing to each other?'

'Of course we are. How else are we supposed to discuss my work when I'm not on the phone?' Dotty answered defensively. Every time they passed a newsagent's she had to stop herself from rushing in and buying every copy of *Woman's Heart* she could find. She doubted she would ever get over the thrill of seeing her name in print each month.

'Well, I would have thought it would be just a matter of posting them a story off each month and waiting for the cheque to arrive. But never mind about that – what are you going to wear? You can't wear the same outfit again.'

'Mm, I hadn't thought of that.' Her London outfit, as she now thought of it, was the only decent one Dotty owned, but Annabelle did have a point. The trouble was, there wasn't much choice in the shops any more.

'You could always borrow one of my blouses and wear it with your suit skirt,' Annabelle offered. 'At least it would give it a different look. What about the blue one with the Peter Pan collar that you like? You could wear my string of pearls to go with it too.'

'I think I'd be too afraid of losing them,' Dotty answered. 'But I will take you up on the offer of the blouse, if you're sure you don't mind?'

'I wouldn't have offered if I did, would I?' Annabelle said in her usual forthright way. They were at the steps of St Michael's Cathedral by then, and on the spur of the moment Lucy suggested, 'Why don't we go in and light a candle and say a prayer for all the people who we're missing?'

Annabelle shrugged but followed the other two into the enormous cathedral just the same. After stepping out of the bright sunshine the interior was gloomy and they all blinked as their eyes adjusted to the light, but then the cathedral worked its magic on them and they all stared up in awe at the beautiful stained-glass windows. Dotty and Lucy had visited the cathedral many times, and it never failed to move them. It was so peaceful within that it was hard to believe that even as they stood there, men and women were fighting to save their country and magnificent buildings like this. Even Annabelle was silenced for a time. Eventually they approached the altar, where they each took candles and lit them, then they sat on the hard wooden pews, bowed their heads and said silent prayers for the loved ones from whom they were parted.

Strangely enough, they all felt a little happier and more optimistic as they made their way back to work.

Lucy slumped onto the sofa when she got home from work. She was shattered and had just started to drop off when there was a tap on the door and she opened it to find Mr P standing on the step.

'Oh, I was going to pop round when I'd had something to eat and—' Her voice stopped abruptly as she noted Mr P's red eyes. He looked as if he had been crying and was shuffling from foot to foot uncomfortably.

'What's wrong?' A cold hand closed around her heart and she knew that she was going to hear bad news.

'I er . . . I were wonderin' if you'd come round an' see the missus?' he said miserably. 'We've had bad news, see. A telegram.'

'Oh no!' Lucy's hand flew to her mouth. 'Is – is it young Freddy?'

He nodded. 'They say he's missin', and I can't do a thing wi' our gel. Would yer come, love? I'd appreciate it. She thinks the world o' you an' yer might be able to stop her cryin'. I certainly bloody can't.'

'Of course I'll come.' Lucy ran back into the kitchen and turned the kettle off, and seconds later she was following Mr P across the shared yard to his back door.

She found her neighbour sitting clutching the telegram with tears streaming down her face.

'Look, love, young Lucy's here,' Fred told her, but for a while Mrs P didn't even seem to hear him. She was locked away in her own little world of grief.

'See what I mean?' he muttered brokenly as his own eyes brimmed with tears. 'She don't even seem to know that I'm here.'

'Mrs P?' Lucy said gently, but she got no reaction whatsoever. It was only when she tried to take the telegram from the woman's hand that she suddenly rounded on her. ''Ere, gerroff, will yer,' she yelled. 'That's *my* telegram tellin' me about me lovely lad.'

Then slowly her eyes seemed to focus and she fell limply into Lucy's arms as sobs shook her big body. 'Eeh, me lovely boy's gone.'

'You don't know that,' Lucy said soothingly as she rocked her to and fro. 'The telegram says that he's *missing* – and unless you hear otherwise you have to hold on to that. He's most probably alive somewhere. It doesn't say he's dead, does it?'

Mrs P's sobs subsided as she looked at Lucy hopefully. 'Do yer really reckon that might be the case?'

'Yes, I do.' Lucy nodded firmly. 'You must *never* give up hope. He might have been injured and be in a hospital somewhere, admittedly, or he might even have been taken prisoner, but either of those options are better than being told that he's dead, aren't they?'

'Yer right,' Mrs P said, clutching at straws. 'An' when they find him they'll let me know, won't they?'

'Of course they will,' Lucy said with an assurance she was far from feeling. 'So it's all the more important that you don't give up on him, isn't it? And now I'm going to make you and Mr P a nice strong cup of tea and I'm going to put a drop of brandy in it. Do you have any left over from Christmas?'

'Aye, it's in that cupboard over there. That's a good idea, love,' Mrs P said in a croaky voice. She was still badly shaken up but at least Lucy had given her a glimmer of hope. She hated to think of Freddy hurt or captured by the enemy, but anything was better than being told he was dead, and the war couldn't go on forever, could it?

By the time Lucy got back to her own little house she felt as if she had been wrung out like a dishcloth. She hated to see Mr and Mrs P so upset, they were such good people and they had been so kind to her and Joel and Mary. She just hoped that she had managed to make them feel a little better, but deep down she wondered if Freddy really was all right. Only time would tell now.

On Thursday Robert was waiting at Euston for Dotty and when she stepped down from the train his face broke into a friendly smile.

'Why, you look lovely!' he exclaimed as he pulled her arm through his and headed in the direction of the nearest café. 'Let's go and have a cuppa, eh? I've no doubt you'll be ready for one after your journey.'

Her cheeks pink from the compliment, Dotty said, 'But won't they be waiting for us at the office?'

'Ah, well, that's the nice thing about being the boss,' Robert told her with a wink. 'I can come and go pretty much as I please, although to be honest I don't think they'd really miss me if I never went in. Laura has that place running like clockwork. Between you and me, I don't know what I'd do without her.'

Dotty felt an unexpected stab of jealousy. It sounded as if Robert was very fond of Laura, but then she asked herself, why shouldn't he be? Laura was a very attractive woman, and clever and efficient too, going by what he had just said.

They were in a small café now and he sat her down at a vacant table before rushing off to the counter. She watched him through a blue haze of cigarette smoke, and was impressed at how well he could manage with just one good hand. In no time at all he was back with a thick china cup and saucer for her, and then another one for himself. He pushed the sugar bowl towards her.

'Laura is really looking forward to seeing you again,' he told Dotty. 'She's delighted with the stories you've been sending in and I'm really looking forward to having a peep at this book you've been writing. I know it's not finished yet, but you did bring it with you, didn't you?'

She nodded as she patted her bag before saying, 'Well, yes, I did – but I didn't think the magazine would be interested in novels – and it really isn't that good,' she added hastily.

'You are right – the magazine wouldn't be interested,' he acknowledged. 'But being in this business, I have a lot of editor friends who might be. And as for it not being that good . . . Well, I'll tell you truthfully what I think of it when I've read it.'

Soon afterwards they strolled to the magazine headquarters arm in arm. Laura was waiting for them and was full of praise about the stories that had been printed so far.

'They're just so . . .' she sought for the right words to describe them before saying, 'simple, I suppose is the word I'm looking for, and what I mean by that is, your characters are very believable, so much so that our readers feel they can relate to them.'

'There you are then,' Robert teased. 'If Laura says they're good then they're good, madam!'

Again Dotty felt a twinge of jealousy as she noted how easy Robert and Laura were with each other. She left her book with Laura – or what she had written so far, all neatly typed – and then Robert once again insisted on taking her out to lunch.

'Where would you like to go?' he asked.

Dotty shook her head. 'I really don't mind, but it doesn't have to be anywhere too expensive.'

'In that case, how about we go and feed the pigeons and call into a café somewhere for lunch? Then we might even have time to take a boat-ride along the Thames before you catch your train home.'

Her face lit up at the thought of it as he steered her towards a taxi and soon they were at the steps of St Paul's Cathedral throwing the seed he had bought for her to the hungry birds. There seemed to be thousands of them and Dotty couldn't stop smiling. When they entered the beautiful building Dotty was rendered momentarily speechless, even more so when they climbed up to the Whispering Gallery and on up to the inner Golden Gallery. And then they were on the outer gallery and London lay spread around them, so changed since the beginning of the war. She was breathless by then after climbing over five hundred steps.

'There's Wimbledon Common over to the west there – look,' Robert pointed out. 'And over there is Tilbury Docks. That's Greenwich and the Observatory over to the south-east.'

Still breathless, she could only nod.

After their visit to St Paul's, he took her into a modest café where they ate fish and chips, and finally they sailed along the River Thames. Robert gestured at the Tower of London with his good arm and Dotty beamed. She would have so much to tell Annabelle and Lucy when she got home. She was just sad that the day had to end.

'Everywhere is just so huge!' Dotty exclaimed as she gazed about her. It was exciting to see all the buildings rearing up on each bank of the river. But even here she could not escape from the fact that there was a war on. There were very few young men about and those who were, were mainly in some sort of uniform.

Robert smiled indulgently. Because he lived in London he took all these sights for granted, but it was gratifying to see Dotty enjoying herself, and the more she relaxed the more he thought what a truly nice young lady she was. 'Where would you like to go now?' he asked, having as good a time as she was.

Glancing at the cheap watch on her wrist, Dotty said regretfully, 'As much as I'd like to carry on, I think I ought to be heading back to the station now or I might miss my train.' The day had passed in the blink of an eye.

'Right you are then, but on the way we'll call in for a cup of tea, eh?'

They stopped off in a Lyons Corner House and the tea was accompanied by a sticky bun. After she had eaten it, Dotty joked, 'It's a good job I don't come here too often. The way you feed me up I'd soon be as fat as a pig.'

He shook his head. 'I doubt that very much. You aren't as far through as a clothes prop!'

Again a stab of jealousy reared its ugly head as a picture of Laura's womanly figure flashed in front of Dotty's eyes, but she forced a smile as he chivalrously helped her back into the lovely blue swing coat that Miranda had given her. She wondered why it should bother her so much. After all, Robert had never behaved as anything less than a perfect gentleman and a friend.

When they arrived back at Euston in time for her to catch her train she told him sincerely, 'Thank you for another wonderful day.'

Again he was struck by how young and naïve she was.

'I'm glad you've enjoyed it,' he told her. 'And if ever you and your friends fancy a weekend in London, just say the word and you can stay at my flat. In your own rooms, of course,' he said quickly, not wishing her to get the wrong idea. 'It's just a shame that there's a war on. You haven't really seen London at its best, but then I dare say everywhere is the same at the moment.'

She nodded in agreement as her train wheezed into the station. 'I'd better go and get aboard then,' she told him awkwardly. 'I don't want it going without me, do I?' In actual fact she couldn't think of a single thing that she would have liked more, but she couldn't tell him that, of course.

'I'll write to you just as soon as Laura and I have had time to look at your manuscript,' he promised. 'And in the meantime, ring me next week so that we can talk about next month's story.'

'I will.' She stood uncertainly for a moment, resisting the urge to peck him on the cheek, then turned and fled – and as he watched her go, he smiled fondly.

Chapter Seventeen

Lucy began to rush home from work each evening to check on Mrs P. She was a changed woman since receiving the telegram informing her that Freddy was missing, and seemed to spend half her time on the doorstep now looking for signs of the postman. She was convinced that he was going to bring her good news, saying that Freddy was in hospital or had been taken prisoner. But each day left her sadly disappointed and a little more withdrawn from the world. It was Lucy now who took her ration books each week to get her shopping and helped her with her washing and ironing.

'I really appreciate this, lass,' Mr P told her one Sunday morning as Lucy fed a clean white sheet through the mangle in the back yard before pegging it onto the line where it flapped like a living thing in the breeze. 'If it weren't fer you over the last few weeks I doubt we'd have so much as a clean towel in the whole house. An' her allus so houseproud before.'

As he shook his head sadly Lucy's heart went out to him. But she didn't have time to stand and chat. It was a Sunday, and still as regular as clockwork she disappeared off at the same time every Sunday afternoon without a mention of where she was going. Mrs P missed having Mary as she had used to. At one time the woman had been consumed with curiosity and had tried everything to get it out of the girl but nowadays she had more pressing things to worry about, namely her son.

'It's all right, Mr P,' Lucy puffed as another wet sheet fell into her arms. 'It's the least I can do after all you and Mrs P have done for us. And try not to worry too much. I'm sure she'll come through this eventually.'

'Let's hope yer right, wench,' he remarked as he jammed tobacco into the bowl of his pipe.

Once the washing was done and Lucy was sure that the couple had all they needed, she hurried across the yard and into her own house where she hastily changed before rushing off.

'There she goes again,' Mrs P remarked from her seat in the front window. Her husband had told her that there was no post on Sunday, but it made no difference.

Over in her flat, Dotty was composing the second letter of the week to Robert. They wrote to each other so regularly now that the letters sometimes crossed in the post, and lately they had become more intimate.

I'm so looking forward to seeing you again, he had written in his last letter. *Is there no chance of you coming for a whole weekend? You could stay at my flat and you would be very welcome. There are so still so many places of interest you haven't seen.*

The very thought of it made her heart pound, although she wasn't too sure what Miss Timms might think of it! A young unmarried girl staying with a bachelor? Dotty giggled as she thought of the woman's reaction, although she knew that now she was no longer in the kindly woman's care it was really none of Miss Timms's business what Dotty did with her spare time. But she had no wish to upset her, although the offer was very tempting. And of course she realised that Robert was only inviting her as a friend – so what could be the harm in that? Dotty knew that she and Robert could never be anything other than friends. They had come from different worlds. He had had a private education and been brought up in the lap of luxury from what she could make of it, and besides that, he was so much older than her. And of course, on top of that it was clear that he and Laura were close too. Just the thought of the woman made Dotty scowl. Laura had always gone out of her way to make her feel welcome each time they had met and yet Dotty still felt inadequate and dull in her company. She wished that things could have been different.

'That's it then!' Annabelle threw her last pair of nylon stockings down in a temper. 'They're laddered too! What am I going to wear?'

'Woollen ones like the rest of us,' her mother answered drily from the settee where she was darning a pair of her own stockings.

'Oh, I'm so *sick* of this having to make do and mend,' Annabelle complained bitterly. 'I'll be damned glad when this rotten war is over. Nothing is any fun any more. It's just work and bed!'

'I dare say your father and our boys at the front are saying the very same thing,' her mother said acidly. 'And I dare say they have a lot more to worry about than we do. Like staying alive for a start-off.'

Annabelle had the good grace to flush. Put that way, she supposed that having to do without nylon stockings was petty, but she still hated the fact that they were no longer readily available.

'Lucy was saying that Mrs P has been unravelling all her family's old jumpers and cardigans and then reusing the wool to knit larger ones for them,' she commented.

'A lot of people are doing that,' Miranda said. 'Most of the new wool is being used to make uniforms for the forces now. But what are you getting dressed up for? Are you going out?'

'Yes. I thought I'd go and see Dotty for an hour or two,' Annabelle sighed. 'There's not much else to do, is there? And it's no good going to see Lucy. She still disappears every Sunday afternoon and we have no idea where she goes.' She stared musingly off into space for a moment before asking, 'Do you think she's going to meet a boyfriend?'

'I shouldn't think so. Not after the way you told me she reacted to that young man at the dance. Perhaps she's going to visit a relative?'

'No, she isn't. She told me and Dotty that since losing her parents she only has Mary and Joel.' Annabelle frowned as she thought of Joel. It seemed such a long time since she had seen him and sometimes now it was hard to picture his face.

'I expect Dotty will be mooning over Robert again when I get there,' she said next. 'Between you and me, I think she's rather smitten with him – although she won't admit it.'

Miranda had grown very fond of Lucy and Dotty in the previous months and she grinned. 'Well, he's certainly pushing the boat out to help her. Didn't you say that he'd forwarded Dotty's novel to an editor friend of his?'

'Yes, he has, but she hasn't heard what the editor thinks of it yet. She's almost finished it now. Always typing away, she is.' Annabelle pulled a face. 'Apart from at work and on the night we do the first aid course at the Red Cross I hardly get to see her now, although I have persuaded her to come and see a film at the Rex in a couple of weeks' time.'

Miranda hid a smile. All three girls had regularly attended the first aid classes, but it was Annabelle who seemed to be getting the most out of it – which had come as a complete surprise to her mother, for Annabelle rarely took an interest in anything other than her appearance.

'Well, if you must go out, just try and be back in before it gets dark,' her mother advised, and with a nod Annabelle hurried away to finish getting ready. It was when she came back downstairs that Miranda suddenly told her, 'By the way, there's a letter that came for you yesterday. I'm so sorry, darling, but I'd forgotten all about it. You'll find it on the dresser in the kitchen.'

Annabelle's heart began to thump. Could it be from Joel? Closing the kitchen door after her, she snatched up the letter and instantly saw from the postmarks that it was. Tearing it open with fingers that were suddenly trembling, she began to read, and as she did so her eyes filled with tears.

Dear Belle,

Sorry I haven't been able to write for a while. Things are pretty grim out here as you might imagine. I sometimes wonder if we'll ever come home. (The next two lines had been censored but then it continued.) *One of the chaps I'm serving with became a father last month and he still hasn't seen his new baby yet. It's so sad. But then I suppose I shouldn't complain. At least we are still alive, which is a lot more than can be said of some of the chaps I came out here with. I have seen things that I don't think I shall ever be able to forget. I miss Mary and Lucy more than I can say and pray that they are both well. And you too, of course. Perhaps when I come home we might go to see a film or something? If you are still free, that is. I don't know when I might be able to write again but I pray that you are well and think of you often. Look after yourself.*

Love

Joel

Annabelle blinked – he had signed the letter *Love, Joel*! The last one had ended in *Kind regards*. Could it be that he felt the same attraction for her as she did for him? And he had asked her if they might go to a film together. She thumped the table in frustration then. If only she could have written back to him, as he sounded very down – but of course that was impossible. He probably didn't know where he was going to be from one day to another. But then she smiled. At least she knew now that he hadn't forgotten about her. In a slightly happier frame of mind she put on her coat and set off.

It was well after teatime when Mrs P noticed Lucy hurry past her front window on her way home. Mrs P frowned. It was unusual for the girl not to call in, but perhaps she was going to take her coat off first. The weather had certainly taken a turn for the better, which was something to be thankful for at least. Shrugging, she turned her attention back to the cardigan she was knitting for Beryl, her youngest.

An hour later, when Lucy had still not put in an appearance, she asked Fred, 'Pop round next door, would yer love, an' just check that young Lucy is all right? It ain't like her not to call in from wherever it is she disappears off to every Sunday.'

Fred gave a long-suffering sigh as he folded the *New of the World*. He knew better than to argue with his Gladys nowadays. If he so much as said a wrong word he got his head bitten off.

Without a word he let himself out of the back door and crossed the yard, avoiding banging his shoulder on the tin bath that hung outside the back door. It always upset him to see it. Sundays had always been bath night for the kids before they'd been evacuated and the house had always rung with laughter as Freddy, Barry and Beryl took it in turns to bathe in front of the fire. Then Gladys would grip each of the younger ones' heads between her knees in turn as she went through their hair with a fine-toothed nit comb. It was funny how he missed the little things he had always taken for granted.

Pausing at Lucy's back door, he lifted his hand to knock, then stopped himself. He could see her through the window sitting at the table and it looked as if she was crying. He shuffled uncomfortably from foot to foot. Perhaps it was 'women's things' as his missus always called them. At certain times of the month she would have a weepy time and walk about like a bear with a sore head, although now that he came to think about it, she was like that pretty much all of the time now. He hovered, wondering what to do, but then decided that he'd rather face Lucy than his Glad if he hadn't done as she asked.

Lucy glanced up at the first knock and he saw that his assumption was correct. She had been crying but she hastily swiped the back of her hands across her cheeks before hurrying through the kitchen to let him in.

'Are you all right, love?' he asked timidly, and to his

horror she burst into tears again. Quickly placing his arm about her shaking shoulders he led her through into the kitchen and plonked her down on the chair.

'Er . . . can I get you a drink o' water or somethin'?' He felt totally useless and didn't know what to do.

'N-no, thank you.' Lucy gulped as he looked helplessly on. 'I-I just had some bad news this afternoon but I'll be fine, honestly. You get back to Mrs P.'

'Well, if you're quite sure.' He then turned and fled.

'So why ain't she been round then?' Mrs P demanded the second he set foot back through the door.

'I ain't got a clue, Glad,' he answered, 'but the lass is in a rare old state, I don't mind tellin' yer. Sobbin' 'er little heart out she is, an' you know I ain't no good in situations like that.'

Mrs P's knitting needles stopped clicking as she stared at him. 'Didn't yer ask her what were wrong then?'

'Course I did,' he defended himself. 'But all she'd say were that she'd had some bad news. P'rhaps it would be better if you went round.' He secretly hoped that she would. She hadn't gone over the doorstep since the day they'd had the telegram about Freddy, and even going across the yard would be a start, surely?

'I dare say I should,' she muttered, although she felt as if he'd asked her to climb a mountain. She had got used to being confined within her own four walls and the thought of venturing out was terrifying. But then he'd said that Lucy was crying, and she'd come to look on the girl as one of her own. Laying her knitting aside, the big woman took a deep breath and rose from her seat, then forcing herself to place one foot in front of the other she crossed the room and stepped out into the sunshine. It felt strange to breathe the fresh air but she didn't linger to enjoy it, merely kept on going until she was safe in Lucy's kitchen. Only then did she realise that she was shaking like a leaf, but still she held herself together as she approached Lucy to ask, 'What is it, love?'

'Oh, Mrs P.' Lucy flung herself into the woman's arms and the tears came fast and furious until Mrs P was convinced that she was going to drown in them.

'That's it, you cry it all out now an' when you've done I'll make you a nice hot cup o' sweet tea an' you can tell me all about it.' Sod the sugar ration, thought Mrs P as she continued to hold Lucy tightly. At last the sobs subsided to dull hiccuping whimpers and Mrs P tenderly stroked the damp hair from Lucy's sweating forehead. The poor lass had worked herself up into a rare old lather, there was no doubt about it.

She gently pressed her back into the chair and minutes later when Lucy sat with a steaming mug of tea in front of her, the woman asked, 'Now how about yer tell me what's wrong, eh? They reckon a trouble shared is a trouble halved.'

Lucy seemed to be remarkably calm now. Too calm by half, Mrs P privately thought, as if she'd had all the stuffing knocked out of her.

'Is it Mary – or Joel?' she asked softly.

Lucy shook her head. 'No. It's . . . it's my mother. She died today.'

Chapter Eighteen

'Yer *mother*! But I thought yer said yer mother had died just afore you moved here?' Mrs P gasped.

'I told everyone that,' Lucy answered dully, 'but she didn't. She's been in a hospital since just after my dad died – well, an asylum really. An asylum for the insane. That's where I've been going every Sunday, to see her. And today . . . she died.'

'Oh, luvvie.' Mrs P was horrified. And to think that this poor girl had kept that terrible secret to herself for all this time. No wonder she and Joel had always clammed up whenever she had probed about their parents. 'But whyever didn't yer tell me? There's no shame in the poor soul bein' mentally ill.'

'There's a lot more to it than that,' Lucy whispered. 'But I can't tell anyone about it – *ever*! I promised Joel.'

Mrs P was confused now but she wisely held her tongue. 'So what will you be doin' about the funeral?' she asked tentatively. Perhaps Lucy would need some help in organising it. She was very young to have that sort of responsibility on her shoulders.

'It's all being taken care of by the asylum,' Lucy croaked. 'They have their own burial ground there. All I have to do is turn up for the service on Wednesday.'

It all sounded very cold and clinical and Mrs P shuddered. 'But won't there be people who you'll want to be there to give her a send-off?'

Lucy shook her head. 'No, it will be just me. And Mrs P – I'd be very grateful if you didn't mention this to anyone.'

'Of course I won't if you don't want me to, apart from my Fred, but he'll not say nothin',' the woman promised her. 'But there must be *something* I can do for yer. Would yer like me to come with you?'

'No, I appreciate the offer but I'd rather go alone.'

'So be it then, but if yer change yer mind, the offer's there.' Mrs P was secretly appalled at the thought of the poor woman having such a wretched turnout for her funeral. But then if that was how Lucy wanted it, it wasn't her place to interfere or express her opinion. Everyone grieved differently and it appeared that Lucy just wanted to get it over with as quickly and as quietly as she could.

She stayed with the girl for another half an hour, although she soon realised that she might as well not have been there. Lucy had become very quiet and distracted, so eventually she told her, 'I'm goin' now, love, but I'm only next door should yer need me. Are you sure you'll be all right on yer own? You could always come an' stay wi' me an' Fred tonight?'

'Thanks, but I'd rather be on my own for now if you don't mind.'

Mrs P slipped quietly away and soon she was back in her own four walls.

'You ain't *never* gonna believe what I'm about to tell yer,' she told Fred, and when she went on to do just that, his mouth gaped in amazement.

'But she never breathed a word about her mam still bein' alive. Do yer think she were ashamed of her?' he asked.

'No, it don't sound like she were,' his wife said. 'In fact, she's broken-hearted an' you ain't like that if you've been ashamed o' someone. It appears she really loved her mam, so I can't make head nor tail of it. An' what makes it worse is the fact that she can't even let Joel know. He could be anywhere, God bless him.' The same as my Freddy, she thought, and the pain was there again, as sharp and acute as the day she had received the telegram telling her that he was missing. Life could be bloody cruel at times, there was no doubt about it.

Lucy didn't go into work the next day and Dotty and even Annabelle were concerned about her.

'It isn't like her not to turn in,' Dotty fretted when they met in the lift on their way to the staff dining room. 'I've never known Lucy miss a day; even when Mary was evacuated she came in late, and if she'd had anything planned she would have mentioned it to us.'

'We could always pop round after work if you haven't got anything planned,' Annabelle suggested. 'Mother won't be in until later anyway so she wouldn't miss me.'

'We'll do that then,' Dotty answered with quiet determination. 'Unless she decides to come in late, and then we can stop worrying.'

But Lucy didn't come in, so straight after work the girls

headed for the bus station and boarded a bus to the end of Lucy's street in Tile Hill.

'Crikey, her curtains are all drawn,' Dotty said worriedly as they approached the house. 'You don't think she's had bad news about Joel, do you?'

Annabelle's stomach lurched at the very thought of it but she hid her feelings well as they turned up the whitewashed entry that led to Lucy and Mrs P's shared back yard. Mrs P was at her kitchen window when Dotty opened the gate and she hurried out to them looking upset.

'Young Lucy's had some bad news,' she confided in a hushed voice. 'In a right two an' eight she is, bless her soul.'

'It's not about Joel, is it?' Annabelle's eyes were stretched with fear, and relief flooded through her when Mrs P shook her head.

'No, it ain't about him,' she whispered. 'But happen she'll want to tell yer about it herself. Go on in, the door's open. I've only just checked on her not half an hour since.'

Dotty nodded, then after tapping lightly on Lucy's door the girls entered the small kitchen. Lucy appeared in the doorway almost instantly and they saw at a glance that her eyes were red-rimmed and swollen from crying.

'Oh Lucy, whatever's happened? You look awful.' Dotty dropped her bag onto the table and seconds later Lucy was in her arms sobbing her heart out again, which was funny when she came to think of it because she'd been sure that she didn't have a single tear left in her whole body.

When she finally stopped crying and pulled herself together, she seemed to be struggling to come to a decision. She then gave a loud sigh and after motioning for them to sit down, she sat opposite them and began twisting her fingers together.

'You may as well know, my mother died yesterday,' she

said quietly, and for a while the silence was all-consuming as her friends stared at her in shocked disbelief.

It was Dotty who broke it eventually when she said, 'B-but I thought you lost both your parents a few years ago.'

'It was easier to tell everyone that,' Lucy said, 'but in actual fact my mum was in a mental asylum.'

'Is that where you disappeared off to every Sunday afternoon?' Dotty asked gently, and Lucy nodded.

'You should have told us,' Annabelle said. 'We're supposed to be friends, aren't we? We wouldn't have thought any less of you.'

'Well, you know now,' Lucy answered. But not all of it, she thought, never all of it!

'We thought something must be wrong when you didn't turn in to work,' Dotty told her. 'Is there anything we can do to help – with the funeral arrangements, for instance?' Never having had to organise anything like that before she was secretly relieved when Lucy declined the offer.

'No. Thanks for offering, but it's all arranged for Wednesday morning.'

'Blimey, that's quick, isn't it?' Annabelle blurted out. She had never been known for her tact but Lucy didn't take offence.

'The asylum has arranged everything,' she told them in a wobbly voice. 'And Mum will be buried within the grounds with the minimum of fuss.'

Dotty frowned in confusion. 'Are you quite sure that's what she would have wanted?' she asked with concern. 'I mean – wouldn't she have wanted to be buried with your dad?'

'No, *never*!' The words burst from Lucy before she could stop herself and she squirmed with embarrassment. 'I mean . . . it's better this way.'

'Well, if you're quite sure,' Dotty said hesitantly. 'I just hope they haven't talked you into something you're not happy about and that you'll regret later. She was your mum, after all.'

'I *am* sure,' Lucy told her and then rising she asked, 'Would you like a cup of tea? I've run out of sugar, I'm afraid, but I've got some saccharin.'

'I'll make it,' Dotty offered, but Lucy said, 'No, it's all right. I'll do it, I'm better when I'm keeping busy,' and she turned away as the two girls exchanged a confused glance. You could have knocked them both down with a feather. Why hadn't Lucy told them that her mum was alive?

An hour later as they were walking back to the bus stop, Annabelle commented, 'It's strange isn't it? That Lucy never told us her mother was still alive, I mean?'

'Perhaps she was ashamed because she was mentally ill?' Dotty suggested, although that didn't seem like Lucy. They shrugged and moved on. All they could do, the two friends agreed, was to be there for her now, if and when she needed a shoulder to cry on.

Lucy was back at work on Wednesday afternoon following the funeral, and the other two instantly picked up on the fact that she didn't want to talk about it. In fact, it was almost as if it was any ordinary day, and no one seeing Lucy would have guessed that she had just buried her mother.

'Best leave her to deal with it in her own way,' Dotty whispered during the afternoon break while Lucy was being served at the counter. Annabelle nodded in agreement. There wasn't much else they could do.

Dotty had informed Mrs Broadstairs that Lucy was absent due to a family bereavement and to their amazement the woman had gone out of her way to offer condolences the second Lucy had returned to work.

'Crikey, she must be going soft in her old age,' Annabelle had commented.

'Or could it be love that's softening her?' Dotty giggled. 'I've heard rumours that she and Mr Bradley have been seen walking out together.'

'Well, good for her then and long may it last. That kiss under the mistletoe must have done the trick. She's certainly a lot less prickly now,' Annabelle sniggered, and then they hurried back to their departments.

After work they all made their way to the Red Cross first aid course in the church hall near Annabelle's home in Cheylesmore, and again Lucy's mother was not mentioned. The two girls wisely didn't comment, and anyone seeing them all together would never have guessed what a trauma Lucy had been through that day.

'How absolutely awful for the poor girl,' Miranda said as she and Annabelle walked the short distance home after seeing Dotty and Lucy onto the bus. 'All evening I felt as if I ought to say something or offer my condolences at the very least, but it was obvious that she didn't want to talk about it.'

'You're not wrong there,' Annabelle agreed. 'We expected her to come back from the funeral in bits, but it was as if she had put a shield up, and if we so much as looked at her she was off like a rocket.' Annabelle couldn't even begin to imagine how she would have felt if she had had to bury her mother, and in a sudden rare show of affection she tucked her arm through Miranda's and they walked the rest of the way home enjoying their closeness.

As Dotty climbed the stairs to her flat that evening she was shocked to find Mrs Cousins hovering outside on the landing, waiting for her. But this was Mrs Cousins as Dotty had never seen her before. Her hair had been curled and she was wearing bright red lipstick and a low-cut flowered dress that left little to the imagination. The woman almost pounced on her.

'Ah, here you are, love,' she said. 'I've been waitin' for you an' I have a big favour to ask. Could yer keep yer ear out for the kids for me? They're all abed asleep, but I have to go out, see, an' I've no one else to ask. I shouldn't be gone that long – I promise.'

A waft of cheap perfume made Dotty blink in surprise. She had never seen Mrs Cousins in her glad rags before. Dotty had been up since six that morning and had been looking forward to falling into bed. But seeing the look on the woman's face, she felt herself melt.

'All right then, you get off and I'll keep my eye on them,' she promised. 'I'll pop down every fifteen minutes or so to check that they're all right.'

For a moment she was afraid that the woman was going to burst into tears as her heavily mascaraed eyes welled up. She seemed to be a bag of nerves, but then pulling herself together with an enormous effort, she forced a smile.

'You're a good girl, Dotty,' she said quietly, and then she was clattering away down the stairs in her high heels, making enough racket to waken the dead.

Dotty shook her head in bewilderment. I wonder what all that was about? she wondered, then she hurried on inside her flat. Thankfully, the noise travelled up to her flat from Mrs Cousins's rooms and if one of the children should wake and cry she had no doubt that she would hear them.

For the rest of the evening she crept into the children's bedrooms at regular intervals, but luckily each time she found them fast asleep. At eleven o'clock she went downstairs yet again, and she was just leaving when she almost collided with Mrs Cousins.

'Oh – so you're here then, Dotty.' The woman looked acutely embarrassed and as Dotty made to pass her she saw the reason why. Mrs Cousins had a man with her and from the way he was looking at her he hadn't come for tea and cake. As his eyes raked up and down Dotty she saw that he was in uniform and her stomach tightened. She knew how hard things had been for Mrs Cousins, but surely she hadn't resorted to bringing men back to make ends meet?

Mrs Cousins met her eye and she seemed to be silently imploring her not to judge her.

'Right, I'll be off now then,' Dotty forced herself to say in as normal a voice as she could manage. 'They're all asleep, Mrs Cousins. Goodnight.'

Once back out on the landing, she let out a deep breath as she pulled Mrs Cousins's door firmly shut. And then when the initial shock had worn off, she felt sad. Perhaps this was the only way the poor woman could think of to put food on the table for her children. She certainly wouldn't be the first to resort to walking the streets, and servicemen on leave were making whoopee with the local girls and women. They wanted to have a good time, and were prepared to pay for it. Dotty made her way back up the stairs with a heavy heart.

When she got in from work the next evening, Mrs Cousins was waiting for her again but this time she was in her usual clothes with the baby in her arms. 'Look, lass,' she said in a choked voice, 'I just wanted to say – please don't think too badly of me. I had no money for food, see, an' the kids were hungry, so—'

'I don't think badly of you,' Dotty butted in, sensing the woman's shame. 'I know how much you love your children and what a rotten go you've had of it. Sometimes desperate times call for desperate measures.' And with that she patted the woman's arm and shot away, thinking how unfair life could be.

Chapter Nineteen

It was now well into June and the weather was so glorious that the girls had taken to leaving the department store during their lunch break to enjoy a little sunshine. They didn't usually venture far and today was no exception as they strolled around the city centre, window shopping.

Lucy was quiet as usual. She seemed to have lost all her sparkle since her mother's death, and the other two had quickly discovered that even mentioning the poor woman was still strictly taboo.

Dotty, on the other hand, was bubbling over with excitement. 'I can't wait to go to London again next week,' she said. 'Robert is going to take me to meet the editor who is interested in my novel. I can hardly believe this is happening to me – but then he hasn't actually said that he'll be publishing it,' she had told them this about ten times in as many days, 'only that he's very interested and wants to talk to me.

But Robert will tell me more when he comes to visit me on Thursday.' She stopped to admire a leather handbag in a shop window. 'I don't know what he's going to think of my poky little flat though,' she confided anxiously. 'Last time I went to London he took me to see his flat and I think his lounge alone is bigger than the whole top floor of the house where I live. And it's so beautifully furnished. It's full of antiques that his mother collected over the years. I imagine they'd be worth a king's ransom, as she had impeccable taste. He might be selling it soon though,' she burbled on. 'He says it's too big for him, but I have a sneaky feeling he might be getting a place with Laura.' The thought of it made her throat tighten.

The girls had also heard all this before too and they grinned at each other behind Dotty's back. They didn't say anything though; it was nice to hear her so excited about the possibility of her book being published and they hoped that it would be.

'So what are you doing tonight then?' Annabelle asked them when they had managed to drag Dotty away from the shop window.

'Nothing much. I might wash my hair and have an early night,' Lucy answered. She hardly ever went anywhere any more except to work, but she was looking forward to a week off early in July when she was planning on visiting Mary in Folkestone. The kindly lady who was looking after the child had invited Lucy to stay for a few days if she wished, and the thought of seeing the little girl again was just about all that was keeping Lucy's spirits up at the moment. She wrote to her regularly and her kindly carer, Mrs Manners, assured her that she read the letters to Mary, not that the child would understand them, but the act obviously made Lucy feel a little better.

'And what about you?' Annabelle now looked questioningly at Dotty.

'I'm meeting Miss Timms after work for tea and so she can have a quick look at my book, then I shall be going home to carry on working on it. I want to try and get it finished for when Robert comes. But don't worry – I haven't forgotten that we're going to the pictures later this week.'

Annabelle sighed dramatically. 'You two are just no fun at all,' she drawled. 'So I dare say I shall have to stay in as well.' She checked the line she had drawn up the back of her leg with an eyebrow pencil then to make sure that it hadn't rubbed off.

'I really don't know how you manage to get those lines so straight,' Dotty commented. 'When I tried to do it, the lines were all over the place. And your legs are such a lovely colour!'

'I wash them in cold tea,' Annabelle told her. 'I get Mum to save the tea leaves now but it's a terrible palaver to get them this colour, I don't mind admitting. It was so much easier when you could just take a new pair of stockings out of the drawer.'

The girls then hurried back to work and the rest of the day passed uneventfully.

When they parted outside Owen Owen that evening, Dotty went back into the city centre where she had agreed to meet Miss Timms. The woman's face lit up as Dotty came towards her and she asked, 'How about we go into that little restaurant over there for tea? I've looked at the menu while I was waiting for you, and some of the meals seem quite nice. My treat, of course.'

Dotty felt embarrassed. She would much sooner have paid for her own meal, but not wishing to hurt the kindly woman's feelings or appear ungrateful she said, 'That would be lovely.'

Once inside they settled themselves at a table and ordered their food, which didn't take long as there wasn't a huge variety of dishes to choose from. While they were waiting for their sardines on toast to be served, Dotty took her manuscript out of her bag and handed it to Miss Timms to look at.

Miss Timms began to read, and was soon so enthralled that she almost forgot that Dotty was there.

'Miss Timms,' Dotty whispered after a time, 'our food is here.'

The woman shuffled the pages back together, looking flustered. 'I'm so sorry, my dear. I got quite carried away there and didn't want to stop. This is really excellent.'

Dotty blushed at the praise. She put a lot of store on what Miss Timms thought. They ate their sardines and then finished the meal off with home-made apple pie and custard, which was delicious.

'I don't think I shall be able to eat another thing for at least a month,' Dotty declared as she rubbed her full stomach.

Miss Timms smiled, making her appear years younger. 'I'm rather full too,' she beamed. 'But now I'm afraid I shall have to love you and leave you. I've left our neighbour with Mother, and no doubt the dear soul will be tearing her hair out by the roots by now. I'm afraid Mother isn't the easiest of patients.'

She insisted on paying the bill, and once outside she asked, 'Will you be all right getting home by yourself, dear?'

'Of course. You get off, I shall be fine, and thanks for the treat,' Dotty answered as she leaned forward to kiss the woman on the cheek.

The woman raised her hand and touched the spot that Dotty had kissed and a wave of tenderness shot through the girl. Miss Timms really was so kind and Dotty knew that she owed her a lot. Without Miss Timms her childhood would have been very lonely and sad. She watched the woman stride away, her back as straight as a broom handle, and then she hurried off to the stationer's, which was open until 7 p.m., to get some more ribbons for her typewriter. She just prayed that Mrs Cousins wouldn't want her to babysit tonight as she hoped to get some serious writing done.

Lucy arrived home to find a wonderful surprise waiting for her. It was a letter from Joel; albeit short and heavily censored, it helped her to believe that he was still safe. Or at least he had been when he wrote the letter, which she saw was well over a month ago. Without even waiting to take her cardigan off she sat down to read it, and as she saw his dear familiar writing he suddenly seemed a little closer.

Dear Lucy,

I hope you, Mother and Mary are all well. I am bearing up although I miss you all terribly. I am now in Dunkirk, (she only just managed to decipher this word as that and the next couple of lines had been blanked out, but then he went on), *things are pretty grim here but try not to worry, one day we'll all be together again and we'll try and put this blasted war behind us. Old Hitler has a lot to answer for and the conditions we are living in are pretty harsh, but then it can't go on forever, can it? Will you remember me to Mr and Mrs P and give Mary and Mum a big kiss from me and tell them that I think about them all the time. It's only the thought of coming home that keeps us lads going. I have written to Belle too and will write again to you both as soon as I can. Till then look after yourselves.*

Love,

Joel x

Annabelle also received a letter saying much the same and it threw her into a complete muddle.

My dear Belle,

I am hoping this letter will reach you as I may not be able to write again for some time. Me and the other chaps are going to the front tomorrow and who knows what might happen? I never realised what it would be like to have to point a gun at someone and pull the trigger but it's a case of kill or be killed. May God forgive me. I can't help but think that some of the Germans are probably only here because they have to be, like our lads, and the thought doesn't make it any easier. They are all someone's son, boyfriend, brother or husband after all, aren't they? I am sorry to be so morbid but I can't write my feelings to Lucy, she has enough on her plate. Bless her. You will keep an eye out for her if anything should happen to me won't you? I know this is a lot to ask but I feel that you, Lucy and Dotty have grown to be very close and she may have need of your friendship in the days ahead.

We are living in tents at the moment and the food is atrocious. If I come home I intend to take us all out for a slap-up meal! They are setting up the Army medical tents tonight for those that will no doubt be injured tomorrow and it's a daunting sight as you can imagine.

Anyway, that's enough from me. Stay safe, pray for me and know that I am thinking of you too.

With much love

Joel x

Annabelle shuddered as she folded the sheet of paper and pictured the conditions that Joel must be living in and what was before him. His life was in God's hands now and she could only pray that he would survive to return home.

Recently she had been able to push him to the back of her mind, but now she was forced to think of him again and she found herself wondering if their friendship might have turned into something more had he been able to stay around. In a way she was glad that he was gone. He wasn't at all the sort of chap she usually went out with, and nothing like the sort of husband she had always envisaged for herself. She wanted someone tall, dark, handsome and *very, very* rich – and Joel was none of those things. And yet she was forced to admit to herself that there had been an attraction between them from the start.

She read the letter through twice more before stuffing it into the back of a drawer. There was no point in thinking about it now. Joel might never come home for all she knew, so it was perhaps as well they hadn't grown too close. But still it was hard to forget him as she tried to turn her thoughts to other things.

On Thursday morning, Dotty was waiting for the train when it drew into Coventry station and she glanced expectantly into the carriages as it slowed. And then there was Robert walking towards her with an enormous bunch of flowers clutched in his good hand and her heart did a somersault.

Without being able to stop herself she raced towards him and then stopped abruptly in front of him feeling a complete fool. What must he think of me? she asked herself. It's hardly the way for a friend to behave. Yet deep down she knew that she thought of him as much more than a friend now, even though her feelings would never be returned.

He hugged her to him with his short arm while holding the flowers out to her with the other.

'Th-they're lovely,' she managed to stutter, deeply conscious of the passers-by who were smiling at them indulgently.

'Not half so lovely as you,' he answered, then it was his turn to blush as he took her arm and led her across the smoky platform to the exit.

It was on the bus to her flat that Dotty began to wonder if she had done the right thing in inviting Robert to her home. What would he think of it? It was so different to what he was used to – but it was too late to do anything about it now.

The smell of stale cabbage assailed them as they stepped into the hallway and she glanced at him apologetically. Unfortunately, it always smelled worse in the warm weather but there was nothing she could do about that either. The residents' staple diet nowadays seemed to consist mainly of Spam and any vegetables they had managed to grow in the small garden at the back of the house. The sight of a lush green lawn was a rare sight now, in this area at least, as everyone was using every available inch to grow food to supplement their rations – when they could fit them around the Anderson shelters, that was.

'It's up on the top floor,' she told him, avoiding his eyes, and they began to climb the steep narrow staircase.

As they passed Mrs Cousins's flat they heard the baby

crying and Dotty whispered, 'A widow lives there with her three young children. It's very sad – she lost her home when she lost her husband, and I know that she struggles now.'

'How awful for her.' Robert looked genuinely concerned as Dotty led him up the last flight of stairs.

'Phew, no wonder you're so thin,' he teased breathlessly as she finally put her key in the lock. 'That's quite some climb.'

'Well, we can't all have lifts,' she told him with a grin and she then beckoned him into her little home.

He looked about with interest before saying, 'You've got this really comfortable, Dotty. Very cosy, in fact. You have the same flair for home-making that my mother had.'

She looked around, trying to see it as he must but could see nothing very special about it, although she did keep it as neat as a new pin. Today she'd made an extra-special effort because he was coming. Every single thing in the room was second-hand but she had made it her own with cheerful cushions and a few cheap ornaments that she had bought from the market. The curtains had come from a rummage sale at the church hall and she had found the rug lying in front of the fire in a pawnshop.

'I'll make us some tea,' she said, and hurried across to the tiny kitchenette to put the kettle on. She'd saved up her food coupons for the last three weeks and now the smell of a lamb casserole slowly cooking wafted around the room. The oven was a very hit-and-miss affair, working when it felt like it, and she offered up a silent prayer of thanks that it hadn't let her down today.

'Something smells good,' he commented when she came back a few minutes later with a pot of tea. She knew that Robert had a sweet tooth so she had saved up her sugar ration too.

'Oh, it's just a lamb casserole,' she said casually, avoiding telling him that she had been up until late the night before reading recipe books. She found a jug to put her flowers in, and once they were standing in pride of place in the centre of the table she edged her manuscript towards him, telling him shyly, 'There you are. It's done. I finished it late last night, and I made a copy with carbon paper. There are another couple of short stories for you to look at too.'

He was just thinking what a remarkable young woman she was, when he suddenly remembered something. Taking a velvet box from his coat pocket, he handed it to her.

'I er . . . brought you a little gift,' he said. 'I hope you'll like it.'

Dotty was flummoxed and it showed. 'But you already bought me flowers,' she objected. 'There was really no need to bring anything at all.'

'Even so I want you to have it. Open it, please.'

She hesitated before taking the box from him, and when she opened it her eyes stretched wide and she was rendered temporarily speechless. Inside on a bed of silk was a gold locket on a fine gold chain. A red stone that was set into the centre of the locket glittered in the sunlight that was filtering through the window.

'That's a ruby,' he told her softly. 'And it belonged to my mother.'

Now she did react. 'Then I really can't take it,' she told him hastily, 'It . . . it must be very precious to you.'

He shook his head. 'No, I want *you* to have it – and I have a feeling that if my mother could have known you, she would have wanted you to have it too. It was her mother's before her, and seeing as I have no sisters to pass it on to, it's a shame for it to lie in its box. You *do* like it, don't you?'

'Like it?' Dotty was stunned. 'But *of course* I like it! It's the most beautiful thing I've ever seen – but I'm afraid it must be very valuable.'

He shrugged. 'It probably is, so it's only right that it should go to someone who will treasure it, and I have a feeling that you will.'

'But Robert, you hardly know me,' Dotty protested. 'I don't think you should be giving this away.'

'But I'm not exactly giving it away, am I?' He smiled now as he lifted it from the box. 'I'm entrusting it to someone who will love it as much as my mother did. Now turn around while I fasten it on for you.'

Dotty did as she was told as Robert struggled with the tiny catch. It wasn't easy with his withered hand but at last he told her, 'There you go. Have a look in the mirror over there. What do you think?'

Dotty crossed to the mirror and gently stroked the gift, still feeling in a state of shock. She had never owned a single piece of jewellery in her whole life and still didn't feel quite comfortable accepting it. But she knew that if she didn't, she might hurt his feelings and she didn't want to risk doing that.

'I really shall treasure it,' she told him in a choky voice. 'But I'll only accept it on the understanding that should you ever want it back, you would tell me. We'll consider I have it on loan.'

'Fair enough, but it will be a permanent loan,' he told her with a twinkle in his eye. 'I don't think it ever looked as good on Mother as it does on you. And I'm sure she wouldn't mind me saying that.'

She impulsively leaned over and kissed him then; thanking her lucky stars for the day she had met him and thinking what a lovely woman his mother must have been.

He looked momentarily surprised but then he lifted his mug of tea and the awkward moment passed.

Their time together raced by all too quickly. They had the lunch that Dotty had prepared, which Robert insisted was delicious, and then at his request she took him back into the city centre to see St Michael's Cathedral. They then had afternoon tea at a restaurant – home-baked scones with jam and cream – a rare treat indeed – before slowly making their way back to the railway station.

'I've had a wonderful day,' he told her sincerely as they stood on the platform waiting for his train to pull in. 'I almost don't want to go home. The time seems to have flown by.'

Dotty felt the same and merely nodded because the lump that had formed in her throat was stopping her from saying anything. He had a bag with her manuscript tucked safely away inside it and now he told her, 'I shall get this to Paul, my editor friend, first thing in the morning. I know he's longing to read the rest of it, and between you and me, by the time you come next week I have a funny feeling I might have good news for you.'

Dotty felt bereft as he stepped onto the train after giving her a quick hug. Then he appeared in a carriage window and she waved until she felt as if her arm was about to drop off.

'Until next week,' he mouthed through the glass as the train chugged back into life. And then she was walking and running alongside it until she reached the end of the platform and the train disappeared in a cloud of smoke.

She moved disconsolately to the entrance and headed for the bus station, but she had gone no further than a few hundred yards when a piercing siren sounded. People were panicking and scattering in every direction as they rushed for cover, and it was then that she realised what the sound was: one that the people of Coventry had hoped never to hear. The siren was warning them that an air raid was imminent. For a moment Dotty was rooted to the spot and strangely her first fear was for Robert. A moving train on an open track would be an easy target from the air, and were the Jerries to drop a bomb on it, the people inside would stand no chance. But then surely they would be targeting the factories?

As her footsteps slowed, someone suddenly grabbed her elbow and barked, 'Come wi' me, love. There's a shelter just down 'ere as will 'ouse at least a hundred people.'

Dotty made to pull away as panic engulfed her, but the man hauled her along as if she weighed no more than a feather and soon he was shoving her ahead of him into a dimly lit space that seemed to be full to overflowing with terrified people all talking and crying.

As Dotty's eyes adjusted to the light she saw a young woman with a baby clutched tightly to her chest with tears streaming down her cheeks. There were people of all shapes, sizes and ages, but fear was on all their faces. The siren seemed to rip through every part of her, setting her nerves jangling – but then suddenly another noise sounded and leaning forward she stared up into the sky to see a large dark mass fast approaching high above. For a start it appeared like an enormous swarm of bumblebees, but as it drew closer the drone became louder and she saw that it was enemy planes.

'Shut the door, for Christ's sake,' someone shouted from the back of the shelter and instantly two men leaped forward and there was a loud clang as the metal door slammed shut. Every sound was magnified as Dotty found herself in total darkness and she put her hands out wildly until they connected with another person. Then someone started to light some candles and suddenly the darkness was not quite so all-consuming. At the same instant, the ack-ack guns roared into life as they tried to intercept the enemy. Dotty clapped her hands over her ears and shrank against the wall as she prayed for the raid to end. And yet deep down she wondered if this was only the beginning.

Chapter Twenty

Time became irrelevant as the people in the shelter sat white-faced, wondering if they would ever get out of there in one piece. And if they did, what would they be going out to? Would their homes still be standing, their loved ones still alive?

And then the sound of an enormous explosion reached them, followed shortly by another and then another.

No one could have any idea what was being targeted, but one man muttered, 'God help us, some poor buggers are coppin' it.'

'Looks like it's our turn now,' someone else said fearfully. 'They must be givin' them poor sods in London a night off.'

Dotty wrapped her arms about herself as her thoughts returned to Robert. London had been under attack for weeks and she worried about him every single day, although up to now the Germans had been targeting the docks and the East

End. The first wave of bombs had hit the Royal Victoria Docks, and soon after the East and West India Docks had become prey to the Messerschmitts and Heinkels that had now become a far too familiar sight in the skies above London. Madame Tussaud's had also been destroyed. The Tower of London had been hit, though not too badly, and some of the West End shops had also suffered damage. She wondered what Robert would be going home to.

There was nothing to be heard within the sanctuary; everyone was holding their breath, and as they stood huddled there in the semi-darkness, two more explosions sounded. And then the roar of the planes could be heard again as they turned from wherever they had been bombing and flew back directly over them. The roar became a drone before fading to a distant buzz, then dying away altogether.

'Do yer reckon they've gone?' A woman's terrified voice broke the silence but for a while no one answered.

And then someone said, 'Do yer think it's safe to go back out there yet?'

'Not until the all-clear sounds,' someone else warned. 'They might come back again.'

The woman clutching the baby began to cry, yet strangely the child was silent; he had fallen fast asleep impervious to the danger they were all in.

And then at last the sound they had all been waiting for came and two men wrestled to pull the heavy metal doors open. It was growing dusk by now but even so, the dim light that flooded the shelter was the most welcome sight that Dotty had ever seen.

They staggered out into the cooling evening and looked about, then someone said, 'Over there – look. Seems they've hit Ansty Aerodrome from the direction o' the smoke.'

In the distance a great pall of smoke was rising into the sky like some ugly great giant, but thankfully, the area around them appeared to be untouched.

People began to drift away, intent on getting home in case the Germans should return. Dotty stood for a time silently staring at the smoke in the distance and then she too set off, her shaking legs barely able to take her weight. She headed for the bus station, relieved to see that this, too, was untouched, and soon after she boarded the bus.

When her home came into sight, Dotty rushed towards it and as she climbed the stairs Mrs Cousins came out to meet her on the landing.

'Oh love, I'm so pleased to see yer,' she babbled. 'It says on the wireless that the bastards 'ave bombed Ansty Aerodrome, but no one's said if anyone was hurt yet.'

'I can't see how there couldn't have been any casualties,' Dotty answered sombrely. 'I got dragged into the shelter up by the station, but even from there we all clearly heard five explosions. Are the children all right?'

'They're all fine. Thankfully the oldest two were fast asleep an' the little 'un is too young to understand what was happenin'.'

'But didn't you get them all down into the cellar?' Dotty asked.

Mrs Cousins shook her head. 'No, I didn't. If I'd woken 'em up they'd 'ave been terrified so I decided to risk it an' stay where we were.'

'But you wouldn't have stood a chance up here,' Dotty pointed out and Mrs Cousins shrugged.

'At least we'd 'ave all gone together,' she muttered. 'The older two won't be around fer much longer anyway. I've agreed they can go wi' the next lot of evacuees, then I'll only 'ave the little 'un to worry about.'

'It might be wise,' Dotty agreed, but she felt so sad for the woman. She'd already lost her husband and soon she would be losing two of her children too, for a time at least.

She had been at home for less than an hour when she heard someone clattering up the stairs and Miss Timms burst into the room without knocking. Dotty had been so shaken up that she had forgotten to lock the door.

'Oh thank God you're all right,' the woman croaked breathlessly when she saw Dotty. 'I was so worried that something might have happened to you. I've left Mother with a neighbour while I came to check.'

The woman was red in the face and breathless and Dotty led her to a chair before fetching her a drink of water. She was deeply touched that Miss Timms had been so concerned about her.

'I'm fine, as you can see,' she assured her, 'although I have to say when the siren went off it nearly scared me to death. I'd just seen Robert off at the railway station and started for home when it happened, but some man dragged me into a shelter and I stayed there until the all-clear sounded.'

Miss Timms gulped at the water and nodded, then was instantly on her feet again. 'Well, I can't stay, dear. The sirens shook Mother up too and I don't want to leave her alone for too long. But promise me that if this happens again, you'll take shelter.'

'Of course I will.' Dotty saw her to the door where she kissed her on the cheek, deciding she would give it another couple of hours and then she would walk to the phone box and ring Robert just to make sure that he had arrived home safely. The day had been perfect until the sirens sounded – which just went to show that you never knew what life had in store for you.

*

'I went into Mrs P's Anderson shelter,' Lucy told them the next morning at work.

'And Mother and I went down into the cellar.' Annabelle shuddered at the thought of it. She had been so confident that the raids would never reach them, but she wasn't so cocky now. 'It was horrible,' she groaned. 'And so *cold.* It was lucky that Mother had remembered to take blankets down there. You don't think it will happen again, do you?'

'I think we should prepare ourselves just in case,' Lucy said quietly. Just over an hour ago the staff had been called together and told by the manager that should the sirens go off during work hours, they were all to make their way down into the basement in an orderly manner. 'No running or panicking the customers, mind,' he had warned them.

'As if we *wouldn't* panic,' Lucy had scoffed behind her hand to the other two. 'I reckon there'd be a right scramble, customers and staff alike.'

Mr Bradley had posted signs around the shop telling customers where to go in case of a raid.

'I don't mind admitting I nearly wet myself when the siren went off,' Lucy told the others. 'I thought it was a false alarm at first until I heard the planes overhead and then I was off around to Mrs P's like a shot from a gun.'

Suddenly what they had all dreaded was a reality and there was no getting away from it any more.

'It wouldn't do us much good down in the basement anyway,' Annabelle grumbled. 'Not if the store took a direct hit. There'd be mountains of rubbish on top of us and they'd never dig us out.'

'It's amazing that no one was killed at the aerodrome,' Dotty agreed. 'But I do think that now they've been once, the German planes will come again. It said on the wireless this morning that they think they'll target the factories next.'

They all looked at each other glumly knowing there was nothing at all anyone could do to stop it now. The Phoney War had become all too real.

The next raid happened the following evening.

Lucy and Dotty had accepted Annabelle's invitation to go to tea, but they had barely set foot in the door after a long day at work when the sirens screamed into life.

'Each of you grab some food off the table and follow me down to the cellar,' Miranda told them as calmly as she could, and the girls quickly did as they were told. Dotty picked up a large bowl of salad and a plate of bread scraped with margarine, whilst Lucy lifted up the tray with the tea things on it and Annabelle picked up a plate of thinly sliced brawn and pickled beetroot.

Miranda threw open the door at the far end of the kitchen and one by one they climbed down the steps into the dark cellar. The walls were damp and the place was dismal despite Miranda's best efforts to make it comfortable.

'There are only two chairs down here,' she shouted above the screech of the sirens. 'But there are some crates over there we can sit on. Come on, we may as well eat. There's nothing else we can do.'

And then they heard it, the slow buzz of the enemy aircraft approaching followed by the sound of the ack-ack guns firing into life. They all glanced up at the ceiling fearfully as the buzz became a drone and then a snarl.

'They must be directly above us now,' Miranda whispered as she made the sign of the cross on her chest. The sound slowly subsided, followed by the bang of the first explosion and they all jumped. Then there was another and another, and Annabelle panicked and clasped her hands over her ears to try and shut out the noise.

'It's all right, darling,' her mother comforted her as she pressed her close. 'We'll be quite safe in here.'

Within minutes they all realised that this was far worse than the first raid. The explosions seemed to go on forever and they sounded so close that the four women had no idea where the bombs might be falling. The food lay on an upturned crate untouched; everyone seemed to have lost their appetites although Miranda did manage to pour them all some tea and urged them to drink it. 'It will warm you up,' she told them and they each did as she asked.

'What time do you think it is?' Annabelle asked in a small voice after what felt like an eternity. The sounds of the enemy planes flying over them were so loud that they were sure they would crash into the roof of the house.

'I don't know, but I've got some candles somewhere.' Miranda stood and began to rummage about until she found them. She quickly lit one with a box of matches she had ready beside them. A flicker of light illuminated their pale faces as the wick began to burn and Miranda gave them all a wobbly smile.

'There. That's better, isn't it?' But they could barely hear her for the planes growling overhead.

The candle slowly burned down and soon they had lost all sense of time as they crouched there wondering what they were going to come out of the cellar to – *if* they ever came out, that was. Dotty dropped into an exhausted doze and Miranda rose to find another candle. It was as she was lighting it that the tumult outside began to quieten down and she said hopefully, 'Listen . . . I think they've gone.'

But they sat on until at last they heard the all-clear.

Dotty woke and one by one they climbed the steep cellar steps. It was dark when they entered the kitchen and

Miranda hurried to the window and closed the blackout curtains before switching the light on.

'Let's see if there's anything on the wireless,' she suggested as she twiddled the knob. It crackled into life and soon the announcer's grave voice reached them.

'The Hillfields area of Coventry was heavily bombed tonight, but as yet no one can say how many fatalities there have been. The Army are digging people from the rubble of what were their homes, and it is feared that many lives have been lost. Meantime, those whose homes have been damaged are asked to report to their nearest church hall where they will be provided with food and temporary shelter.'

Dotty clapped her hand over her mouth as they looked towards her and without a word being said they were all thinking the same thing. Would her home still be standing?

Miranda snapped to attention at the sound of ambulance bells and fire engines clanging past the end of the drive.

'I must go,' she said, reaching for her coat. 'I'm off to Hillfields. The WVS will need all the help they can get, but I want you all to promise me that you will stay here. I don't want you two girls trying to get home tonight, and if the siren goes off again you are to head straight back down into the cellar. Will you promise me that you'll do that?'

'But how will you get there?' Annabelle asked. 'I doubt there will be any buses running.'

'In the car, of course. I've saved some cans of petrol in the garage so I have some at hand for emergencies.'

'I'm coming with you,' Dotty stated with determination.

'I don't think that's a good idea, love,' Miranda told the distraught girl. 'Why don't you let me go first and see how bad things are? I can check that your house is still intact. You'll be quite safe here.'

'You don't *understand*!' Dotty said urgently as she grabbed her coat. 'I don't care about the house – that's just bricks and mortar – but what about Mrs Cousins and her children? They're my neighbours and I have to know that they're all right.'

'In that case we'll come too,' Lucy piped up. 'Won't we, Annabelle? There might be something we can do to help as well.'

Miranda looked decidedly unhappy about the suggestion but it was three against one and she saw no point in arguing.

'Very well then,' she reluctantly agreed and the girls followed her out to the garage.

As they approached Hillfields they felt as if they were driving into a nightmare. Thick black smoke and flames were belching into the sky from what only hours before had been people's homes, and the police had set up road-blocks to prevent traffic from entering the bombed area.

'We shall have to park here and walk the rest of the way,' Miranda told them as she pulled into the side of the road. 'The WVS will have set up food and shelter for those that need it in the church hall in the next street. I'm sure they'll be glad of as much help as they can get.'

They all clambered out of the car and made their way on foot into the chaos. Army lorries were parked higgledy-piggledy, and they could see the men digging frantically in the rubble for survivors.

'Over here, I thought I heard something!' one young private shouted, and the other men raced towards him to help.

Appalled, Dotty stared at the pile of bricks, certain that no one could survive if that lot had toppled on them, but the men worked furiously, determined to get to anyone who might still be alive.

They walked on a little further and Lucy's eyes filled with

tears as she saw a bloodstained teddy bear lying in the middle of the road next to yet another bombed house.

'My God, it must have been blown out through a window when the bombs struck,' she wept. 'Some poor child must have been holding it.' She couldn't help thinking about her little Mary. In fact, not a second passed when she didn't think about her. Lucy broke down and dropped to her knees, sobbing as her small frame rocked in distress. Annabelle reached for her and held her, rubbing her back in comfort. And then at last Lucy managed to pull herself together enough to proceed and they moved on.

When the church hall came into sight they pelted towards it, but the sight that met their eyes when they opened the door made them all stop in their tracks. Injured people were lying on the floor on blankets everywhere they looked, as the women from the WVS darted between them trying to do what they could. And then Dotty's eyes settled on a tiny figure and she gasped. An ambulance man was leaning over it but she knew instantly that this was Mrs Cousins's baby. She would have recognised her anywhere.

'I know this child,' she told the man breathlessly. 'But where are her mother and her brother and sister?'

'I don't know, love,' he breathed sadly. 'But I do know it's too late for this poor little mite.' Even as he spoke he gently closed the baby's eyes and Dotty began to cry.

'What are you doing?' she sobbed. 'Stop it! She *can't* be dead. She's just a baby.'

He rose wearily and patted her arm. The sights he had seen that night would stay with him forever – and the night was far from over yet.

'I'm afraid she didn't stand a chance,' he said. 'The terrace of houses where we found her took a direct hit.'

Dotty's heart sank. That could only mean that Mrs

Cousins and the other two children must have been inside too. Mrs Cousins hated the shelters and made no secret of the fact that if a raid came she would rather stay put and take her chances. Now her decision had cost her dearly and Dotty also realised that her own little flat must be gone. But there was no time to worry about that for now.

Miranda was already helping the women, carrying drinks of water to the wounded and putting temporary dressings on their wounds as the ambulance men and women gingerly walked between them trying to see who needed to get to the hospital first.

'Come on, girls,' Miranda told them. 'It's time to put your first aid training into practice. All the bandages and dressings are on a table over there, look. Just do what you can.'

And so began the longest night of the girls' lives.

Chapter Twenty-One

As the night progressed, things in the church hall became even more chaotic as ARPs, ambulance men and women and Army personnel carried more injured into the hall on makeshift stretchers.

Those who were beyond help were carried to a far corner which was curtained off, and they were covered with a blanket until they could be identified. For now, everyone's attention must be centred on the living. Above the hall searchlights still swept the sky and people held their breath, praying that there would be no more raids that night. Even more people arrived; those who had emerged from their shelters to find their homes nothing more than a pile of rubble. White-faced and dazed, they were served tea from the large urns that had been set up at one end of the hall, and wrapped in warm blankets. Some of the luckier ones had friends and neighbours who came and took them into their own homes. The less fortunate would stay the night in the hall once all the injured had been transported to hospital, until they decided where they were going to go. And through it all the fire engines struggled to bring the flames of the various fires under control whilst the soldiers continued to dig amongst the debris for survivors.

At one stage, Miranda paused to see what the girls were doing. She was binding a badly fractured leg and was shocked to see Annabelle cradling an old woman in her arms as she gently poured water into her mouth. Miranda's heart melted at the sight of her normally selfish daughter showing such compassion, and her chest swelled with pride. Annabelle had enjoyed the first aid classes, and now what she had learned was being put to good use. Lucy was serving tea to the homeless and Dotty was cradling a child of no more than five years old in her arms as he cried pitifully for his mother.

And then the door opened and two Army corporals appeared carrying two small children who lay limply in their arms. The men's faces were blackened with soot and one of them was crying unashamedly.

Miranda instantly turned to another WVS worker and once she had taken over binding the man's leg, Miranda crossed to the curtain at the end of the room and held it aside as the soldiers carried the little bodies behind it.

Dotty saw them from the corner of her eye and vomit rose in her throat as she hastily passed the child she was nursing to the woman nearest to her. She hurried across the room and as the soldiers gently laid the children down with the rest of the dead, she began to cry.

'It's Mrs Cousins's other two children,' she choked. 'But wasn't there a woman with them?'

One of the soldiers answered her wearily. 'If there was, we haven't come across her yet.' He looked ready to drop with fatigue. 'But we're still digging, so we could still find her.'

Dotty squeezed her eyes tight shut, knowing full well that if she hadn't gone to Annabelle's for tea she too might well have been lying with the bodies behind the curtain. And then suddenly a woman erupted into the hall and began to wail.

'My babies . . . where are my babies?'

Dotty blinked, scarcely able to believe her eyes as Mrs Cousins staggered towards her. She was dressed in her Sunday best although she looked decidedly dishevelled now, and when she saw Dotty she grabbed her arms and began to shake her.

'Did yer get the message I left taped to yer door?' she asked desperately, her eyes wild. 'An' what have yer done with the kids? Are they safe?'

Dotty stared at her in confusion. 'I didn't go home after work tonight,' she told her as calmly as she could. 'So I have no idea what you're talking about, Mrs Cousins. But I'm afraid . . .' she gulped deep in her throat before forcing herself to go on. 'I'm afraid the children are all in here. These soldiers have just brought the older two in.'

The woman pushed past her and as her eyes settled on the two little broken bodies she started to shake as she dropped to her knees at the side of them.

'And the baby?'

'I'm afraid she is here too. Over there.'

'This is all my fault,' the woman muttered brokenly. 'I had to go out to earn some money, see? Otherwise the kids would have had nowt to eat tomorrow. So I thought, if I go now, young Dotty'll keep her ear open for 'em when she gets in.' Her head wagged from side to side in shocked disbelief. 'But Dotty didn't come in, which meant the kids would 'ave been all alone when the raid started. They must 'ave been so scared! An' when the warnin' went off I were over the other side o' the city, but I told meself, "They'll be all right, Dotty'll get 'em into the shelter."' When she looked Miranda in the eye, Miranda saw the light of madness shining there and she took the woman in her arms as tears started to her own eyes. What comfort could she give her under such horrific circumstances?

'I might as well 'ave killed 'em meself,' Mrs Cousins said in a voice barely above a whisper, and then she laughed – a horrible, grotesque laugh that grated on the nerves of everyone who heard it. 'I left me kids to die alone. What sort o' mother does that make me, eh?'

'I'm sure you had good reason for doing what you did,' Miranda soothed. 'But now please come away. I'll get you a nice hot drink.' The words seemed so inadequate. This poor woman was almost beside herself with grief, and quite understandably so. It would have been tragic if she had lost one child – but to lose all three? Miranda couldn't even begin to imagine the suffering she must be going through.

Mrs Cousins allowed Miranda to steer her through the sea of people as if she were in a trance, and Dotty watched with tears pouring down her grimy face. Poor Mrs Cousins. First she had lost her husband and now her children. Knowing how much the woman had loved them, Dotty wondered how she would bear it. If only she had gone straight home after work and seen Mrs Cousins's message, she might have been able to get the children into a shelter.

'Someone will have to fetch more water from the stand-pipe,' one of the volunteers shouted then. 'The tap's run dry. The water-pipe in the road must have ruptured.'

'I'll go,' Dotty said as she took a large tin bucket from the woman and headed for the door. Right then anything was preferable to having to watch the look of absolute misery on Mrs Cousins's face. Once outside she stumbled through the debris until she came to the temporary standpipe that the Army had set up at the end of the road. On one side of the road a woman was digging through the rubble of her home with bare hands trying to find any undamaged possessions and Dotty thought it was one of the most desolate sights she had ever seen as she quickly averted her eyes. She wasn't sure how much more she could take. Once she had filled the bucket she staggered back the way she had come, wishing with all her heart that she could be a million miles away.

As the first light of dawn tinged the sky the last casualties were finally transported to hospital. Many of the homeless had already fallen into an exhausted sleep right where they sat but the women then made up makeshift beds for those who were still awake. And then, at last, when they were quite sure that there was nothing else they could do for now and other WVS helpers had come in to take over from them, the four women walked out into the early morning light, bone weary and sick at heart at the sights they had witnessed, promising that they would be back as soon as they had had some rest.

Miranda had spent most of the night trying to comfort Mrs Cousins. A doctor had seen her and given her a sleeping draught, and at last the poor tormented woman had slept from complete exhaustion. Miranda had fussed over her like a mother hen and now she was drained both mentally and physically.

There was no thought of the girls turning in to work for that day at least. One of the Red Cross workers had managed to get the address of Mrs Cousins's sister, who lived in Wales, and Dotty was hoping that she would come to fetch her once the Red Cross were able to contact her. Meanwhile, she would be cared for at the church hall. There was nowhere else for the poor woman to go, and although Dotty was aware that there were those who would condemn her once they found out that she had left her three children in alone, Dotty knew that she had only done it out of desperation.

'I must phone Robert,' she said now, rubbing her eyes, which were gritty from lack of sleep. 'He'll be worried sick if he hears on the news that Hillfields has been bombed. But first I need to go and see what's left of my flat.'

'Are you sure that's wise, dear?' Miranda asked. 'It can only upset you and you're more than welcome to stay with us for as long as you like.'

Dotty shook her head. 'No, it's something I need to do. But I do appreciate your offer.'

They walked in silence through the shattered streets, appalled at the sights they witnessed. Soldiers, who looked almost dead on their feet, were still frantically digging amongst tons of bricks, their ears strained for the least sound that might tell them that a survivor was buried beneath the mess. They had worked tirelessly throughout the long night and Miranda couldn't help but admire them.

'If our boys at the front are half as good as these men, we'll win this bloody war eventually,' she declared defiantly, hoping to give the girls a sliver of hope. Annabelle raised her eyebrows, surprised to hear her mother swear. It was a first, but then so was what they were witnessing.

Fire engines were still damping down fires, and ash floated in the air, settling on their clothes and making them all appear a ghostly grey. And then at last they turned the corner into Dotty's road and her flat, or what was left of it, came into view.

She pressed her knuckles into her mouth to prevent a sob

from escaping as it came to her that she now had nothing more than the clothes she was standing up in. The house was merely a towering heap of smoking rubble.

'Come away now.' Miranda placed her arm about the distressed girl's shaking shoulders. 'We'll go and find the car then we'll go home and have something to eat and a short rest before we come back to the church hall. We'll need to get changed as well. We all stink of smoke.' She refrained from mentioning the bloodstains on their clothes from the many wounded people they had helped during the night. And all the time her mind was firmly fixed on her husband. If things were so awful for them, who were only left to deal with the aftermath of the attacks, what must it be like for Richard and his comrades, who were fighting on the front line? She could only pray that he would stay safe.

'There's one problem with your suggestion,' Dotty said wryly. 'What do I change *into?*' Her heart broke afresh as she thought of the one beautiful outfit she had possessed, hidden now beneath tons of rubbish. Thank God, she thought, that she always wore the locket, and that most of the stories were safe in the London offices of *Woman's Heart*. Ah, but her precious typewriter . . .

'That's not a problem,' Annabelle assured her, squeezing her hand. 'I've got loads of clothes you can have.'

They were back at the end of the road by now, and Lucy told them, 'I'm going to head home now, if you don't mind. Mrs P will be worried sick and I need to let her know that I'm safe. But I'll see you all back at the church hall this afternoon, shall I?'

'I doubt that there will be any buses running yet,' Miranda said. 'Come on, I'll give you a lift home on our way back.' And so they all trooped on until they came to the car, which was covered in a thick layer of ash and brick dust.

*

When Dotty managed to find a telephone box and rang Robert later that afternoon, she heard the relief in his voice when he answered.

'Thank God you're safe,' he told her. 'I've been going out of my mind with worry. In fact, I was about to see if the trains were still running normally and to come up to try and find you.'

'I'm fine,' Dotty assured him. 'But my flat isn't. It was razed to the ground unfortunately, so I'm going to stay with Annabelle and her mother for the time being.'

'But you could come here,' he suggested quickly, and Dotty's heart warmed at his obvious concern for her as she fingered the gold locket he had given her, which was hanging safely about her neck. When he had first given it to her, she had been almost afraid to wear it, it was so precious. But now she was glad that she had chosen to, otherwise it would have been lost forever beneath the shell of her burned-out home.

'I appreciate the offer, Robert, but I'm all right, really. And I still have my job to go to, which is something.'

'Hmm.' He didn't sound too happy about things. 'Then I shall come to you on Thursday instead of you coming to me. You won't have the money for the fare now so I shall bring you some cash to tide you over,' he said in a voice that told her he wouldn't take no for an answer. 'And we'll go shopping and get you some new clothes and basic essentials too. You must have lost everything.'

'I have,' she admitted, fighting back the tears which were always dangerously close to erupting at the moment. 'But I don't want you spending your money on me. It wouldn't be right.'

'Very well then, if you feel like that I shall give you an

advance on your fees. Shall we say the next twelve months?'

'But a lot of my stories were in the flat,' she explained in a small voice.

He snorted. 'That's the least of your worries. You can write some more, and luckily I have quite a few here that you gave me to look at, so you won't be under any immediate pressure.'

Once again Dotty thought what a remarkable man he was and she felt slightly better. And at least she could look forward to seeing him again now. It would give her something to focus on.

Mrs P was highly relieved too, when Lucy walked through the door.

'Yer look like somethin' the cat's dragged in, love!' she exclaimed, drawing Lucy towards the settee. 'Wherever have yer been? I thought yer were goin' to Annabelle's, so how have yer got in this state?'

The girl quickly explained as Mrs P put the kettle on to boil and the woman sighed. 'It's a bad do, ain't it? But then I think we all knew deep down that it were comin'. An' accordin' to my Fred, this is only the beginnin'. God help us!'

At that moment someone rapped on the front door and Mrs P looked up. 'I wonder who that is? Most people I know always come round to the back.'

She pottered away, tightening her flowered pinny about her waist as Lucy sat fighting to stay awake.

Lucy heard her open the front door, but then there was nothing and she started to get concerned. Struggling to climb off the overstuffed settee, she walked into the front room to find Mrs P staring down at a brown envelope in her hand, her face the colour of putty.

'It's a telegram,' she breathed fearfully.

'Perhaps it's good news. Perhaps they've found Freddy somewhere?' Lucy said hopefully. 'Aren't you going to open it?'

Mrs P's head wagged from side to side. 'I daren't. Will you open it for me, luvvie?'

With a sick feeling of dread Lucy took the envelope from the woman's hand. She slit it open with her thumb then quickly read what was written on it before looking at Mrs P gravely.

'He's dead, ain't he?' Mrs P's voice was dead too.

Lucy found that she couldn't speak for the lump in her throat so she merely nodded.

'I knew it,' Mrs P muttered. 'In here I knew it.' She placed her hand over her heart. 'Right from the day when we had that first telegram sayin' he were missin' I had this empty place inside an' I knew that he were gone. I'd 'ave felt it if he were still alive, God bless his soul.'

Lucy felt completely and utterly devastated. This, on top of what she had witnessed the night before, was just too much and she had the urge to run away and hide. But of course, she couldn't do that. Mrs P needed her.

Hurrying out of the front door, she shot off down the next entry where she found Mrs Bloomfield, her next-door-but-one-neighbour hanging out her washing in the yard.

The woman looked at the state of her in amazement, but before she could comment, Lucy gasped out, 'Mrs Bloomfield, Mrs P has just had some really bad news. Do you think your Eric could go and fetch Mr P from work?'

'Of course he will, love,' the woman said, guessing what the bad news was. She had seen the telegram boy through her front window and felt guilty because she was so relieved he hadn't stopped at her house. Derek, her youngest, was away in the RAF.

Not stopping to thank her, Lucy then ran back to find Mrs P still standing exactly where she had left her. She could hear the kettle whistling its head off and went to switch off the gas.

The next three-quarters of an hour passed interminably slowly as Lucy watched the hands of the clock on the mantelpiece. Mrs P sat where Lucy had put her as if she had been carved in stone, with not a tear in sight, until at last, Mr P burst into the room.

'So what's to do then, ducks?' He threw his snap tin on the table as his wife handed him the telegram and once he had read it, his face crumpled. Then surprisingly it was Mrs P comforting him.

'Come on now,' she soothed. 'It's strange . . . but I think I've already done my grievin'. In fact, in a funny sort o' way it's a relief to know what's happened to him, official-like. I knew he were gone from the time we had the first telegram, but now we can hold a memorial service fer him. Our lad were a hero, Fred, an' we must *never* lose sight o' that. We can be proud he died fighting for his country an' what he believed in.'

She glanced towards the photo of young Freddy standing next to the clock on the mantelpiece all upright and proud in his soldier's uniform, with a watery smile on her face, and suddenly feeling in the way, Lucy slipped out of the back door leaving the bereaved parents to grieve in privacy.

Chapter Twenty-Two

Robert did manage to get to Coventry on the following Thursday and Dotty as usual was waiting at the station to meet him wearing clothes that she had borrowed from Annabelle.

'She and her mum have been marvellous to me,' she told him once they had greeted each other. 'And they've made me feel so welcome. But between you and me it isn't like having your own front door. I think I might start to look around for another flat to rent soon when things have quietened down. And of course I shall have to get myself another typewriter.'

'*If* they quieten down,' Robert commented grimly. 'The newspapers reckon this is only the beginning, which is why I wish you'd come to London with me, Dotty.'

'But it will be no safer there than it is here,' Dotty pointed out. 'And I've had no shortage of offers of a home. Miss Timms said I could go and stay with her too, bless her. Her mother died of a heart attack on the night of the raid, although I don't think it was entirely unexpected. She's been poorly for a long time, and reading between the lines I think she ran poor Miss Timms ragged. She wasn't a very easy patient and was quite a strict, highly religious person from the bits that I've picked up on. Mind you, she was still her mother at the end of the day, wasn't she?'

Seeing the sadness that flitted across Dotty's face, Robert's heart went out to her. It couldn't have been easy for her being brought up in an orphanage not knowing who her parents were, or even why they had chosen to abandon her, which was why he was so surprised at how nice Dotty had turned out to be. She didn't seem to have a single nasty bone in her body and always had a kind word for everyone.

'How about we head for the centre?' he suggested now. 'I'm determined to get you some clothes of your own before I go back. I've brought some cash and clothes coupons.' He tapped his coat pocket and winked at her. 'You'd be surprised what money can buy, even in wartime. It's like they say – money talks. Oh, and we'll get you another typewriter as well while we're at it. We can't have you slacking, can we?'

Dotty knew that he was only trying to cheer her up, but she was so down in the dumps that she doubted anything would do that.

Once outside the station they decided to walk into town. It was a beautiful day and they both wanted to take advantage of the sunshine while they could. On their way, Dotty told him all about Mrs Cousins and her children, shedding tears, and he sucked in his breath and squeezed her hand in his good one. Dotty still felt terribly guilty because she hadn't gone straight home that dreadful night and found the note that poor Mrs Cousins had left for her, and she knew that she always would.

'Her sister came to fetch her to go and live with her and her family in Wales,' Dotty said, wiping her eyes, 'but Mrs Cousins wouldn't go until they had buried her children. I went to the funeral. Poor thing, I think she'll always blame herself – if only I had gone straight home!'

'You couldn't have known what was going to happen, and she was only doing what she had to do, to feed her children,' Robert said with no condemnation whatsoever. 'I think this war is making a lot of people do things that they wouldn't normally dream of doing.'

Dotty glanced at him in surprise. He was so understanding and kind that he never failed to amaze her.

'Laura has been worried sick about you too,' he told her then, and the old familiar jealousy instantly flared up at the mention of her name. Dotty had allowed herself to get a little carried away when he had offered to come and see her, but now she realised once more that he had come merely as a very dear friend and she became silent.

Once in the city centre they went into a café for a cup of tea, then Robert bought her some new clothes so at least she felt as if she had something of her own again, and a typewriter – another second-hand one from a pawnshop as Dotty refused point blank to allow him to buy her a brand new one. Then they headed back to Annabelle's to unload the purchases, which were far too heavy to carry about for the rest of the day.

'I'm afraid I'm going to have to catch the four o'clock train home to London,' Robert told her on the way. 'Otherwise I might get stranded here. Not all the trains are running.'

Dotty felt a stab of disappointment but knew they would just have to make the best of the time they had.

Miranda greeted them warmly and winked at Dotty as Robert took his coat off, making the girl blush. They settled him in the parlour then went through to the kitchen to make some tea.

'What a nice-looking young man,' Miranda said archly. 'And he's so polite. I think you may have struck gold there, Dotty.'

'We're just friends.' Dotty blushed an even deeper red.

'Well, *you* might regard him as a friend – but judging by the way he looks at you, I'd say he regards you as rather more than that,' Miranda said knowingly.

Dotty felt a flash of irritation. How could Miranda ever imagine that someone like Robert would ever look at her in a romantic light? She was under no illusions; she was a plain Jane and always would be, and she was sure that Robert was in love with Laura. And why shouldn't he be? she asked herself. Laura was everything that she would have liked to be. But not wanting to upset the woman who had shown her such kindness, she decided that it might be best to ignore the remark and so she busied herself getting the tea tray ready.

'So what are you two planning on doing for the rest of the day?' Miranda asked.

'Oh, we'll probably just go back into the centre and have a wander around until it's time for Robert's train.'

'You'll do no such thing!' Miranda said. 'You can both stay here. Annabelle's gone out and I'm going out too, shortly, so you may as well make the best of having the house to yourselves for a while.'

'Are you quite sure you don't mind?' Dotty asked hesitantly.

'Of course I don't. Now get that tray into the parlour before it goes cold and I'll see you later.'

Dotty did as she was told after flashing a grateful smile,

and it was as she and Robert were sitting together drinking their tea that he suddenly put his cup down and regarded her seriously.

'Actually, Dotty, there's something I need to tell you, which is one of the reasons I've come today.'

'Oh?' Dotty raised her eyebrow quizzically as Robert looked slightly uncomfortable.

'The thing is, I know how awful everything has been for you over the last few days and I'm not sure that this is the perfect timing for the news, but . . . . well, the long and the short of it is, Paul, my friend who agreed to look at your book, got in touch with me yesterday and told me that he'd like to publish it.'

Dotty stared at him speechlessly. *'What?'* she managed to croak eventually. 'Is this a joke?'

'It most certainly isn't,' Robert assured her. 'Of course, he wouldn't discuss your advance or anything like that with me. But he told me that he absolutely loved it and he'd like to meet you at the earliest opportunity.'

Dotty continued to stare at Robert in amazement. Her book was going to be published and she could hardly believe it. After all the terrible things that had happened recently, it was a dream come true.

'So . . .' His face broke into a wide smile now. 'When do you think you'll be able to come and meet him?'

'Not before next week,' Dotty squeaked. 'I can only make it on a Thursday, my day off. Unfortunately Annabelle, Lucy and myself have lost a few days off work over the last week helping the WVS out. Mrs Broadstairs, our boss, has been very understanding, but I don't think she would be if she knew I wanted more time to go gallivanting off to London.'

He chuckled. 'Well, you might not need to work at Owen Owen when you become a bestselling author.'

Dotty didn't like the sound of that. She enjoyed working in the department store; it was her security and she had no intention of giving her job up.

'I suppose I could make it next week, that's if the trains are running all right,' she said as the wonderful news finally began to sink in.

'Next week it is then. I'll tell Paul,' he answered and they then went on to talk about the plot of her novel – Dotty became quite animated as she spoke of 'War-Torn Londoners' and the hardships her main characters were forced to endure throughout the book and Robert listened, enthralled.

The afternoon seemed to race away and all too soon Robert glanced at the ornate French clock and told her regretfully, 'I ought to be getting back to the station now. Do you think Miranda would mind if you used her phone to call me a taxi?'

'Of course she wouldn't. I'll do it now and when it comes, I'll go to the station with you,' she said, springing up from her seat.

'No, I'd rather you didn't,' he told her in a no-nonsense sort of voice. 'I'd rather you stayed here where you can get down into the cellar should there be another raid. I'd never forgive myself if anything happened to you because you'd seen me back to the train.'

Dotty went to ring a taxi firm and fetch his coat, holding it close to her as she went back to the parlour, feeling miserable. They seemed to have had so little time together and it had gone so fast, and now she would have to wait for another whole week before she could see him again.

They were standing in the hallway waiting for the taxi to arrive when Robert suddenly took her hand and awkwardly drew her towards him.

'Promise me that you won't go taking any silly risks,' he said urgently. 'You are very precious to me, Dotty.'

She was so shocked that she could only nod in reply. And then he leaned forward and just for an instant his lips brushed hers and longing rose in her.

'B-but won't Laura mind you kissing me?' she asked him in a choky voice when he released her and he looked at her, baffled.

'What on earth would it have to do with Laura?'

'W-well, I thought . . . that is, I assumed that you and she . . .'

When her voice trailed away Robert threw back his head and laughed aloud before telling her, 'You silly goose. Whatever gave you that idea? Laura and I have been friends since we were children; our mothers were very close. But Laura is happily married as it happens, with two lovely children to show for it. It's actually her husband who wants to publish your book. Did I not mention that before? He's an editor in a very big publishing house. The poor man is like me – we're stuck at home unable to join the other chaps in giving Hitler a pasting. I've got this damn arm, and he's in a wheelchair after a brush with spinal TB.'

'Oh, I see,' Dotty stammered, feeling more confused than ever.

'Ah, that sounds like my taxi,' he said, looking slightly embarrassed now. 'Ring me and let me know what time your train gets into Euston next week, and I'll come and meet you. We can talk more then,' he promised. Then he turned on his heel and she stood as if rooted to the spot as the door closed behind him.

She heard the taxi draw away before slowly raising her hand to her lips. They were still tingling. Her thoughts then moved on to the wonderful news he had brought for her: her novel was going to be published! She hugged herself as a shiver of delight coursed through her, but she wasn't clear whether it was because of the kiss or the thought of becoming the author of a published novel. She felt as if all her birthdays and Christmases had come at once – and Robert had told her that she was precious to him. And the way he had kissed her – could it be that he felt something for her too? Suddenly she was so happy she could have climbed a mountain.

Over the next few days, life returned to something resembling normality. The girls all went back to work and their daily routine, and the people of Coventry cleared up the mess and got on with their lives. There was nothing else they could do. But the respite was brief and within days the sound of the sirens had them all repeatedly scurrying for the cover of the shelters and the cellars again. Thankfully each time proved to be a false alarm, although other places weren't so lucky. Everyone wondered how long it would be before the Luftwaffe came back – and which part of the city would be in the firing line next time.

It was on a Wednesday as Lucy was serving a customer that she looked up to see the lift doors open and Mr P standing there. She hastily took the money from the woman she was serving and placed it in the large brass till then hurried towards him with her heart beating fast. He was as white as a sheet and she wondered what could have happened now. He saw her coming towards him, and taking his cap off he twisted it in his hands as he shuffled uncomfortably from foot to foot.

'Er . . . is there somewhere we could go to talk, private-like?' he asked, obviously feeling totally out of place.

'Wait here for a minute,' Lucy instructed him. 'I'll just get

Miss Lawson to cover for me then we'll go up to the staff dining room.'

Seconds later, they were riding up in the lift towards the top floor. Once the lift stopped, Lucy glanced through the glass doors leading into the dining room before asking him, 'So what's wrong, Mr P? Has something happened?'

'Aye, I'm afraid it has, love.'

When he didn't go on, she urged, 'Well, what is it then?'

He sighed heavily before answering. 'The missus sent for me from work again. Yer know she ain't so good at venturin' out since we lost our Freddy. But the long an' the short of it is, a woman from the Red Cross came to see yer this mornin' an' seein' as yer weren't in, the missus invited her into our house. She left this letter for yer but she couldn't stay, so Gladys promised that she'd see as yer got it.'

Lucy looked confused. Why would anyone from the Red Cross be coming to see her? For a start she had been terrified that it might be a telegram informing her that something had happened to Joel, but surely that would have come from the War Department, not the Red Cross.

'I'm afraid it's really bad news,' Mr P said in a small voice. 'An' I wonder if yer shouldn't come along home wi' me before openin' it.'

'Do you know what's in it then?'

'Aye, I do.' He dropped his eyes as Lucy stared at the letter he had passed her as if it might bite her. 'The lady told our Glad.'

And then suddenly all the strength drained out of Lucy as a thought occurred to her. It must be something to do with Mary, but she was safe in Folkestone and she was going to see her on Saturday. She had booked a day off work especially and had the train tickets all ready at home. She had been looking forward to it for weeks.

Perhaps Mary was ill and they were writing to ask her to postpone the visit? She opened the envelope but when she started to read what was inside it she had to lean against the wall as her legs threatened to buckle.

'It-it says that they deeply regret to have to inform me that M-Mary and the people who she was staying with were all k-killed last Saturday night,' she stammered incredulously. 'They say the unused bombs that the Germans were carrying were dropped on Folkestone before they set off back across the Channel.'

She stared at Mr P appealingly, as if she were begging him to tell her that it was some horrendous practical joke, but the expression on his face told her that it was true.

'B-but Mary *can't* be dead,' she sobbed as a picture of the little girl's innocent face floated in front of her eyes. 'I'm going to visit her on Saturday, you see. I've got her a new dolly and some fairy storybooks and . . .' her voice trailed away as she slithered to the floor in a dead faint.

She woke up to find herself lying on Mrs P's settee and for a moment she wondered why and how she had got there. Then suddenly it came flooding back and she threw herself into the older woman's arms and began to sob heart-rendingly.

'There, there,' Mrs P soothed, weeping herself for the loss of the little girl she too had loved. 'Our Fred got one of the staff to fetch yer home in his car. There were no way yer could have stayed at work after receivin' news like this.'

'Tell me it isn't true,' she pleaded, but Mrs P could only hang her head.

'I'm afraid it is, luvvie,' she whispered, then blew her nose. 'This war is a terrible thing an' cruel.'

Lucy was almost beside herself with grief and when Lucy

and Annabelle suddenly rushed in she could only stare at them vacantly, her face ravaged.

'We heard what happened and felt we had to come,' Dotty explained as she looked at Lucy with concern. 'Oh Lucy, we're *so* sorry! We all know how much you loved your little sister. We loved her too.'

Lucy laughed bitterly and they all gazed at her uncomprehendingly. Perhaps the shock had unhinged her mind?

Lucy then gazed into the fire before saying, 'You all know that my mother died in a mental asylum, but perhaps it's time you knew why. It was because . . . because she stabbed my father to death. He was a bully, you see.' She shuddered as she remembered and the people in the room stared in horror.

Lucy scrubbed at her eyes with the back of her hands before forcing herself to go on.

'I think it was Mary's birth that was the final straw for her. She'd been ill in bed on and off for years – she was never strong,' she said tremulously. 'And one night shortly after Mary was born, Joel saw Dad hitting her and he went at him with fists flying, calling him all the names he could think of. But Dad was a big man, and he started to knock Joel about the room. That's when Mum disappeared and when she came back,' Lucy sucked in her breath as she relived the scene in her mind, 'Mum was holding a knife. She screamed at Dad to leave Joel alone and called him a wicked bastard, but Dad just kept on hitting Joel again and again. So then she . . . she ran towards them and stabbed Dad in the heart. He died instantly. If she hadn't done that, I think it would have been Joel that was killed. After that, all hell broke loose. One of the neighbours had heard the commotion and called the police, and when they arrived they arrested Mum for murder. She had no life at all with Dad, he had knocked her from pillar to post from as far back as I can remember, and me and Joel too if it came to that. Yet strangely she still loved him, and once she knew that she had killed him, something inside her just switched off. By the time they took her to court it was clear that she was mad, so they sentenced her to life in a mental asylum. That was when we moved here. Joel decided that we needed a fresh start where no one knew us . . . so now you know the truth.'

'Dear God above.' Mrs P was so shocked that she had to force the words out.

It was Annabelle who eventually laid her hand gently on Lucy's shoulder as she told her, 'I'm *so* sorry, Lucy. But whyever didn't you tell us all this before? We're your friends, we could have helped you.' She suddenly felt very guilty as she thought of the privileged upbringing she had had while poor Lucy must have been going through hell. Her own father had cosseted and pampered her and she was ashamed of the way she had treated him. There and then she determined that she would make it up to him when he came home, God willing, if he ever did.

Dotty meanwhile was sobbing openly. Her own childhood had been lonely, but she had never suffered as Lucy must have and she wished that she could magic all the hurt away. Of course she knew that she couldn't, but she *could* be there for her and she swore that she always would be.

Mr P too had tears on his cheeks after listening to the sad tale, and for a while he felt ashamed of being a male. It was just beyond him how any man could do that to a woman, especially his own precious wife.

So many things suddenly made sense now. Lucy's reaction to the chap who had come on to her at the dance hall for a start-off. No wonder the poor girl couldn't stand a man to touch her after seeing the way her father had treated her mother. The reason why Joel had been so fiercely protective of both Mary and Lucy. At one stage both Dotty and Annabelle had been secretly concerned that his possessiveness was a little unhealthy, but after this awful confession they could understand why. And for the girl to have to carry a secret like that trapped inside; it just didn't bear thinking about. And now little Mary was dead and they all wondered how Lucy would cope with this new loss when she had gone through so very much already.

'We're your friends, Lucy, and we'll help you to get through this together,' Dotty promised now and Annabelle backed her up. As Mrs P looked on tearfully, she saw the strong bond that had developed between the three girls and thanked God for it. She had a feeling that in the dark days ahead, Lucy was going to need all the support she could get.

Chapter Twenty-Three

At her own insistence, Lucy travelled alone to Folkestone to identify Mary's body. She was led into a large, bleak morgue where Mary's body, along with a number of others, lay on cold stone slabs covered with white sheets. Some of them had name tags tied to their big toes, but others were as yet unidentified. As Lucy gazed down on her beloved girl's ashen face, she felt as if a part of herself had died too, but she shed no tears. For now, the pain she was feeling was beyond tears.

Mary was buried in a tiny churchyard in Folkestone overlooking the sea. The Red Cross had offered to have her body transported back to Coventry but Lucy felt that there was no point. The little girl was gone and it didn't really matter where she was laid to rest.

Mrs Broadstairs had been marvellous about the whole thing and told Lucy that she must take off as much time as she needed. Only the people that Lucy had made her dreadful confession knew the real truth and none of them would ever repeat it. Annabelle and Dotty fussed over her and pandered to her every need, but although Lucy was grateful to them, she felt dead inside. She told them her mother had never wanted Mary, yet from the moment the child had been born Lucy had adored her unconditionally. After all, it wasn't Mary's fault that she had been born and now that she was gone, as well as her mother, and with no word from Joel, the girl sometimes wondered if life was worth living. It was only the tender ministrations of Dotty and Annabelle that kept her going and she knew that she would never be able to repay them for their kindness.

It was as they were going to Primrose Lodge after work one evening that Annabelle told them, 'I'm going to be twenty-one next week.'

'Really? Then we should do something special to mark the occasion,' Dotty said excitedly.

Annabelle reared up. 'Huh! What *is* there to do? There's warnings going off nearly every night, and even when they turn out to be false alarms you have to cope with broken sleep. Daddy promised me a big posh party but we still haven't heard from him. It's been months now,' she added gloomily.

Dotty and Lucy exchanged a glance, wondering what Annabelle was most upset about. Was it the fact that she hadn't heard from her father and had no idea of his whereabouts, or the fact that she couldn't have a big do for her twenty-first? Annabelle could still on occasion be remarkably selfish and self-centred, although she had mellowed considerably during the time they had known her. Dotty refrained from mentioning that her own twenty-first birthday had passed without acknowledgement the week before, except from Miss Timms, who had bought her a lovely silver charm bracelet. She hadn't even bothered to tell anyone about it, since the way she saw it, there wasn't much to celebrate. They were all tired and the war was still raging on. Everywhere they looked, posters had been pasted up warning them that *Careless Talk Costs Lives* or urging them all to *Make Do and Mend*. Kindertransport trains containing Jewish children who were fleeing their homelands were pouring into the country and the tales of the persecution of the Jews who couldn't escape were horrendous. Norway had been overrun by Hitler's army, as had Belgium and Holland, and thousands of men had been slaughtered on the beaches during the Battle of Dunkirk; the country was still reeling from the shock of it.

There had been over 370 siren alerts in Coventry although only forty-one actual raids had taken place, and everyone's spirits were low with no prospect in sight of the war ending.

Only Dotty was managing to stay cheerful as she had now been to London twice to see Robert and Paul Parsons, Laura's husband, who was the senior editor at Huntes Publishing House, who were going to publish her book. Paul's disability did not prevent him from being a force to be reckoned with: Dotty found him to be a real live wire.

'I might decide to write under a pseudonym,' she told them one day during their afternoon break. 'Dorothy Kent is *so* boring, isn't it? What name should I write under?'

'Something completely different and romantic,' Annabelle told her stoutly. 'If you're going to change it you may as well go for something glamorous. What about Genevieve Moriarty or something like that?'

Dotty had dissolved in a fit of laughter as she tried to imagine what Robert would say if she suggested such a name, but happy times like these were getting scarcer now.

They moved on towards Cheylesmore, each lost in their own thoughts, until Lucy noticed a stray dog scavenging in a dustbin just ahead of them. Strays were an all too regular sight across the city now as people's homes were blown to smithereens and their pets were left without anyone to care for them.

Lucy scrabbled in her bag for the remains of the sandwich she had bought in the staff dining room that day and not bothered to finish. She had the appetite of a bird nowadays. 'I bet he'd enjoy this. It's only bloater paste but he looks as if he's starving. Here, boy.'

'Ugh, don't encourage the scabby thing,' Annabelle said, horrified. 'He might have the mange or any number of different diseases. Just look at the state of the mutt. He's absolutely *filthy*!'

'So would you be filthy if you were forced to live on the streets,' Lucy retorted as the creature took a step towards her. He seemed reluctant to come too close but when he saw the food in Lucy's hand his hunger overcame his fear and he lurched forward, snatched it off her, gulped it down, then wagged his tail as he looked at her expectantly.

'Ah, he's still hungry,' Lucy said sadly.

'So what?' Annabelle retorted cold-heartedly. 'So are the hundreds of other strays roaming around the city. And we can't feed them all, can we?'

Dotty dug her in the ribs then and glowered at her, and Annabelle piped down. Dotty meanwhile was thrilled to see Lucy showing an interest in something again, even if it was only a stray dog.

Lucy had bent to stroke him by then and his tail was going ten to the dozen as he lapped up the attention. He wasn't the prettiest of animals, she had to admit. In fact, he was a real mongrel. He was of medium size with legs that looked too short for his thin body, which was short-haired whilst his long ears and his tail were bushy. It was hard to decide what colour he was too under all the layers of dirt, but when he looked up at her from trusting soulful brown eyes Lucy felt something inside her stir into life. He was helpless and vulnerable just as Mary had been, and in that moment she knew that she was going to take him home and care for him.

'I'm going to adopt him,' she stated and Annabelle almost choked.

'Adopt him? You must be mad! If you must have a pet, surely you could choose a prettier one?'

'He will be pretty when he's had a bath and a brush,' Lucy said with a determined glint in her eye. 'He's coming home with me and that's the end of it. I just have to work out how I'm going to get him there now, but I'll walk him home if I have to.'

'But you don't even have a collar and lead,' Dotty pointed out sensibly and Lucy's face fell. 'And although he's scrawny, he'll be too heavy for you to carry him far.'

Lucy nodded, knowing when she was beaten, but it broke her heart to leave him to fend for himself.

'Sorry, boy.' She scratched him beneath his chin and he arched his back with pleasure. She sighed. 'Come on then. We may as well get on. I just hope that he'll be all right.'

Annabelle sighed with relief, glad that Lucy had come to her senses. But her relief turned to astonishment when the dog fell into step with Lucy and began to trot along beside her.

Lucy chuckled with delight. 'Looks like I don't need a collar and lead. I think he's made his mind up too.'

Annabelle sniffed. 'Well, he'll have to stay outside when we get home,' she said irritably, thinking that Lucy had lost her marbles. 'There's no way Mummy is going to allow him into the house smelling like that! He could be covered in fleas as well, ugh!' She marched on, hoping that the dog would get fed up of following them, but by the time Primrose Lodge came into sight he was still ambling along with his eyes fixed adoringly on Lucy.

'Actually, I think he could be quite cute if he were to be cleaned up a bit,' Dotty smiled.

Annabelle snorted. 'It would take more than a clean-up to improve that ugly creature!'

They were walking up the drive to Annabelle's home by then and Lucy began to feel nervous. What if Miranda was horrified at the sight of him? But then she decided that if this were the case she would just set off and walk him home. It was a good way off admittedly, but if the poor thing had been roaming the streets he was probably used to walking long distances by now.

They decided to enter by the back door and as they went through the gate they found Miranda on her knees in the garden pruning the roses.

She smiled in welcome, but as her eyes settled on the dog she asked, 'So who is this then, and where did he come from?'

'He's a stray and I'm going to adopt him,' Lucy answered with her chin in the air. She was expecting Miranda to scold her as Annabelle had, but to her surprise the woman's eyes filled with sympathetic tears.

'Oh the poor thing,' she muttered as she hurried up the path to stroke him. 'There are so many strays about now, it's heartbreaking. He looks as if he's starving. Bring him into the kitchen and I'm sure we can find him something to eat.'

Annabelle's mouth gaped in amazement. 'But he smells like an open sewer!' she objected.

'Ah, but he won't if we give him a good bath, will he?'

Miranda appeared to be almost as enamoured of the little dog as Lucy was. 'But first things first – let's get him fed, bless him. I think I've got some corned beef and a cold potato or two left over from last night.'

Within minutes the new arrival was wolfing down his meal as if he couldn't believe his luck. Meanwhile Miranda had fetched the old tin bath from the shed and was filling it with warm water.

'You'll have to give him a name,' she told Lucy. 'We can't just call him Dog, can we?'

'Hmm . . .' Lucy stared thoughtfully off into space for a moment before saying, 'I think I'll call him Harry. It was my grandpa's name and he was such a lovely man.'

'I think it suits him,' Miranda agreed but Annabelle had to be contrary.

'You can't call a dog Harry,' she objected. 'It's a person's name. What's wrong with Rover?'

'Nothing at all, but I like Harry and that's what I'm going to call him.'

'Then Harry it is,' Miranda said as she coaxed the dog towards the bath.

Fifteen minutes later, with his fur – which they saw now was a lovely red-gold colour – gleaming, Harry was unrecognisable. He had been dried and brushed to within an inch of his life, and although he was still frighteningly thin, even Annabelle grudgingly had to admit that he was actually quite cute.

'See! Didn't I tell you he was lovely?' Lucy laughed as she bent to his level and hugged him. He returned her show of affection by licking every inch of her he could reach.

Meanwhile Miranda looked on happily. Lucy had been so quiet and depressed since she had lost Mary that it was wonderful to see her smiling again.

As always she fussed over the girls and raced about fetching them tea and biscuits and Dotty couldn't help but be a little envious. Miranda was much as she had always liked to imagine her own mother might have been, and often she couldn't help but think that Annabelle took her for granted.

'I ought to be thinking of getting back now,' Lucy said eventually as the light outside began to wane. 'I don't want to be out in the open on the way home with Harry if there's another air-raid warning tonight.'

They all became solemn then. The warnings had been so frequent of late that a lot of people were now choosing to sleep through them in their own beds and ignore the sirens. Sadly it had cost some of them their lives when the Germans had dropped their bombs on the city. Almost every night, Miranda had found herself in some church hall with the other WVS volunteers, tending the sick and catering to the homeless, and she was glad to do it. At least while she was busy she did not have time to fret about her husband. There was still no news from him, but each day she managed to persuade herself that no news was good news and that he was safe wherever he was.

'I shall run you and Harry home tonight,' Miranda told Lucy now. 'It's too far for you to walk.'

'Oh no, I can't let you do that,' Lucy objected. 'Petrol is too precious to waste on that.'

'No, it isn't.' Miranda fetched her car keys from the pot on the dresser then told her, 'Come along, young lady. I won't take no for an answer so let's get Harry into the car. There's a dry towel he can sit on here. And isn't it tomorrow you lot are all going to see *Gone With the Wind* at the Rex?'

When the girls nodded she went on, 'Then in that case I

don't mind looking after Harry, if you're worried about leaving him on his own.'

'Thank you, but I'm hoping that Mrs P will volunteer,' Lucy explained. 'I'm going to have to ask her if she'll let him out in the day for me while I'm at work too,' she confided, 'Between you and me I don't think she'll object too much. She used to have a dog of her own when we first moved next door to her and she really loved him. Sadly he died of old age a couple of years ago and I know that Mrs P was heart-broken and really missed him, so I'm hoping that she'll enjoy having Harry about. She doesn't have anyone else to spoil at the minute.'

Her face became sad then and they all knew that she was thinking of Mary, so Miranda said hastily, 'Come along then, let's get him home to meet her. The light will be gone before we know it and I don't fancy driving through the streets without my headlights on after dark.'

When she dropped Lucy and Harry off some time later right at their front door, Lucy impulsively leaned over and kissed the woman on the cheek, making a warm glow spread through Miranda. Annabelle, Dotty and Lucy were all as different as chalk from cheese and made unlikely friends, and yet she had watched the closeness between the three girls grow and had rejoiced in it. Miranda felt that Dotty and Lucy were good for her daughter. Lucy was a sensitive, kind girl, while Dotty was shy and rather lacking in confidence, but full of surprises.

She pecked Lucy on the cheek then drove away, her thoughts already on what the night ahead might hold for them.

'Well, bless my soul!' Mrs P exclaimed when Lucy marched Harry into her kitchen a short while later. 'Who have we here then? An' who does he belong to?'

'His name is Harry and he belongs to me,' Lucy told her proudly. 'We've sort of adopted each other.'

Mr P, who was reading his newspaper in the chair at the side of the fireplace, looked at Harry over the top of the glasses perched on the end of his nose, then smiled and disappeared back behind the paper again.

'Ah, bless him,' Mrs P said, dropping onto her knees and stroking his long silky ears. 'Ain't he just the loveliest little thing yer ever did see, our Fred?'

'I'm glad you think that,' Lucy said sheepishly. 'Because I have a big favour to ask of you. I was wondering if you would pop round and let him out into the yard during the day for me while I'm at work?'

'I can do a lot bloody better than that,' Mrs P declared. 'He can come round here an' spend the whole day wi' me when you're out an' about. We can keep each other company.'

'I was hoping you'd say that,' Lucy grinned and it was so nice to see her smile that Mrs P felt a lump form in her throat. 'But now I'd better get His Lordship here round to his new home and get him settled in. Bye for now.'

Mrs P watched her cross the yard and said to her husband, 'Life's a funny thing at times, ain't it, Fred?'

'It is that, Glad,' he agreed quietly, as a picture of Mary and their Freddy flashed before his eyes.

Next door, Lucy dragged a wooden packing crate from the cupboard under the stairs. She had already sorted out an old warm blanket, and once she'd tucked it into the crate she was satisfied that it would make a very comfortable bed for her new friend. She then selected two deep dishes from the kitchen cupboard, one for his food and one for water.

'There you are, Harry,' she told him. 'We'll soon have you done and dusted now.' He wagged his tail as if he could understand every word she said, and she suddenly realised that she hadn't minded coming home tonight for the first time in ages. The house felt more like a home again now, and it was all thanks to Harry.

'Cooee!' Mrs P shouted as she puffed into Lucy's kitchen half an hour later. 'I got to thinkin' after you'd gone and realised that I still had these.' She held out a collar and lead, saying, 'They were my Prince's an' I couldn't bring meself to get rid of 'em when we lost him. Lookin' at Harry, the collar should fit a treat.'

'But are you quite sure you want to part with them, Mrs P?' Lucy asked doubtfully. She knew how much Mrs P had loved her dog and how devastated she had been when he died.

Her neighbour nodded. 'I'm quite sure, luvvie. They're only lyin' in a drawer an' it will be nice to see 'em bein' used again.'

'Then thank you very much,' Lucy said gratefully as she took them from her and tried the collar on Harry. It did indeed fit very well and he wagged his tail as if in appreciation.

'I reckon he were well loved at some time,' Mrs P said then. 'He's such a lovely-natured dog he must have been well treated.'

They both became solemn then as they each thought of the circumstances that might have led to him becoming a stray. Perhaps his family home had been destroyed in one of the raids? It was a sobering thought, but not wishing to spoil Lucy's happy mood the older woman commented, 'At least all's well that ends well – in his case, anyway. But now I'm goin' to leave you two to bond.' Even as the words were being spoken, Harry dropped his head into Lucy's lap and Mrs P chuckled. 'I take that back. Looks to me like he already has. G'night, love.'

Lucy stroked him lovingly, wondering if perhaps she shouldn't let him sleep in her room that night. He was in a strange place, after all, and she didn't want him to feel lonely. The decision was taken out of her hands when the sirens began to wail just as she was preparing for bed. 'Oh not again!' she groaned, wondering how much longer it might be before they could all get an unbroken night's sleep.

'Come on, Harry,' she encouraged. 'Looks like it's the shelter again tonight.'

As she stepped out into the yard she almost collided with Mr and Mrs P who were just coming out of their back door. Mrs P had her metal curlers in and was clutching a rubber hot-water bottle. Mr P was in a string vest with his braces dangling around his backside.

'Bloody Jerries,' the older woman complained as enemy planes sounded in the distance. They all looked up at the sky and saw a darker mass zooming towards them in the distance. The sky lit up with searchlights and Mrs P hurried them all towards the shelter now as the drone of the planes became a roar.

'Looks like some more poor sods are in fer it tonight,' she said.

Mr P had barely closed the door behind them when the Bofors guns and the ack-acks growled into life and Mrs P wrapped her faded old dressing-gown more tightly about her. Harry shrank against Lucy's leg and she stroked him gently.

'It's all right, boy,' she soothed him. 'You're quite safe in here with us.' And then they all settled back, trying to close their ears to the deafening explosions going on all around them.

Chapter Twenty-Four

'Oh Lord, I'm so tired,' Annabelle yawned the next morning at work during their break. 'I doubt I got two hours' sleep all night.'

'Well, neither did we,' Dotty said rather indignantly. 'I heard on the wireless this morning that the Rex took a direct hit last night and it's nothing more than a pile of rubble now so we won't be going to see *Gone With the Wind* tonight.'

'Oh, that's just wonderful!' Annabelle rolled her eyes. 'I was looking forward to that. I dare say I shall have to spend another night at home now.'

'At least you still have your birthday party on Saturday to look forward to,' Lucy pointed out, but if anything that only made Annabelle more disgruntled.

'Oh yes. And some party it's going to be, isn't it? Just us, Mummy, Grandpa and Grandma. I was hoping to have a room in a posh hotel, a band, a wonderful spread laid on – instead it will be our front room and a home-made cake!'

Suddenly something in Dotty snapped. 'You can be so selfish sometimes,' she hissed in a rare show of temper. 'I happen to know that your mother has been saving her food rations for weeks to make you that cake, and it took her absolutely hours to ice it! And here's me who would give anything in the whole world just to know *who* my mum was – let alone have her bake me a cake!'

Annabelle's cheeks reddened, and she lit a cigarette.

'Sorry,' she mumbled. 'I suppose I did sound a bit ungrateful, but I'm just so tired.'

Dotty shrugged, regretting her outburst, but it couldn't be taken back now and they were relieved when it was time to part and go back to their separate departments.

Dotty felt guilty when she got back to the haberdashery department. She was still living very happily at Annabelle's, and Miranda had made her very welcome, but her mind was in turmoil. Recently, she had been going to London every so often on her day off to spend time with Robert and Paul, her publisher. Paul had told her that her debut novel would be released in a year or so, depending on the availability of paper. They were even discussing ideas for book covers now, and Dotty could barely wait to see her first novel in print, however long it took. Meantime she was busily working on another novel, as well as keeping the magazine supplied with a fresh story each month.

It was her feelings about Robert that she was finding confusing. Each time she saw him waiting on the platform for her at Euston her heart would lift, and it became harder each time they met to say goodbye. Finally she was having to ask herself if she was in love with him. But never having been in love before, she had no idea how to know what love was. Was it the way he could produce butterflies in her stomach with just a smile? Or the longing she sometimes got to just reach out and touch him? However, she knew that even if she did love him, there could be no happy ending for them. Robert was rich, successful and attractive. She, on the other hand, was plain and boring. A shop girl who didn't even know where she came from. Why would he ever look at her when he could surely have his pick of any woman he chose?

Admittedly he had never shown her anything else but kindness, and he had told her that she was precious to him. He had even entrusted his mother's locket to her, which she wore all the time. But she had an inkling that he had done this because he felt sorry for her. And so what should she do about it? Would it be better to walk away now before she got hurt? She supposed it would, and each time she came back from London she promised herself that she would never see him again. But it was so much easier said than done, and her need to be near him drove common sense away. And then there was something else that was playing on her mind. Recently the need to find her real family had resurfaced as it had at different times throughout her life. But she was older now and after making enquiries at the local Welfare Department she had been told that the Red Cross might be able to help her. Of course, she realised that as there was a war going on it wouldn't be the best time to approach them, but the war couldn't last forever, could it? And when it was over she would begin her search in earnest. It gave her something to look forward to.

'Things ain't looking good for our lads,' Mr P commented the next night when Lucy rushed round there to collect Harry. He put the *Daily Mail* down and said, 'They reckon the seas are red wi' blood after some o' the battles. Ee, the Jerries are pickin' our lads off like flies.'

Lucy and Mrs P shuddered simultaneously as they

pictured the heaving seas full of the dead and dying men who would never see their families again. It was too awful to contemplate.

'Coventry and London ain't the only cities bein' targeted now either,' he went on gravely. 'The Jerries have bombed Southampton, Liverpool, Bristol, Portsmouth an' Birmingham an' all now, an' they reckon folks are leavin' all the major cities in droves, pushin' what's left o' their belongings in old prams, wheelbarrows – anythin'! Yet Churchill still reckons we'll beat the buggers! I think it's only his optimism that's keepin' the country's spirits up.'

'Let's just hope as he's right then,' Mrs P muttered, but then she forced a smile as she changed the subject and told Lucy, 'This chap 'ere 'as been as good as gold. I ain't known I've had him. But he's pleased to see you – look. If his tail wags any faster it'll be in danger o' fallin' off.'

Lucy bent down to hug Harry and was rewarded with a licking.

'He's set me to thinkin' that perhaps we should get another dog,' Mrs P said musingly and her husband glanced up in surprise.

'But I thought yer said yer'd never have another pet after we lost Prince?'

'Happen I did,' she admitted sheepishly. 'But that was then an' this is now, an' God knows there's enough strays needin' a good home.' She patted Harry affectionately. 'Back then when we lost Prince I had the little 'uns to run around after an' keep me busy,' she told him matter-of-factly. 'But the truth o' the matter is, I get lonely now wi' our Barry and Beryl gettin' up to Gawd knows what in the country, an' our Freddy . . .' She gulped before going on. 'Anyway, wi' you two at work all day I've no one to talk to so maybe I've changed me mind.'

'Well, they do say as that's a lady's prerogative,' Fred teased. 'An' if you've a mind to get another dog I'll not stand in yer way. Happen he'll be good company fer this 'un here.'

Lucy smiled as she headed for the door, saying, 'I'm off then, and thanks for having Harry for me. Let's hope we get a good night's sleep tonight, eh?' And thankfully they did and all got up feeling a lot better for it the next morning.

That same evening, as Annabelle arrived home from work she was surprised to find her mother walking around the house with a stranger, an elderly gentleman, showing him into the rooms.

'Oh, hello darling. You're early.' Miranda appeared flustered as she told her, 'Go and have a cup of tea – there's plenty left in the pot. Mr Buxton will be leaving shortly and then I'll join you.'

Annabelle went off to do as she was told, wondering what was going on.

It was fifteen minutes later before her mother joined her and she asked bluntly, 'So what was that all about then? Why were you showing that chap around the house?'

Annabelle had removed her make-up and was smoothing Pond's cold cream across her face at the kitchen table, a habit her mother abhorred, but just this once Miranda chose to ignore it as she told her, 'I'm afraid there is something I need to speak to you about. The truth is, I've been putting it off because I don't think you're going to be too pleased about it. But the long and the short of the matter is . . . Mr Buxton is an estate agent. I'm going to sell the house.'

'You're going to *what*?' Annabelle was completely flabbergasted. 'But why? This is our home! I can't remember ever having lived anywhere else and I don't *want* to move.'

'Neither do I,' Miranda answered as tears welled in her

eyes. 'But I'm afraid we don't have much choice any more, darling. Times are hard for everyone and the money your father left us to manage on is dwindling rapidly.' She spread her hands as she looked around her beautiful home, each room furnished and decorated with love and care over the years. 'The trouble is, it's such a huge house to keep. The heating bill alone is astronomical, which is why I don't light the fires in all the rooms any more. And I'd rather sell it now than wait until we have to, and then accept some ridiculous offer – if we can, that is. According to Mr Buxton, properties aren't selling well at all at the moment! So if it doesn't sell . . . Well, we'll just have to tighten our belts a little more and shut some of the rooms off. But it isn't all doom and gloom. If I do manage to sell it, we can buy a smaller house somewhere that's more economical to run. You can come with me to look. That'll be nice, won't it, choosing it together?'

'No, it damn well *won't*!' Annabelle spat churlishly. 'I want to stay here!'

'Then that's a shame because I'm afraid we are moving if we get the chance, whether you like it or not. It isn't a matter of choice any more. It's necessity. I want a home for your father to come back to and we're so much luckier than most. Many people don't even *have* a home any more. They're leaving the city in droves to live with relatives or anyone who'll take them in, God bless them. So I suggest you forget your tantrums for now, young lady, and count yourself amongst the lucky ones. Everyone is having to make do and mend at the moment!' And with that Miranda turned and stamped from the room, leaving Annabelle to stare after her mother open-mouthed. She was beginning to hate that phrase – make do and mend! It seemed that that was all everyone did any more.

*

When Robert next met Dotty off the train at Euston he instantly noticed a change in her, although he couldn't quite put his finger on what it was. She was as polite and friendly as ever, but then he realised that she hadn't welcomed him with a kiss today, which was unusual. Normally she would hold his hand too as they strolled along, but today she had put some distance between them as if she didn't want to get too close. It hurt him far more than he could say, although he didn't comment on it. After all, Dotty was a young girl compared to him and she'd probably met someone who was nearer to her own age. Robert was just surprised that some lucky chap hadn't snapped her up before.

'We'll go and see Paul first,' he suggested. 'I think he has a cover design to show you for *War-Torn Lovers*.'

'Really?' Dotty's face lit up. She had made a conscious effort to put their relationship back on a more professional level, but it was proving to be very difficult, especially now, after hearing that she might get a glimpse of her very first book cover. Her first instinct was to throw herself at Robert and kiss him soundly, but she had finally decided that there was no point in becoming any more involved. It could only lead to heartache and she had already had enough of that in her lifetime.

Even so, she was determined to enjoy the day. Who knew how long it might be before she could get to London again? The Germans were targeting train lines and stations all over the country now, especially the ones that were transporting the parts that were needed for the tanks and the aeroplanes. And so many stations were being closed down while men worked frantically trying to repair the mangled tracks.

She casually mentioned this to Robert as they walked through the busy streets. 'I wonder if it wouldn't be better if we just stuck to corresponding via post and telephone for the time being after today?' she suggested, and was shocked to see his face fall. 'What I mean is, the raids are coming so regularly now I never know if I'm going to be able to get here.'

Unwilling to show her how hurt he was, he answered curtly, 'Of course, if you think that's best. I understand how busy you must be with writing and working, and I wouldn't want to impose on your time.'

Now it was Dotty's turn to be hurt but she hid it well as she hastily changed the subject and told him all about Harry and how Lucy had adopted him.

'It might turn out to be the best thing she's ever done,' he said. 'I mean, you've told me how devastated she's been since she lost Mary and I believe that animals are meant to be very therapeutic.'

Dotty nodded. She had told him about Mary's death but not the fact that Lucy's mother had stabbed her father to death. That knowledge would stay strictly between the people that Lucy had confided in, although sometimes Dotty wondered how Lucy had managed to cope with keeping such a terrible grisly secret for so long. It must have been eating away at her.

She and Robert spent the rest of the day pleasantly. After going to have a peep at Dotty's book cover that featured a handsome young soldier in uniform and a pretty girl who looked exactly as Dotty had described her, which she positively swooned over, they then went back to the magazine headquarters where Laura made tea and fussed over Dotty like a mother hen. She was very fond of Dotty and sometimes felt like banging Robert over the head with something heavy to bring him to his senses, because she had a sneaky suspicion that he was in love with the girl but was too shy to tell her so. From what she could make of it, Dotty was taken with him too, yet today for some reason the pair were skirting around each other like ballet dancers. It was all very frustrating. Why couldn't they see what was right under their noses? But of course she kept her counsel and said nothing, tutting in exasperation when they finally left together to go for some lunch.

'Would you like to join us?' Robert had asked politely.

Laura had grinned. 'No, thank you. You know what they say – two is company, three is a crowd.' She had winked at them blatantly but all her comment managed to do was make both of them blush and so she gave up and went back to work.

The rest of the day passed in a blur and all too soon the couple were standing on the platform of Euston station again.

'That's my train in over there,' Dotty said, suddenly feeling as if the cat had got her tongue. 'I er . . . I'd better get on otherwise I might not get a seat. It's always so busy at this time of day.' She had booked her return journey for two hours earlier than she normally departed and now she was wishing that she hadn't.

'Yes, yes, of course.' Robert too was feeling awkward and as much as he longed to give her a kiss, her stand-off attitude throughout the day had made him fear that his advances might be unwelcome. And so they shook hands formally and soon Dotty was staring from the carriage window looking for a sight of him. He usually waved until she was out of sight but today he had disappeared amongst the crowds and had not bothered waiting for her train to leave. Everything had gone exactly as she had planned, so she wondered why she felt so empty.

Chapter Twenty-Five

It was on Annabelle's birthday that the next bombshell was dropped, but it wasn't by the Germans. They were all gathered in Miranda's luxurious front room late in the afternoon and everyone was impressed by the buffet she had managed to put on, assisted by Dotty. Everyone but Annabelle, that is, who had been in a bad mood ever since Lucy and her grandparents had arrived. Lucy had presented her with a pretty silver ring, which Annabelle barely glanced at, and Dotty had bought her a bottle of the latest bright red nail polish and matching lipstick that were so popular at the time. Both Dotty and Lucy took to Annabelle's grandparents immediately. In their late sixties, they were impeccably dressed and very well-spoken but they were also very friendly, so the atmosphere was light, or it would have been if Annabelle had tried a little.

Her grandmother presented her with a beautiful solid gold brooch in the shape of a delicate leaf, set with emeralds, that had everyone's eyes on stalks as they admired it. Neither Lucy nor Dotty had ever seen anything quite like it. But in her usual self-centred way, Annabelle merely glanced at it.

'I do hope you like it, dear?' her grandmother said as she noted Annabelle's reaction to it. 'And that you're having a nice birthday?'

The girl was thinking of the birthday party she felt she should have had, and her mood worsened each time she caught a glimpse of the *For Sale* board at the end of the drive through the front window.

'I suppose it's very nice but it would have been better still if someone had managed to get their hands on some silk stockings. I'm sick and tired of having to wear these awful thick lisle things! They're so unbecoming.'

'Annabelle, really!' her mother scolded as she squirmed with embarrassment. 'I'm sure the brooch is much better than any number of pairs of stockings. It's something you'll be able to keep forever. And one day you might be able to pass it on to your own daughter and tell her that it was a twenty-first gift from your grandparents.'

'I suppose so,' Annabelle said ungratefully, dropping it onto the sofa as if it was nothing more than a cheap trinket from Woolworth's.

Her grandmother pursed her lips disapprovingly, but not wishing to spoil the occasion she told Miranda, 'The tea looks lovely, dear. Quite a feast, in fact, when food is in such short supply. Did you make those sausage rolls and that trifle yourself? They look quite delicious.'

'Yes I did,' Miranda said proudly. 'And the cake.'

'Then I suggest we all tuck in,' the older woman said with a bright smile. 'Just looking at it is making me feel hungry.'

As Annabelle glanced at the table she scowled, thinking again of the birthday party she had envisaged. This was certainly a far cry from what she had wished for.

'Come on, darling. You go first,' her grandmother encouraged. 'You are the birthday girl, after all.' She held a plate out to Annabelle but she declined it.

'No thanks,' she muttered ungraciously. 'I've never been that keen on meat paste. If Daddy was here we'd be in some big hotel somewhere celebrating properly! With *decent* food to eat.'

'Yes, but he isn't here, is he?' Mrs Hamilton Gower was losing her patience now. 'He's away at war fighting to try and keep us all safe. I would have thought you would be more concerned about your father's safety than celebrating your birthday.'

'He chose to go,' Annabelle said nastily. 'He didn't even wait to be called up – and why shouldn't I celebrate my birthday? I won't be twenty-one again, will I? What do you expect me to do? Wait until this damn war is over?'

Her grandmother seemed to swell to twice her size at the girl's blatant selfishness, and before she could stop to think she blurted out, 'How could you be so unfeeling? Do you never think of anyone but yourself, girl? Your father could be *killed*. He might never come home again. But then I always feared that you would turn out like this. Your parents have ruined you since the day your father fetched you!' She clapped her hands over her mouth then and the colour drained from her face.

Annabelle frowned. 'What do you mean, since the day my father *fetched* me? I don't understand. Mummy, what's she talking about?'

Miranda and her mother exchanged a glance and to everyone's horror, the older woman began to cry. 'I'm so sorry, dear,' she sobbed as she looked at Miranda imploringly. 'I never meant to say it. It just sort of slipped out.'

'Oh, for goodness sake! Will someone just tell me what's going on here,' Annabelle ranted.

'I always warned you this day would come,' Miranda's mother told her now in a voice barely above a whisper. 'Secrets like this are too hard to keep forever. But I never meant it to happen like this, I swear it, darling.'

Annabelle was stamping her foot with impatience now, so with a resigned sigh her mother turned to her. The moment she had always dreaded had finally come.

'Perhaps we should go into the kitchen where we can talk in private?' she suggested, but Annabelle shook her head.

'I don't want to go into the kitchen,' she spat. 'You can say whatever you have to say right here. There's only family here, and Dotty and Lucy are my friends. I don't mind them hearing whatever it is you're going to say.'

'Very well then.' Miranda drew a long shuddering breath as she chose her words carefully, but she feared that once they were said, things would never be the same again.

'The thing is,' she started hesitantly, 'when your father and I got married we planned to have a big family. A *huge* family, in fact!' She smiled nostalgically as she remembered how happy they had been, but then her eyes grew sad as she went on tremulously, 'We tried for a baby from the second he put the ring on my finger, but time went by and each month I would cry with disappointment when I discovered that I wasn't pregnant. Eventually we had to accept that it wasn't going to happen for us and I sank into a depression. And then one night your father came home with a young girl. She was homeless and she had been hanging around his garage because he slipped her food and gave her a little money here and there. He felt sorry for her. But the thing is – she was heavily pregnant and she told your father that she didn't want to keep the baby. So, he offered to buy the baby from her when it was born. She agreed, so then your father put her into a small hotel and paid a woman to go and deliver the baby when her time came. You were the result, and within hours of the girl giving birth he went and fetched you home and paid her. We haven't seen or heard from her since.'

Annabelle's eyes were starting from her head. It was just too much to take in. 'B-but who was she?' she croaked. 'You must have known who she was and where she was from?'

'All we ever knew about her was that her name was Carol and that she had run away from home when she found out that she was pregnant. She never even told us who your father was. I'm so sorry you had to find out like this, darling! I always hoped you would never need to know. But it doesn't change how daddy and I think of you, I promise. You've been our own since the very first second I set eyes on you, and I couldn't have loved you any more even if I had given birth to you myself.'

'You're telling me that my mother was a runaway unmarried mother?' It was too unbelievable to be true, and Annabelle felt as if the bottom had dropped out of her world.

Then temper took hold and she shouted accusingly, 'You're *lying*! Tell me you're lying! Why are you doing this to me – and today of all days too?'

But one glance at her mother's pallid face told her that it was true, every single word of it, and she sagged onto the nearest chair.

Dotty and Lucy glanced at each other feeling totally in the way and wondering if they should leave. This was such a private moment and they felt that Annabelle should have some time to come to terms with what she had just learned.

'I er . . . think I should be going now,' Lucy mumbled, getting unsteadily to her feet.

'Yes,' Dotty agreed, hastily joining her. 'I think I might go and stay at Lucy's with her and Harry for the rest of the weekend too – if Lucy doesn't mind, that is?'

When Lucy shook her head, Dotty said, 'Right then – I'll just go and shove a few clothes into a bag and we'll er . . . see you at work on Monday, shall we, Annabelle? And have a happy . . .' the words trailed away. How could what was left of Annabelle's birthday possibly be happy now after the disclosure of such a momentous secret?

No one tried to stop them. It was as if everyone in the room had been rendered speechless, so Lucy and Dotty made a hasty retreat.

'Phew!' Dotty said some minutes later as they walked away from the house with Dotty clutching a small bag. 'That was some party, wasn't it? Poor Annabelle. She's always been so full of herself, hasn't she? I mean, she truly believed that she'd been born with a silver spoon in her mouth, so this is going to hit her like a ton of bricks.'

'Hmm, seems like I'm not the only one who had a secret in her past, doesn't it?'

They walked on in silence for a time until Dotty suddenly took Lucy's hand and gave it a gentle squeeze. 'Whoever we all are I'm glad we met and became friends,' she said quietly. 'And neither you nor Annabelle should feel ashamed of your past. Neither of you had a say in it, none of what happened was your fault.'

'I just hope Annabelle will look at it like that,' Lucy answered stoically.

The two girls then moved on, their thoughts firmly fixed on Annabelle, who had possibly just had the worst birthday ever.

*

'Oh, good morning, Miss Smythe,' Mrs Broadstairs said in astonishment the following Monday morning as she walked through the cosmetics department. Annabelle was behind her counter, but this girl looked nothing like the Annabelle that the woman was accustomed to seeing. Annabelle was usually so glamorous but today she was bordering on downright dowdy. Her beautiful blonde hair was scraped back into a severe ponytail at the nape of her neck and her face was bare of make-up.

'Are you feeling unwell, dear?' she asked as she stared at the transformation. She had often had cause to tell Annabelle off for being too glamorous, but now she realised that she actually preferred the glamorous to the dowdy.

'I'm fine, thank you, Mrs Broadstairs,' Annabelle answered meekly and again the woman was shocked. The girl had always been so full of herself and lippy into the bargain, but today she seemed positively subdued.

'Good, good,' she muttered and quickly moved on. Ah well, she thought to herself, we're all entitled to our off days. Perhaps it's the wrong time of the month? No doubt she'll be back to her usual confident self tomorrow. She then continued with her inspection and moved on to the next department.

'How are you feeling?' Dotty asked when they all met up in the dining room for their break.

Annabelle shrugged. 'How would you expect me to be feeling? I dare say you've both had a good laugh at my expense now you know what I really am.'

'What do you mean, what you *really* are? You're Annabelle Smythe, the same person you've always been.'

'But I'm not though, am I?' Annabelle stared down

into her mug. 'I'm the daughter of a common runaway girl.'

'How do you know she was common?' Dotty said indignantly. 'Don't you remember Mrs Cousins, my neighbour from Hillfields? She resorted to walking the streets, bless her, to put food on the table for her children. But she certainly wasn't a bad person or common. Circumstances made her do what she did out of desperation. Perhaps it was the same for your mum? From what I could gather she was very young so perhaps she had no way of keeping you. She probably let you go because she wanted the best for you.'

'Oh yes, how romantic,' Annabelle said sarcastically.

Dotty lowered her head then before saying cautiously, 'I went to meet Miss Timms yesterday afternoon and she's asked me again to move in with her, so I thought . . . Well, I'm very grateful for all you and your mother have done for me but I think it's time to give you both a bit of space. You have a lot to come to terms with at present.'

'If that's what you want,' Annabelle answered carelessly.

Lucy and Dotty exchanged a worried glance, but they didn't say anything. It was as if Annabelle had put up a brick wall and there was no getting through to her at the moment.

That evening after work, Annabelle and Dotty travelled home together on the bus and Dotty told Miranda of her decision to move out.

Miranda cried a little. She had grown very fond of Dotty and enjoyed having her around, but she didn't argue with her. At the moment she was trying to spend as much time as she could with her daughter and Annabelle was her priority. Dotty packed her belongings quickly and efficiently. The whole of her worldly possessions amounted to no more than a small suitcase full of the clothes that Robert had bought for her, and her typewriter, which she packed carefully into its small hard case. She said her goodbyes to Miranda and within an hour was back on the bus on her way to stay with Miss Timms, who had written her address down for her. She lived on the main Kenilworth Road and when Dotty toted her cases off the bus she chewed her lip in agitation. The houses all looked very grand, even grander than Annabelle's, and she felt out of place. They were all a very far cry from the orphanage she had been brought up in and her little flat in Hillfields, but she had no choice but to go on now. Perhaps she could just stay for a few days and then start to look for somewhere else of her own again the following weekend?

She walked on a little further until eventually she came to the number Miss Timms had given her. She took a deep steadying breath before setting off up the path and tapping on the door. It was a lovely old timbered house painted in white with the timbers painted black and its leaded windows sparkled in the early evening sun. Just like Miss Timms it looked very spick and span.

The woman answered the door almost immediately. So quickly in fact that Dotty wondered if she had been watching out for her.

'Oh you're here at last,' Miss Timms said happily as she took Dotty's case from her. 'You are so welcome and I have your room all ready for you. I do hope you'll like it. I've put you in the back one overlooking the garden. But first you must eat. I have a meal all ready for you.'

Dotty was overwhelmed at the greeting. It was almost as if she was visiting royalty.

'I er . . . hope you don't mind,' she said as Miss Timms hauled her into a spacious hallway where a highly polished parquet floor shone in the dull light, 'but I rang Robert and gave him your phone number this afternoon. I didn't want him worrying about where I was.'

'Ah, that's your boyfriend in London, isn't it? Of course I don't mind. Your friends are welcome to ring you or call whenever they wish. This is your home now.'

'Well, just temporarily,' Dotty answered quickly. 'And I really appreciate this but I think I might start to look around for another flat at the weekend. I can't keep putting on people forever. And Robert isn't my boyfriend. We're just friends,' she added.

'Oh, but you can't think about leaving when you've only just arrived!' Miss Timms exclaimed. She spread her hands then. 'This place is far too big me for now that Mother is gone,' she confided. 'In fact, it was too big when Mother was alive. We rattled around in it like peas in a pod, but she wouldn't hear of moving. I'm afraid she was a terrible snob. Not an easy woman to live with at all, to be honest.' She glanced nervously over her shoulder then as if the dead woman might magically materialise at any moment. But then she smiled again as she took Dotty's elbow and led her towards the back of the house. Dotty was amazed as they moved on and felt as if she had stepped back in time. The house and its contents were very dated and fussy, and all the heavy furniture gleamed as if it had been polished to within an inch of its life. She got the impression that Mrs Timms must have been quite a slave-driver.

Miss Timms led her into an enormous kitchen, and Dotty's eyes goggled. It was like a picture she had seen of a kitchen in the last century, but once more everything was as neat as a new pin with not a single thing out of place.

'I got some fish from the stall in the market,' Miss Timms told her, 'and I've done you some potatoes that I grew in the vegetable patch in the garden and broccoli to go with them. You do like cod, don't you, Dotty? I seemed to remember you did when you were at the orphanage.'

'I love fish,' Dotty assured her, touched at how hard the woman was trying to please her. 'But you really don't have to go to all this trouble every day. I can get a meal in the staff dining room at work.'

Miss Timms sniffed disapprovingly. 'That isn't the same as having a good home-cooked meal,' she said. 'And you're so thin. But never mind, now that you're here I shall soon get you fattened up a little.'

Dotty grinned, thinking that Miss Timms had made her sound like a Christmas turkey, but she didn't object because she knew that the dear soul only meant well.

The meal was actually delicious, and Dotty cleared her plate – much to Miss Timms's delight.

'And now I must show you your room,' she said when she had plied the girl with soft stewed fruit from the garden and thick custard.

Dotty followed her upstairs where Miss Timms showed her into a very pretty bedroom. A chintz bedspread lay across a large brass bed and matching curtains hung at the window, which overlooked a very neat garden, most of which was clearly being used to grow fruit and vegetables. There was a heavy oak wardrobe, a chest of drawers and a thick wool rug on the floor at the side of the bed.

'Why, it's lovely!' Dotty exclaimed and Miss Timms beamed.

'Then I'll leave you to unpack,' she chirped merrily. 'The bathroom is the third door on the right along the landing. I've put you some fresh towels in there but do let me know if there's anything else you need.'

'I will,' Dotty promised as the woman backed out of the room looking very happy. She must be very lonely if she's so pleased to have me here, Dotty thought and then set about unpacking her case.

Later that evening, Robert telephoned Miss Timms and asked if he could speak to Dotty. The woman tactfully left Dotty to speak to him in private, then came back into the hall when she heard the receiver go down.

'Are you all right, Dotty?' she asked, seeing the girl's glum face.

'Oh yes, I'm fine,' Dotty assured her a little too quickly.

Miss Timms stared at her thoughtfully. 'You love that young man, don't you?' she asked bluntly, and when Dotty immediately lowered her eyes, her suspicion was confirmed. For months Dotty had talked of little else but Robert, but recently she had seemed very subdued and had scarcely mentioned him.

'Of course I don't,' Dotty responded rather heatedly. 'We have to stay in touch because of my writing, but that's all there is to it. Robert regards me as nothing more than a friend – I think.'

'And how do you regard him?'

Dotty squirmed uncomfortably. 'As a wonderful man,' she admitted. 'But we live in different worlds. And Robert is older than me too. I think he sees me as just a silly kid who has a flair for writing.'

'I doubt that very much,' Miss Timms said quietly. 'And age and class between two people who care about each other should be no barrier at all.'

Dotty sighed and moved away, and as the older woman watched her go her heart was heavy. Poor Dotty, life had not been kind to her, but Alice Timms hoped that from now on, she could make things a little easier for the girl.

Chapter Twenty-Six

During the autumn air raids continued on a regular basis, although thankfully many of them turned out to be false alarms. And then they were into November, with Christmas racing towards them again.

'Crikey, it's enough to freeze the hairs off a brass monkey out there,' Mrs P shivered one night when Lucy called to collect Harry after work. Lucy couldn't imagine being without him now and blessed the day she had found him. Apart from when she went to work they were inseparable, and Mrs P loved him too, although she still hadn't got herself another dog.

'An' how were things at work today?' she asked now as Lucy ruffled Harry's silky ears.

'Well, depending on how you look at it, Annabelle and her mother have had some good news. They had a telegram saying that Mr Smythe has been taken prisoner of war.'

'An' that's good news?' Mrs P said uncertainly.

'Well, it's better than being told that he's been killed, isn't it?' Lucy instantly felt guilty as she thought of Mrs P's son and added hastily, 'At least he won't be in the firing line any more. And hopefully when the war is over he'll return home. I think Miranda is quite relieved. She's been going out of her mind with worry because she hadn't heard from him.'

'Aye, well I know what that feels like,' Mrs P said sadly. 'An' so do you, love, wi' still no news from your Joel.'

'Joel will survive,' Lucy answered determinedly. 'He has to, because he's all I've got left in the world now apart from Harry.'

Mrs P nodded and gave her a hug. 'An' how's Dotty? I ain't seen her fer a while neither. Nice girl she is.'

'Oh, she's fine and still living with Miss Timms. She reckons she wants a place of her own again now but I don't think she likes to leave her.'

'Well, her short story in *Woman's Heart* were brilliant last week,' Mrs P commented. 'I reckon she's gettin' better all the time, an' I can't wait fer her book to come out. I shall be at the front of the queue to buy that, I don't mind tellin' yer. An' what's more, I reckon in the not too distant future she'll be earnin' a livin' writin' full-time. But what's goin' on between her an' that London bloke now?'

'Not a lot, as far as I can gather.' Lucy stifled a yawn. They'd spent half of last night in the shelter again, and she was worn out. 'And I think it's a real shame because I believe Dotty loves him even if she hasn't admitted it to herself yet. Suddenly she's stopped going to London, and between you and me she's as miserable as sin half the time. I just don't understand it.'

'Hmm . . . Well, no doubt it'll sort itself out. They do say the path of true love never runs smooth,' Mrs P commented.

Lucy yawned again. 'I dare say you're right, but now if

you don't mind I'm going to take Harry round home and get an early night. I could do with matchsticks to prop my eyes open at the minute. In fact, today during a quiet spell I almost fell asleep at work. I dread to think what Mrs Broadstairs would have said if she'd found me snoozing.'

Mrs P chuckled as she envisaged the scene. She loved to hear about the staff that Lucy worked with, and some of the customers she served. Mrs Broadstairs was now apparently making no secret of the fact that she and Mr Bradley were finally a couple.

Once back in her own home, Lucy fed Harry then warmed up some soup she had made the day before for herself. She was just too tired to bother to cook tonight, and praying that she would get an unbroken night's sleep – but it wasn't to be. She was just washing up her dishes when the air-raid sirens began to wail. Glancing at the clock she saw that it was only just gone 7 p.m. and she groaned as Harry rushed over to her and hid his head in her skirt. He hated the sirens. Grabbing him by the collar, Lucy led him out into the yard where Mr and Mrs P were emerging from their back door.

'I reckon it's gonna be a bad 'un tonight,' Mrs P told the girl as she ushered her towards the Anderson shelter. 'Our Fred's just had the wireless on an' they reckon the first wave o' bombers have just flown across the coast at Dorset. They're headin' our way an' all, God help us.' Glancing up at the sky, she sighed. 'An' on such a beautiful night an' all! Would yer just look at that moon an' them stars. There must be at least a million of 'em.'

But even as she spoke, the drone of the planes sounded above the sirens. 'Christ Almighty, they're droppin' incendiaries. Get into the shelter quick!' Mrs P pushed Lucy ahead of her but not before the girl had time to see the first bomb float down towards the city. The sight was followed by the sound of a deafening explosion and Harry began to whimper pathetically as Lucy sat down and pulled him to her.

'Bastards!' Mrs P shouted as her husband managed to slam the door shut, and then the shelter shook as another bomb dropped dangerously close to them. Lucy felt about for the candles and matches that Mrs P always kept in there, and once she had located them she lit two candles with trembling fingers. She had never known the bombs to drop so close before. Normally the Germans targeted the factories, but tonight it appeared that they were aiming for the city centre. Once, when Fred dared to peek outside, he saw wave after wave of bombers flying overhead and dropping their loads with terrifying regularity. Within minutes the smell of fires reached them and he could see flames licking up into the sky. The Bofors and the ack-acks had growled into life now and searchlights probed the sky as they swept this way and that, but the attack was so severe that the guns on the ground were having little effect. They heard the bells on the fire engines as the men raced to do what they could, but somehow they all knew that whilst so many bombs were dropping, the firemen would be fighting a losing battle.

Then came the sound of the high-explosive bombs, and Mr P said worriedly. 'If they hit the water-pipes, the firemen will have nothin' to fight the fires with. They're droppin' them to make holes in the roofs. Then it sounds like they're droppin' the incendiaries to light the fires.'

He placed his arm protectively around his wife's shaking shoulders and they sat there feeling totally useless as the lovely city of Coventry was destroyed around their ears.

Over at Primrose Lodge, Annabelle and her mother were down in the cellar.

'Here, put this round your shoulders to keep you warm,' Miranda told her daughter.

The girl took the blanket from her without a word, showing no emotion whatsoever. But then Miranda was not surprised. Annabelle had been like this ever since the disclosure about her birth at her twenty-first party.

'Don't worry, darling, it will be over soon,' Miranda told her as they listened to the terrifying drone overhead, followed by a loud bang.

Annabelle shrugged. She wasn't much bothered how long it went on now; in fact, she wasn't much bothered about anything any more. Admittedly her mother still treated her exactly the same as she had before, but as far as Annabelle was concerned nothing was the same now that she knew about her true parentage. And so they sat on in silence as Miranda desperately tried to think of something to say that would bring her daughter back to her. At last, however, Miranda rose, saying apologetically, 'I shall have to leave you now, sweetheart. I shall be needed tonight and I must get to the church hall. But you should be quite safe here.'

'I'll come with you,' Annabelle said dully. 'Anything is better than just sitting here not knowing what's going on, and I dare say it will be a case of the more hands the merrier if the bombing continues.'

Miranda chewed on her lips, hating the thought of this precious girl being out on the streets during a raid. But she knew better than to argue with Annabelle once she had made her mind up, so she allowed the girl to follow her up the cellar steps.

Over on the Kenilworth Road Miss Timms and Dotty were also sheltering in their cellar. Dotty was almost beside herself with fear as she thought of Robert in London. Was he safe? And then she finally had to admit to herself that she loved him, *truly* loved him, and she knew that if anything should happen to him there would be no point in living. It was funny when she came to think of it; she had seen so many hurdles between them – his age, his upbringing – and yet none of that mattered now, and had he been there, she would have told him how she felt even if she risked learning that her feelings were not returned.

When she began to cry, Miss Timms cuddled her.

'Don't cry, sweetheart,' she urged tenderly. 'I've got you safe and I won't let anything happen to you.'

'I – I wasn't crying for me,' Dotty whimpered. 'I was crying for Robert. Oh Miss Timms, I've been such a fool. I think I've loved him since the first second I set eyes on him, but I was too afraid to tell him. I felt that I wasn't good enough for him so I've deliberately backed off and held him at arm's length. And now I may never get the chance to tell him. What shall I do if anything happens to him?'

'Oh, my poor Dotty.' The woman was distressed to see the dear girl so upset. 'If it's God's will he'll survive,' she murmured, and Dotty could only pray that she was right. And then the very room trembled and they both cowered as lumps of plaster rained down on them.

'I think the house has taken a hit,' Miss Timms murmured as she spat out plaster dust.

Dotty's eyes stretched wide with panic. 'Then that means that we are trapped down here,' she breathed.

'If we are, they'll dig us out,' Miss Timms said calmly, although her own heart was beating fast now. But then if she was to die she could think of no one she would rather be with, and suddenly the time for the truth was upon her. She didn't want to take her secret to the grave with her.

'Dotty . . . I have something that I must tell you,' she

began. 'And I fear that once I have told you, if we get out of here alive you may never want to see me again.'

Dotty peeped up at her, her face pale in the light from the flickering candle.

'The thing is . . .' the woman went on, 'I know how much you have always wanted to know who your mother was – and well, I happen to know. You see, *I* am your mother.'

'What?' Dotty eyes were transfixed on the woman now and Miss Timms squirmed uncomfortably.

'B-but you *can't* be,' Dotty breathed, feeling as if she was caught up in some sort of a dream. 'And if you really *are* my mother, why did you abandon me and leave me in the orphanage all those years?'

'I – I had no choice,' the woman informed her brokenly above the roar of explosions. 'But please let me at least explain and then you might understand.'

When Dotty did not object she took a deep breath before going on. 'My mother was a very strict religious woman, as I think I may have told you,' she began. 'I was her and Father's only child and I had the best education that money could buy. I went to a private convent school as Mother wanted me to make something of myself and marry well.' She snorted then. 'Unfortunately, although I had the brains, I was somewhat of a plain Jane, so the last part might have proved to be somewhat difficult. Anyway, I left school and enrolled at a secretarial college. I quite enjoyed it, and when I had completed the course I found a job as a receptionist in an office. I soon developed a crush on one of the bosses there. I had never been in love before and was sadly lacking in confidence, but amazingly he found me attractive and before I knew it we were having an affair.' Miss Timms sighed. 'He was some years older than me and before too long I discovered that he was a married man and my whole world fell apart. The problem was, he kept telling me that he was going to leave his wife so that we could be together. Young and naïve as I was, I believed him.'

She shook her head as memories rushed back. 'Then another woman in the office began to suspect that there was something going on between us, and she privately tried to warn me off him. She said I was a fool and that nothing could ever come of it, but I wouldn't listen to her. Of course, I was furious and told her to mind her own business. I know now that she was only trying to help me. Perhaps she had been in a similar situation herself, once. You think you know it all at that age, don't you? And then one day I came home to find a very attractive woman in the kitchen with Mother. She was his wife and she'd gotten wind of our affair. Mother was absolutely furious and forbade me from ever seeing him again. She even locked me in my room for a few days until I agreed. But of course, she couldn't lock me away forever, and as soon as she let me out I headed back to the office to find him. That was a big mistake. He told me that he did love me, but found he couldn't bring himself to leave his wife because of the children. I was totally devastated, and yet I admired him for putting his children first. He was a good man, you see? And then I missed my next period.'

Miss Timms gulped deep in her throat as a tear plopped off the end of her nose. 'I'm ashamed to admit that I thought of getting rid of the baby but I didn't know who to go to or who to ask for help, so I just said nothing and foolishly believed I could keep it a secret. Eventually Mother confronted me and I had to admit that I was pregnant. We had lost Father by then and she had taken his loss badly, so although I wanted to keep my baby I knew that I couldn't leave Mother all alone. I never stepped out of the house again after that for months. And I didn't tell your father about you either. It wouldn't have been fair on him.

'On the night that you were born, Mother paid someone to come to the house to deliver you. I never knew who it was, but you were such a beautiful baby and I realised then that I couldn't bear to part with you. I told her so. And then a couple of days later I woke up one morning to find that you were missing from your crib. I begged Mother to tell me what she had done with you, but she refused to say. She just said that you were safe and that I must put it all behind me now. And then a few days later I read in the newspaper about a baby being abandoned on the steps of the orphanage and I guessed that it could only be you. So I went and applied for a job there. I knew that I could never bring you home, Mother would never have allowed that and it would have caused a terrible scandal if I had admitted that you were mine. But at least by working there I could see you and be near you every day.'

Miss Timms leaned forward and said passionately, 'Oh Dotty, I was so proud as I watched you grow up, and you'll never know how many times I was tempted to tell you who I was. I knew how much you longed to know your true parentage and it tore me apart when you told me about your mummy who would come for you one day. But by then Mother was gravely ill with a heart condition and I knew that the shock would kill her, and much as I hated her I couldn't bear to have her death on my conscience. And then she died and I thought, At last I can tell her! I almost did, but by then I was too afraid of how you would react. I feared that you would hate me and never see me again. Somehow your father found out that I'd given birth to you shortly after Mother took you away. I often wonder if it was she who told him when she knew that it was too late for him to do anything about it. That's just the sort of malicious thing Mother would have done. He was utterly distraught to know that he had a daughter somewhere whom he would never know. But I sent him away. There was nothing either of us could do without hurting his family, and they didn't deserve that. But one day when the time is right I will tell you who your father is, Dotty. I think this is more than enough of a shock for you to take in. I'm *so* sorry, my dear. So very, very sorry.'

As if in a trance, Dotty stared into space as visions flashed in front of her eyes. Miss Timms working late, so that she could read her a bedtime story. Miss Timms picking her up and kissing her better when she tripped and fell. The many little treats the woman would sneak into the orphanage for her. It all made sense now and surprisingly, rather than be angry she felt as if a lead weight had been lifted from her heart. For the first time in her life she could hold her head up and know who she belonged to. It was a curious, wonderful feeling.

'I think I understand,' she told the woman softly. 'And I appreciate you telling me now. I know it couldn't have been easy for you.'

'Do you really mean that?' the woman asked incredulously as a look of pure joy spread across her thin face.

'Yes, I do,' Dotty answered sincerely. 'And when we get out of here we'll shout it to the world and I'll be proud to tell them that you're my mum. And then we'll have the rest of our lives to make up for what we've missed.'

'Oh, darling. You'll never know what that means to me,' the woman sighed, but just then there was another deafening explosion and they heard the windows in the house above them implode as the cellar walls juddered with the force.

Simultaneously they both looked towards the ceiling and Miss Timms threw herself over Dotty as another explosion sounded, but they had no time to say any more before the roof of the cellar collapsed in on them.

Chapter Twenty-Seven

The raid lasted all night and the people of Coventry faced an inexorable assault of terror as wave after wave of bombers flew over, dropping their deadly cargoes on the city. Finally, at just after six o'clock in the morning, the all-clear sounded and people began to emerge from their shelters to a scene of hell on earth. The beautiful Cathedral of St Michael's lay in ruins, as did most of the city centre – and everywhere they looked flames were licking into the sky. Sometime later it was reported that the fires had been so severe that people who lived 100 miles away could see the glow in the sky. Thousands found themselves homeless. Water mains and major roads had been targeted first, making it almost impossible for the fire engines to reach or tackle the blazes. Seriously wounded people and dead bodies littered the streets, and many more families were trapped beneath piles of smouldering rubble that only hours before had been their homes.

'God help us,' Mrs P sobbed as they looked about them. Mangled water-pipes rose out of the roads like grotesque sculptures and not a window in the whole street had any glass left in it. The whole landscape had changed, with rows of houses in ruins as if they had never been. Thankfully their house was still standing, although they could see a large hole in one corner of the roof.

Mr P rushed inside and fiddled with the wireless until the latest news reports began to filter through.

'It ain't just us that's took it,' he told Mrs P and Lucy when they joined him. 'London's been raided an' all by twenty-one bombers, poor sods. We took the brunt o' nearly four hundred an' fifty o' the bastards, an' only two of 'em shot down.' He shook his head sorrowfully, wondering where it was all going to end, before straightening his shoulders and telling his wife, 'Well, standin' here gripin' ain't goin' to do no good, is it? I'm off to see where I can help. There might be people buried under the rubble, an' the Army lads'll need all the help they can get. An' there ain't much point turnin' in to work, I doubt there's a factory left standin'.' And so saying he went to put his work boots on as Mrs P looked around her home in alarm. The severity of the close blasts had covered every surface with soot from the chimney, and broken glass from the windows was strewn all across the floors.

'I bet my house won't be any better,' Lucy said, gripping Harry's lead. 'I'll leave you to it now and go and make a start on mine, Mrs P.'

'Aye, you do that, love,' the woman told her as she went to collect a broom. It looked like they would both have enough to keep them busy that day.

Miranda and Annabelle had just walked back into Primrose

Lodge later that morning when the phone rang. Miranda hurried to answer it, aware that they were very lucky indeed that the phone was still connected. Many of the telephone exchanges across the city had been bombed.

'Hello, is that Mrs Smythe?'

Recognising Robert's voice, Miranda answered, 'Yes, it's me, Robert. Are you all right?'

'I'm fine,' he assured her. 'It's good to know that you are too. I just wanted to know if Dotty's OK. I think Miss Timms's phone is down because I can't get through.'

Miranda felt misgivings but tried to sound confident as she said, 'I'm sure she is, but most of the phone lines are down here. I've no doubt the girls will be in touch with each other later on, and as soon as they are, I'll get her to ring you.'

'Thank you, I'd appreciate that.'

Hearing the concern in his voice, she sighed wearily. It had been a hellish night and during it she had seen sights that would stay with her forever – but when were these two idiots going to admit what they meant to each other? She despaired of them sometimes!

Once she had placed the telephone receiver down she caught sight of herself in the hall mirror and gasped. Her hair was caked with thick dust, her clothes were blood-spattered and smelly, and there were dark bags beneath her eyes from lack of sleep. An exhausted Annabelle had collapsed onto a chair in the kitchen. When Miranda entered she found the girl with her head on her arms, fast asleep.

'Come along, miss,' she told her. 'I'm going to make you a good strong cup of tea and I'll put the water heater on. Then you're to have a nice hot bath and get yourself into bed for a few hours. And Annabelle, I was really proud of you last night, you worked so hard.'

'So did everyone else,' Annabelle replied ungraciously. Miranda sighed as she filled the kettle at the sink. Thankfully they still appeared to have running water, which was more than the majority of Coventry had.

'That was Robert on the phone, checking that Dotty was safe and sound,' Miranda went on, and at the thought of her friends, Annabelle sat up straight.

'After I've had a rest I'll go and see them,' she decided. 'Although I don't know how I'm going to manage it. I heard the Army chaps saying that the majority of the trams and buses have been destroyed. I suppose I could go on my bike though. In fact, it might be easier that way.'

'Just so long as you have a rest first,' her mother told her. 'You look all in, and if you don't get some sleep soon you'll make yourself ill. I'm sure that Dotty and Lucy will be fine.'

As it happened, in fact, before Annabelle got a chance to go out, just after lunchtime Lucy arrived on her bicycle looking pale and worried.

Miranda had managed to snatch a couple of hours' sleep by then and have a wash and change of clothes, and felt slightly better.

'Ah, Lucy, Annabelle was going to come and check on you and Dotty later when she'd had a rest. Are you all right, sweetheart?'

'I'm fine, but I can't get through to Dotty,' Lucy told her. 'And I was just talking to some soldiers on the way over here who told me that her side of the city had taken a lot of hits. You don't think Miss Timms's house has been bombed, do you?'

'I don't know,' Miranda said. 'But Robert rang earlier on, and he was worried because he couldn't get through to her either.'

'That's it then,' Lucy said as she strode purposefully back towards the door. 'I'm going over there to see what's happening. Oh, and could you tell Annabelle not to bother going in to work tomorrow? Owen Owen is flattened apparently, and the police and the Army have had to clear off looters who were sifting through the rubble for undamaged stock.'

'Oh dear.' Another shock. Miranda placed her hand over her mouth. That meant that all three girls were out of work now, but then that seemed unimportant after what she had been forced to see the night before, like the tiny baby who had died in her arms. He would never grow up now to ever have a job. It all seemed so utterly pointless – and all because of one wicked man's greed for power. Adolf Hitler had a lot to answer for!

'I'll tell her,' she promised. 'But don't get fretting about that for now. That's the least of our worries. At least we still have a roof over our heads and we're still alive.'

Lucy hurried outside and clambered onto her bicycle. She just needed to know that Dotty was safe now and then she could go home and get some blessed sleep. She had left Mrs P to watch Harry and Mr P covering her windows with sheets of plywood, and with any luck he would be done by the time she got back.

As she rode along she tried to avert her eyes from the scenes of devastation all around her, but she often had to get off her bike and pick her way across rubble and smouldering piles of bricks. People were sitting dejectedly on the kerbstones with the few possessions they had managed to salvage from their ruined homes scattered around them, and the sound of children crying and ambulance and fire-engine bells filled the air. But then at last she came to the Kenilworth Road and she stared in horror at the scene before her. She was covered from head to foot in the ash that was floating in the air from the numerous fires by now, and her lungs felt as if they were on fire too. But even so she spurred herself on until she came to Miss Timms's house. The roof was completely gone and half of the house was flattened. Lucy's stomach sank. Dotty had told her quite clearly that she and Miss Timms always sheltered in the cellar if the air-raid sirens sounded, and there was no reason why last night should have been any different. So could it be that they were still trapped down there?

Throwing her bike to the ground, she raced towards a number of soldiers who were digging through the rubble of the house next door and told them breathlessly, 'Please, you have to help – my friend must be trapped down in the cellar next door.'

A young soldier whose eyes looked immeasurably weary shrugged as he covered the bodies of an old lady and an old man they had dragged from the ruins.

'We may as well come and have a look then,' he answered with a nod towards his colleagues. 'The neighbours the other side reckoned there was only an elderly couple that lived here and we've got them both out. Not that it will do them much good,' he answered sadly.

Lucy knew she would never forget the sight of those broken bodies for as long as she drew breath.

They all trooped over to what had once been Miss Timms's treasured vegetable patch and looked around them. Half of the house was still standing, giving it a grotesque appearance, and even as they watched, an oak dressing-table slithered over the edge of the floor in what must have been Miss Timms's room to land in a shattered heap on the rubble below.

'Where would the cellar door be?' the young soldier asked

Lucy now and she chewed perplexedly on her lip as she tried to remember. She had only visited the house a few times.

Then she pointed towards the area where the kitchen had been. 'On the left-hand side over there, I think,' she told them.

They instantly lifted their spades and began to dig. It was mid-afternoon by now and the light was fast fading. Added to that, it was bitterly cold. The men had worked non-stop all through the long night, and now they were so tired that they barely knew what they were doing.

Feeling useless, Lucy suddenly joined in, flinging bricks and rubble aside with her bare hands, but after an hour the young soldier she had spoken to informed her wearily, 'Sorry, miss, but I think we'll have to stop now. There's been no sound of anyone still alive and my men are about dead on their feet. I'm going to get them back to the barracks for a rest and we'll start again in the morning.'

'But you can't just leave them trapped down there!' Lucy cried, horrified. And then she began to shout: *'Dotty! DOTTY*, can you hear me?' Over and over she shouted until her voice became hoarse as the soldiers leaned heavily on their spades watching her. Lucy's hands were cut and bleeding by now and she was openly crying, the tears leaving grimy tracks down her cheeks. But the only sound they heard was the collapsing of the damaged houses around them.

The soldiers turned to leave and it was then that it came to them, dully at first but then a little louder.

'Help! HELP!'

Lucy's face lit up as she threw herself at the rubble with renewed vigour. 'You see?' she breathed triumphantly. 'They *are* alive down there!'

The young soldier gave an order to his men and within seconds they were digging again. Lucy smiled gratefully at them and side by side they worked on. It was almost dark when at last they reached the cellar door, and the sight of it seemed to spur everyone on. Finally, they managed to drag it open.

'Thankfully, the steps are clear,' the young soldier told them as he shone a torch down into the gloomy room below. 'Come on, chaps.' Then to Lucy, 'It might be best if you stayed here, miss. We don't want you trapped down there an' all if any more of the roof collapses.'

Lucy's hands clenched into fists of frustration as she watched two of the men tentatively moving down the dark staircase, testing each step as they went to make sure that it would hold their weight. Time stretched on and at one point Lucy would have gone down to join them, but another soldier gently held her back, telling her, 'They know what they're doing, miss.'

Lucy sincerely hoped so and stood there on tenterhooks as the sound of rubble being carefully moved carried up the steps to them. It seemed that only part of the cellar roof had collapsed, but they all knew that the rest could go at any time and then the two young soldiers would be trapped down there too. But then at last when Lucy was sobbing with emotion, a shout came to them.

'We've found them! Radio through for an ambulance – we're fetching them out now.'

A young private hurried away to do as he was told as Lucy chewed on her knuckles. And then minutes later there was a sign of activity at the bottom of the steps and the two men appeared carrying a limp form between them. It was impossible to tell if it was Dotty or Miss Timms for now as the body was thickly coated in dust, but as they inched cautiously further up the stairs Lucy cried out with relief when she recognised Dotty's haircut.

The men emerged at last and gently laid the figure down whilst another soldier leaned over her and began to wipe the dirt from around her mouth. Then suddenly Dotty's eyes flew open, the whites of them glaring in the dim light.

'M-my mum!' she muttered weakly as Lucy dropped to her knees beside her and took her hand.

Lucy stared down at her, perplexed. What was Dotty talking about? Perhaps she had concussion?

'It's all right,' she soothed, stroking the matted hair from Dotty's forehead. 'You must have had a bang on the head, but don't worry, the ambulance is on its way. You're going to be fine, I promise.'

By now the men had disappeared back down into the cellar and it was as the sound of the ambulance bells reached them that they reappeared, carrying another figure.

'They've got Miss Timms,' Lucy told Dotty. 'Everything is going to be all right now. You're both safe.'

Within minutes, both women had been lifted onto stretchers and placed in the ambulance, Lucy hastily told the ambulance men their names, and then it raced away with its bells clanging.

'Thank you so much.' Lucy turned to the soldiers who had been so valiant. 'Which hospital do you think the ambulance will take them to?'

'It'll be the Coventry and Warwick,' one of them told her. 'Though God alone knows how long they'll have to wait to be seen. It's pandemonium there an' all, as part of the hospital took a hit.'

Lucy was sickened to know that not even a hospital was safe from the Luftwaffe's raids.

'Thank you again,' she said with all her heart, then turned

and raced towards her discarded bicycle as the soldiers threw their spades into the back of an Army jeep. Her legs were going like pistons on the pedals again as she flew back towards Annabelle's to tell her and her mother that Dotty was safe.

Both Annabelle and Miranda breathed a sigh of relief at the news.

'Well done, Lucy darling. Now come in and clean yourself up a bit,' Miranda urged kindly. 'I'll boil a kettle so you can have a good wash. There's no point in racing off to the hospital tonight. We'll all go first thing in the morning, and perhaps by then we'll be allowed to see them both. In the meantime I can ring Robert and tell him that Dotty is safe. He rang again while you were gone and he's almost beside himself with worry, bless him. He wanted to come today but the train lines are down so his friend is going to drive him here tomorrow. If Dotty is discharged she can come here to stay. Please stay here tonight too if you wish, my dear. I really don't like the thought of you going home on that bike in the dark and I'd never get the car through.'

But this offer was gently turned down. 'Thanks, but I have to get back. Mrs P is watching Harry and if I don't go home she'll think something's happened to me,' the girl explained.

Miranda nodded understandingly. 'Very well then, but promise me you'll be careful. And if the sirens should go on the way, you get into the nearest shelter, right?'

'I will,' Lucy agreed. It had been one of the longest days of her life and all she wanted to do now was throw off her filthy clothes, get clean and drop into bed, where she'd snuggle up to Harry, and try to forget some of the atrocities she had witnessed today.

Chapter Twenty-Eight

The three women arrived at the hospital early the next morning to total chaos. Injured people were lying in the corridors on stretchers waiting to be seen by doctors and the reception area was swamped by people trying to trace their loved ones.

'I reckon this is going to be a long job,' Annabelle commented gloomily. 'Looking at that queue, it's going to be at least an hour before we even get to talk to anyone.'

'Then so be it,' Miranda said stoically as she joined the back of the straggling queue. 'We may as well get on with it. There's no point in just standing here moaning.'

Harassed-looking nurses and doctors were hurrying to and fro whilst porters struggled to find somewhere to leave the injured. People were crying and Annabelle shuddered. It was like a waking nightmare, yet they had no choice but to wait their turn. Eventually they reached the reception desk and a nurse asked sharply, 'Yes?'

'A friend of ours was brought in here last night with the lady she lodges with,' Miranda told her politely.

'Very well. Names?'

'Miss Dorothy Kent and Miss . . . Timms.' Miranda and the girls suddenly realised that they didn't even know Miss Timms's Christian name. She had always been just Miss Timms to them.

The woman began painstakingly to go through endless lists of admissions and at last she told them, 'Miss Kent is in Ward Three, but I have no entry for a Miss Timms. Are you sure that they were brought in together?'

'Quite sure,' Lucy told her solemnly. 'I was there when they put them into the ambulance together to bring them here. Miss Timms was unconscious.'

'I see.' The nurse gave her a strange look, then taking up another list she began to scan that too until eventually she asked, 'Was Miss Timms admitted from the Kenilworth Road?'

When Lucy nodded, she told them curtly, 'Just wait here a moment, would you? I'll get a doctor to see you.'

'But isn't Miss Timms on the same ward as Dotty?' Lucy questioned.

The woman ignored her and hurried away, only to come back some minutes later to tell them, 'Take a seat over there, please. A doctor will be out to see you as soon as he can. Next, please!'

The three women trooped back to the seats to begin yet another long wait, but eventually a doctor appeared and after having a hasty word with the reception nurse who pointed towards where they were sitting, he approached them.

'I believe you are here looking for Miss Timms?'

When they all nodded, he shook his head gravely. 'Then I

am very sorry to inform you that Miss Timms was pronounced dead on arrival at the hospital.'

'B-but she can't be!' Lucy spluttered. Yet one look at his face revealed that he was telling the truth.

'I'm afraid she is. She has been taken to the hospital morgue at present,' he informed them. 'But you are welcome to go and see Miss Kent if you wish. Luckily, apart from a broken arm and cuts and bruises, she escaped unharmed. It appears that the older woman shielded her with her body and took the full brunt of the collapse of the cellar roof, thereby sustaining serious internal damage that proved fatal. I'm very sorry to have to be the bearer of such bad news, but now if you will excuse me I really must get on.'

'Of course,' Miranda muttered as she placed her arm protectively about Lucy's shoulders. 'But just one question before you go, Doctor. Has Dot . . . Miss Kent been informed of Miss Timms's death?'

'No, we were waiting for her next of kin to do that. Would you happen to be related to her?'

'Well, not exactly,' Lucy told him. 'But I think we are the nearest people she has. Dotty was an orphan, you see.'

He nodded. 'Then perhaps it would be best if you broke the news to her,' he agreed. 'Goodbye.'

The three women stared at each other in horror, wondering how Dotty was going to take the news. They all knew that Miss Timms had been the only constant person in Dotty's life and were all too aware of how fond Dotty had been of her. Their friend was going to be absolutely heartbroken.

'I dare say we should go and see her now,' Miranda said, eventually breaking the stunned silence. 'At least Dotty survived, which is something to be grateful for.'

'Yes, but how will she feel, knowing that Miss Timms may have died protecting her?' Lucy answered numbly.

'I think we shall have to cross that bridge when we come to it,' Miranda said sensibly. 'For now, Dotty needs to know we are still here for her. Come along.' And so the three women set off, following the signs for Ward Three with heavy hearts.

The ward they were shown into was every bit as chaotic as the reception area had been, with beds jammed down the middle of the room and along each wall.

'You'll find Miss Kent just along there,' the unsmiling Sister told them, and after thanking her they walked in the direction she had indicated. They were each dreading what they might find, so were surprised to see Dotty sitting in a chair at the side of her bed.

Their first glimpse of her caused them all to gasp with shock, for the poor girl was almost unrecognisable. Both her eyes were black and swollen, and every inch of her that was visible was covered in cuts and bruises, and yet as she caught sight of them her face broke into a radiant smile causing her to grimace with pain.

'I knew you'd come,' she croaked painfully as they stared at her arm, which was in a heavy plaster cast supported by a sling. 'The ambulance men told me that you saved my life by insisting that the soldiers searched for me, Lucy. Thank you so much. I thought I was a goner down there in that cellar for a time. The only trouble now is that I can't find where they've put Miss Timms. Well – she's not Miss Timms any more really but I'll tell you all about that in a minute. It's something so wonderful you won't believe it. I can still hardly believe it myself – but hark at me rabbiting on. Have they told you where they've put her? And has there been any word from Robert? I heard some ladies further down the ward saying that London had been bombed, too, last night and I've been worried sick.'

Here at least, Miranda was able to put her mind at rest as she told her, 'Robert is safe. In fact, even as we speak he's on his way. His friend is driving him from London. But how long will you have to stay in here?'

'Ah well, that's a bit more good news.' Dotty attempted another smile, making her cracked lips split open again. 'Because there's such a shortage of beds they said I can go home. Normally they would have kept me in longer, but with things as they are . . .' She shook her head. 'Trouble is, I shall have to come home in the clothes they found me in. They're in the locker there but they had to cut off the sleeve of my blouse to get it off my arm before they set it and the nurses have washed me as best they could and put me in this gown, but my hair . . .' Her voice trailed away as her one good arm rose to stroke the tangled filthy mess that was her hair. 'I'm afraid I must look a dreadful sight,' she whispered. 'And I don't quite know where Miss Timms and I are going to go – when I find her, that is.'

'Ah well, there's no need to worry about that,' Miranda told her, forcing a smile. 'You're going to come home with me for as long as you need to, and we'll soon get you washed and brushed up. We don't want Robert seeing you like this, now do we?'

'But what about Miss Timms?' Dotty persisted, her eyes concerned now.

Ignoring her question, Miranda whipped the curtains about the bed as she told the girl, 'We'll talk about that in a while. But first we're going to get you dressed and take you home. I'm sure there will still be some cabs running. Lucy, could you go outside and see if you could find one whilst I help Dotty?'

Only too glad to escape, Lucy hurried away, but Dotty was not going to let the subject of her beloved Miss Timms drop so easily.

'But can't she come home too?' she asked as Miranda pulled the hospital gown over her head.

'No, I'm afraid she has to stay here for now,' Miranda answered. 'But I'll explain everything when we get home.'

'Then can't I at least see her before I go?'

Miranda shook her head, too full to speak, and for the next few minutes she concentrated on getting Dotty dressed. In no time at all she and Annabelle were helping the girl down the stairs to the reception area. Dotty was as weak as a kitten and leaned heavily on Miranda, and for now she was silent as a terrible sense of foreboding took hold of her. Why were they whisking her away so quickly without letting her see her mother first? Another little thrill spliced through her. *Her mother!* She had never been able to say that before, but now at last she knew who she belonged to, where she had come from. Her mother had promised that she would soon reveal who her father was too. For the very first time in her life she felt complete and could hardly wait to share her good news with her friends.

The bad feeling lifted a little as she saw the chaos all around her. Doctors were tending to the most seriously injured patients first as others lay on stretchers groaning with pain. Ambulance and Army men were wheeling yet more casualties in and the whole place was heaving, with bodies everywhere. Perhaps her friends hadn't managed to locate Miss Timms yet in such pandemonium? But later on when she had cleaned herself up a little she would come back. Things might have calmed down by then and she would find her.

Outside, they helped her into the cab and the driver told

them, 'I'm afraid it's goin' to take some time to get yer to Cheylesmore, missus. There are diversions everywhere, an' half o' the roads are closed off, but I'll do me best.'

It was the first sight of the city Dotty had had since being trapped in the cellar and she was horrified. Fires were still blazing, and people with all that was left of their worldly possessions packed in barrows, prams or anything that would carry them were making a mass exodus from the city.

'Th-the cathedral?' Dotty gasped as they drove along.

'I'm afraid it's flattened,' Miranda told her gravely. 'And so is most of the rest of the city centre – including Owen Owen. But don't worry about that for now. At least we are still alive. You had a miraculous escape, Dotty, and we must be thankful for that.'

The car drove slowly on beneath the huge cloud of smoke that hung over the city as the three women gazed solemnly at the wreckage all around them. Would Coventry ever recover and be the same again?

Back at Primrose Lodge they helped Dotty inside and Miranda rushed off to heat some water to wash in. 'We shall have to be careful not to get your plaster wet,' she told her, as she helped her undress, then, 'Annabelle, run and find some of your clothes for Dotty to wear, would you?'

Dotty sighed as a feeling of déja vu washed over her. Once again she was homeless and forced to borrow Annabelle's clothes, but at least she was still alive. She was beginning to feel a little like a cat that had nine lives.

An hour later, with all the dirt washed from her hair that was combed out to dry, with a towel round her shoulders, Dotty sat dressed in fresh clothes at the kitchen table with the others, a large pot of tea in front of them – and she said joyously, 'Now at last I can tell you my news. It's something really wonderful and you'll never guess what it is – not in a million years!'

'So tell us then,' Annabelle said, puzzled to see Dotty looking so happy. What did she have to be happy about, after all? She had just lost her home– *again* – which didn't seem to be something to rejoice over.

'Well, it's like this . . .' Dotty went on to tell them about Miss Timms's confession down in the cellar and they all gaped in amazement as the tale unfolded.

'That poor woman,' Miranda sighed as she poured them all some tea. 'How hard it must have been for her all those years, seeing you almost every day but unable to tell you who she was. Her mother must have been a very harsh woman.' But not as harsh as life, she was thinking. 'That's really wonderful, Dotty,' she forced herself to say eventually. 'Now at last after a lifetime of wondering, you know who your mother was and how much she loved you. No one will ever be able to take that away from you . . . but I'm afraid I have some tragic news. You see,' Miranda's voice died away and she cleared her throat. 'You see, poor Miss Timms – your mother – didn't make it. It appears that she threw herself across you when the cellar ceiling collapsed to protect you, and this brave action meant she took the brunt of it. She was pronounced dead on arrival at hospital. I'm so sorry, darling.'

The colour drained out of Dotty's cheeks and she looked even paler than she had before, if that was possible. She stared at Miranda uncomprehendingly.

'B-but she can't be dead!' she stuttered. 'I only just got to know who she was! I can't have found her and lost her all in the space of one night! It's not *fair*.'

'None of this bloody war is fair!' Lucy exclaimed as her

heart broke for her friend and then she drew Dotty carefully into her arms and let her sob out her grief as the others looked helplessly on.

Robert arrived in Coventry mid-afternoon, appalled at what he had seen along the way. Ministry of Information vans were touring the streets with loudspeakers telling the homeless where they could obtain food and shelter, and he passed tramlines that now rose from the ground in twisted grotesque metal loops. Everyone knew now that the raid had been named *Moonlight Sonata* by the Luftwaffe and it was clear that they had targeted well, causing destruction. The morgues were full of unidentified bodies and the Coventry people's spirits were at an all-time low as everyone wondered how they could ever come back from such a catastrophic raid.

Robert had been travelling from London since early that morning, and by the time he arrived he was heart-sore at the things he and his friend Duncan had witnessed.

'Oh Robert, I'm so pleased to see you,' Miranda told him when she answered the door. She smiled weakly at Robert's friend. 'This is Duncan Fellows,' Robert introduced him. 'He has very kindly brought me here because the trains aren't running.' Then, seeing her red eyes, Robert's heart plummeted as he asked, 'Has something happened to Dotty?'

'Well, yes, she has been injured, but not seriously. She's in there.' Miranda gestured towards the front parlour before ushering Robert and Duncan in the direction of the kitchen. 'But there's something you should know before you see her. I'm afraid she is rather upset.'

Once the two men were safely out of earshot, Miranda quickly explained about Miss Timms.

'Poor Dotty,' Robert exclaimed. 'Fancy discovering who your mother is, only to lose her almost immediately. The poor love must be distraught.'

'She is,' Miranda said quietly. 'But I hope she'll perk up a bit when she sees you. She's been so worried about you.'

She then offered Robert's friend a bed for the night and a proper meal, but he politely refused, it saying that he really had to get back to London as he was on fire watch. Robert then saw him on his way, and once he was back inside the house he asked, 'May I go in to her now?'

'Of course,' Miranda answered. 'And you can stay as long as you like, dear. We have plenty of bedrooms and I think Dotty would be glad of your company during the next few days whilst we organise the funeral. If you can spare the time, that is?'

'I shall be here for as long as she needs me,' he said grimly, and after taking a deep breath he tapped at the parlour door and entered.

Dotty was sitting quietly staring off into space and he had to swallow his shock at first sight of her. The bruises and swelling were really coming out now and her face looked deformed.

'Oh, Dotty . . .' For now it was all he could say as he looked at the plaster on her arm and saw the state of her. But then she turned her head to look at him and his heart swelled as she tried to smile.

She held her one good hand out to him and tried to get out of the chair to greet him, but he pressed her back down and awkwardly put his arms around her, trying his best not to hurt her.

'Oh darling,' he muttered into her sweet-smelling hair. 'I can't believe what you've been through. I'm so very sorry.'

Tears began to trickle down her cheeks now. She didn't

care any more if he realised that she loved him. She was just grateful to have him there.

'I . . . I found my mother,' she whispered brokenly. 'After all these years of not knowing who she was, I found her – and then on the very same night I lost her.'

'I know.' He held her a little tighter, feeling her pain. 'Miranda just told me. But at least you know who she was now. And you know who you are too. And now we're going to give her the very best funeral that money can buy.'

'B-but I can't afford a big affair,' she sobbed. 'Owen Owen was bombed so we're all out of a job now and all I have left is my writing money.'

'Don't worry about that for now.' He stroked her cheek as he smiled at her lovingly. 'I shall see to the funeral.'

'But I can't let you do that,' she objected.

'Shush. We'll worry about that later. For now I'm just grateful that you survived. I don't know what I would have done if anything had happened to you, Dotty. You see . . . I know it's ridiculous because I'm so much older than you and you would never look at me. But the thing is . . . I have feelings for you, deep feelings that started to grow the very first time I ever set eyes on you.'

Dotty blinked, convinced that she must be hearing things. 'B-but I *would* look at you,' she stammered. 'I have feelings for you too. That's why I've been holding you at arm's length, because I didn't ever think that you could care for someone as plain as me.'

'You plain?' he said incredulously, lifting her chin. 'But Dotty, you're one of the most beautiful girls I have ever met – both inside and out, may I add.'

Since hearing the news about her long-lost mother, Dotty had been in a dark place, almost as if she was still buried in the cellar, but now suddenly there was light again and something in her heart stirred as Robert gently kissed her on the lips. And when he finally broke away, she smiled at him tremulously through her tears. Perhaps there was still something worth living for, after all.

Chapter Twenty-Nine

On 16 November 1940, the people of Coventry's spirits were lifted when King George VI visited the city to view for himself the devastation caused by the Blitz. He walked through the ruined city centre and there were those that said they saw tears in his eyes when confronted with the ruins of the once magnificent St Michael's Cathedral.

Along the way he stopped and spoke to many townspeople, offering his condolences and heartfelt sympathy, and by the time his visit was over, they were ready to stand and fight for what they believed in once more.

During the raid, over 4,330 homes had been destroyed and 554 men, women and children had been killed. Some of them were still missing, trapped beneath the piles of rubble, but now troops were drafted in by the hundreds to dig for their remains whilst the Royal Engineers worked to restore electricity, gas and water supplies.

Meanwhile, labourers worked day and night to dig graves for the victims, and on Wednesday 20 November, the first mass burial took place in the London Road Cemetery. Normally a quiet place of curving paths and graceful trees, on this day more than 1,000 mourners attended the service, which was conducted by Dr Mervyn Haigh, the Bishop of Coventry.

Dotty, Robert, Annabelle, Miranda and Lucy were amongst the mourners, as Robert had not been able to find an undertaker with time to do a single burial. Miss Timms would be laid to rest with the other victims of the 14 November Blitz in a plain oak coffin with nothing to distinguish it from the next apart from a small label with her name written on it. They found themselves standing at the side of two deep trenches into which the coffins were lowered side by side and stacked three high, and Dotty felt as if her heart was breaking. As the trenches were slowly filled, the top coffins were then covered in Union Jack flags and people openly wept at such a senseless loss of life. But life had to go on for those left behind, who were determined that they would not be defeated.

Once the service was over, Dotty, Annabelle, Miranda and Robert returned home, while Lucy went off for a job interview at a munitions factory. As she had pointed out, she couldn't afford to stay at home – and who knew how long it would be before Owen Owen was rebuilt, if it ever was? Each of the three girls knew that they would miss working together, although their friendship was forged now and they vowed never to lose touch.

Back at Primrose Lodge, Miranda offered everyone a sherry. They were all still a bit numb after the funeral, and she hoped that the sherry would revive them. She raised her own glass. 'To Miss Timms – Dotty's mother,' she said, and the other three echoed the toast.

As she put her sherry glass down, Dotty's eyes strayed to the letter lying on the table in front of her. Shortly after her own mother's death – Dotty's grandmother – Miss Timms had left the name of her solicitor with Dotty, asking her to contact them should anything ever happen to her. Dotty had complied with her wishes, calling in at their offices the day before, where she had been handed this sealed letter addressed to her. Deciding that there was only one way to find out what was in it, she asked Robert to open it for her as it was too difficult to manage by herself with only one good arm.

He took a sheet of paper from the envelope and handed it to her, and as her eyes scanned the contents, she went even paler than before. 'My God,' she muttered. 'Miss Timms has left her house and the sum of ten thousand pounds to *me*!'

'Don't you mean *half* a house?' Annabelle quipped, and Miranda glared at her.

'And why shouldn't she?' she said quickly. 'You were her daughter, after all, and when this is all over you will be able to have the house restored. It's wonderful news, Dotty. You're a wealthy young woman now and you won't need to work if you don't want to.'

'B-but I *do* want to,' Dotty answered in a daze. It was all just too much to take in.

'I'm pleased to hear it,' Robert butted in, 'because there's an idea I've been meaning to put to you, but I didn't like to broach it until the funeral was over.'

When Dotty looked at him quizzically he went on, 'Well, the thing is, Laura was saying that we could do with a new typist in the office and she also said that if you didn't mind moving to London, you could stay with her and her family for the time being. That would still give you time to write too. You could stay with me, but we wouldn't want to set tongues wagging, would we? What do you think?' He really wanted to tell her that he would be only too happy to support her but was afraid of rushing things, and possibly offending her.

'I . . . I don't know,' Dotty murmured, her mind in a spin. Everything was happening so fast, but then what was there to keep her here now, apart from her friends, and they would always stay in touch. If she did go to London she would be close to Robert and the thought was tempting, to say the least.

'Well, I can't do much typing like this,' she pointed out, tapping her plaster cast, and Robert chuckled.

'There's no one cracking a whip. Of course you'd need time to recuperate. In fact, you could take as long as you want. You're hardly desperate for the money now, are you?' he teased.

'I suppose not.' She read the letter again just to make sure that she'd understood it correctly, but the facts were still there in black and white.

It was Miranda who joined in the conversation then when she told Dotty, 'For what it's worth I think it's an excellent idea, although we'll miss you, of course. But you must think of yourself, Dotty, and at least I wouldn't worry, knowing that Robert was there to take care of you.'

'Oh, I'd do that all right,' he promised.

'Can I just have a little time to think about it?' Dotty asked, feeling as if she was on a roller coaster.

'You can have all the time in the world,' he told her with a twinkle in his eye. 'Just so long as you say yes at the end of it because I'm not going anywhere without you.'

Miranda felt a lump rise in her throat as she saw the look

that passed between the two young people. At last they were making some sort of progress. It sounded as if Lucy was going to be all right too. Now she just had to get her own daughter back on track.

The next three weeks passed in a blur as the people of Coventry tried to restore some sort of normality to their city. But three young women were still coming to terms with the secrets from their past that had changed all their lives forever.

'So 'ow did yer get on then, luvvie?' Mrs P asked when Lucy returned from her job interview at what had formerly been known as Morris Engines in Coundon.

'I got the job,' Lucy informed her, 'and I start next Monday morning. The only disadvantage to it is I'll be working shifts. One week I'll work ten p.m. till six a.m. and the next week I'll work seven thirty a.m. till five thirty p.m. That means that Harry will be alone all night every other week, unless you wouldn't mind having him round here?'

''Course he can come round here, bless his 'eart,' Mrs P assured her. 'Poor little bugger'ud be scared stiff if he were on his own an' them bloody sirens went off. No, don't you fret, he'll be safe as houses round here or in the shelter wi' me an' Fred. But what are the wages like?'

'I'll get two pounds and four shillings a week, so I should be able to manage.'

Lucy sank wearily into the fireside chair, squinting in the gloom. The windows were still covered in any old pieces of wood that Mr P had been able to get his hands on, and it looked like they might have to stay that way for some time to come. Glass wasn't easy to get hold of, but then it seemed nothing was any more, and people were beginning to get used to having to manage on rations. Mrs P had now unpicked nearly every woolly she could find and then used the wool to knit balaclavas and socks for the troops. It made her feel that she was doing her bit for the war effort. 'We all have to make do and mend' was her motto and now whenever she said it, Lucy and Mr P would wink at each other.

Now Mrs P put the kettle on and carefully measured two teaspoons of tea leaves into the warmed teapot. She'd found that if she used a little less tea but left it to mash for just a while longer, the weekly ration lasted just a bit better.

'An' how is young Dotty doin' now?' she asked a few minutes later as she carried the teapot to the table.

'Well, the bruises and the cuts are healing nicely, but she'll have to have her arm in plaster for at least another three weeks, and of course she's still very upset about Miss Timms.'

'That's understandable,' Mrs P said as she stirred the tea before carefully straining it into the two mugs. Unknown to Lucy and Fred she would save the tea leaves to reuse for herself whilst she was alone, to ensure that she always had a decent cuppa for them. But then she'd never been fond of strong tea, so she didn't really see it as a sacrifice. 'Who would ever have thought her mam were there right under her nose all that time, eh? An' then fer the poor girl to go and lose her like that. Still, on a brighter note it seems as if her an' Robert may make a go of it now, so happen she'll pick up eventually.'

'I hope so,' Lucy answered sadly.

'Off out again are you, darling?' Miranda asked as Annabelle picked up her coat and headed for the door. Along with Robert and Dotty, they had been having breakfast together.

Annabelle merely nodded.

'Then wrap up warmly,' her mother advised. 'It's so cold. I wouldn't be surprised if we didn't have some snow before too long.' She would have liked to ask Annabelle where she was going but didn't fancy having her head snapped off. The girl was unbelievably touchy at present, but then Miranda blamed herself for that. Perhaps her mother had been right all along and she should have told Annabelle about her true parentage a long time ago. But she had only been trying to protect her, and right from the first time she had held her, Miranda had never thought of the girl as anything other than her own.

'I wonder where she's off to?' she said as the door closed behind her daughter with a sharp click. 'She's been going out at the crack of dawn every day for ages and not coming back till late afternoon. Has she told you where she's going, Dotty?'

'No, she hasn't.' Dotty dabbed at her lips as she placed her toast down on her plate. She had never realised how difficult it must be for people like Robert who only had one good arm, and couldn't wait to have her plaster cast off now. 'Perhaps she's job hunting?' she suggested.

'Hmm, you could be right but if that's the case, why is she making such a big secret of it?'

'I don't know,' Dotty admitted. Then, glancing at Robert, she gathered her courage and said to Miranda, 'Actually, we were thinking of leaving for London at the end of the week, if that's all right with you? Will you and Annabelle be all right on your own?' She was more than grateful that Robert had chosen to stay with her but knew that he was keen to return to London now.

'Of course we will, but are you sure you're up to the journey? And what about your plaster?' Miranda asked.

'Oh, I'll be fine,' Dotty said. 'And Robert will take me to a hospital in London to have the cast off when it's time. We just feel we've imposed on you enough now, and once I've seen Miss T— Mother's solicitors again tomorrow to make sure that everything's in order, we can get out from under your feet.'

'You haven't been under my feet,' Miranda told her, and she meant it. 'I just wish you could have stayed again under happier circumstances.' Dotty had been very brave since the day of the funeral, helped by Robert's presence, but Miranda sometimes glimpsed the grief and regret in the girl's eyes when she thought that no one was looking.

'Well, I appreciate what you've done, but it's time to get on with the rest of my life now,' Dotty said softly and Robert smiled at her. They had been back to the cemetery the day before, where yet another mass burial had taken place, and Dotty had laid flowers, although she had no idea at all where in the grave her mother might be. She just hoped that she was in a better place and at peace now, but she felt aggrieved that they had never had time to spend together as mother and daughter. Her mother had given her own life to save hers, and Dotty would never forget it.

When Annabelle came home late that afternoon she sat down at the table, folded her hands in her lap and told her mother calmly, 'I've joined up to be a VAD.'

'*What?*' Miranda almost dropped the saucepan of potatoes she was straining into the sink.

'It's the Red Cross Voluntary Aid Detachment—'

'I *know* what it is,' Miranda snapped. 'But what do you mean, you've joined?'

'Exactly what I said.' Annabelle stared coolly back at her. 'That's where I've been going – to do the training – and now that's done and out of the way, I filled all the forms in today.

I'm going to be mobile as well but I don't know where I'll be posted as yet.'

Wiping her hands down the front of her apron, Miranda sank heavily onto the nearest chair as she tried to take in what Annabelle was telling her.

'But why?' she asked numbly. 'And why couldn't you have stayed around here? Do you know how hard VADs have to work? You'll be doing all the menial jobs like emptying bedpans and doing bed-baths. It's nothing at all like being a qualified nurse.'

'I'm quite aware of that,' Annabelle responded, her voice curt. 'But I have enjoyed helping the WVS out and this is like the next step. All the hospitals are crammed with wounded and they're crying out for help. I thought you'd be proud of me.'

'I *am* proud of you, darling,' Miranda insisted. 'But I ask again – why do you have to go away?'

'Because I think a little time apart will do us good,' Annabelle answered. 'I need an opportunity to try and come to terms with things.'

'Oh, I see.' Miranda looked so bereft that Annabelle felt a twinge of guilt, but it was too late to do anything about it now. Everything was signed and sealed and she had been informed that she would be notified of where she was to be posted within the next few days. Miranda would just have to get used to the idea.

'So don't you have any inkling where you might be going?' What if Annabelle was sent to France? Miranda was only too aware that a lot of VADs were being posted abroad.

'Not for definite, but they did say there was a good chance I would be sent to Haslar.'

Miranda was only slightly mollified. 'But that's at Gosport on the coast.' Visions of the beach covered in barbed wire in case of an invasion by sea flashed in front of her eyes and she felt weak. If the invasion came, Annabelle would be first in the line of fire. But then one look at the determined glint in her daughter's eye made her realise that nothing she could say or do would make her change her mind now. Annabelle was twenty-one years old and no longer needed parental consent to do anything.

'In that case we must start to get together the things you might need,' she said, forcing a brave smile.

'We're to be issued with uniforms so there won't be much I need to take,' Annabelle answered. Just then the front door opened and seconds later Robert and Dotty came into the kitchen, their cheeks glowing from the cold outside.

Looking from one to the other of them, Dotty wondered if they had had a row. There was obviously something amiss if Miranda's white face and glistening eyes were anything to go by. She turned to leave the room, not wishing to intrude, but Miranda stopped her when she said, 'Annabelle has just informed me that she's going to be a VAD.'

Dotty's reaction was much as hers had been. Her mouth gaped as she blinked before saying, '*What?*'

'I don't know why everyone is making such a big thing of it,' Annabelle growled. 'I'm not completely useless, you know?'

'I never thought that you were useless,' Dotty objected. 'And I think it's a wonderful thing to do. But I believe it's very hard work.' Somehow she couldn't picture Annabelle doing some of the menial jobs she had heard VADs did.

'Hard work never hurt anybody,' Annabelle retaliated. 'And we should all be doing our bit, or so Churchill keeps on telling us. In fact, when the war is over I might go on and do the training to become a proper State Registered Nurse.'

Robert and Dotty exchanged a glance then offered their congratulations. Dotty was actually quite impressed with her friend, even though she found it hard to imagine her in such an unglamorous job. Her mind was already whirling after the appointment with Miss Timms's solicitor. Mr Jenkins had been so lovely that he had brought tears to her eyes as he offered her his condolences, and he hadn't been able to do enough for her.

'I spoke to Miss . . . your mother shortly after her own mother's death,' he had told her. 'Mrs Timms had left everything to her and she in turn wanted to ensure that should anything happen to her, it would all then come to you. She was adamant on that point, and now that I am in possession of a copy of her death certificate I can release some funds to tide you over until all the legalities are completed.' He had then told her sadly, 'Your mother was a remarkable woman. I've known her for many years and she was truly selfless. She was very like her father in nature. He was a lovely man too, whereas your grandmother was . . . dare I say, slightly formidable? But should you need anything, anything at all, please don't hesitate to contact me. It has been a real pleasure to meet you.'

Dotty had come away thinking what a truly nice gentleman Mr Jenkins was and Robert had agreed with her.

Friday morning found Lucy and Annabelle standing on the platform of Coventry station with Dotty and Robert to say their goodbyes. Thankfully the train lines were now back in use although the raids had continued. As fast as the railmen repaired the tracks, the Jerries blew them up again.

Each of the three friends was aware that they were all on the verge of a new life, and none of them quite knew what to say to each other. But in that moment they all realised how much they would miss the others, and how much their friendship meant to them.

'Well – this is it then, for now at least.' It was Lucy who broke the silence as Robert walked a discreet distance away to allow them to say their goodbyes in private.

'Good old Owen Owen, eh?' Dotty blinked to hold back the tears. 'If it wasn't for working there, we might never have met.'

'True, and poor old Mrs Broadstairs and Mr Bradley,' Annabelle said quietly. She hadn't always seen eye to eye with the woman or the manager, but the girls had all been saddened when they learned that the couple had not survived the night of the Blitz.

'We'll write to each other regularly and we must meet up at least once a year.' Dotty held her good hand out and the others placed theirs on it and gave their word. After seeing each other almost daily for so long it felt strange to think of them all being apart and leading separate lives.

'Good luck at Haslar,' Dotty told Annabelle. Her posting had arrived only that morning and in just a few short days she would be on her way. 'And good luck in your new job too, Lucy. Give Harry a kiss from me, and that handsome brother of yours when you get to see him.'

'I will,' Lucy promised chokily and then they all hugged as Robert came and took Dotty's elbow.

'I'm afraid we're going to have to get aboard now,' he apologised as the platform-master began to walk along, slamming the carriage doors.

They gave each other one last kiss then Robert lifted their cases aboard as Lucy and Annabelle waved furiously.

'Goodbye, goodbye, take care,' Dotty shouted as she waved from the carriage window and the two girls stood and watched as the train carried Dotty away to her new life.

Chapter Thirty

Annabelle stared from the window of the train as it pulled into the Portsmouth Harbour station. It certainly didn't look like any station she had seen before, as it appeared to be built on stilts – and when she climbed down from the train clutching her small suitcase, she could see the waves beneath the decking she was standing on. There were lots of people in Navy uniform hurrying to and fro, so after taking a deep breath she approached a woman dressed in a nurse's uniform and asked, 'Could you tell me the way to Haslar Hospital, please?'

'Oh, yes of course. You'll need to get the pinnace across to it.'

'Pinnace?' Annabelle looked bewildered and the nurse grinned.

'It's a small naval launch. It's over there – look – and if you hurry, you might just catch it.' She pointed towards a small boat, and Annabelle smiled her thanks and hurried towards it.

The boat was almost full of other young women in civilian clothes carrying suitcases, and Annabelle wondered if they were going to be VADs too. It certainly looked that way. The smell of seaweed was heavy in the air and she could taste the salt from the sea. It was a far cry from the smoky streets of Coventry and she looked around with interest. Boats of all shapes and sizes were rocking on the choppy waves in the harbour and Annabelle felt a little tingle of excitement. She had not had a good day up to now, since the parting from her mother had been painful, but now she knew she must concentrate on the job she had come to do. She looked down from the quay into the pinnace with trepidation. It looked an awfully long way down if she should fall, but then the other girls had managed it so she had no doubt she would.

'Give us your hand, miss,' a cheerful sailor said as he helped her into the boat, and in no time at all she was seated next to a plump girl with lovely green eyes and a friendly smile.

'Goin' to be a VAD, are you?' the girl asked conversationally.

Annabelle nodded. 'Yes, are you?'

'Yes, I am, an' I have to admit I'm a bit nervous.'

The boat engine clicked into life and the boat began its short journey across the frothy waves to Haslar.

'I didn't realise we'd have to get a blooming boat across to the horspital,' the girl muttered, then holding out one hand while she clutched the side of the boat with the other, she told Annabelle, 'I'm Hilary, by the way. Hilary Slater. But me mates call me Hils. What's your name?'

'Annabelle Smythe.'

'Cor blimey, that's a bit posh, innit?' The girl had a broad Cockney accent, but then they had no time to say more, for as the boat picked up speed they were too intent on clinging onto their hats and staying in their seats.

As the pinnace bounced across the waves, Annabelle stared around the big harbour. There seemed to be everything there, from huge steel-grey battleships to small sailing dinghies, and there wasn't a square foot of water that didn't have a vessel anchored on it. She began to feel a little queasy but thankfully the journey took no more than a matter of minutes and almost before they knew it they had passed through the main harbour and turned into a creek with another small quay ahead of them.

The seaman expertly drew the boat alongside of it and told them, 'This is it then, ladies. Good luck.'

Another sailor up on the quay helped them all to disembark before telling them, 'The hospital is straight ahead. You can't miss it.'

The girls began to walk in a straggly line until they came to an enormous gateway.

'Do you reckon this is it?' the girl called Hilary asked nervously. 'It looks more like some sort of stately bloody home.'

'I suppose it must be,' Annabelle replied as she marched on towards the enormous iron gates where two sailors holding rifles stood.

'We're VADs,' Annabelle told them imperiously and with a nod they moved aside as the row of girls scooted past them. They were then confronted by a massive red-brick building with an arched colonnade.

Hilary whistled through her teeth. 'Phew, it's bloody massive, ain't it? How are we ever supposed to find our way about that place?'

'I dare say we'll manage,' Annabelle responded. Hilary seemed to have latched onto her and she wasn't sure that she liked it. She'd come to get away from everyone and to lick her wounds in peace.

Once inside the building the new intakes were directed towards an office where a stern-faced woman in uniform was waiting for them. Annabelle felt as if she were back at school and being sent to the headmistress.

'I am Miss Dewhurst,' the woman introduced herself. She was standing behind an enormous desk and the girls formed a circle around it. 'I am the Red Cross Commandant and during your time at Haslar you will all be answerable to me. You will address me as Madam at all times and should you have any concerns, I will always be available to listen to you and help wherever I can. However, you must all remember that you are here to work, you are *not* on holiday, and I shall expect the best of each of you. Initially, you will all be assistant nurses to the Queen Alexandra Royal Naval Nurses or the QUARNNS as we tend to call them. But of course if we have a sudden influx of patients, you will be doing real nursing. We shall provide you with proper training for this and as part of that training you will attend lectures given by naval doctors, QUARNNS and myself. You will all be addressed by your surnames whilst you are here. Are there any questions you would like to ask?'

Miss Dewhurst looked along the line of girls and when all of them remained silent she told them, 'Right, I'm sure you must all be tired and hungry after your journey and I still have another intake to greet yet. So I will get someone to take you over to the mess where you can have something to eat and then you'll be shown to your dormitories and you can settle in.'

When the woman stood up to dismiss them, Annabelle saw that apart from her stern expression she was quite attractive, with a slim figure and fair hair drawn back into an elegant chignon beneath her nurse's cap. Madam summoned a QUARNN who then led them to the mess hall where they were served with a surprisingly tasty meal of beef stew followed by rhubarb and custard.

'Blimey, I could get used to this,' Hilary remarked with a grin, wolfing hers down. 'At least we know we ain't goin' to starve.'

Once the meal was over they were shown to a dormitory that at first glance appeared to house between twenty and thirty black iron beds spaced down either side of the room. On each of them was a white blanket with a blue anchor embroidered in the centre of it and a pillow. Between each bed was a comfortable chair and a locker where the girls quickly placed the few possessions they had brought with them. They had been advised that they would be issued with their uniforms the following morning.

In the centre of the room was a large iron stove and Hilary held her hands out to it appreciatively. 'We ain't goin' to freeze either,' she remarked with a grin. 'I reckon I'm gonna like it 'ere.'

In no time at all the room began to look more homely as pictures of loved ones appeared on the lockers, and once they were unpacked some of the girls settled down to write letters home. There were three large windows across the end of the room but as it was dark now the blackout blinds were firmly in place and Annabelle wondered if they would have a sea view. She would have to wait until the morning to find out.

Once Miss Dewhurst had spoken to the girls again after supper that evening, they all trooped off back to their dormitory and Annabelle curled up in the chair at the side of her bed and pretended to read a book. She didn't feel much like socialising and felt curiously homesick. Hilary had enough to say for both of them, however, and Annabelle listened to her chatting away to the other girls gathered around the stove as they all got to know each other.

One girl who lived in Portsmouth was giving them all a history lesson about Haslar. 'It was opened in 1750,' she informed them, enjoying their attention, 'and thousands of men have been buried here over the years.'

'How come you know so much about the place?' Hilary asked curiously, and the girl, who had introduced herself as Janet, smiled.

'Because I live close by, of course. We did all about Haslar in history lessons at school.'

Annabelle listened with half an ear. She was tired by now after the long journey and more than ready to settle down, although she wondered how she was ever going to sleep surrounded by so many other girls. She had never had to share a room before. She did sleep, however, the second her head hit the pillow – and didn't wake until a bell sounded early the next morning. The girls all hastily washed and dressed then made their way to the mess room for breakfast. Once they had eaten they were told that they had half an hour until they had to report to Miss Dewhurst again, so Annabelle decided to do a little exploring. Seeing her leave the room, Hilary hurried after her.

Once outside they turned their coat collars up against the biting wind that was blowing in from the sea and headed for the gate that was set in the wall surrounding the hospital. They opened it – and there before them was the sea. A protective sea wall sloped down from the road, and they saw that they were outside the harbour, with Portsmouth to one side of them and the Isle of Wight on the other.

'Cor, we could swim from here!' Hilary announced with delight and Annabelle shuddered.

'Not in this weather we couldn't. And from what Miss

Dewhurst has told us, I don't think we'll get much time for swimming anyway.'

'Well, we've got to have some free time,' Hilary pointed out. 'They can't work us twenty-four 'ours a bleedin' day, can they?'

'I suppose not,' Annabelle conceded. 'But come on now. We don't want to be late the first morning, do we?'

'Nah, you're right,' Hilary agreed, with one last glance at the choppy grey waves.

Soon after returning to the hospital the girls were taken to the clothing store where they were issued with their uniforms. Plain grey dresses, a navy petersham belt, white aprons, flat black shoes, a red cape, thick lisle stockings and white caps. They were then allowed back to their dormitory to get changed.

'Cor, I feel like a proper nurse now, though I don't know why we ain't never goin' to be allowed to wear our own clobber any more,' Hilary declared, twirling in the only mirror the room boasted. 'But can somebody help me wiv this blasted cap? It don't wanna sit right for some reason.'

Annabelle adjusted it on the girl's thick fair hair for her and then twiddled with her own. Fixing it on wasn't as straightforward as it looked, but she eventually managed it with the help of a few Kirby grips. They all then set off for the next lecture.

'It's like bein' back at flippin' school,' Hilary grumbled beneath her breath. 'I wonder when we'll get to do some proper nursin'?'

After the lecture a senior VAD was elected to give the girls a tour of the hospital, and half an hour later, most of them were beginning to panic.

'It's ruddy enormous! We'll never find our way round 'ere,' Hilary whispered to Annabelle. The wards were full of men with injuries ranging from broken limbs to burns and bullet wounds.

'Poor bugger,' Hilary muttered to no one in particular as they passed a bed where a man lay with his face covered in severe burns. A QUARNN was dressing them for him with the curtains partially open around his bed so they couldn't help but see. 'I hope he ain't got a wife or a sweetheart waitin' at home for him, else she's in for a shock.'

After a tour of the wards they were shown down into the cellars.

'When the sirens sound we bring the patients who are able to be moved down here for safety,' the nurse explained to them. 'Unfortunately, some of the patients are too ill to be moved so they have to stay on the wards and take their chance. We also have operating theatres down here and part of your job will be keeping them as spic and span as the ones upstairs. Cleanliness is of major importance. If the patient should pick up an infection through lack of hygiene during an operation it could be fatal.'

The girls all nodded solemnly, suddenly understanding that although they weren't fully qualified nurses, they still had an important part to play in the welfare of the patients.

Once the tour was over the QUARNN regarded them all seriously as she advised, 'I suggest you spend the rest of the day getting to know your way around the place. It's vitally important to know where you are going, as you will probably be somewhere different every day to start with, especially if we have an emergency and there's an influx of patients. Madam won't be thrilled if she has to waste valuable time sending out search parties for you. But don't look so worried.' She smiled at their expressions. 'You'll find your way about a lot quicker than you think. It always feels a bit daunting when you first start. Now I advise you all get over to the mess first for something to eat, and be sure to get a good night's sleep. You'll all be on the wards tomorrow.'

Annabelle felt a bit shaky at that thought. It had been fine practising resuscitation and bandaging up people who weren't really injured during her training, but it would be different doing it on real patients. Still, it was too late to back out now so she would just have to get used to it. And after all, what was there back at home for her now? She didn't even have a real mother and father; it seemed as if her whole life had been a lie. Feeling very sorry for herself, she followed the other girls to the mess.

The next morning after breakfast in the mess the girls were shown to their wards, and from then on Annabelle didn't know if she was on her head or her heels. One of the QUARNNS showed her the sluice room and where the bed-pans were kept, and her first job was to ensure that all the patients that needed one got one. She found herself blushing furiously for the first half of the morning as she helped the men to clamber on and off them, but by lunchtime she had gone past caring. One male bottom was much the same as another after a time. Then she was shown where the cleaning utensils were kept and soon she was busily mopping and dusting every surface in sight. The Ward Sister's standards of hygiene were high and Annabelle soon learned that for now at least it was up to her to maintain them.

Mid-morning wasn't so bad when she was asked to go around the ward with the tea trolley and some of the men teased her.

'New are you, love?' one chap asked her with a cheeky wink. He had both his legs in casts suspended from an evil-looking device at the end of the bed.

Annabelle nodded. 'Yes, it's my first day.'

'And where are you from?'

'Coventry.'

'Oh, I hear they took a right blast not so long ago, poor sods,' he said sympathetically. Now for the first time Annabelle was seeing the real results of war, and it was humbling. Here was she, feeling sorry for herself, when half the men in this ward would probably never be able to lead normal lives again. Many of them had had amputations, others were horrifically scarred and burned, and yet they still tried to be cheerful; it was really quite amazing. And then there were the ones whose injuries were not quite so bad. They would recover and return to fight again, and she wondered how they could face it.

'Phew, I don't know if I'm on me arse or me soddin' elbow,' Hilary complained at lunchtime after making a beeline for Annabelle in the mess. 'They've had me cleanin' out bedpans for most o' the mornin', ugh!' She wrinkled her nose in disgust and Annabelle couldn't help but grin.

'Me too,' she admitted as she spooned some sugar into her tea. There was sausage and mash for dinner today served with thick onion gravy, and Hilary attacked it as if she hadn't eaten for a month.

Well, at least the job she's been doing hasn't put her off her dinner, Annabelle thought wryly.

When Hilary had finally cleaned her plate she suggested, 'Do you fancy going over in the pinnace to the town tonight? We could have a nose round and perhaps find a café where we could have a cuppa? It would beat sittin' up in the dormitory, an' I overheard some o' the other girls sayin' they were goin'. Apparently there's a hall where they have a dance at the weekends an' all. That'd be nice wouldn't it?'

'I suppose so,' Annabelle answered unenthusiastically. She didn't feel in the mood for going out, but then she couldn't stay in forever, and if the rest of the week turned out to be as hard as her first morning had been, she would no doubt be in the mood to escape for a time by the weekend.

Hilary beamed at her. It seemed that she had skin as thick as a rhinoceros's, and even Annabelle's stand-offish attitude wasn't going to stop her befriending her. Annabelle's thoughts turned to Lucy and Dotty then, and she wondered how they were faring. She was missing them both far more than she had thought she would.

Chapter Thirty-One

Lucy trudged home through the snow, looking forward to seeing Harry and getting a few hours' sleep. After the shop work in Owen Owen she found her job in the munitions factory very repetitive and the shifts had totally disorientated her. It felt strange to be coming home early in the morning when most other folks were going to work, but then she knew she shouldn't grumble. At least she still had a home to go to, which was a lot more than some people had. The snow that had been holding off for days had now started to fall, and the thin covering on the ground disguised the piles of rubble left by the Luftwaffe's attacks, making everywhere look clean and bright, apart from the damage caused by the raid of the night before. The results of that were still very much in evidence as firemen damped down the remains.

At last she arrived at Mrs P's, and after stamping the snow from her boots she entered the kitchen to find Mrs P making the fire up in an old candlewick dressing-gown with her hair clad in metal curlers. Harry wagged his tail as he scampered over to greet her, and Mrs P yawned.

'Eeh, I'm right glad to see yer,' she remarked. 'I hates it when there's a raid an' you're stuck in that ruddy factory. Half the night we were up again, an' it's enough to freeze hell over in that shelter now. I even wrapped Harry up in a blanket in there last night. But how are you? Yer look fit to drop.'

'I am tired,' Lucy said. 'But I'm fine. A cup of tea wouldn't go amiss though.'

Whilst Mrs P pottered away to put the kettle on Lucy's eyes strayed to the sideboard, which was covered in photographs of Mrs P's three children, as was the wall behind them, at various stages of their lives. She had seen the woman dust them lovingly every single day since the two younger ones had been evacuated. She must miss them so much, she thought to herself, and once again found herself thinking of Mary. It was really hard to enter her own home now without her and Joel there, but what choice did she have? She just had to get on with life as the other people of the city were having to do.

Thankfully she didn't have to work that night, so she had arranged to go and see Miranda in the afternoon, once she'd had a sleep. Unless there was another raid, of course, and then Miranda would be at some church hall somewhere tending to the injured or homeless or driving an ambulance. It seemed that there was no job that was closed to women now, and the days of them staying at home to raise their families were long gone. With most of the men absent, fighting the war, the women had been forced to step into the breach – and a fine job they were making of it. It was commonplace to see women driving trams and buses now. A lot of the single women had gone to become Land Girls whilst others like Annabelle had become VADs. And then of course there were the others like Lucy herself who were busily making parts for Spitfires and tanks in the munitions factories. Each job was as important as the next and Lucy was glad to be able to do something worthwhile, although she still missed working with her friends.

After sharing a cup of tea with her kindly neighbour, she crossed the yard to her own home where she fed Harry, gave him a few moments in what was left of the garden, then dropped into bed exhausted and was asleep the instant she closed her eyes.

'Ah, here you are, darling,' Miranda greeted her late that afternoon when Lucy arrived at the house. The *For Sale* board was still in the garden but Miranda had given up hope of selling the Lodge now. Few people were willing to spend money on a house that could be razed to the ground at any time. And so instead she had 'pulled her belt in' as Churchill had instructed the nation to do. Many of the rooms were shut off now, especially since Annabelle had gone, and Miranda spent her time between the kitchen and the bedroom.

Now she nearly dragged Lucy through to the kitchen as she waved an envelope at her. 'I had a letter from Annabelle this morning,' she told the girl, as if the Crown Jewels had dropped through her letterbox. 'And she's safe and well, thank goodness.'

'I had one from her too,' Lucy smiled. 'And one from Dotty.'

Her face dropped then and Miranda squeezed her hand. 'You miss them too, don't you, pet?' she asked, and Lucy nodded and blinked back tears.

'I do, but they both said that they're going to try and visit over Christmas so that's something to look forward to, isn't it?'

'That's if Haslar doesn't have another sudden influx of patients and Dotty can get a train,' Miranda pointed out. The constant attacks by the Jerries were soul-destroying for the railwaymen, who were working around the clock to try and keep the trains running. Then brightening a little she asked, 'And how is Dotty doing in London?'

'Well, the letter was quite brief,' Lucy told her as she unwound her scarf from about her neck. 'But then it would be, wouldn't it, seeing as she's still one-handed at the minute. But she sounded cheerful enough, although she's frustrated because she can't type. Robert's bought her a new typewriter and she says Laura has made her feel really welcome. She asked me to give you her love and to tell you that she'll write you a nice long letter just as soon as her cast is off.'

'I'll look forward to that then.' It was growing dark now and Miranda hurried across to draw the blackouts before asking, 'Have you eaten yet? I've got a Spam casserole and a semolina pudding in the oven, and it's far too big for me. I can't seem to get used to cooking for one. You will share some with me, won't you?'

'If you put it that way, how can I refuse?' Lucy said with a twinkle in her eye, but inside her heart was heavy. Miranda was obviously missing Annabelle far more than she would let on, if her pale, drawn face was anything to go by. The girl knew that she worried about her husband too, but there was nothing she could say that would ease the woman's pain. Only having her husband and daughter safely home again could do that – and who knew how long that might take? The newspapers were still full of doom and gloom and the war seemed to be intensifying, if anything.

'Are you going to get a Christmas tree this year?' Lucy asked, hoping to lift the mood a little.

Miranda shrugged. 'I can't see much point, to be honest. The money could be better spent on other things at present and on Christmas Day I'll go over to visit my parents so I won't be here that much to see it. I might try to find some holly though, just to perk the place up a bit in case Annabelle does manage to get home. What are you planning to do?'

'I shall spend it with Mr and Mrs P.' Lucy fetched the tablecloth and spread it across the table. She had visited so many times now that she knew where everything was and didn't need to be asked.

'It would be nice to get an unbroken night's sleep for a change, wouldn't it?' Miranda yawned when they'd finished their meal. 'It's not just us copping it now though. London is being hit pretty badly too, according to the papers. I just wonder if Dotty is safe, that's all.'

'Well, she's got Robert to look out for her now,' Lucy said. 'I just hope those two make a go of it, as they obviously think the world of each other. I reckon Dotty used to believe that she wasn't good enough for him, but Miss Timms has changed all that, bless her. Now Dotty knows that she came from a good family and she's a fairly wealthy young woman in her own right, she may have a little more confidence in herself from now on.'

'And what about you, darling?' Miranda smiled at her gently. 'When are you going to put the past behind you and look around for a nice young man? You can't let what happened between your mother and father spoil your life too. Not all men are like your father.'

'I don't need a man to make me happy. I've got Harry,'

Lucy retorted immediately. 'And once Joel comes home we won't need anyone else.'

'I shouldn't be too sure about that,' Miranda told her worriedly. 'If I remember rightly, Joel and Annabelle seemed to be quite attracted to each other before he went away, so the chances are that even if they don't get together he'll meet a girl eventually and want to lead his own life.' When Lucy's face fell, she hurried on, 'That doesn't mean to say that he won't still care about you. Of course he will! You are his sister and you'll always be important to him – but both of you are too young to face a life alone.'

'We'll see,' Lucy sniffed haughtily, and realising that she had inadvertently upset the girl, Miranda hastily changed the subject and got back on to safer ground. Lucy was always as prickly as a porcupine, when her family were mentioned, and Miranda vowed that she wouldn't speak about them again. When she came to think about it, Lucy was becoming increasingly withdrawn and touchy, but then it was to be expected. What with no word from Joel, losing her mother and then her little sister, it was hardly surprising that the girl wasn't a ray of sunshine. Miranda suppressed a shudder as she thought back to the secret Lucy had shared with them. It must be very hard for her, coming to terms with the fact that her mother had been a murderer. Even so, as far as Miranda was concerned, none of it was the girl's fault and she wished she could shake her out of her melancholy. Miranda thought of her own daughter then and the traumatic impact on her of the secret she had kept from her for all these years. Poor Annabelle. She seemed to be floundering, not knowing who she was any more. And then there was Dotty, torn between being thrilled to finally discover who her mother was, and anger at losing her so quickly.

All three of the girls had an awful lot to come to terms with, Miranda concluded, and sadly, they were all going to have to work out their problems for themselves. No one else could do it for them.

Chapter Thirty-Two

'Don't look so glum, Dotty,' Laura said bracingly after she had returned from taking her children to school. 'It won't be long now and your plaster will be off, then you'll be able to get cracking on your writing again.'

'Sorry, I didn't mean to be a moaning minnie. It's just that I get so frustrated at only being able to use one arm,' Dotty apologised.

'I can understand that. I know Paul has his moments, being stuck in that wheelchair, and I dare say I would be just the same,' Laura answered sympathetically as she straightened the cushions on the settee. 'But why don't you just relax this morning? You could listen to some music on the wireless or read. As it happens, I'm only doing half a day in the office today so how about we go and do a bit of Christmas shopping this afternoon?'

Dotty instantly brightened. 'I'd like that. I need to get something for Annabelle and her mum – and Lucy, of course. Robert is going to come with me back to Coventry one day next week so that I can see them all before Christmas – if Annabelle manages to get home, of course, but I hope she will.'

'Hmm, I can imagine the nurses are being kept very busy with all the raids we're having.' Laura paused in the act of pinning her hat on.

Dotty couldn't stop herself from grinning as she replied, 'Actually, from what I can make out in her letters, the poor thing hasn't been doing much actual nursing. It sounds like all she's done up to now is clean the wards and empty bedpans. The nearest she's got to proper nursing was being allowed to roll bandages when they had a bit of spare time. I just can't imagine her doing menial and mucky jobs like that somehow. She was always so fastidious.'

'Well, someone has to do it,' Laura pointed out. 'And keeping up the standards of hygiene in a hospital is as important as doing the actual nursing. I've no doubt she'll be able to do more with the patients eventually. But will she be staying at Haslar? I know a lot of VADs have been shipped abroad to nurse the troops.'

'She hasn't said anything about a move,' Dotty shrugged, then, 'Is there anything I can do for you this morning while you're at work? One-handed, that is.'

Laura chuckled as she fastened her coat. 'Nothing at all. The cleaning lady will be in as usual, so you just relax. I'm sure Robert said he was dropping by to see you on his way into work so that will break the morning up for you. Bye for now.'

And with that she went off, leaving Dotty to pace the floor like a caged animal and curse her broken arm. She had never realised before how frustrating it must be for the men who had lost limbs in the war, and she felt guilty for complaining.

After all, she was only temporarily incapacitated. They would have to learn to live with their disabilities for the rest of their lives. Annabelle had written to tell her horror stories about some of the men on the wards and Dotty felt tearful every time she thought of them, poor things.

Now she tried to think more cheerful thoughts, and first on the list was her visit to Coventry. She had really missed her friends, even though Laura and Paul had made her feel more than welcome. Laura's children were adorable too. Simon was seven and a real little imp, always up to mischief, but lovable with it, and his five-year-old sister Elizabeth, affectionately known as Lizzie, was a real little sweetheart, never happier than when Dotty was reading her a story.

Her stay with the Parsons family in Whitechapel had been a time of adjustment for Dotty. Leaving her home town had not been easy, and discovering who her birth mother was had been a bittersweet experience. After all the years of dreaming, she had finally found her mother, but the chance for them to really get to know each other on this new, more intimate footing, had been cruelly snatched away from her. And then there was Robert and her admission of the love she felt for him. He had made it more than clear that he felt the same way about her, but was too much of a gentleman to rush things. With his inbuilt sensitivity, he was happy to give Dotty time to come to terms with everything that had happened.

As in Coventry, the spirits of the people of London were low. It seemed that the war was escalating, with the German forces dominating and Dotty wondered where it was all going to end. Her broody thoughts were interrupted then as Mrs Wiggins, Laura's daily help, breezed into the room wielding a tin of wax polish and a large yellow duster.

''Ello, me owld duck,' she said cheerfully and Dotty

instantly perked up. No one could stay sad around Ada Wiggins for long. Born and bred within the sound of Bow bells and proud of it, she was like a ray of sunshine. She was short and plump with a wicked sense of humour, and Dotty had taken to her at first sight. Today Mrs Wiggins was clad in her customary flowered wraparound apron and she had a headsquare tied turban-like around her steel-grey hair with one metal curler sitting on her forehead. Sometimes she put Dotty in mind of Mrs P. A Woodbine dangled from the corner of her mouth, something she wouldn't have dared do had Laura been at home. But she had already sussed that Dotty could be trusted not to tell on her. Her husband, Jim, worked on the London docks and her family were all grown and long flown the nest. 'I don't really need to work,' she had confided to Dotty shortly after the girl had arrived there, 'but it gives me a bit o' pin money to do as I like wiv, which is no bad fing is it, dearie?'

'Absolutely not,' Dotty had agreed, trying hard to keep a straight face, and their friendship had grown from there. The woman fussed over Dotty like a little round mother hen. It soon transpired that Mrs Wiggins had worked for Laura for years and they thought the world of each other, which was hardly surprising as the housekeeper kept the house clean as a new pin with never a word of complaint. She would even meet the children from school if Laura was tied up in the office, and then she would look after them till their mother or father arrived home. She had told Dotty that the children had been evacuated to a small village in Kent earlier in the war, but they had pined for their parents so badly that Laura had eventually brought them both home, much to Mrs Wiggins' relief. Now Mrs Wiggins spoiled them both shamelessly.

'She has this knack of being able to conjure a meal up from almost nothing,' Laura confided to Dotty one day. By her own admission, Laura had never enjoyed cooking, so the meals Mrs Wiggins regularly prepared for the family were more than welcome.

Now she dusted her way across the sideboard before asking, 'How long's it been since you 'ad a warm drink, dearie? Or per'aps I could tempt you to a bit o' somefink to eat? You ain't as far through as a stick o' celery.'

Dotty chuckled at Ada's attempts to feed her up as she watched the postman walking up the path through the snow-white net curtains. The post was very hit and miss nowadays, and she wondered if he would have anything for her. 'I'm fine for now, thanks.' She smiled at the woman then hurried into the hall to retrieve the letters from the letterbox. It was no easy task with only one hand but eventually she came to one with her name on and instantly recognised Mr Jenkins's stamp. He had written to her often since she had come to London, keeping her informed of what was happening about her late mother's estate, so now she took the envelope into Mrs Wiggins and asked, 'Would you mind opening this for me, please? It's rather awkward with only one hand.'

'Course I will, ducks,' Mrs Wiggins said obligingly and she did as she was asked before handing the letter inside to Dotty and waddling off towards the kitchen. 'I'm goin' to fetch some more coal in an' get these fires made up,' she told her. 'It's like the bloody Arctic in 'ere. Almost as cold as me muvver-in-law's heart.'

Dotty guessed that the dear woman was really just looking for an excuse to leave her to read her letter in private.

The letter began: *Dear Dorothy, I hope this letter finds you well and settling happily in London. I am writing to update you on the current position of your late mother's, Alice Louise Timms's, estate.*

Dotty felt her legs go all wobbly. Surprisingly she had never known the woman's Christian names before. To her, she had always been simply 'Miss Timms'. Now that she did know them, it somehow made her mother feel more real. *Alice* – it was such a pretty name and Dotty wondered why she had never tried to find out what it was before. The rest of the letter just went on to tell her how much longer it might be before her inheritance was wholly signed over to her. Mr Jenkins also asked if she was still all right for funds and told her to contact him immediately should she need more. He then ended the letter by wishing her a very Merry Christmas, and wrote that he was looking forward to seeing her again in the New Year when they could finalise the transfer of Miss Timms's estate into her name.

Dotty sighed as she awkwardly folded the letter and poked it back into the envelope. Mr Jenkins really had been remarkably kind and helpful, considering he had never met her before. But then she supposed he was used to dealing with people who found themselves in her position. She glanced at the clock then before moving to the window. Robert should be here soon and as always she waited for a glimpse of him.

'I have to say it isn't easy buying presents with the strict rationing in force, although thankfully I did manage to get some toys for the children,' Laura remarked just before one o'clock that afternoon as they shopped in the Strand. Oxford Street had been heavily bombed in the Blitz. 'I know most people have resorted to knitting and sewing presents for their nearest and dearest, but I'm afraid I've never been much good at that sort of thing,' she giggled. 'I'm not much of a cook either, as you know, so I sometimes wonder what my Paul ever saw in me.'

'I imagine he saw what everyone else sees,' Dotty told her. 'A kind, beautiful woman who would turn out to be a wonderful wife and mother. And clever too. You keep the magazine running like clockwork. I don't know how you do it, but I do know Robert would be lost without you. He's always singing your praises.'

Laura blushed at the compliment before asking, 'How are we doing on the present front anyway?'

'Well, I got some lavender bath salts for Miranda, a pretty hat for Lucy, and some perfume for Annabelle. I just have to get something for Robert now. Do you have any suggestions?' She had already bought presents for Laura and her family the week before when she had gone shopping with Robert, but she didn't mention that, of course. The gifts were safely hidden away in her room.

'Hmm.' Laura tapped her lip thoughtfully with her gloved finger before suggesting, 'How about a nice scarf for him?'

Dotty pulled a face. It didn't seem like much of a gift considering all he did for her, and she could easily afford something more expensive with the allowance Mr Jenkins had forwarded to her.

'I know,' she said suddenly as an idea popped into her head. 'How about a pen? A really nice pen, I mean. One that he could keep.' She thought regretfully of the one that her mother had bought for her, now buried beneath tons of rubble and lost forever.

'I think he'd love that,' Laura said, and taking Dotty's elbow she propelled her in the direction of a shop where she had a feeling she would find just what she was looking for.

An hour later they caught a bus to Liverpool Street, and from there walked home feeling content with their purchases. Dotty had bought Robert a solid silver fountain pen and could hardly wait for Christmas morning when she could give it to him. Back indoors, they drank a pot of tea before Laura rushed off to fetch the children from school.

'An' what are you plannin' on doin' tonight then?' Ada Wiggins asked as she cleared the dirty dishes into the sink.

'Robert is taking me to the Finsbury Park Empire to see Max Miller, the Cheeky Chappie, and I was wondering if you'd mind helping me wash my hair again, please, Mrs Wiggins?'

'O' course I don't mind,' the woman told her cheerily. 'We 'ave to 'ave you lookin' yer best. I must say I'm quite envious. I do like Max Miller meself an' they reckon it's a grand show, but you wouldn't get my old man to anyfink like that, not if 'e was under threat of death. Let's just 'ope Jerry stays away, eh? We don't want no raids to spoil it fer you.' She then scurried off to put the kettle on for some hot water and an hour later Dotty sat by the fire as the woman rubbed at her hair with a towel.

Robert arrived promptly at seven o'clock in a taxi to pick her up and as they drove towards the theatre he whispered, 'You're looking really lovely tonight, Dotty.'

She blushed furiously. She was still not used to compliments and never quite knew how to respond to them.

'I er . . . was wondering if you still think we might be able to get back to Coventry for a brief visit before Christmas?' she asked hopefully, keen to change the subject.

'Actually I was thinking the day after tomorrow, the day before Christmas Eve, if that suits you?' Robert was pleased when he saw her face light up. He knew that she regarded Lucy and Annabelle as her nearest and dearest, although they were only friends

'Oh, that would be marvellous. Thank you, but are you sure you can spare the time?'

'The Christmas and New Year edition of the magazine went to print first thing yesterday morning, so after tomorrow evening when I've tidied a few things up, I'm all yours for the holiday,' he assured her. 'All we have to do now is hope that the trains are running.'

She sent up a silent prayer that they would be.

'Dotty, Robert, come in! Oh, it's so lovely to see you! We weren't sure that you'd make it with the weather being so appalling.' Miranda hugged Dotty with delight, being careful not to hurt her arm, which was still in a sling tucked beneath her coat. She nearly dragged the young couple into the hallway, where she shouted, 'Annabelle! Lucy! Guess who's here?' She turned back to them then and helped Dotty to take her coat off. 'It's perfect timing,' she told them gleefully. 'Annabelle got home late last night and Lucy's popped round to see her.'

At that moment the two girls appeared in the drawing-room doorway and they too were thrilled to see her, although Dotty instantly noticed that Lucy didn't look at all well.

They all greeted each other fondly, hugging Robert too in welcome, then while Miranda hurried away to fetch some refreshments, Dotty asked, 'Are you all right, Lucy? I think you've lost some weight and you're awfully pale.'

'I'm fine. It's just these night shifts are taking some getting used to, that's all,' Lucy replied. 'I never realised how cushy we had it at Owen Owen till I started in the munitions factory. It's damned hard work, I don't mind telling you, standing on a production line for hours on end. The women I work with are a decent lot though.'

'And how is your job going?' Dotty asked Annabelle.

The girl shrugged. 'Fine. I've actually been taken off

bedpan duty now and I'm in the operating theatres sterilising the instruments, which is an improvement.'

They chatted about this and that, and as the afternoon wore on they all exchanged presents with promises that they wouldn't be opened until Christmas morning. It had been arranged that Lucy would spend Christmas Day with Annabelle and Miranda, who had decided to stay at home rather than go to her parents, and Boxing Day with Mr and Mrs P.

'And what will you be doing?' they asked Dotty.

When she glanced at Robert uncertainly he grinned. 'She'll be spending the day with me,' he told them with a wink. 'I've got something pretty special lined up for her but I can't tell you what it is because I don't want to spoil the surprise.'

Dotty was intrigued as she tried to imagine what it might be, but then Robert looked at the clock and told her regretfully, 'I'm sorry, darling, but we ought to be heading back to the station now if we're to have any chance of getting back to London tonight. It was bad enough on the way here,' he explained to the others. 'Because of the weather conditions the train got diverted twice and it might be even worse now because it hasn't stopped snowing.'

'Well, you're more than welcome to stay here. In fact, you can stay over Christmas if you like,' Miranda offered generously. She was actually dreading Christmas without her husband, so it was a case of the more the merrier as far as she was concerned – especially as Annabelle had to return to Haslar the day after Boxing Day. Now that Annabelle had managed to get leave, Miranda was determined to make the most of every second they had together, which was why she had decided to stay at home, for who knew how long it might be before her daughter was able to get leave again?

Miranda just prayed that they might get some respite from the air raids. She'd almost forgotten what it was like to have an unbroken night's sleep, and now even when she did she found that she lay there waiting for the sirens to wail.

Robert told her, 'That's really kind of you and I appreciate the offer, but Laura will be in a tizz if I don't deliver Madam here back home to her.'

Miranda bustled away to get their coats and hats and when the couple were ready, everyone saw them to the door. Dotty hugged them all as best she could with her one good arm. 'The next time I see you, I hope I'll have got rid of this thing,' she told them tearfully, and then she and Robert set off, watched by the others until the thickly falling snow swallowed them up.

Robert arrived at Laura's bright and early on Christmas morning with a spring in his step and a twinkle in his eye.

'Merry Christmas,' Laura greeted him from the hearthrug where she was playing with Simon and his new train set.

'Uncle Robert . . . look what Santa brought for me!' Lizzie flung herself at him, proudly showing off her new doll, and he shook his head in mock amazement.

'Why, she's just about the prettiest dolly I ever saw,' he told her seriously. 'But not quite as pretty as you, of course.'

Lizzie giggled with delight before skipping off to examine her other presents. Robert thought how festive the room looked. A large Christmas tree standing in the corner of the room in a sturdy bucket was decorated with tinsel and paper garlands that the children had made, and glossy sprigs of holly were placed on every surface, the red berries looking festive. A fire was burning in the grate, adding to the cosy atmosphere, and Robert hoped that one day he too would have a lovely family like Laura's.

'So, is she almost ready?' he asked.

Laura nodded. 'Yes, she's all spruced up and ready to go, and dying to know what the surprise is. In fact, we all are.'

He grinned but shook his head. 'You'll know soon enough.'

Dotty came in then looking very pretty in a pink twinset that Laura and Paul had bought her for Christmas, and a smart black skirt. She usually avoided bright colours but they all thought how much it suited her.

'You look beautiful,' Robert told her and Dotty flushed self-consciously.

'I might look better without this,' she answered, tapping her plaster cast, and everyone laughed. It was very colourful now as Simon and Lizzie had crayoned pictures all over it.

'Right, well, if Madam is ready, her carriage awaits.' Robert bowed gallantly, making the two children snort with laughter. They had never seen their Uncle Robert do anything like that before and found it highly amusing.

'But where are we going?' Dotty asked as Laura helped her into her coat.

'Ah, now that would be telling and it wouldn't be a surprise then, would it?'

He led her out to a waiting car and soon they were manoeuvring through the streets of London as Dotty tried to guess their destination.

Chapter Thirty-Three

When they pulled onto the little road that led to the grand entrance of the Savoy Hotel, Dotty gaped.

'That's right,' Robert told her, looking pleased with himself. 'We're going to have our Christmas dinner in the River Restaurant.'

'B-but Winston Churchill goes there. I know because I read it in the papers. Won't it be awfully expensive?' Dotty still couldn't accept the fact that she was now a wealthy young woman. Robert was rich too, but she didn't want him spending all his money on her. It didn't feel right.

'It's Christmas Day,' he scolded gently. 'Surely I'm allowed to spoil you today of all days?'

'Well, if you're quite sure.'

She allowed him to help her from the taxi and before she knew it they were in the most luxurious foyer she had ever seen. Robert looked totally at ease there but Dotty felt like a fish out of water. She was shocked to see how many people were there, many of them officers in uniform with pretty girls on their arms drinking cocktails, smoking and appearing to be having a really good time. As Robert moved to the desk she glanced around in awe at the sweeping staircase and the huge crystal chandeliers that were sending rainbow prisms all about the room. Her feet felt as if they might disappear into the thick-pile wall-to-wall carpet and she was stunned that such luxury existed, especially as there was a war on.

When Robert came back, she whispered, 'Robert, I'm going to look such a fool. I can't even cut my own food up with only one hand.' Dotty was mortified to think of people laughing at her, but he instantly reassured her.

'Don't get worrying about that. It's all in hand, trust me.'

Seeing that she didn't have much choice, Dotty followed him to the restaurant where they were met by a head waiter in a black suit, white shirt and bow-tie.

'Ah, Mr Brabinger, how nice to see you again,' he greeted him smoothly. 'Do follow me, sir. We have your table all ready for you.' He then nodded politely at Dotty before whisking them through the tables to a spot near the rear window, overlooking the Thames. So he's been here before then, Dotty found herself thinking. I wonder who with? She instantly felt annoyed with herself for being so possessive. Robert could have brought lots of women here in the past! What business was it of hers?

Awed, she stared at the table laid with its crisp white cloth, shining silver cutlery and cut-glass goblets. She was still concerned about how she was going to manage to cut up her food, but she needn't have worried. When the meal was served she found that every morsel in the large silver salvers had been chopped into bite-sized pieces, even the turkey. It seemed that Robert had thought of everything and saved her a lot of embarrassment. It never ceased to amaze her how well Robert coped with his withered hand. But then she supposed that he had had a lifetime to adjust to it and it certainly didn't seem to stop him from doing most things.

'Thank you,' she whispered across the table and he smiled as a waiter approached with a bottle of champagne. Again Dotty tried not to think about how much all this must be costing. After pouring out two foaming flutes, the waiter left them.

'I hope you didn't mind me ordering for us,' Robert said as he raised his glass to her. 'But I somehow thought you'd be the sort of girl who would like the traditional Christmas fare. I can always order you something else if you don't like it though,' he added, hoping he hadn't overstepped the mark.

'It's perfect,' Dotty said happily, giggling as the champagne bubbles went up her nose. 'Merry Christmas!' They toasted each other, and suddenly it was really Christmas!

Each course was perfectly cooked, and within an hour Dotty groaned and rubbed her stomach as she told Robert, 'That was really delicious but I think I shall burst if I eat so much as another mouthful.'

'I'm glad you enjoyed it,' he replied as the waiter removed the dishes that had contained their Christmas pudding. 'But you must make room for some coffee and a mince pie before we leave, just to finish it all off.'

'If you insist.' Dotty was really enjoying herself now that she had relaxed and knew that she would never forget this day. It had been perfect. And then Robert did something quite unexpected and amazing as they waited for their coffee to be served: he produced a small velvet box from the pocket of his jacket and took a deep breath as he looked Dotty in the eye.

'Dotty, I . . .' He gulped then forced himself to go on. 'I have something here that I'd like you to have.' He snapped the lid open and she found herself gazing down at a beautiful emerald and diamond ring. 'It was my mother's and—'

She held up her hand to stop him as she fingered the locket about her neck. 'I'm afraid if you were planning on giving it to me, I shall have to refuse,' she told him primly. 'I already have her locket and I treasure it, but I really can't accept any more of her jewellery. It just wouldn't be right.'

'But you don't understand,' he flustered. 'This was Mother's engagement ring.'

'Then that is all the more reason why you shouldn't be giving it away.'

'Oh dear.' Robert ran a hand through his thick wavy hair which would not be tamed by any amount of Brylcreem. 'I'm afraid I've handled this all wrong. You see, Mother always said that she wanted the woman I chose to marry to wear this ring. What I'm *trying* to say is . . . Dotty, will you do me the very great honour of becoming my wife?'

When Dotty simply stared vacantly back at him, he stumbled on, 'I wanted to give this to you as an engagement ring – but of course, if you didn't like it you could choose another one. Any one you liked. If you'll only say you'll marry me, that is. I mean, I know I'm not much of a catch with this arm and being so much older than you, but . . . Oh Lord. I've made the most frightful hash of this, haven't I? I suppose I should have gone down on one knee and done things properly. And I so wanted everything to be perfect.'

He looked up to see tears in Dotty's eyes as she reached

across to take his hand, hardly able to believe her luck. This dear man was asking her to be his wife.

'You, Robert Brabinger, are the most *wonderful*, kindest man I have ever met and I would be honoured to be your wife.'

'What? Do you really mean it?' he asked incredulously, and when she nodded, he slipped the ring onto her finger and kissed it tenderly, heedless of the glances they were attracting.

'Perhaps sir would like me to pour some more champagne,' the waiter who was standing at the side of the table with a tray of coffee asked with a broad smile. 'It appears that a celebration is in order. May I be the first to offer my congratulations?'

'You certainly may,' Robert answered as he leaned across the table to give Dotty a smacking kiss on the lips, and when a cheer went up from the other diners he beamed like a Cheshire cat while Dotty blushed to the roots of her hair.

Everyone raised a toast to them as Dotty stared at the magnificent ring on her finger and wondered if she was dreaming. Finally she would have someone to call her own. Sadly, she had thought the same when she discovered her mother – but that had not been meant to be. Surely with Robert it would be different?

In the cab back to Laura's, Robert spoke excitedly about their wedding.

'Of course you'll want a church wedding, won't you?' he assumed. 'I believe every girl dreams of that, and you can have whatever you want just as soon as you want.'

She tapped her plaster. 'Actually, I'd quite like to have this off first.' And then she shocked him when she went on, 'And to be honest I'd much prefer a very quiet affair. It is wartime, after all and . . . Well, I suppose finding my mother and losing her all in one night made me realise just how fragile life is for everyone at the moment. And as neither of us have any close family there wouldn't be much point in a big do. Why don't we just go to the Register Office and have Laura and Paul as witnesses?'

'But what about Annabelle and Lucy?' he asked. 'I know how much you think of them. Surely you'd want them to be there?'

'I'd *love* them to be there,' she said. 'But with Annabelle so busy at Haslar and Lucy working in the munitions factory, it wouldn't be easy for them to get time off and I wouldn't want them to feel pressured.'

He nodded understandingly. 'Then if that's how you want it, that's how it shall be,' he promised. 'Although I think you may have a bit of a battle on your hands when we tell Laura. She's a sucker for a white wedding and she won't approve of a Register Office do at all, if I know her.'

'You just leave Laura to me,' Dotty said as she snuggled into his side feeling like the happiest girl in the world.

Robert's remark proved to be correct when they marched into Laura's front parlour a short time later and broke the happy news to her.

'Oh, this is wonderful,' she declared, clapping her hands with delight, then: 'Paul, let's open that bottle of champagne we've been saving for a special occasion, shall we, darling? They don't get more special than this.' She picked up Dotty's hand then to admire her ring.

'It was Robert's mother's,' Dotty told her and Laura nodded.

'Yes – I never saw her without it on her finger whilst she was alive, God rest her soul. But I know she would have fully approved of Robert's choice of a wife and would have been thrilled to know that you will be wearing it from now on. We must all go out tomorrow evening to celebrate your engagement properly, or better still we could go on New Year's Eve and make it a double celebration. I have a wonderful dress that you could borrow, Dotty – it would look just lovely on you. And of course, we must start to make some plans. When were you thinking of? June is always a lovely time for a wedding and that would give us time to book the church and a venue for the reception. Oh, and of course we shall have to start to look around for your wedding dress straight away. And there are the flowers and the photographer to organise, and—'

'*Whoa!*' Dotty held up her hand to stop her flow. 'To be honest, Laura, Robert and I were thinking of getting married within the next few weeks – just as soon as I can get this plaster off, in fact. And then we're going to have a very quiet affair. I've never been one for a lot of fuss and palaver, and what with the war and everything . . . it just doesn't seem right to go overboard when people are having it so hard.'

'Oh!' Laura seemed to deflate like a balloon, but then as Paul came back into the room on his crutches, the champagne tucked under one arm, she brightened again. She hadn't entirely given up on getting her own way – not yet.

'Well, we have plenty of time to talk about the arrangements,' she declared warmly as she fetched some glasses from the cocktail cabinet and Paul popped the cork noisily. 'For now let's just celebrate your engagement. I really couldn't be happier. I'm sure you two were made for each other, although over the last months I did sometimes wonder if either of you would ever acknowledge it.' She gave them a mock-stern glance. 'I don't mind admitting there were times when I felt like banging your heads together. You couldn't seem to see what was staring you straight in the eye. Still, all's well that ends well. Here's to you both, wishing you a long and happy future together with lots of squalling babies and lots of love.'

'I'll drink to that,' Robert answered as he raised his glass and pulled Dotty into his side. Surely things couldn't get much better than this?

They never did get to go out and celebrate New Year's Eve because the city was targeted yet again, and they all had to hasten down into Laura's cellar to take shelter in their finery as the sirens wailed.

'That's it!' Laura said crossly as she ushered them all ahead of her, Mrs Wiggins included. The woman had come to babysit and there was no way Laura was going to allow her to walk home until the raid was over. 'I am going to get one of those Morrison shelters and put it in the drawing room. We could use it as a table for the children to play on during the day, and at least then when the sirens go we can stay upstairs in the warm. It's so damp and dismal down here. And it would be much easier for Paul than struggling down these stairs.'

'Whatever you think best, darling,' Paul answered indulgently as Lizzie and Simon clambered onto his lap. The children had been down to the cellar so many times during the air raids that they didn't even cry about it any more and took it all in their stride.

During the long night that followed, over ten thousand incendiary bombs were dropped and one historic building after another was razed to the ground.

As the New Year dawned, people finally crept from their shelters to scenes of hell on earth. Buildings that only the day before had formed landmarks were now no more than smouldering piles of rubbish, and all across the city fires raged out of control as a pall of smoke blocked out the sky.

What a horrendous beginning to the new year. Would life as they had known it ever be the same again?

For the people of Coventry, the Christmas holidays had passed blissfully peacefully, with no air raids and nothing to spoil the religious festivities. People wondered if they had been spared because of the atrocious weather conditions, or if it was because Hitler had renewed his attacks on London. They certainly didn't believe that the Führer would respect the religious holiday. But whatever the reasons, they were grateful for the respite.

Dotty had rung Miranda late on Christmas Day, to pass on the happy news of her engagement and as Annabelle and Lucy were there, she had been able to talk to them too. Of course, they were both thrilled for her, although disappointed that they wouldn't be able to attend her wedding. However, they assured her that they would be there in spirit and looked forward to seeing her as soon as possible.

Dotty and Robert had decided that they wanted to get married in February. Dotty's plaster would be off her arm by then and the couple saw no point in waiting. After all, who knew how long any of them might have? It was whispered that Hitler was going to intensify his attacks, and they wanted to spend every second they could together as husband and wife, just in case. No one was safe in these dangerous times, as Dotty had discovered to her cost. She was still suffering from terrible nightmares about the time she had spent trapped in the cellar with her mother, and would wake up at night in a cold sweat as she relived those long, terrifying hours.

Laura wasn't too thrilled with the speed of the plans but already she had found that Dotty could be very stubborn when she wanted to be, so she had resigned herself to seeing the pair married in a Register Office, although she was still trying to talk Dotty into having a conventional white wedding gown.

'You'll regret it in years to come when you look back on your wedding photographs,' she had warned, but Dotty had just grinned and told her that she would be happy to marry Robert dressed in a brown paper bag. As far as she was concerned, being with the man she loved was more important than pomp and ceremony – and put like that, Laura didn't have much of an argument; deep down, she knew that this was just as it should be.

Chapter Thirty-Four

After Christmas the people began to view their brief respite as the calm before the storm as Hitler's Luftwaffe renewed their attacks on all the major cities. London, Coventry, Plymouth, Birmingham, Gosport all came under fire. The sea battles also increased, which meant Annabelle and the staff at Haslar were working round the clock. Even the hospitals were being targeted now, which meant that the underground theatres were in continual use with each influx of injured men.

Every time the air-raid siren sounded, it was part of the VADs' job to get the patients that could be moved down to the safety of the cellars until the all-clear sounded. Those who were too sick to be moved had to remain on the wards. Annabelle hated leaving them there so vulnerable, but the majority of the men were extremely brave and would tell her and the other nurses, 'We're all right, loves. You just do what you have to do.' And so the young women did, because they really didn't have any other choice.

Within a week of being back at work after Christmas the staff at Haslar were exhausted, but as Madam continually pointed out to them, 'These are brave men who have landed here: they have sustained their injuries fighting for our king and country, so it is our duty to do our best for them *at all times* – whether we are tired or not. Do I make myself clear? Second-best just will not do.'

And so the weary staff carried on doing the best they could, although often by the time the patients were delivered to them it was too late to do anything other than draw a white sheet across their pale faces and wheel them down to the morgue or hold their hands and offer what comfort they could until the men drew their last breath. At first, Annabelle found it soul-destroying to see young men killed in their prime, but eventually she began to accept it. What other option did she have?

The rest of the VADs and also some of the QUARNNs now regularly took the 'floating bridge' across the harbour from Gosport into old Portsmouth in the spare time they did have. From there it was only a mile into Southsea and they would go to dances at the Savoy, which was close to the South Parade Pier. It was popular with sailors and soldiers alike as it had many top acts playing there, including Vera Lynn, Tommy Trinder, Gracie Fields and Joe Loss. But up to now Annabelle had preferred to stay in the dormitory and read, and eventually the other girls, some of whom had formed close friendships, stopped inviting her along and she gained the reputation of being 'a bit of a loner'.

It was during such a night, when she was looking forward to going to bed early, that a senior QUARNN suddenly stuck her head round the door and asked, 'I know it's your night off, Smythe, but we've just been put on standby for another influx of patients. You couldn't come and help us out, could you?'

Annabelle's hopes of a cosy night tucked up in bed flew out of the window. 'I suppose so,' she said wearily. 'I'll be with you as soon as I've got back into my uniform.' She cursed as she quickly got dressed again. Perhaps she should have gone with the other girls, after all. But it was no use mithering about it now, so she set off for the front door where she knew the new intake would be brought. They began to arrive almost instantly, some of them supported by nurses, others on stretchers and trolleys, and she began to list their names, checking the dog tags of the men who were unconscious or unable to tell her their name.

Looks like it's going to be a very long night, she thought to herself as the next injured soldier was wheeled towards her – and then her heart missed a beat as she stared down into a face that she had often seen in her dreams. The young soldier was unconscious and covered in blood from his wounds but she would have known him anywhere, even after all this time.

'Is there a problem, Smythe?'

Madam's sharp voice sliced into her shock, and flustered she answered, 'N-no, Madam.'

The woman swept across to her. 'Ah, I see he isn't wearing his dog tag.'

'His name is Joel. Joel Ford,' Annabelle answered before she could stop herself.

Madam raised an eyebrow as she looked at the sheet attached to the end of his trolley listing his injuries. 'And do you know this young man?'

'Slightly. He is my friend's brother,' Annabelle answered, keeping her eyes downcast to hide her reddened cheeks.

'Well, whoever he is, he needs to go to surgery immediately,' Madam told her efficiently. 'Take him straight down to theatre, Smythe, and inform the surgeons that he is an emergency case, then report back here. By the look of this lot we may be here all night.'

'Yes, Madam.' Annabelle quickly grasped the trolley and headed for the cellars, and all the way she was silently praying, '*Please don't die, Joel.*' It would be just too cruel if Lucy were to lose her brother so soon after losing her little sister and her mother.

Once she had entrusted Joel to the theatre nurses who would prepare him for surgery, she hurried back upstairs to muck in, and the rest of the night passed in a blur as she and the other VADs registered the new intake of casualties. There was little time to wonder if Joel had survived until at last, early the next morning, Madam told the exhausted girls, 'Go to your rooms now and rest for a while. None of you are any good to me if you are too tired to work. But be back down here for lunchtime. I fear we have a very busy few days ahead of us.'

The girls trudged away, stifling their yawns, and then Annabelle finally had time to think of Joel again. She had glanced at his notes on the way down to theatre and three words had jumped out at her. *Possible leg amputation?* She hoped with all her heart that the surgeons had managed to save his leg. She had seen hundreds of amputations during her time at Haslar. Indeed, sometimes the theatres had been so busy that the amputated limbs had had to be piled outside the theatre doors until the porters had time to wheel them away to be incinerated. It was a terrible sight, and the first time she had witnessed it, Annabelle was ashamed to admit that she had vomited. The stench of rotting flesh and blood had been too much for her, but it was yet another sight that she had been forced to get used to. But somehow, knowing that one of those limbs had belonged to someone you knew personally, made it a thousand times worse.

She wondered if she should try and find out which ward Joel had been transferred to, but then decided against it for now. Madam and the Ward Sisters were very strict about there being no fraternising between the staff and the patients, and she was sensible enough to realise that she stood more chance of seeing Joel if she played their friendship down. And so she returned to her dormitory along with the other girls who had also pitched in to help when they got back from their night out. She was ready to drop, and yet even when she was tucked in bed, sleep refused to come as pictures of Joel's pale face kept flashing before her eyes.

Later that day, after making discreet enquiries of the other girls, she discovered which ward Joel was on and also that the surgeons had managed to save his leg, although it would never be the same again.

'That poor bugger won't be seein' service again,' Sandra Pritchard, one of her roommates, told her in a matter-of-fact voice. Annabelle felt torn between sympathy for Joel and relief. He might be maimed but at least he was still alive, which was a lot more than could be said for many of the men who had arrived the night before and who were now lying in the hospital morgue. During the next couple of days, telegrams would be going to their nearest and dearest informing them of their deaths, and yet more families would be devastated. It all seemed such a terrible waste of life. But as the VADs had learned early in their training, it wasn't their job to dwell on the fate of the departed. There was nothing that anyone could do for them. Their job was to do their best for the survivors, with a cheerful word or a shoulder to cry on when the men were feeling down.

Sometimes Annabelle thought that this was one of the most important aspects of their job, although had anyone asked her if she was capable of doing such a thing just a short while ago, she would have scoffed at them. Why would Annabelle Smythe, the girl who had been born with a silver spoon in her mouth and who had been pampered and spoiled all her life, demean herself to such a low level? But as she was now painfully aware, that girl no longer existed. Had never existed really, and so she just got on with the job she had chosen to do as she tried to work out who she was now.

Two days later, Annabelle found herself on duty in the ward to which Joel had been admitted, and she had to force herself not to rush over to him as she worked her way down the row of beds seeing to the patients' needs. Madam had set up a new rota, and she was no longer required in the theatre for the time being. And then at last she was standing next to him. He was lying very still with one arm in a sling and his leg suspended from a pulley in the ceiling.

'Good morning, Mr Ford,' she said officially as she swished the curtains around the bed to create some privacy. 'I've come to change your dressings. How are you feeling today?' She began to rummage on the trolley for fresh bandages as Joel turned dull, reddened eyes towards her, and then as recognition dawned those eyes lit up and he held his hand out to her. Every visible inch of him seemed to be covered in cuts and bruises, and he had lost a tremendous amount of weight – and yet she still felt the pull of him as she had when she had first met him.

'Belle,' he said weakly, and she grinned. She had always

considered shortened names to be common, yet coming from Joel she quite liked it.

'Yes, it's me,' she whispered. 'But we mustn't let the Sister think that we know each other, or she won't let me nurse you.'

He was obviously very weak but he nodded to acknowledge that he understood what she was saying. She began to unroll the bandage from his arm and after checking that the wound beneath was clean she painstakingly applied a fresh one.

'I – I got blown up,' he managed to tell her. 'I was trying to help my friend who had been shot, back to one of the trenches, b-but he didn't make it anyway.' His head rolled from side to side in distress. 'H-he was just twenty-four years old and married with a new baby. He didn't even get to meet his child.' A tear rolled from the corner of his eye and sliced its way down his stubbled cheek, and deeply affected, Annabelle gently wiped it away. And then her heart plummeted as she suddenly realised that Joel didn't know about his own little sister's and his mother's death. She was in a dilemma. Should she tell him, or would any more bad news tip him over the edge? She decided to say nothing for now. She didn't want to do anything to impede his recovery, but she could at least let Lucy know that he was alive and perhaps she could write to him and tell him? Deciding that this might be the best course of action, she finished dressing his wounds, then after washing him and making him as comfortable as possible she moved on to the next bed, promising that she would be back as soon as she could.

That night, before retiring, she wrote to Lucy telling her that Joel was alive and in Haslar, then she hurried down to the reception area and placed her letter along with the others that would be collected and posted the next morning. Lucy wrote back immediately, begging for more news of her brother and asking how serious his injuries were. It was almost a week later before the letter arrived, and thankfully by then Joel was a little stronger, but he still had a long way to go before he made a complete recovery. His leg had been so badly broken in three places that the bones had actually been protruding through his skin, and although the surgeons had managed to save it they had told him that he would always have quite a bad limp and would probably have to walk with the aid of a stick. Thankfully his other injuries had been fairly superficial and now as the bruises started to fade his skin was a kaleidoscope of yellows, reds, purples and blues.

Annabelle wrote to Lucy again, telling her that she could write to Joel although there were no visitors allowed at Haslar. She explained about the severity of his injuries but said that he would survive, hoping to put her mind at rest – and then she also told her that as yet, he had not been informed of Mary or his mother's death. And then once that letter, too, was posted, all she could do was wait.

'I've heard of Joseph's coat of many colours, but skin is ridiculous,' Annabelle would tease him as she gently bathed his fading bruises.

Slowly his speech improved over the weeks as he regained his strength, and he began to watch for a sight of her walking into the ward.

'I think young Mr Ford has a soft spot for you, Nurse,' the Ward Sister teased her one day, and Annabelle blushed and quickly walked away to cart a bedpan off to the sluice. Being back on the wards meant she could spend as much time as possible with Joel, without making it look too obvious. When she had first met him, she had felt drawn to him, despite her reservations. That same attraction was still there, but now she felt as if they had more in common. She was a working girl now for a start-off and not the spoiled young madam Joel who had once known, who felt that the world was at her feet.

The day came when she received another reply from Lucy. It arrived just as she was about to go to breakfast, which meant that Joel's letter might well have arrived too. When she walked into the ward a short while later, Annabelle saw instantly that Joel had received his sister's letter. His eyes were bloodshot, much as they had been when he first arrived, and there was no welcoming smile today.

'Did you know about Mary and my mother?' he asked as she approached his bed and made a pretence of straightening the blankets.

'Yes. I wanted to tell you but I didn't feel it was my place. I'm so sorry, Joel.'

He stared up at the ceiling. 'Poor little mite didn't have much of a life, what with one thing and another, did she? Neither did my mother if it came to that. She was an invalid for most of her life,' he muttered, and Annabelle felt her throat constrict.

'But at least Mary was loved during the time she did have,' she answered softly. 'She couldn't have had a better brother or sister. And I'm sure your mother knew that you all loved her too. Her death might have been a blessed release, from what Lucy told us.'

He looked at her strangely, and knowing that she had said too much, she rushed on, 'Lucy told us – about your mum, I mean. I think she needed to confide in someone.'

'Oh yes? And what exactly did she tell you?' He was frowning now and she felt suddenly nervous.

'W-well, just that your dad was a . . . a bully and one night she couldn't take any more so she er . . . stabbed him to death and ended up in a mental home.'

Joel's lips pursed into a thin line but he remained silent, and feeling extremely uncomfortable, Annabelle told him, 'I must get on now, but I'll be back as soon as I can.'

There was no response and as she set off back down the ward she cursed herself. Why had she had to go and blab that out, about Lucy telling them her secret? Joel was obviously none too pleased about the fact that she knew, but it had just come out as she'd tried to comfort him. But what was there to be ashamed of? She just hoped that she hadn't got Lucy into bother, but for now she had a list of jobs as long as her arm to think about, so there was no time to dwell on it. With luck, by the time she saw Joel again he would have had time for the first shock to subside. She just prayed the bad news would not impede his recovery.

Chapter Thirty-Five

On St Valentine's Day, 1941, Dotty and Robert were married in a short ceremony at Marylebone Register Office as Laura and Paul looked on. Dotty had the low-key affair she had wanted, although Laura had insisted on her having a new outfit and carrying a small bouquet of pink roses, and everyone who saw the bride commented how absolutely beautiful she looked. She wore a pale blue costume with a navy hat and shoes, and happiness seemed to radiate off her in waves as the registrar pronounced them husband and wife.

Laura sniffed tearfully into a scrap of handkerchief as the newlyweds came out onto the steps after the ceremony, and Paul took some photographs on his Kodak Brownie camera. A professional photographer had been impossible to find in these difficult times, but that didn't matter to Dotty or Robert. All they cared about was being together. Laura then showered them in rice and Paul whipped them all away to a restaurant at Marble Arch for a slap-up meal.

'To our dear friends!' Paul declared a toast as he raised his glass and Robert kissed his wife tenderly as he asked, 'Are you happy, Mrs Brabinger?'

'Couldn't be happier,' she assured him, and if a tiny part of her was wishing that her mother and her father could have been there to share this most special occasion, she hid it well. She was determined that nothing should spoil the day and thankfully nothing did – until later that night when she shyly climbed into bed with her new husband in the sumptuous hotel bedroom in the Charing Cross Road. He had promised her a honeymoon somewhere exotic when the war was over, but for now this was the best he could do and Dotty had assured him that it was just perfect. She had just been admiring the congratulation telegrams that had arrived early that morning from Miranda, Annabelle and Lucy, and was deeply touched that they had all thought of her. But now she suddenly felt nervous. She had never had anyone to tell her about what would be expected of her on her wedding night, and she was praying that Robert would not be disappointed in her. However, sensing her unease, he didn't rush things but slid his arm about her shoulders and asked, 'Have you enjoyed the day, darling?'

'Every minute of it,' she told him truthfully as she gingerly inched across the mattress towards him in the lovely silk nightdress Laura had bought her especially for the occasion. Dotty had never owned anything so fine in her whole life and she almost hated to crease it. She knew that it must have cost an absolute fortune, but then that was Laura down to a T – generous to a fault, bless her. Fingering the gold band on her finger, nestling next to her later mother-in-law's engagement ring, she resisted the urge to pinch herself. Could this really be happening to her, plain old Dotty? But yes it was. She could feel the heat of Robert's leg lying next to hers and there was something sensuous about his closeness. She had never lain with a man before, and yet from now on she would lie next to him every single night for the rest of her life. It gave her a tingly feeling just to think of it, and when his hand settled gently on her thigh it felt like the most natural thing in the world and something deep inside her responded to him.

'Oh Dotty, I can't believe that you're really my wife at last,' he muttered as he covered her eager lips with short hot kisses. And it was then that the air-raid sirens sounded, and for a moment they were both so shocked that they lay motionless.

'Oh no, I don't believe it,' Robert groaned. 'On tonight of all nights too! Bloody Adolf wants shooting!' But he got no further because Dotty had dissolved into giggles and they were so infectious that soon he saw the funny side too. 'Come on,' he ordered, dragging his wife from the bed and draping her dressing-gown about her. 'It doesn't look like we'll forget our wedding night in a hurry.'

'But there will be other nights,' Dotty told him naughtily, as she took his hand and led him downstairs to the hotel's air-raid shelter. 'Lots and lots of them.'

'Now is there anything else that you need?' Annabelle asked as she tucked the blankets about Joel's legs. He was no longer in traction, which was heaven for him, although his injured leg was still in splints. She was about to go off duty for the night and was so tired that she didn't know where ached the most.

'No, I'm fine,' he said – just as the sirens began to wail.

'Oh no!' Annabelle glared towards the ceiling as if she could somehow magically see straight through it to the German planes that would soon be droning overhead. 'It looks like we're in for it *again* tonight. Come on – let's get you into this wheelchair and down to the cellar.'

'Go and see to some of the other chaps first, Belle,' he instructed her, but she shook her head and with a determined glint in her eye, began to help him out of bed.

'I'll come back for them,' she said firmly. 'But not until I've got you down there first.'

He sighed with resignation as she manhandled him into the wheelchair. They had grown close during the weeks that she had tended to him, and he sometimes wondered how he would have got through this without her. Sometimes he would wake from a terrible nightmare where he was once again on the battlefield crawling through stinking mud as he tried to get to his friend to help him. And then he would once more feel the impact as the landmine exploded and threw him into the air like a rag doll. But then he would wake and she would be there, holding his hand and mopping his sweating brow, and he was more grateful than he would ever be able to tell her. Now they joined the queues of nurses in the corridors wheeling patients to safety.

'I reckon there's more chance of a wheelchair crash in this mob than being bombed,' he half joked. 'I'd much sooner take my chances on the ward with the blokes that can't be moved.'

'Well, that's just too bad, because you're going whether you want to or not,' Annabelle told him bossily. How could she tell him that a lot of the men who were left on the wards were too critically ill to be moved and were not likely to make it anyway? For some of them, death would be a blessing and a liberation.

Joel grinned. She was a tough little bird when she wanted to be, there was no doubt about it. In fact, sometimes it was hard to believe that she was the same girl he had met back home in Coventry. Then all she had seemed to care about was what she wore and enjoying herself, and he wondered what had brought about this transformation? Perhaps it was the nursing that had changed her. Whatever it was, he thought the change was for the better – not that they could ever be more than friends, he thought regretfully. Once the war was over she would go back to her privileged lifestyle whilst he . . . What could he do now with this gammy leg? He would be very restricted in what jobs he could take on. Driving would be out of the question for a start-off. And then there was Lucy. She needed him, and after what they had been through together, he could never think of leaving her alone. He sat back in the chair and depression settled about him like a cloak.

'Oh Lawdy, not again.' Mrs P sighed as the sound of the siren sliced through her fragile sleep. Then digging poor Fred in the ribs she ordered, 'Come on, luvvie. Looks like it's the shelter again tonight fer us lot.'

A mumbled groan sounded as Fred tried to pull the blankets over his head but his wife was having none of it. She whipped them off him.

'You go an' get young Lucy an' Harry, an' I'll stay here an' take me chances,' he muttered, groping for the eiderdown.

'Then I'll stay an' all,' she said stubbornly as she leaned back against the headboard and crossed her arms across her plump chest, which made him pull himself up onto his elbow. It was one thing risking his own life, but quite another to risk his old girl's. Clambering out of bed he pulled his trousers on over his long johns, then snapping his braces into place he told her resignedly, 'Come on then. But I hope you've put some extra blankets in that bloody shelter. It were freezin' in there t'other night.'

'Happen bein' freezin' is better than bein' dead,' she told him perfunctorily and he followed her from the bedroom as meekly as a lamb, knowing that she was quite right.

'You give Lucy a knock while I go in an' light the candles,' she told him once they were in the yard. It was bitingly cold and he nodded as she hurried towards the shelter.

Lucy joined them five minutes later, just as the drone of the enemy planes reached them.

They glanced at each other in the dancing flames from the candles, each wondering if this would be their time to die.

It was the early hours of the morning before they emerged, feeling dazed and disorientated. It had been a particularly bad raid again, and at one point the very ground beneath them had shaken and Mrs P had started to pray, sure that the time to meet her maker had come.

Again they saw that the sky above their city was as bright as daylight from the many fires that were burning, and fire engines and Army troops in jeeps were rushing to the worst-affected areas.

'Looks like there'll be a few more graves to be dug in London Road Cemetery,' Mrs P said bleakly. 'Come on, we may as well go an' have a cuppa – if they ain't hit the water mains again, that is.'

In London, Dotty was very happy getting used to being Mrs Brabinger and living in newly wedded bliss with Robert. It was just a week now until the release of her first novel, *War-Torn Lovers*, and she was very excited about it. She was now also happily working part-time in the *Woman's Heart* office and still producing her short stories for them on a monthly basis. Sometimes she wished that there were a few more hours in each day.

'You're doing far too much,' Robert would scold her. 'There's really no need for you to work, Dotty. It isn't as if we need the money.'

But she would simply smile and tell him that she enjoyed it, which she did.

At breakfast this morning she was delighted to find that there was a letter from Annabelle and one from Lucy in the post. She quickly read them as Robert put a tiny bit of marge on his toast and poured the tea. It still gave her a thrill to see the name *Mrs Brabinger* on the ones that were addressed to her.

'What do they have to say?' Robert asked.

'Well, Annabelle sounds OK. She says Joel is well on the way to recovery now,' she confided, 'Between you and me, I think she and Joel have a little spark between them, although they haven't admitted it yet.'

'I dare say they will when the time is right, if they're anything like we were,' he answered with a grin. 'And what does Lucy have to say?'

Dotty glanced at the other letter again. 'Not a lot really. But then she never does just lately. She just hasn't been the same since she lost her mother and Mary. She seems to have sort of gone into herself, if you know what I mean?'

'Time is a great healer,' Robert answered as he scraped some marmalade onto his toast.

Dotty nodded, hoping that he was right, then lifting the last letter she frowned. 'It's from the solicitors,' she told her husband as she slit it open with the end of her teaspoon. Then as she scanned the page, she went on, 'He's asking when I'm next visiting Coventry as he would like to see me on a personal matter. What do you think that might be?'

'I've no idea,' Robert replied. 'But perhaps he has some papers or something for you to sign?'

Dotty shook her head. 'I doubt it. I think I've done all that part of it now, and he does say it's personal.'

'Well, you were hoping to go back to Coventry in the next couple of weeks for a visit anyway, weren't you? You could perhaps call and see him then.'

'I will,' Dotty agreed, and then there was a mad scramble as the couple got ready for the office.

'Young Lucy is worrying me,' Mrs P remarked a few days later as she got Fred's snap tin loaded for work. He'd enjoy his dinner today; cold tongue and mustard was one of his favourites. 'She just seems to have gone into herself, don't she?'

'I suppose she is a bit quiet,' Fred agreed as he wound his scarf around his neck. 'But then everyone is out of sorts at present. Seems the whole bloody world is at war now. There's the Japs, the Italians, the poor bloody Jews . . . they're all involved now an' still there's no end in sight. I'll forget what me kids look like at this rate,' he added gloomily.

Mrs P glanced towards the photographs on the sideboard and her eyes filled with tears. 'An' they'll be shootin' up an' all,' she said in a wobbly voice. 'Happen nothin' will fit our Barry an' Beryl by the time they come home.' She and Fred had written to tell them that their elder brother had died bravely in combat, and to think of him as a hero. But oh, how Gladys Price had longed to comfort her little ones in person!

'That's the least of us worries, so long as they do come 'ome safe an' sound,' Fred retorted, and then after planting a hasty kiss on his wife's cheek, he snatched up his snap tin, went out into the yard to collect his bicycle and pedalled off for work.

Alone with her thoughts, Mrs P pondered about Lucy, who had just collected Harry after working a night shift. It was hard to get more than two words out of the girl nowadays, and she seemed to have lost all her vitality and sense of humour. Admittedly, Lucy had always been very guarded when it came to discussing anything about her family life, but things were going from bad to worse. Still, Mrs P thought optimistically, the girl had mentioned that Dotty and Annabelle were coming home for a visit the following week, so happen that would cheer her up a bit. Humming 'Smoke Gets in Your Eyes', she shook out her duster then and began to polish her children's photographs, just as she did every single day. It was as close as she could get to them for now, and the way she saw it, that contact was better than nothing.

'So what made you become a VAD then?' Joel asked one day as Annabelle plumped up his pillows and straightened his blanket ready for Madam's inspection. 'What I mean is, you lot seem to get all the dirty work to do, what with emptying bedpans, washing smelly bandages and cleaning. Wouldn't you have preferred to become a State Registered Nurse?'

'I have thought about doing that once the war is over,' Annabelle replied, 'but when Owen Owen was bombed I needed to get a job fairly quickly so I became a VAD instead. After all, someone has to do the dirty jobs, don't they? I was helping out in the operating theatres, but I don't mind being back on the wards. As Madam always tells us, keeping the patients happy and the wards clean is as important as the job the trained nurses do.'

'I suppose it is when you put it like that, but I still never pictured you doing something like this. You always seemed so . . .' He tried to find a tactful way of saying what he was thinking, but Annabelle actually finished his sentence for him.

'I always seemed so self-centred and spoiled? Is that what you were going to say?'

'No, no of course I wasn't,' he muttered hurriedly.

'Well, looking back, I was,' she told him calmly.

'So . . . what happened to change you?'

Annabelle straightened and eyed him thoughtfully, wondering if she could confide in him. The secret her grandmother had let slip had been festering like a boil inside her and it would be nice to speak to someone about it. But now wasn't the time, not with Madam's ward inspection imminent. 'I'll tell you another time,' she said, then collecting the dirty sheets she had just changed she walked briskly away, leaving Joel to stare after her.

As Madam was leaving the ward, she stopped Annabelle, who was entering the sluice room, to tell her, 'I'd like to see you in my office, Smythe. Shall we say about two o'clock after you've had your lunch?'

Annabelle's heart skipped a beat as she tried to think of what she had done wrong, but she nodded politely. 'Certainly, Madam.'

The woman walked away with the doctors as Annabelle chewed on her lip. Try as she might, she couldn't think of a single thing that might have annoyed the woman . . . but as worrying about it wasn't going to get the rest of her jobs done, she hastened away and got on with things. VADs were famous for being good at that. They had to be.

'So, Smythe, the Ward Sister has spoken very highly of you,' Madam told Annabelle as she stood before her desk a few hours later. Annabelle still felt apprehensive, but at least the woman's opening words had sounded hopeful. Perhaps she wasn't in trouble, after all?

'As you know, I don't usually encourage friendships between staff and patients, but the Ward Sister has informed me that your company seems to act like a tonic for young Mr Ford, which is why I have let you stay on that ward.'

Annabelle shifted uneasily from foot to foot but remained tight-lipped as the older woman went on, 'Because Mr Ford is so much improved now, we are thinking of transferring him to a convalescent home sometime next week. We desperately need the beds and find that patients tend to recuperate much better when their relatives can visit. However, I understand that Mr Ford has recently lost two members of his family and so I hoped that you would be able to tell me if there is anyone left to visit and care for him when he is eventually discharged?'

'Oh yes, there is,' Annabelle told her. 'My friend, Lucy, is Joel – Mr Ford's sister. They share a house in Coventry.'

'And do you think she would be capable of caring for him? I'm afraid his leg is still very fragile and it may be some long time before he can get about on it properly again, even after he leaves the convalescent home.'

'I'm sure Lucy would cope. In fact, I know she'd be delighted to have him home. He is all she has left in the way of family now.'

'In that case I shall arrange a transfer just as soon as I can. Thank you, Smythe.' Annabelle smiled and turned to go, but Madam stopped her then when she added sternly, 'And Smythe, whilst I accept a friendship, I would frown on a romance. Do you understand what I am saying?'

'Yes, I understand, Madam,' the girl said quietly. 'And I assure you there is nothing between Mr Ford and myself other than friendship.'

'I'm pleased to hear it. It just wouldn't do to go setting a precedent for the other girls, would it?'

Annabelle's chin set as she marched back to the ward. It was commonly known that the patients flirted outrageously with the nurses and most of the girls could give as good as they got. Annabelle had even heard of the odd romance or two that had flared up. But she could understand why Madam insisted on that rule. Not that there was anything to worry about with her and Joel. He had never behaved as anything other than a perfect gentleman, and even if he had – what good would it have done? Who would ever want her now when they discovered that she didn't even know who her birth mother was? Shaking her head, she went off to resume her duties. She had learned the hard way that there was no sense in wallowing in self-pity. She just had to make the best of things now.

Chapter Thirty-Six

The Ward Sister was waiting for Annabelle when she got back onto the ward and without preamble she told her, 'I'd like you to go and sit with young Private Reed in the side ward if you wouldn't mind, Smythe.' She shook her head sadly. 'He's deteriorating rapidly now and there's nothing more that we can do for him, poor soul. But at least somebody can be there to hold his hand at the end. That's the least we can do for him, isn't it? No one should face death alone. His name is Johnny, by the way.'

Annabelle was saddened but not really surprised considering the state the poor young man had been in when he arrived. His innards had been spilling out of his stomach and although the surgeons had worked diligently to repair him, an infection had set in and everyone knew that this might be the end for him. She had sat with many other men in much the same situation; the ones suffering with gangrene were the worst. Nothing could remove the foul smell of their afflicted limbs, and one poor man had been so bad that she had been forced to sit holding a handkerchief over her nose and mouth until he died.

As she turned to go and do as she was told, the Sister warned her, 'I'm afraid he's delirious and keeps calling for his mother.'

'I'll cope,' Annabelle replied, and seconds later she stood looking down on the wretched boy lying in the bed. He can't be more than eighteen or nineteen, she found herself thinking as she wrung out a cloth from the bowl at the side of the bed to wipe his sweating brow. His eyes instantly sprang open and he reached out to grasp her hand. His was feverishly hot.

'You *must* tell me mam that I love her,' he muttered chokily and Annabelle nodded reassuringly.

'Sh-she's special, see? Me real mam couldn't keep me when I was a babby an' she took me in out o' the kindness of her heart an' treated me the same as her own.'

Annabelle swallowed deeply as she looked gravely down at him. His breath was laboured but even so it seemed that he wasn't going anywhere until he had passed on his message.

'O-one in a million, she is. Yer will tell her, won't yer?'

'I'll make sure she gets your message, I promise, Johnny,' Annabelle whispered, and a look of contentment settled across his face as his eyes fluttered shut. She sat down on the chair at the side of the bed, gently stroking his hand until at last his chest became still and the sound of his rasping breaths ceased. He was at peace now.

Annabelle sniffed and swiped a tear from her cheek with the back of her hand as her thoughts raced to the woman she had always thought of as her mother. Since the night she had learned of her true birth mother's existence, she had held

Miranda at arm's length. She had even joined the VADs to get away from her. Yet this boy had only loved his adoptive mother all the more for bringing him up and loving him as her own. For the first time she wondered if perhaps she had been a little harsh, but this was not the time to be thinking of it now, so she folded his arms across his thin chest, then after gently drawing the crisp white sheet across his face, she quietly left the room.

It was much later that evening when she was returning from a walk along the sea wall that she spotted Joel sitting in the day room having a cigarette. One of the nurses must have pushed him down there to give him a change of scenery, so she made a detour and popped in to join him, removing her red cape from her shoulders as she entered the room.

'Hello there,' he greeted her. 'Care to join me?'

'Don't mind if I do,' Annabelle answered, taking a Woodbine from the packet he offered. He lit it for her with a match then asked, 'Been for a stroll, have you?'

When she nodded, he went on, 'Bad do about that poor young Johnny Reed, wasn't it? I saw the porters come to take him to the morgue.'

It was just the chance that Annabelle had needed and now she told him, 'He asked me to pass on a message to his mother – only she wasn't his mother, not really. He said she'd taken him in when he was a baby because his real mum couldn't keep him, and she brought him up.'

'Then she *was* his mother, wasn't she?' Joel said in a matter-of-fact voice. 'That's the way I see it anyway. She was the one who no doubt nursed him through his childhood illnesses. She was the one who read him bedtime stories and kissed him better when he fell over, so in my eyes that makes her his mum.'

Annabelle gulped. 'Do you *really* believe that?'

'Absolutely. Why do you ask?'

Her lip trembled, and before she knew it she had blurted out the whole sorry tale of what had been disclosed on her birthday. Joel wisely let her get it all off her chest without interruption.

When she was done, he fished a clean handkerchief from the pocket of his dressing-gown and handed it to her, and she blew her nose noisily. 'How the mighty are fallen, eh?' she said shakily. 'There was me, all airs and graces, thinking I was a cut above everyone else when all the time I was a nobody!'

'What do you mean?' he asked, puzzled. 'You're still the person you were before. Nothing's changed, only how you think of yourself.'

'B-but my mother was a *runaway*! Who would ever want me now?'

He shook his head. 'That's not the way I see it,' he told her. 'Look at it this way: your mother is at home in Coventry and you would still think of her as your mother if your grandmother hadn't let slip what happened after you were born. Does she *really* deserve to lose you now after all the years she's loved you? We all have secrets in our past,' he went on bitterly, 'but we have to learn to live with them and get on with our lives. And as for who would want you now . . .' he suddenly took her hand and bowed his head. '*I* would, Annabelle. You must have realised how I feel about you. But I have a secret too, so much worse than yours, and it would be *you* who wouldn't want *me* if you knew what it was, believe me.'

Despite being so upset, she was intrigued now. 'If it's about your mother dying in a mental asylum, Lucy already told us about that,' she whispered.

'Huh, but she only told you *half* the story,' he answered, and then squeezing her hand, he asked urgently, 'Do you think you might ever have been able to care for me, Annabelle, even a little, if I had been someone else? Someone from your own class with a bit of money?'

'None of that matters now.' She squeezed his hand in return. 'That's one thing this war has taught me. When you love someone, nothing else matters. But what's this secret that's so terrible?'

Shutters suddenly seemed to go down across his eyes. 'That's something I can never share,' he told her. 'Just know that while Lucy is alive, I can never leave her for anyone.'

Annabelle was shocked. 'What? You're telling me that you'll *never* leave Lucy?'

He nodded, his eyes bleak, and without another word she quietly rose and left the room. It seemed that there was nothing more to say. In one breath he had told her that he had feelings for her – and in the next that he would never leave his sister. None of it made any sense.

Miranda saw a distinct change for the better when her daughter returned home for a two-day leave the following week. Annabelle didn't seem so stand-offish any more, and within minutes of being home she had enquired if there had been any news of her father. The Red Cross had been trying to track him down for months.

'Actually there is,' Miranda told her, 'although I'm not sure if it's good news or bad, to be honest. He's in a German prisoner-of-war camp, and we all know the horror stories we read in the papers about those places. I just pray that he'll survive.'

'He will,' Annabelle told her with conviction. 'And once the war is over he'll be home, you'll see.'

Miranda raised a smile, hoping her daughter was right. 'Dotty and Lucy should be here soon,' she told her. 'That'll be nice. I'm so looking forward to seeing them. How is Joel, by the way?'

'He was transferred to a convalescent home in Watchet, in Dorset yesterday,' Annabelle said, and there was something in her tone of voice that made her mother raise her eyebrows.

'That's good,' she replied cautiously. 'It must mean that he's on the mend.'

Annabelle nodded and without another word, lifted her small case and went upstairs to put her things away as her mother watched her go with a bemused expression on her face.

When the other two girls arrived they were all shocked to see the change in Lucy. She had lost so much weight that her clothes hung off her, and there were dark circles under her eyes. However, they all tactfully said nothing as Dotty proudly handed them copies of her new book hot off the press.

'I can hardly wait to read it,' Miranda told her, thinking how well Dotty looked. She was a complete contrast to Lucy and seemed to have filled out a little. Her skin and her eyes were glowing, and it was obvious that she was happy.

'I've just got to pop out to see Mum's solicitor in a while,' she told them apologetically within minutes of arriving there. 'But I shouldn't be long and then I'll stay until the morning, if you don't mind, Miranda.'

'It would be a pleasure to have you,' Miranda said sincerely. 'But I thought you'd dealt with all the legalities now?'

'I have,' Dotty agreed. 'But Mr Jenkins wrote to tell me that he needed to see me about a personal matter.'

'Then you'd better go and find out what it is and put us all out of our misery,' Miranda teased her.

An hour and a bus ride later, Dotty was shown into Mr Jenkins's office. The kindly gentleman rose from his desk to greet her, and shook her hand warmly.

'May I say how well you are looking, Mrs Brabinger?' he smiled. 'Married life must be suiting you.'

'It is,' Dotty answered. 'But I'm very curious as to why you want to see me, Mr Jenkins.'

'Hmm.' He steepled his fingers as he sat back down and regarded her over the top of them. 'I sincerely hope that you won't think that I'm an interfering old fool,' he said quietly. 'But the thing is, as I've come to know you over the last months, I've realised how much it meant to you, to know who your mother was.

Dotty nodded, looking perplexed.

'With that in mind, I felt that you might also like to know the identity of your father.' Seeing her shock, he hurried on, 'I happen to know who your father was, and seeing as he is now deceased, I see no harm in you knowing too – if you want to, that is?'

'Oh I do!'

'Very well then. I'll begin by telling you that when your mother first started work, she was employed here, in this very office, as a receptionist. My dear, your father worked here too, as a solicitor. His name was Jeremy Matthews and he was a very nice chap. Anyway, it transpires that after a time he and your mother began an affair. Now I know you might condemn him for that, but his wife, to be perfectly honest, was a shrew of a woman. However, they did have two lovely children – which is why your father chose to stay with her. He had no idea that your mother was having you until after you were born, by which time it was too late to do anything about it. But I can tell you that he was absolutely mortified and riddled with guilt, and before he left the firm to join the RAF he entrusted to me a sum of money, with the instructions that should you ever be found, it would be passed to you on his death, which sadly occurred when he was out on patrol with his squadron recently.' Mr Jenkins went over to a safe in the wall, opened it and returned with a large envelope.

'He wanted you to have this,' he told her solemnly. 'And he also asked me to tell you how sorry he was, and that in other circumstances, he would have been proud to be your father.'

'I see.' Dotty stared at the envelope as if it might bite her. She had no idea how much was in it, nor did she care, for there was a feeling of pure joy racing through her veins. Now she *truly* knew who she was, and although she would never have the chance to get to know her father or enjoy spending time with Miss Timms in the knowledge that she was her mother, she felt complete.

'Thank you, Mr Jenkins,' she said sincerely. 'Not just for the money but for helping me to understand. It seems that neither of my parents truly abandoned me, and you'll never know how much it means to me to learn that. Now I can hold my head high and name both of them if asked, and I can also get on with the rest of my life.'

'You are very welcome, my dear,' the kind-hearted man said with genuine warmth. 'I shall only be a phone call away, should you ever need my services, and may I say it has been a pleasure to know you. I think both of your parents would have been very proud of you indeed.'

Dotty rose and walked towards the door, clutching the envelope. She really must find a phone and ring Robert to tell him the happy news. At last she felt truly at peace and one day she hoped she would be able to tell her own children the names of their grandparents – Alice and Jeremy.

'Can't you tell me what's wrong, darling?' Miranda asked later that night. Lucy had set off for home and Dotty had gone to bed, and now she was snatching a few precious minutes with her daughter.

'I . . . I think I've been rather unfair to you,' Annabelle answered in a small voice and Miranda instantly drew her into her arms and kissed the top of her head.

'My back is broad, I can stand it,' she told her affectionately. 'Let's just try to put what's happened behind us and go back to the way we were, eh? But are you sure there isn't anything else bothering you?'

Annabelle didn't answer immediately but then she said slowly, 'Before he left the hospital, Joel told me that he could never leave Lucy. But don't you think that's strange? I mean, she's only his sister, isn't she?'

Ah, so that's it, Miranda thought. My girl is in love and doesn't know what to do about it.

'Perhaps he just feels responsible for her and doesn't want to leave her alone after what happened to Mary and her mother?' she suggested, but Annabelle shook her head.

'No, there's more to it than that,' she answered. 'He said that Lucy had only told us half of the secret. You don't think that they're . . . Well, you know – more than brother and sister, do you?'

'Absolutely not, you're just letting your imagination run away with you,' Miranda said firmly. 'But why are you so concerned anyway? Do you have feelings for Joel?'

Annabelle opened her mouth to deny it but then promptly clamped it shut again. She had never been able to lie convincingly to her mother. 'I . . . I suppose I do,' she sighed. 'And he told me that he had feelings for me too, so why is he putting Lucy first?'

'I don't know,' her mother told her honestly, 'but I've no doubt you'll find out all in good time. Although I have to say, Joel is hardly the sort of chap I thought you'd fall for. What happened to tall, dark, handsome and rich?' Then, more seriously: 'Didn't you say that Joel would be permanently crippled?'

'I wouldn't care if he didn't have any legs at all, let alone a limp,' Annabelle responded, then she grinned sheepishly. 'Perhaps I've changed my values.'

'I rather think you have, and I must admit I approve of them.' Miranda kissed her on the cheek. 'But just try to be patient, eh? Things will come right in the end, you'll see.'

'I hope so.' Annabelle snuggled closer to her mother and they sat that way for some time, enjoying being together. It was something they hadn't done for what seemed like a very long time. She's coming back to me, Miranda thought, and her heart rejoiced.

The following weekend Lucy made the journey to Watchet to visit her brother. The train she travelled on drew into a quaint little station and after a brisk walk and asking directions she eventually found the convalescent home nestling on top of some cliffs overlooking the sea. She could see at once how men might recover here. The scenery was breathtaking and it was so peaceful that it was hard to believe that there was a war raging.

Brother and sister were both shocked when they first saw each other. The time they had spent apart had not been kind to either of them. Joel was sitting in the day room, which had a view of the sea, and he greeted her with concern.

'How are you?' he asked.

'Shouldn't it be me asking you that?' she responded, thinking how gaunt he looked. He had actually put a little weight back on during his stay at Haslar, thanks to Annabelle's insistence that he eat, and her unwavering care, but she could have no way of knowing that.

'I survived, which I suppose I should be thankful for,' he answered caustically, and taking a seat next to him she folded her hands primly in her lap. Now that she was actually here she found that she didn't quite know what to say to him. He felt almost like a stranger, and yet before he went away they had been so close. And then he broke the silence that had settled between them when he said, 'It will be strange when I come home without Mary being there . . . and poor Mum dead and buried.'

Lucy lowered her head in agreement but then suddenly asked, 'You didn't tell Annabelle our secret, did you? The way she talks about you, it sounds as if you two have grown very friendly.'

He met her eyes. 'Of course I didn't. I swore to you that I never would, didn't I? And what's wrong with us being friends?'

This seemed to satisfy her for the moment and she glanced around at the other men in the room, all obviously recuperating from their injuries. Many of them had visitors too and a nurse was going around with a laden trolley supplying anyone who wanted it with a cup of tea.

'I have a dog now,' she suddenly told him. 'His name is Harry.'

'So Annabelle said,' he answered, then seeing the set of her chin he wished he hadn't. She clearly felt threatened by Annabelle, although she had no reason to be. He had once made their mother and Lucy a promise, that he would always be there for her, and he had no intention of breaking it even for Annabelle, although he ached just thinking about her. In another life he knew that he could have happily spent the rest of his life with her, but it wasn't meant to be.

Chapter Thirty-Seven

Before Dotty left to return to London, the three girls stood in Miranda's hallway and hugged each other. Annabelle was also returning to Haslar soon and Lucy had come to say goodbye to them both before they left as it was one of her rare days off.

'Let's promise each other that whatever happens we'll all meet up and have a big party when the war is all over,' Dotty suggested. She had visited her old doctor early that morning and could hardly wait to get home to Robert now, for she had some very exciting news to share with him. She had told Miranda that she was just nipping into the city centre, or what remained of it, to pick a few things up and would have loved to share her news with them all, but she felt that Robert should be the first to know.

'It's a deal,' Annabelle and Lucy agreed. Lucy had been very quiet, but the others had refrained from asking too many questions as she clearly didn't want to discuss it.

Annabelle had dared to ask, 'How is he?' and something about the way she said it made Lucy glance at her strangely. Annabelle had flushed and looked away, and from then on the subject had been carefully avoided.

They had one last hug as Dotty told them, 'I'm afraid I really must go now. If I miss the train I'll have to wait hours for another one, and you know what a worrier Robert is. And anyway . . .' she blushed prettily. 'This is the first night we've been apart since we got married and to be honest I can't wait to get back home to him.'

Miranda smiled indulgently. She was no fool, and despite the fact that Dotty hadn't said a word, she had guessed her secret the minute she arrived. She had the glow that all pregnant women have, and she prayed that all would go well for the young woman. She appeared to be truly happy for the first time in her life and Miranda felt that she thoroughly deserved it. Dotty was scarcely recognisable now from the shy retiring girl Annabelle had once brought home. She was happy and confident, not to mention quite wealthy, and Miranda was thrilled for her.

As she looked at the girls, Miranda realised that, in fact, they had all changed. Annabelle had struggled to come to terms with the secret she had discovered about her true mother, but finally she seemed to have worked through that, although Miranda sensed that she was still sad and knew that it was because of Lucy's brother. She clearly loved him, and if what Annabelle said was true, he loved her too – and yet he had told her that he could never leave his sister to fend for herself. It was all very strange.

And then there was Lucy. Poor Lucy, she seemed to be wandering about like a lost soul lately with no purpose to her life and no sense of direction. But what could Miranda do about it? She decided that she would try and persuade

Lucy to stay until after the other two had left. Perhaps she could get her to open up about what was wrong then? It was worth a try, she decided.

Two hours later, after seeing Annabelle off with her kitbag and her gas mask flung across her shoulder, Miranda led Lucy into the kitchen and suggested, 'How about a nice cuppa? I could just do with one, couldn't you?' Lucy looked hesitant but Miranda wasn't about to give up that easily. Somehow she sensed that her daughter's happiness was at stake here.

She made the tea, then once they were both seated at the kitchen table and she had poured out two steaming cups, she asked bluntly, 'So what's wrong, Lucy? And don't say "nothing" because I'll know that you're fibbing. You haven't been yourself for ages and I feel it isn't just due to losing your little sister and your mother any more, so why don't you tell me what's troubling you? You know the old saying, "a trouble shared is a trouble halved".'

For a terrible moment she thought that Lucy was going to take to her heels, but Miranda reached across the table and gripped her hand. 'You do know that Joel and Annabelle are in love, don't you?' she asked, seeing no reason to beat about the bush.

Just for a brief moment Lucy looked stricken, but then she shrugged.

'Why is it that he told Annabelle he had feelings for her but that they could never come to anything because he could never leave you?' Miranda persisted. Her question was met with another shrug and Miranda began to think that she was banging her head against a brick wall.

And then suddenly, Lucy's shoulders sagged and she started to cry, great heaving sobs that shook her thin frame.

'Oh, darling, I'm so sorry. I didn't mean to upset you. I was only trying to help. You just seem so unhappy all the time lately and I hate to see you like this.' Miranda was around the table in a second, and when she gathered the sobbing girl into her arms, Lucy clung to her as if she were a lifeline. Miranda let her cry until the sobs subsided to dull hiccuping whimpers and then holding her at arm's length she asked softly, 'Do you feel a bit better now?'

Lucy took a shuddering breath before mumbling, 'I shall never feel better. Oh, everything is *such a* mess!'

Miranda rocked her to and fro, wise enough not to push any more until the girl was ready to open up of her own accord. And finally she did.

'I've done something really terrible,' she said hoarsely, her eyes deep wells of pain. 'And because of what I did, Joel's life is over before it's even begun.'

'I'm sure it couldn't have been anything that bad,' Miranda soothed. 'And they do say there's a solution for every problem if you face it head on.'

'Not for this one there isn't!' Lucy took a great gulp of air as if she was coming up for breath. She had carried her secret for so long but now the weight of it was bearing her down, and despite the promises she had made to Joel and her mother she knew that she couldn't carry it any longer. She seemed to be struggling with something deep inside her as Miranda watched varying emotions flicker across her face, and then she said in a voice so quiet that Miranda had to lean close to hear it, 'My mum didn't kill my dad . . . *I did*!'

Miranda's heart was threatening to leap out of her chest, but she kept her expression calm as she waited for the girl to go on, and eventually she did.

'I once told you that my dad was a bully, and that bit was true,' she whispered. 'What I didn't tell you was that after my mum became really ill and took to her bed, Dad started to come into my room in the night and he . . . he raped me. He told me that if ever I said anything to Mum or Joel, he would deny it and I would get into trouble. I believed him, so I kept quiet. I was really scared of him. It started when I was just thirteen. Eventually I missed a period and I didn't know what to do, but eventually Mum noticed my swelling stomach and asked outright if I was pregnant. I so wanted to tell her then – in fact, it was the nearest I ever came to it – but her heart was so weak that I was afraid the shock would kill her. She still loved Dad, you see? So I made up some story about this boy I had been seeing after school and told her that the baby was his. Obviously, Mum didn't want it to become common knowledge about the baby, so I stayed in for the rest of the pregnancy then, and on the night that Mary was born Dad paid someone to come in and deliver her, then they told everyone that Mary was Mum's baby.'

Lucy blew her nose and took a trembling breath. 'I'd just left school by then and no one questioned it as I'd never got out much, what with looking after Mum and everything. So Mary wasn't really my little sister, she was my daughter – and the odd thing was that the second I set eyes on her, I loved her. Yet all through the pregnancy I had prayed that the baby would die.'

The girl stopped again as more tears threatened. 'The good thing was that Dad stopped coming to my room for a while. But then one night when I was feeding Mary he came in again and something inside me just snapped. I knew that I wouldn't be able to bear to have him touch me again so I started to scream and fight him. But he was stronger than me and he had just knocked me onto the bed when Joel heard the commotion and burst in.'

She screwed her eyes tight shut as the memories flooded

back before forcing herself to go on. 'Joel saw straight away what was going on and he pulled Dad off me and started to punch him. Then suddenly Mum was in the doorway and I shall never forget the look on her face for as long as I live. Mary and Mum were both screaming by then and Dad was thumping Joel about the room. I thought he was going to kill him and I think he would have done, but suddenly I saw the pair of scissors that I had been using to cut out material for some nightdresses for Mary on my bedside table . . . and I snatched them up and I . . . *I stabbed Dad right through the heart*. I swear I didn't mean to kill him. I meant to stab him in the arm so that he'd stop hurting Joel, but he turned and . . . Anyway, he went down like a lead weight and we all just stood there hardly able to believe what had happened. It was then that Mum told us we must say that *she* had stabbed him. I argued and said I wouldn't agree to it but she told me that her life was almost over anyway.'

Lucy stared at the tabletop, clearly seeing the scene in her mind's eye. 'And then there was knocking at the front door. The neighbours had heard the rumpus and had called the police. Mum picked up the scissors and when the police came upstairs they found her still holding them and arrested her for Dad's murder. I think I must have been in shock by then because I just stood there like a dummy. After that, Joel decided we should move. The newspapers had had a field day with the story and we knew that none of us would ever get any peace if we stayed where we were. That was when we packed up and moved here. Meantime Mum was kept in custody until her case went to court, but by the time it did she was too ill to be tried so they put her into the mental asylum. We went to see her every single week and she made Joel promise that he would always look after me and Mary. She said that I had suffered enough and blamed herself for not realising what was going on right under her nose.'

Lucy lifted her head and looked straight at Miranda with a desolate expression. 'So now you know why Joel feels responsible for me. But I don't *want* him to any more and I've told him so. The trouble is, he's as stubborn as a mule and he says he would be breaking his promise to our mother if he ever left me. But now I just want him to be happy and I want Annabelle to be happy too and I feel as if I'm standing between them. It's all my fault that they can't be together!'

'Oh, you poor, poor thing!' Miranda could hardly believe what she had just heard, and yet now she could vaguely remember reading about the case in the newspapers some years ago. 'You must never blame yourself for what's happened,' she told the girl. 'None of this situation was your fault. Your father abused you and your mother was a very brave woman who saved you from a possible death sentence. You, too, saved your brother's life. But you have to put it all behind you now somehow and go on with your life.'

'And how am I supposed to do that?' Lucy cried bitterly. 'I'm soiled goods; no man would ever want me now. And while I'm here, Joel won't get on with his life either and all because of a promise he made to our mother.'

Miranda hugged her again as she tried to think of a solution to this whole sorry mess, but for now, no ideas were forthcoming.

Lucy stayed for another hour although Miranda tried to persuade her to sleep at Primrose Lodge. She didn't like the thought of the girl being alone in the state of mind she was in, but Lucy argued that Mrs P would worry if she didn't go home to collect Harry.

And so Miranda found herself alone again and poured

herself a large glass of scotch. She felt that she needed it after hearing Lucy's story, even though she wasn't much of a drinker. She lit a cigarette too and as she sat there in the darkness she thought how incredible it was that all three of the girls had such huge secrets in their past one way or another, and once they had been revealed, this had changed all their lives. Dotty's for the better admittedly; at least she knew who her real parents were now. But it was a different story for Annabelle and Lucy. Lucy's terrible secret had obviously been weighing heavily on her mind and she had seemed almost relieved to finally share it.

As always, Miranda's thoughts returned to her daughter and her husband Richard. The thought of him being at the mercy of the Germans filled her with dread. The newspapers were full of the atrocious way the prisoners were being treated and the horrendous conditions they were forced to live in, and she wondered if he would survive it. And if he did, and came home, would he be the same man who had left? She didn't see how he could be. No one could witness and endure things like that without it affecting them permanently, but she loved him so much she just wanted him home, whatever state he might be in.

And then finally there was Annabelle. Her heart ached as she thought of her. The girl had changed so much since the night she had learned of her adoption that sometimes Miranda barely recognised her now and she blamed herself. But Annabelle had been slightly more affectionate on her last visit, so perhaps she had turned a corner? If only she had told her daughter earlier that she was adopted this might have been avoided, but of course it was all too late for if onlys. She thought back to the time when Annabelle had started at Owen Owen and smiled wryly. The girl had been incensed at the thought of having to work for a living, yet after a time she had made a couple of friends and seemed to actually be enjoying it.

Miranda could remember clearly how surprised she had felt, the first time Annabelle brought Lucy and Dotty home to meet her. They had been so different from Annabelle's usual choice of company and yet Miranda had warmed to them immediately. There was Dotty, so plain and shy, who wouldn't say boo to a goose. Then there was Lucy, so protective of her family and so guarded when it came to speaking of her personal life. And now it seemed that Annabelle was in love with Lucy's brother and poor Lucy felt as if she was standing between them. Everything was so complicated . . . Miranda just wished that she could put everything back to the way it had been before the war. Of course she couldn't do that, so she poured herself another large scotch. It seemed to take the edge off all the sad things – and that couldn't be a bad thing, surely?

Chapter Thirty-Eight

'You're an early bird, ain't yer?' Mrs P said the next morning as Lucy appeared in the kitchen doorway with Harry. She was raking out the dead ashes before setting the fire and cooking breakfast, and she stared at Lucy curiously. 'An' ain't that yer best coat yer wearin'?'

'Is it?' Lucy answered, looking flustered. 'Oh, it was the first one I grabbed from the cupboard under the stairs. Never mind though. I don't get to wear it much any more. I dare say an airing will do it good.'

'Hmm.' Mrs P stared at her more closely through narrowed eyes. The girl was as jumpy as a kitten and looked ready to burst into tears at the drop of a hat. But then that was nothing new lately. She lit the paper beneath the faggots of wood and held a newspaper over the hearth to create a vacuum and let the fire draw. Then she threw some coal onto the flames. Once she was sure that it had caught she rose off her plump knees and asked, 'Seein' as yer so early, do you want a cuppa afore yer go?'

'No thanks, I won't if you don't mind. We've got some training on at work and that's why I'm early.' No need to light the fire today – I'll be back in time to do it myself.' The girl fumbled for a hankie.

It sounded plausible enough so Mrs P nodded as she bent to stroke Harry. 'In that case then, you'd best be off. This one here'll be fine wi' me, won't yer, matey?'

Lucy seemed to pause, but then she strode towards the door before turning to say quite unexpectedly, 'You've been really golden to me, Mrs P. Almost like a second mum. And I really appreciate your kindness. I just wanted you to know that.'

Mrs P blushed and chuckled as she waved her hand at her. 'Get away wi' yer. I've just been a good neighbour, that's all. Now get off while me an' Harry here have our breakfast before me old man comes down.'

Lucy's eyes lingered on the dog for a moment then with a little sigh she left the room, closing the door quietly behind her. There was something not quite right – Mrs P could feel it in her bones, though she couldn't for the life of her put her finger on what it was. Her eyes strayed to the photographs of her children and they suddenly brimmed with tears. It was so long since she had seen her younger son Barry and the 'baby', Beryl, and sometimes she wondered if the bloody war was ever going to end. But then with her usual resilience she sniffed and swiped the tears away with the sleeve of her dressing-gown. Sitting there feeling sorry for herself wasn't going to solve anything, so she might as well get on with things the same as everyone else was having to do.

It was seven o'clock that night before Mrs P started to get

really worried. Fred had been in from work for some time and having had his toad-in-the-hole and junket for afters was now snoring softly in the fireside chair with his feet stretched out to the flames and the *Daily Mail* in a heap on the rag rug beside him. Lucy should have been back hours ago, but there was still no sign of her.

Moving into the front parlour, Mrs P tweaked the blackout curtain aside and gazed out for a sign of the girl, but the street was deserted. It was dark and miserable, and rain was lashing against the windows as if trying to find a way in. Shuddering, Mrs P dropped the curtain and scuttled off to the warmth of the back room. Perhaps she's decided to go straight from work to visit Miranda Smythe, she thought, but then dismissed that idea almost immediately. Had Lucy been planning to do that, she would have told her. The girl was very thoughtful that way.

'Fred, I'm just gonna pop round next door to check that young Lucy ain't back,' she said to the slumbering figure in the chair, and after receiving a grunt as an answer she slipped out of the back door and crossed the yard. The house appeared to be in total darkness as she had expected, but after trying the back door with her spare key, she was surprised to find that it was unlocked. She inched it open before shouting, 'Lucy, are yer in, pet?'

There was no answer so she went inside, and after ensuring that the blackouts were in place in the scullery, she clicked the light on. Everywhere was neat and tidy so now she entered the back room and did the same in there. She then noticed an envelope propped up against the cruet on the table and sucked in her breath when she saw that it was addressed to her. She slit it carefully open with a hairgrip, and then as her eyes scanned the page she sank heavily onto the nearest chair.

Dear Mrs P,

I know this will come as a shock to you and I'm sorry if it upsets you, but by the time you read this letter I shall be miles away and I shan't be coming back. I hope that in time you'll come to understand that it's for the best. I know that Joel and Annabelle are in love but whilst I am about he will never leave me to begin any sort of life of his own and he deserves that. He's the best brother in the world and I want both him and Annabelle to be happy.

I have left another envelope on the mantelpiece with enough money to pay the rent until Joel returns home and would be grateful if you would pay the rent man for me until that day arrives. I have also written to Joel and Annabelle to tell them what I am planning to do, but I don't want any of you worrying about me. I have already got somewhere to live and another job lined up in another part of the country and one day I shall come back to see you all.

I hope you will forgive me for leaving this way and one day when you know the whole story of my past you may understand. In the meantime I hope you will adopt Harry for me. I know you love him as much as I do. He will be happy with you and Mr P, and will keep you company until your children come home.

You will never know what your kindness has meant to me since we had the good fortune to come to live next door to you, and I will always think of you with affection.

With much love,
Lucy xx

'Aw lass,' Mrs P muttered to the empty room as her face crumpled and tears rolled down her cheeks. 'I knew somethin' were up this mornin', so why didn't I stop yer goin'?' And yet even as she said it, she knew that there was nothing she could have done. Lucy had obviously made her mind up to go and there would have been no stopping her.

'Poor little sod,' she breathed as she looked about the room. The girl hadn't had much luck in life up to now, but perhaps this would be a new start for her.

When she got back to the warmth of her own room and showed the letter to Fred, he patted her arm comfortingly. 'Well, yer know, I've seen this comin',' he remarked. 'She ain't been right for a while. A blind man on a gallopin' donkey could have seen how unhappy she's been. An' in a funny sort o' way, this might be the makin' o' the girl. What I mean is, it's a whole fresh start fer her, an' happen that's just what she needs. It'll be the makin' o' young Joel an' all now, an' he can live a more normal life as well.'

Mrs P nodded, hoping he was right – but oh, how she would miss her young neighbour!

Joel and Annabelle both received their letters the following week and after opening them it would have been hard to say who was the most shocked.

'I can't believe she's done this,' Annabelle groaned, waving the letter at Hilary who was crouched by the stove in their dormitory painting her toenails. They were off to a dance in Portsmouth that night and she wanted to look her best, seeing as it was her first evening off in three weeks. The VADS had been rushed off their feet after tending to the sailors whose ship had been bombed out at sea, or at least those who had survived it. Over half of the men aboard had perished in the ocean or died of their injuries shortly after arriving at Haslar.

'Can't believe who's done what?' Hilary asked as she stuck her tongue out and tried to reach her little toe.

Annabelle read the letter out to her and when she was done, Hilary grinned. 'Didn't I say that Joel had a soft spot for yer?' she beamed. 'Seems like yer mate knew it too, so now you'll 'ave to go an' see 'im an' put fings right between you. There ain't nuffink standin' between yer now, is there?'

Annabelle frowned uncertainly. She and Joel had never really made any promises to each other, and perhaps she had only imagined that he had felt the same way as she did. She said as much now to Hilary, who snorted.

'Well, there's only one way to find out, ain't there? An' that's to go an' see the feller!'

'But it'll be weeks before I'm due any more leave,' Annabelle objected.

'So? He ain't goin' anywhere soon, is he? An' in the meantime yer could write to 'im.'

'I suppose I could,' Annabelle admitted musingly. 'And I think I ought to write to my mother as well. I'm afraid I've been rather awful to her and Daddy too for a long time now.'

'Ain't no time like the present,' Hilary commented wisely. 'You only get one mum an' dad, be they adopted or otherwise.' She was the only one at Haslar that Annabelle had ever confided in about her true parentage, and from the start Hilary had struggled to understand why Annabelle was so angry with them.

'But they obviously took you in an' loved yer because they wanted to,' she had pointed out. 'Why waste time worryin' about yer real mam when she clearly didn't want yer?'

Now, suddenly, Annabelle could see that she was right and she felt ashamed.

'I'll write to Mummy straight away,' she decided, taking a pen and a writing pad from her bedside locker. 'And then I'll go and see Madam and find out when I've next got leave so that I can pay Joel a visit.'

'Hallelujah!' Hilary rolled her eyes heavenwards. 'The girl *finally* sees sense!'

Annabelle grinned as a little bubble of excitement formed in her stomach. It was time to put things right.

Early in May, Annabelle stepped down from the train in the little station and walked out into the charming cobbled streets of Watchet. It was like stepping back in time as she stared at the pretty thatched cottages, and so peaceful with nothing but the sound of the seagulls to be heard. She breathed in deeply, enjoying the salty tang of the air, then set off in the direction of the convalescent home, which Lucy had told her was perched high on a cliff at the end of the town overlooking the sea.

It was a good half-hour's walk but she enjoyed being outside after the confines of working in the underground operating theatres of Haslar where she was back assisting the surgeons and sterilising their instruments.

She had left the village behind her some time ago before the home came into view and she thought how lovely it looked, with the sun shining down on it. The sea was breathtakingly blue and twinkled in the sunshine, and for the first time she began to have misgivings. Should she have let Joel know that she was coming? And would she be welcome? She paused, but then taking a deep breath she strode on. There was only way to find out.

A fresh-faced young nurse met her in reception. After asking her who she had come to see, the nurse enquired, 'Is he expecting you? And are you a relative?'

'Er . . . . Well, no, he doesn't know I'm coming and no, I'm not a relative,' Annabelle flustered.

'In that case I shall have to have a word with the Ward Sister,' the nurse informed her. 'Follow me, please.'

They moved through a labyrinth of corridors and up several flights of stairs before the nurse said, 'Would you mind waiting here? I'll just go in and have a word with Sister.'

There were men milling about everywhere and some of them looked at Annabelle curiously. Some were in wheelchairs with the legs of their trousers empty and tucked beneath them. The luckier ones were hobbling about on crutches, but they all seemed happy enough and many of them smiled at her. She smiled back as her heart threatened to leap out of her chest and eventually a Ward Sister appeared and said, 'I believe you've come to see Private Ford?'

Annabelle's mouth had suddenly gone dry so she nodded. The Sister looked at Annabelle's uniform and said pleasantly, 'Did you nurse him whilst he was at Haslar?'

'Yes, I did,' Annabelle managed to squeak. 'But he was already a friend before that.'

'I see. Then in that case I can see no reason why he shouldn't have a visitor. He's doing very well. In fact, we're hoping to discharge him in a few weeks. Come this way. I think he's in the day room.'

Annabelle followed the woman down a long corridor and eventually the Sister pointed to a door. 'You'll find him in there. He spends a lot of time in that room. Have a nice visit.'

'I . . . I will. Thank you,' Annabelle croaked, then wiping her sweaty palms down the side of her uniform she pushed the door open. She found herself in an enormous room with a number of windows that all looked out to sea. No wonder he likes it in here, she thought. The views from the windows really were quite stunning. A table-tennis table stood at one end of the room and comfortable easy chairs were scattered about where little groups of men were playing cards and dominoes and chatting. An enormous bookcase with a large quantity of books on it took up another wall and Annabelle thought what a relaxing room it was. Just the place to come and convalesce. But at first glance there was no sign of Joel. And then she saw him. He was sitting alone at the far end of the room gazing out across the sea and her heart skipped a beat. He had put a little more weight back on, and now that his hair had grown out of the harsh Army cut he looked so much more like the young man she had once met what seemed like a lifetime ago now at his home in Coventry.

As she approached, he glanced around and saw her and after the initial look of shock his face lit up and he rose awkwardly to greet her. He was managing to get about on his own now, she noticed, but he would probably always need a walking stick.

'Why, what a lovely surprise! Why didn't you let me know you were coming? I could have dressed up a bit,' he teased.

'You look fine just the way you are,' she said shyly taking a seat next to him, and then they lapsed into silence, each wondering what to say. When they eventually did speak again they both started at once and then both laughed – and it seemed to break the ice.

'Sorry, you go first. What were you going to say?' Annabelle said.

'Just how wonderful you're looking,' he mumbled as colour flooded into his cheeks, and Annabelle had to suppress the urge to take him in her arms and kiss him soundly there and then, because she knew in that instant that she had found her soulmate for life.

They talked about what was going on in the war then, and

about Lucy, and before they knew it it was coming up to tea-time. The afternoon seemed to have flown.

'What time do you have to go?' he asked.

'My train leaves at seven so I'm all right for a while yet. It's only about half an hour back to the station.'

'In that case, let's go outside and get some fresh air before you leave shall we?' he suggested, and Annabelle followed him gladly. It took him a while to negotiate the stairs but he stubbornly refused any offer of help and her heart twisted as she saw the sweat break out on his forehead.

'It – it's good for me to use my leg as much as I can – the doctors told me so,' he informed her breathlessly. 'The old muscles are a bit wasted, I'm afraid, after being in bed for so long, but they will get better if I persevere.'

She gnawed on her lip, wishing he would let her help him, but at last they reached the entrance hallway and emerged into the gardens, which were beautiful. Rolling lawns ran down to the clifftops and he led her towards a large oak tree with a bench placed beneath it in the shade.

'It's lovely here,' she whispered as her eyes stared out over the shimmering water, and then her heart began to race again as he gently took her hand in his. Her whole arm seemed to be on fire and it was all she could do not to throw her arms about him. She knew without a doubt that in Joel Ford she had found the love of her life.

'I heard from Lucy last week,' he told her now. 'She's living somewhere in Cornwall and she sounded happy. She's lodging with a widow, apparently, who has a little girl about the same age as Mary would have been. Needless to say, Lucy is very taken with her and she's working at the hairdresser's that the woman owns.'

'I heard from Dotty too,' Annabelle told him. 'And she's looking forward to the birth of her first baby. Robert is really excited about it, and her book is flying, by all accounts. She's almost finished her second one now.'

'So all's well that ends well for two of the shop girls,' he grinned. 'But what about the third one?'

'Oh I'm all right,' Annabelle said hastily as he played with her fingers and lowered his head.

'Annabelle,' he whispered gruffly. 'You know that I'm never going to be the man that I was before the war, don't you? What I mean is, this leg is never going to be as it was. I'll always be a cripple and that will seriously impede what job I'm able to do. It's highly unlikely that I'll ever be rich or—'

'Shh.' She placed her finger on his lips to silence him, and when he raised his head again he saw all the love she felt for him shining in her eyes and hope stirred in his heart. 'You'll always be more of a man than any other I've ever known – apart from my dad, of course,' she told him with a twinkle in her eye.

'Then in that case I'll say this; none of us knows what's going to happen with this blasted war or even how much longer it may go on for. But if at the end of it you think you might not mind being saddled with a man with a gammy leg . . .'

'Is that a proposal?' she grinned but he shook his head.

'No, it isn't. It wouldn't be fair to tie you to that because as I said, who knows what might happen or if we'll both still be alive? But if we are . . .'

'That's good enough for now,' she sighed, but then she had no time to say any more because he was kissing her and there were more stars behind her eyes even than there had been in the sky on the night of the Blitz – and the war couldn't last forever, could it?

Epilogue

The war raged on so slowly that people began to despair and wondered if it would ever end. Four long years passed. Hitler's next horrors were the V1 and V2 rockets that reduced much of London to rubble, causing countless deaths and immeasurable heartache to thousands. But then in April 1945, as Soviet troops advanced on Berlin and the American troops invaded Okinawa and Nuremberg, Hitler realised that the tide had turned. Not wishing to suffer the same fate as the Italian dictator, Benito Mussolini, who had been killed and mutilated, his body put on public display in Milan, Hitler and his lover, Eva Braun, whom he had married less than forty hours earlier, committed suicide on 30 April in his Führerbunker. The people of England rejoiced as the news reached them, and yet more good news followed at the beginning of May when the German forces surrendered in Italy and Berlin. German forces in Denmark and the Netherlands quickly followed suit, along with the Germans' surrender in Bavaria, the Channel Islands and Breslau.

On 8 May, Winston Churchill made a radio broadcast during which he announced: *'Hostilities will end officially at one minute after midnight tonight, but in the interests of saving lives the "Cease fire" began yesterday to be sounded all along the front, and our dear Channel Islands are also to be freed today!'*

Victory was official, and suddenly celebrations erupted throughout Europe as people tried to take in the wonderful news that the war was really finally over.

'I can hardly believe it,' Mrs P said as she scraped marge on yet another slice of bread to add to the pile already tottering on the table.

'Well, yer can believe it, me old duck,' Fred declared with a broad smile. Mrs P stared at the glass of home-brewed ale in his hand. He'd already drunk enough to sink a battleship and the party wasn't due to start for another hour yet. But then she didn't want to get on at him today of all days.

''Ere, get off that, you little sod,' she said then, slapping her Barry on the back of the hand with the butter-knife as he pinched a slice of bread. The children had arrived home the night before, and Mrs P was still trying to get used to how big they had grown in the time they had been away. Barry had shot up without a doubt and his younger sister Beryl wasn't far behind him. A right little madam now she was, but it was so wonderful to have them home. If only . . . she thought then as her thoughts slipped to her Freddy. It was a day for celebration, but like thousands of other families it would be bittersweet as they thought of the loved ones who would not be coming back.

Her eyes went to his photograph in pride of place on the mantelshelf, and seeing her tear-filled eyes, Miranda slid an arm about the woman's shoulders, feeling her pain. She had come to help with the preparations and hopefully, Annabelle would be arriving from Haslar soon to join them.

'You must always remember he was a hero,' Miranda told the older woman gently. 'And you will always be proud of him.'

'I will that,' Mrs P agreed with a loud sniff as she pulled herself together. This was not the time for tears, today of all days. There was plenty of time for them at night when her Fred was softly snoring at the side of her. 'But what's happenin' about your old man? Any idea when he might be comin' home yet? Oh, an' yer can use some o' that Spam fer the sandwiches, an' some o' that bloater paste an' all,' she added.

'The Red Cross reckon he could be home within weeks,' Miranda told her as she obediently started to fill and cut the sandwiches, pressing the slices together with the flat of her hand. 'But I'm not sure what to expect. It can't have been a bed of roses stuck in that prison camp.'

'Happen yer right but just be grateful he is comin' home,' Mrs P answered and Miranda nodded, knowing that she was right. Whatever state Richard was in she would welcome him with open arms. As they carried the piled-high plates out to the trestle tables that had been draped with white sheets all down the middle of the street, Mrs P chuckled.

'Why, it looks a fair treat, don't it!' she exclaimed delightedly, and indeed it did. Bunting had been strung from lamp post to lamp post and the Union Jack flags that had been hung from the bedroom windows were fluttering in the breeze. The tables were heaving with food and the older woman commented, 'I reckon we'll all starve fer at least a week after today. Rationin's still in place whether the war's over or not, an' I think everyone's emptied their pantries to make today a good spread. But who cares, eh? It'll be worth it.'

Further along the street, someone had dragged a piano into the road and now the sound of someone singing 'The White Cliffs of Dover' was floating towards them.

'That'll be Ma Bennet from number sixty-three,' Mrs P snorted. 'She's always fancied herself as a bit of a songbird, but she won't never be any competition fer Vera Lynn wi' a voice like that, will she?'

'Now put your claws away,' Miranda chuckled as she edged a wobbly jelly over to make room to slide her sandwiches onto the table. The street seemed to be full of children all shouting and laughing and snatching at the treats as they raced by the tables, but today no one corrected them. It was a day to rejoice.

Further along the road was a table full of crates of home-made wine and ale, and most of the men seemed to be congregated there, including Fred, who had managed to escape again.

'He'll be as drunk as a lord, come teatime,' Mrs P confided with a shake of her head. 'They're like bees around a honeypot – look. Never was one fer holdin' his drink were my Fred, but then who cares if I have to put him to bed, eh?'

It was then that Joel hobbled up to them, leaning heavily on his stick, but with a broad smile on his face.

'Hello,' he said, addressing Miranda. 'No sign of Belle yet then?'

'I'm afraid not,' her mother responded with a grin as she watched her future son-in-law glancing up and down the street for a sight of her. 'But rest assured if she's said she'll come, she will.'

Miranda had seen a huge change in him since he had got a job in the local Royal Mail sorting office the year before.

It was a job he could do sitting down and he seemed to have regained some of his confidence since going back to work. She suspected that he felt like a man again now that he could earn a living, although it was apparent that he would never walk again without the use of a stick, and she knew that there were times when the leg still caused him considerable pain. However, he never complained, which she felt was to his credit, and she had grown to be very fond of him.

When she suddenly saw his face light up, she guessed immediately who would be the cause of it. Sure enough, she followed his gaze to see Annabelle picking her way through the people towards them, and before she could say a word, Joel was off, hobbling towards her. Miranda glanced at her watch. Dotty and Robert's train should be in too within the hour and then they could all have a proper reunion. She just felt sad that Lucy wouldn't be there too, for although she and Joel still wrote to each other regularly, she had never made any attempt to return home even for a visit. Miranda could understand it in a way. Lucy could never have had any sort of a life had she stayed in Coventry. There were too many bad memories there to haunt her, but Miranda hoped that in Cornwall she had been able to put the past behind her, to heal old hurts and get on with her life.

She was pulled sharply back to the present when Mrs P dug her in the ribs. 'Well, come on then, gel,' she scolded. 'The sooner all the snap's on the table, the sooner we can get this party started. An' I don't know about you, but I'm ready fer a drop o' that home-made wine meself. Let's get the rest o' them sandwiches out, eh?'

Miranda followed her back into the little terraced house, thinking just how much her own life had changed since before the war. Back then she had had a charlady and someone else to do her washing and ironing for her, but those days were long gone and strangely she found that she didn't miss them. The war seemed to have wiped out class distinction and Miranda thought it was no bad thing. Everyone was on a level footing now, be they a beggar or a queen, and she doubted it would ever go back to the way it had been. During the war, women had had to take on men's roles – and a very good job they had done of it too – so would they ever go back to being chained to the kitchen sink? As Mrs P would say, 'Not on your nelly!'

Further up the road, Joel met Annabelle and she placed her arms about him even though they were in full view of everyone.

'I was worried you wouldn't make it,' he told her as he returned her embrace.

'Well, I only got a temporary reprieve,' she admitted. 'I have to be back at Haslar by lunchtime tomorrow. Even though the war is over there are still an awful lot of sick men to care for on the wards, and my job won't be ended until they're all healed. And of course we have to remember that the war is still going on in Japan, and I've no doubt there'll be more casualties coming from there.'

'So how long do you think that might be?'

She shrugged. 'A few more months at least,' she told him truthfully. 'And then when my VAD time is over and I get demobbed, I thought I might train to become a State Registered Nurse.' She watched him closely for his response and when he looked approving, she sighed with relief.

'I know that's what you want to do, an' I reckon you should go all out for it,' he told her, and once again she thought what a remarkable man he was. He seemed to understand that after the war, women would never be as dependent on men as they had been before. 'Just so long as it doesn't stop you from being my wife as well, of course,' he added.

When her eyes opened wide in shock, he held her to him whilst fumbling in his jacket pocket with his free hand. And then she found herself staring down at a tiny velvet box and he rushed on, 'I did tell you that I wouldn't hold you to anything until the war was over. But it is over now, so Annabelle Smythe, I am asking you if you would do me the very great honour of becoming my wife?'

Before she could even answer, he went on, 'I'm afraid this damn leg won't allow me to drop down on one knee and do it properly. But will you at least look at the ring and consider it?' He then flicked the box open and as Annabelle stared down at the small chip of diamond solitaire he told her hastily, 'I know it probably isn't exactly the rock you always dreamed of, but—'

'Stop right there,' she told him. 'It's absolutely perfect and I would be honoured to be your wife, Joel Ford. In fact, I can hardly wait. Now can I please have my ring?'

He slid it onto her finger as a great cheer went up from the people around them and then he was kissing her and suddenly Annabelle's life was perfect and she couldn't remember ever feeling so happy in her whole life.

'So let's have a look at this sparkler then,' someone said behind her, and as Annabelle tore herself away from Joel to glance around she found Dotty standing there with a cheeky smile on her face. But this was not the shy girl from the orphanage Annabelle remembered from their days at Owen Owen; instead, she was a smart, sophisticated woman. Dotty was holding her new baby girl in her arms, and a little boy in a sailor suit who was the absolute double of his father was clutching at Robert's hand.

'I wondered when you two would see sense,' Dotty chuckled as she admired Annabelle's ring. 'So when is the happy day to be?'

'Well, we haven't had time to think about it yet, but it can't be soon enough for me,' Joel replied as he looked at his new fiancée with pride.

Dotty glanced affectionately at her husband. 'Then I can only hope you'll both be as happy as we are,' she said quietly, and as Annabelle looked at her she couldn't help but be impressed. Dotty's hair, which had grown, was twisted into a gleaming chignon and she was dressed in an elegant navy-blue suit that showed off her slim figure to perfection. Her accessories were white and Annabelle thought she looked as if she had stepped straight from the pages of *Vogue*. Somewhere along the line, the two of them seemed to have changed places. But now that her ring had been admired it was time to view the new arrival, and Annabelle gently drew the shawl from the baby's face.

'Why Dotty, she's just beautiful!' she gasped. 'What have you called her?'

'Alice Louise,' Dotty answered proudly, 'for my mother. And Jeremy was named after my father. He's quite besotted with his new baby sister, thankfully.'

Mrs P had joined them by then, leaving Fred to keep a tipsy eye on Barry and Beryl, and she too dutifully cooed over the new arrival before commenting, 'Crikey, lass. You look a million dollars! No one would believe you'd recently had a baby. How did you get your figure back so fast?'

'I doubt it would have been difficult, seeing as she was never further through than a coat-hanger,' Annabelle teased. The party was getting louder by now and someone was playing 'Roll Out the Barrel' on the piano.

Miranda joined them too then and she hugged her

daughter with delight as Annabelle proudly showed off her ring. She hoped that the couple would wait to get married until Annabelle's father came home. Rations or no rations, Annabelle was her only daughter and she wanted the wedding to be a lavish affair. The Red Cross had informed her that Richard should be home within the next few months and after waiting so long, she was sure that they wouldn't mind waiting just a little longer.

'Well, we said we'd meet up after the war and here we are at last,' Dotty said when everyone else started to drift away to join in the party. 'There were times when I thought it was never going to happen, didn't you?'

'Hmm, but it's a shame there's one of us missing,' Annabelle said sadly as she thought of Lucy.

'I wouldn't be too sure about that,' Mrs P commented as she peered up the street. ''Cos if I ain't very much mistaken, the Missin' Link is on her way.'

And sure enough, as they followed her eyes there was Lucy striding towards them with another woman at her side and a young girl.

Without thinking, Dotty thrust Alice into Mrs P's open arms and suddenly she and Annabelle were racing towards her.

'Oh *Lucy*! You'll never know how wonderful it is to see you!' Dotty cried. 'I can't even begin to tell you how worried we've been about you – but you look *marvellous.*'

'I'm so sorry for clearing off like that,' Lucy apologised when they had all had a hug. 'But I think I had to get away to find out who I really was, and thanks to Julie here, I believe I have now. I just love living in Mevagissy. Then when Joel wrote to tell me about the party, I felt it was time to come back for a visit.' She smiled lovingly towards the woman at her side, then leaned down to fuss over Harry, who was like Mrs P's shadow. His tail wagged furiously – he clearly hadn't forgotten her.

Lucy's companion looked to be slightly older than Lucy and had a kind face, and they took to her instantly. She introduced her daughter as Tamsyn.

'Come on, luvvie, Mrs P said bossily, taking charge. 'You an' the little 'un come along wi' me, Julie. We'll get some grub an' a drink, eh, an' leave these three to catch up, shall we?' she suggested and after flashing a smile at the girls the woman followed her willingly with the little girl trotting happily along behind them, watching the other children playing boisterously in the street.

'It seems like such a long time since we met, doesn't it?' Dotty said musingly as the three old friends stood hand in hand watching the celebrations.

'Yes, and so much has happened to all of us since the night of the Blitz, hasn't it?' Annabelle replied. 'I can still remember that night as if it was yesterday. There were so many stars in the sky that night, weren't there? But what's been happening to you, Lucy?'

'Well, Julie took me in and gave me a job in her hairdressing business as well as a home. She trained me and I'm a fully qualified hairdresser now,' Lucy told them proudly and as her eyes strayed after Julie, Annabelle saw the loving look in them, and a novel idea suddenly occurred to her.

'She's a widow, isn't she?' she asked innocently.

'Yes, she is, but to be honest I don't think she was happily married,' Lucy confided to them both. 'Her husband was the most terrible brute, and like me I don't think she's too keen on men any more, although they did have a lovely daughter, as you can see. Little Tamsyn is a real poppet. I adore her.'

'Well, just so long as you're content, that's all that matters,' Annabelle answered and they then went on to discuss everything that had happened to them all, including Annabelle's engagement to Joel. Lucy was thrilled to hear the news.

'I knew you two would get together eventually if I got out of the way,' she said, then added hastily, 'but that wasn't the only reason I went, of course. I could never have been truly happy here. And in Cornwall I got a brand new start.'

From across the road, Miranda and Mrs P were viewing the reunion with smiles on their faces. Joel had taken Julie and Tamsyn off to watch the fireworks that were being lit at the end of the road, and Robert had gone with them, taking his own two children.

Mrs P remarked casually, 'They seem very close, don't they? Lucy an' Julie, I mean.'

'Yes they do,' Miranda answered, understanding exactly what the other woman was trying to say. 'But you know what I think Mrs P? Live and let live. None of us knows where love is going to strike, and as long as they're happy, who are they hurting? After all that Lucy went through, she deserves to grab her happiness where she can.'

Mrs P nodded sagely in agreement. She loved the girl as her own daughter, and was overjoyed to see her coming to life again. 'Who would have thought it though, eh?' she said pensively. 'All three of 'em had secrets in their pasts that they've had to deal with one way an' another, but I reckon they've come through wi' flyin' colours, an' I think they're better people for it. Since the night o' the Blitz they've turned from slips o' girls into young women. And now we've got a weddin' to plan. But then they do say every cloud has a silver lining.'

'I know,' Miranda said, beaming. 'And I think I can guess who Annabelle will be choosing to be her bridesmaids. But come on, Gladys, I don't know about you but I could murder another glass of that home-made wine. I've got no idea what's in it, but it's working a treat.' And arm in arm the two women set off for the makeshift Victory Day bar at the end of the street.

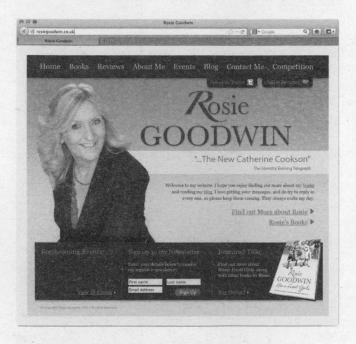